RESCUE ... OR DEATH?

Beverly was sleeping fitfully when the siren came screaming down the street in the middle of the night.

McClain snapped awake about ten seconds after she did. As Beverly sat up, he bolted off the bed and stood in the middle of the darkened room, listening as the siren moaned and died, sounding as if it were only a few yards away from the bedroom. McClain turned back, grabbed Beverly by the throat, and threw her down on the mattress. Squeezing the breath out of her, he whispered, "Do not make a single sound. If you do, I will kill you in a heartbeat."

With that, he raced from the room, leaving the bedroom door open in his wake. Thirty seconds later, McClain stormed back into the room with a pistol in his hand.

From somewhere to their left, Beverly could hear the sounds of footsteps bounding onto the front porch, and then the raised voices of at least two people talking to each other. Then someone pounded on the door and shouted, "Police! Open up!"

Behind her, Beverly felt her captor tense. He laid the barrel of the pistol against the right side of her head . . .

No Place
To Die

No Place To Die

JAMES L. THANE

THOMAS & MERCER

Text copyright © 2010 by James L. Thane
All rights reserved. .
Printed in the United States of America.

Published by Thomas & Mercer
P.O. Box 400818
Las Vegas, NV 89140

ISBN-13: 9781477831250
ISBN-10: 1477831258

For Victoria, finally.

ACKNOWLEDGMENTS

I am indebted to a number of people without whose assistance this book would not have been possible. Principal among them is my agent, Alanna Ramirez, who was the first person to read the book and to believe in its potential. I am also extremely grateful to Barbara Peters, who inspired the book with a chance remark.

Sam Reaves read portions of the early manuscript and made valuable suggestions for its improvement. Thanks to my editor, Don D'Auria, who polished the book. Also at Dorchester, thanks to Tanya Reynolds and to Cindy Johnson.

Karl Huntoon and David Gannon offered legal and medical advice respectively, though I alone am responsible for any mistakes I might have made in utilizing the counsel they provided. Finally, Lieutenant Randy Force of the Phoenix Police Department's Homicide Unit provided insights into the inner workings of the department and patiently answered all of my questions. For the sake of the story, I have taken some liberties with the organization of the Phoenix PD; I hope Lieutenant Force will forgive me.

It is customary at this point for an author to thank his spouse and friends for their contributions to his efforts. I would very much like to do so, but it would be impolite for a writer to lie to his readers. The truth of the matter is that my wife and friends constantly distracted my attention away from this project, insisting that I play golf and tennis, that I go out to dinner or to the movies, and that I do scores of other such things. Without their repeated interference this book would have been finished months earlier than it was. These people know who they are and I will not embarrass them by naming them here, except for Victoria Kauzlarich, Dick and Pat Ballman, Tom and Pat Nauman, Todd and Jane Nicholson, Hal and Rosann Welser, and Bob and Vicky Wyffels.

Come to think of it, my cat was no damn help either.

CHAPTER ONE

Dinner was almost ready when Beverly Thompson was snatched from her garage on a beautiful Wednesday evening early in February.

At forty-three, Beverly was still an extremely attractive woman with thick auburn hair that spilled down to her shoulders, framing an oval face highlighted by deep green eyes and a pair of medium-full lips. She watched her diet carefully and worked out as regularly as she could, and thus remained fit and trim at five feet five inches tall and a hundred and twenty-one pounds.

On that Wednesday evening, Beverly was twenty-seven months into her second marriage. Her first—to a fellow law student—had gradually run out of gas and finally sputtered to an end seven years earlier. Thankfully, it had produced no children.

Through the first four years that followed the divorce, Beverly had dated gingerly, dedicating the bulk of her time and energy to her career as a medical-malpractice attorney in a large firm in downtown Phoenix. But then she met David, a cardiologist who'd testified as an expert witness in a case that she won largely on the strength of his testimony. Following the trial, they had dated for four months and then lived together for another five before formally tying the knot.

At six thirty that evening, Beverly called David and told him that she was finally leaving the office after finishing a particularly grueling deposition. He promised to chill some Bombay Sapphire gin and two martini glasses while he started dinner.

Forty-five minutes later, eagerly anticipating the first sip of the promised martini, Beverly punched the button on the remote to open her garage door. She waited for a moment as the door rolled up, then pulled her Lexus SUV into the garage. She parked, as she always did, to the left of her husband's Mercedes and then pressed the button on the remote to close the garage door behind her.

She was just stepping out of the car when she saw the man, dressed all in black, slip under the garage door as it rolled back down. Instinctively, she jumped back into the Lexus. With her left hand, she hit the button to lock all the doors; with her right, she laid on the horn.

In a heartbeat the intruder was at the door of the SUV, pounding on Beverly's window with the butt of a pistol and yelling, "Lay off the goddamn horn!" Then he stepped back, pointed the gun at Thompson's head and shouted, "Get out of the car, lady. NOW!"

Beverly threw her hands up and the garage went suddenly quiet. Her right hand still in the air, she reluctantly opened the car door with her left. As she did, the kitchen door opened and her husband stepped out into the garage. But before David could even begin to comprehend what was happening, let alone react to the situation, the man spun and fired, hitting David twice in the chest.

David slumped to the floor and Beverly let out a piercing scream. The commotion attracted the attention of Chester, the German shepherd that she and David had rescued from a shelter, who now came bounding out from the kitchen. Again the gunman fired twice, and the dog dropped to the floor, whimpering softly.

As Beverly continued to scream, the gunman jerked her out of the car, slapped her hard across the face, and shouted, "Shut the hell up!"

The man spun her around so that she was facing away from him and wrapped his left arm around her chest, pinning her arms to her sides and effectively immobilizing her. With his right hand he set the pistol on the roof of the car. Then he pulled a rag from his back pocket and clamped it over her mouth and nose.

Beverly struggled, the panic coursing through her body as she tried desperately to stomp on her assailant's foot with her right heel. Unfazed, he simply squeezed tighter and lifted her up off the ground, her legs flailing ineffectively as she tried to kick back at him.

The rag was damp with something that tasted slightly sweet, and she shook her head in a frantic effort to avoid breathing the chemical into her system. But it was futile. Within a matter of seconds she felt herself slipping away. And as she faded into an unconscious state, the last thing she heard was the gunman whispering softly into her right ear, "Hello, Beverly. It's very nice to see you again."

CHAPTER TWO

I was headed from my office to the nursing home a little after eight P.M., when my cell phone began vibrating on the passenger's seat next to me. I flipped open the phone and took a quick look at the caller ID, which indicated that the person so rudely intruding into the rest of my evening was my sergeant. Sighing heavily, I slowed from eighty to sixty-five and connected to the call.

The sergeant was a veteran named Hanneman who'd been with the Phoenix PD since the days of Wyatt Earp. Dispensing with any opening pleasantries, he said, "Richardson? We've got a guy and his dog who've been shot to death in a garage. It belongs to you and McClinton. I'm on the horn to her next."

He gave me the address, which was in an upscale neighborhood on the city's east side, and then disconnected.

Cursing both my luck and the Valley's evening traffic, I took the Shea Boulevard exit off the Piestewa Freeway and headed east. Ten minutes after getting the call, I turned south onto Forty-fourth Street and then east again onto Mountain View.

The flashing lights of three squad cars and an ambulance marked the spot, an expensive home that backed up against the Phoenix Mountains. One city patrolman stood sentinel in front of the home's large three-car garage while two others looped yellow crime-scene tape around a wide perimeter of the scene. In the driveway the ambulance attendants leaned against their vehicle wearing lightweight uniform jackets and the bored expressions of two men who knew that they wouldn't be going anywhere for a while.

Earlier in the afternoon the temperature had climbed into the middle seventies, but now, five hours later, it had fallen into the low fifties. Someone in the neighborhood had built a fire either in a fireplace or in a backyard fire pit, and the scent of wood smoke hovered lightly in the evening air.

Inevitably, all the activity had attracted the attention of the neighbors, about thirty of whom had abandoned their television "reality" shows or whatever the hell else they might have been doing at eight twenty on a Wednesday night. They huddled together behind the crime-scene tape, talking quietly among themselves and gesturing in the direction of the tan stucco house where the action was taking place.

I pulled into a spot behind one of the squads and killed the engine. The front door on the passenger's side of the squad was standing open, and a man sat half in and half out of the car, holding onto a leash. A black Lab was attached to the business end of the leash, and both the man and the dog turned to watch my arrival. One of the patrolmen guarding the perimeter nodded and raised the crime-scene tape so I could duck under it.

"Who caught the call?" I asked.

"Me and Martinez," the patrolman responded, tipping his head in the direction of the uniform who was standing nearest the garage. Pointing to the man who was sitting in the squad, he said, "The citizen is Michael Litwack. He was out walking his dog and heard a commotion inside the garage. Then a Lexus SUV backed out of the garage and went tearing down the street.

"Litwack ran over and saw the body lying there. Then he raced to the neighbors' house and told them to call nine-one-one. Martinez and I responded to the call. We found Litwack standing in the driveway waiting for us. We took a quick look, called for backup, and then checked to make sure there was no one else in the house. The paramedics got here about ten minutes behind us and pronounced the vic. The second and third squads got here a few minutes after that and we began sealing the area."

"Okay," I said. "The crime-scene techs are on their way, along with some additional detectives and uniforms. While we're waiting for them, you and the other patrolmen start circulating through the crowd collecting names and addresses before we start to lose our audience. If anyone has information that would be of immediate interest, let me know."

"Will do," he replied.

I pulled on a pair of latex gloves and walked into the garage. A small sports car sat in the far right stall, covered with a tarp, and a black Mercedes sedan was parked in the middle stall. Toward the front of the garage, in the empty stall on the left, a large German shepherd lay on its side in a pool of blood. Five feet away from the dog, a man who was equally dead lay on his back, having bled out from wounds to his chest.

The victim was wearing jeans and a soft blue shirt with a button-down collar. He appeared to have been in his late forties and in good physical shape. The clothes, though casual, looked expensive, as did his haircut and wristwatch. His fair complexion and soft, well-tended hands suggested that he was a professional man who spent most of his working days indoors, beyond the reach of the Valley's blazing sun. The look frozen on his face suggested a mixture of surprise and abject terror.

I'd come to the department thirteen years ago, twenty-three and fresh out of college. A patrolman for four years, detective for nine, seven years a member of the Homicide Unit. And even after all that time, I'd never gotten used to scenes like this.

I knew that some cops did. Somehow they were able to distance themselves emotionally from the human tragedy that constituted the warp and woof of the job. To them, the crimes were reduced to intellectual problems, the victims simply pieces of the puzzle.

Not for me.

Doubtless my outlook was colored to some extent by the emotional wreckage of my own life at the moment. But rather than becoming inured to and hardened by the violence that human beings so casually inflicted on each other, I found myself growing increasingly distressed by the cataclysm of the lives so cruelly and abruptly interrupted. My first homicide victim was a nineteen-year-old woman who'd been raped and then brutally murdered. I remembered her as vividly as I knew I'd always remember this man—and all of the others in between.

Rising to my feet, I stripped off the gloves and stuck them in my pocket. Then I ducked back under the crime-scene tape and walked over to the squad where the citizen who'd reported the crime was sitting. He was somewhere in his middle fifties with thinning gray hair and eyes so impossibly blue that I wondered if he might be wearing tinted contact lenses. He was perhaps four inches shorter than my six one, and about ten pounds heavier than my one seventy. He wore a Phoenix Suns T-shirt over cargo shorts and a pair of New Balance running shoes. He was obviously badly shaken and looked as though he might yet lose his dinner.

"Detective Sean Richardson, Phoenix Homicide," I said, extending my hand.

"Mike Litwack," he responded, rising to greet me. He shook my hand with a firmer grip than I'd expected under the circumstances and said, "Forgive me, but I'm still in a state of shock here."

"Perfectly understandable," I replied. I reached down and petted the dog, who continued to sit silently and perfectly still, watching the exchange between his master and me. "Can you tell me what happened here this evening, Mr. Litwack?"

He gestured toward Martinez. "Well, as I told the other officers, I live five houses down from David and Beverly. My wife and I finished our dinner a little after seven, and I brought Barney out for his evening constitutional. We were walking by here a few minutes later when I heard somebody honking a horn in the garage. The honking stopped and I heard two shots. A woman screamed and then there were two more shots. Then the noises stopped."

Litwack looked away for a moment, then turned back to me, seemingly embarrassed. "I'm afraid I panicked. I had no weapon and I didn't know what I could do, so Barney and I ran up the street a bit, and then I stopped and turned to watch. The garage door came up and Beverly's SUV came flying out. Then it sped off back toward Forty-fourth Street."

"Could you tell who was driving the car?" I asked.

"No," he replied apologetically. "It was too dark, and I was too far away. Plus it all happened so fast . . ."

"I understand, Mr. Litwack. Could you at least see if the driver was a man or a woman?"

He shook his head. "No, I'm sorry, I couldn't. The windows of Beverly's car are tinted. Plus, of course, it was already dark. I couldn't see anything inside the car, so I just focused on getting the license number so that I could call the police."

"I gather you know the people who live here?"

"Yes—David and Beverly Thompson. He's a cardiologist, and she's an attorney. The dog's name is Chester."

"And that's Dr. Thompson in the garage there?"

"Yes, it is," Litwack replied, his voice breaking.

I looked up to see the Crime Scene Response team's van driving slowly up the street, followed by my partner's beat-up Mazda. Coming to a stop behind them were two more squads and the first of the television news crews.

"Okay," I said. "Thank you, Mr. Litwack. I'm sorry you've had such an unsettling experience here tonight, and I hate to impose on you further, but another team of detectives will be joining us shortly. We'll want you to go downtown with one of them and make a formal statement."

"Certainly," he replied. "Again, I only wish I had something more useful to tell you."

I nodded and walked over to join my partner. She unfolded herself out of the Mazda and I said, "So where's your official ride?"

Grimacing, she replied, "In the fuckin' shop again. I swear to Christ, that car is the most useless piece of shit Detroit ever put on the road. So what do we have here?"

I nodded back in the direction of the garage. "One seriously dead cardiologist and a dog who's in the same unhappy condition. The wife's SUV went racing down the street immediately after the shooting, and since she's nowhere in evidence, I assume that she was in the car. A neighbor walking by heard the shots and called it in. He also heard a woman screaming while the shots were being fired. I'm assuming that the screamer was the wife, whose name is Beverly Thompson.

"Either she shot her husband and the dog and then made her getaway, or an intruder shot the husband and the dog and then took Thompson with him when he left. Beyond that, we don't know anything yet."

"Okay," she sighed, "Let's get to work."

Maggie McClinton had joined the Homicide Unit seven months earlier. She'd come to the department after a stint in the army, and at thirty-eight, she was a year and a half older than I, even though I was four years her senior on the force. The daughter of a white mother and a West Indian father, she'd been gifted with perfectly clear skin the color of light toffee, warm brown eyes, and glossy dark hair that she wore cut to a medium length and in a perpetual state of disarray. She had a bright mind, a razor-sharp wit, and a mouth that would put an outlaw biker to shame.

The department had initially teamed her with a fifty-four-year-old veteran detective who perpetually referred to her as "my girl" and who seemed constitutionally incapable of keeping his eyes off her breasts. She'd ultimately requested a reassignment, and we'd been partnered together for the last five months. I valued her strong work ethic, her intelligence, and her obvious street smarts. In my wildest dreams I could never imagine referring to her as "my girl."

She walked into the garage and stood quietly for a moment, looking over the scene. Then we went over to join the members of the Crime Scene Response team. The lead tech was Gary Barnett. Ben Franklin–style glasses fronted his boyish face, and in truth, he looked more like a small-town high-school physics professor than a senior member of a major metropolitan crime lab. I brought him up to speed. Then Maggie and I left him and his team to go about their business in the garage while we went to take a look inside the house.

The door from the garage to the house was standing open and led into a short hallway. On the left side of the hallway was a powder room; on the right was the laundry room. The end of the hall opened into a spacious, well-designed kitchen that looked as though somebody actually cooked in it. A double oven was built into the wall, and the convection oven on top was preheated to four hundred and fifty degrees.

On a large island in the center of the room, two salmon fillets, brushed with oil and seasoned with what looked like ground pepper and an assortment of herbs, sat in a roasting pan, apparently ready to go into the oven. Someone had been interrupted in the middle of making a salad, and a bowl of mixed greens, a cucumber, a red onion, and a plastic container holding what looked like homemade vinaigrette were arranged around a cutting board in the center of the island. Someone had also been interrupted in the middle of drinking a martini, and a stemmed glass with the remains of the drink stood next to the salad bowl.

We took a quick look through the rest of the house, but as the patrolman had indicated, no one was there, and save for the bodies in the garage, the place seemed undisturbed. We concluded our tour back in the kitchen, and I picked the phone out of its base on the counter next to a large side-by-side refrigerator and freezer. I pressed the button to display calls received, and it indicated that the last call, at six thirty-one P.M., had been from "Beverly Cell."

"So what do you make of it?" Maggie asked. "They have a fight in the middle of making dinner. She grabs a gun. They wind up in the garage. She pops him and then takes off? Or are you leaning toward the intruder alternative?"

I put the phone back in its base, opened the freezer door, and saw a second martini glass standing on a shelf next to a small carafe of what I assumed was either gin or vodka. I closed the freezer door and said, "I'm betting on the intruder, Maggs. One person has started a martini, and there's a second in the freezer. Plus, the wife called home forty-five minutes before it all went down.

"It looks to me like he was making dinner and waiting for her to get home from work or wherever. She drives into the garage and the killer surprises her there. She screams and lays on the horn. The husband and the dog come out to investigate and the intruder shoots them, then takes off with the woman. If it's a straight domestic thing, it probably would have happened here in the house and there wouldn't have been any reason to shoot the dog."

"Yeah," Maggie sighed. "That makes sense. So where in the hell do you suppose they are by now?"

CHAPTER THREE

Carl McClain pulled his nondescript Ford Econoline van into the garage, jumped out of the vehicle, and pulled the garage door down behind him. He secured the door from the inside, then leaned back against it and let out a heavy sigh as the tension and the adrenaline rush of the last ninety minutes slowly drained away.

The house with its attached garage was in a gritty area of south-central Phoenix, a stone's throw from the Sky Harbor Airport. It sat among a group of similarly aged homes, a few of which were now abandoned and others of which were slowly falling into ruin. McClain had rented the place three months earlier from a balding, overweight landlord who seemed exceedingly happy about the prospect of getting the rent and who appeared to care not at all about McClain's plans for the house, as long as he paid the rent on time.

As was the case with many of the other houses in the neighborhood, the windows were protected by iron security bars. The yard, which consisted mostly of dirt, litter, and a few hardy weeds, was enclosed by a chain-link fence. These precautions notwithstanding, McClain had installed a new set of heavy-duty locks on each of the exterior doors. He'd also boarded up the windows in the larger of the two bedrooms, first closing the blinds and then nailing the shabby curtains in between the plywood and the glass. From the outside of the house it would simply look like he always left the blinds closed and the curtains pulled shut.

That done, he'd tacked fiberglass insulation over the walls and ceiling of the bedroom and the small connecting bathroom. The insulation would soak up any sound that might otherwise escape from the rooms in the unlikely event that anyone in the seamy neighborhood would be close enough to hear the noise and in the even more unlikely event that they would care anything about it.

Against one of the walls of the bedroom he'd built a platform, eighty inches long by sixty inches wide and twenty-four inches high. On the platform he'd put a queen-size mattress that he bought at a discount mattress outlet. He'd bolted two heavy iron rings into the wall at the head of the bed, and two more into the floor at the foot of the bed.

By the fifth of February everything was in readiness, and two nights later McClain opened the rear doors of the van and pulled an old painter's tarp off of Beverly Thompson, who was lying on the floor of the van, still unconscious from the chloroform.

A little after nine o'clock that night, Beverly felt herself coming slowly back to life, but everything around her seemed hazy and out of focus, as if her life was happening at a distance. She had a vague recollection of driving into her garage and of shots being fired, then of bouncing on the hard floor of a vehicle that was being driven over a rough stretch of road. She'd had a fleeting moment of semiconsciousness when someone threw her over his shoulder in a fireman's carry, but that was the last thing that she remembered.

As she now came to again, she found herself lying spread-eagled on a bed. Her arms were stretched wide apart over her head and her wrists were handcuffed to a pair of rings hanging from the wall above the bed. Her left leg was secured by a rope that dropped off the foot of the bed and was anchored somewhere out of her sight. Her right ankle was secured in a metal cuff. A thick wire cable trailed from the cuff down to a ring that had been bolted into the floor about three feet from the edge of the bed.

The ceiling above and the walls around her were covered with pink fiberglass insulation, and the ultimate effect suggested a demented cotton-candy maker had run amok in the place. The room was warm, and she found herself perspiring.

Suddenly Beverly remembered the sight of David collapsing to the floor of the garage. She shook her head in an effort to drive the image away and gave a sharp little cry. Then she heard the sound of a chair scraping on the floor somewhere to her right. She turned her head to see a man rise from the chair and walk over to the side of the bed.

"Are we finally awake now?" he asked.

The man appeared to be in his late thirties or early forties, tall and well muscled. He was still dressed in the black jeans and black long-sleeve T-shirt he'd been wearing when he slipped under the door into her garage. Strong features, including an especially prominent nose, filled an oval face. The man was completely bald, and as Beverly's vision drew back into focus, she realized that he also had no eyebrows.

In her mind's eye again she saw David lying on the floor of the garage, and she began to cry. "Who are you?" she pleaded. "Why did you do this?"

The man gave her a hard smile, then climbed onto the bed and straddled her waist. With his right hand he began kneading her left breast, softly—almost carelessly. "You don't remember me, do you, Beverly?"

She shook her head and asked again, "Who are you?"

The man removed his hand from her breast and began slowly undoing the buttons on her blouse. "Don't worry about that now, Beverly," he answered. "We've got plenty of time to get reacquainted."

Chapter Four

A little after nine o'clock, a patrol officer found Beverly Thompson's SUV abandoned on a dark side street only three blocks from Thompson's home. Maggie and I interrupted our canvass of the neighborhood, collected Gary Barnett, and drove over to take a look.

The patrol officer had been smart enough to park her squad well away from Thompson's vehicle, and I pulled in behind her. As Maggie, Gary, and I got out of my car, the officer walked back to greet us. I asked her if she had approached the car.

Nodding, she said, "After I called it in, I walked over to the driver's side and used my flashlight to make sure that the vehicle was unoccupied. From here I could see that there wasn't anybody sitting in the car, but I figured I should make sure that there wasn't somebody lying on one of the seats or in the back who might need medical attention. There wasn't."

"Was there a gun or a purse lying where you could see it?"

She shook her head. "There's a briefcase and a purse sitting on the passenger's seat, but I didn't see a gun."

I nodded and turned to Gary. "Have the patrolmen seal Thompson's house and get your team over here. Do a thorough check of the area around the car, then haul it into the lab and see what you can get out of it. Maggie and I will start knocking on doors."

Barnett reached for his radio, and Maggie and I split up, with her taking the houses on the south side of the street while I did the ones on the north. I assumed that the killer must have transferred Thompson from the SUV into a vehicle that he had parked there before walking the few blocks to Thompson's home. With a little luck perhaps we could find someone who saw it go down.

I started with the house directly behind the Lexus, but the place was dark, and no one answered the door. A couple in the house to the west indicated that they had been home all night. Unfortunately, they'd spent the bulk of the evening out on the patio at the back of their home. They'd not seen any activity in front of their house and could tell me nothing about any vehicles that might have been parked there earlier in the evening.

I thanked them for their time and moved on to the house on the other side of the home where Thompson's car was parked. I rang the bell, and a minute later the door was opened by a girl who was maybe fifteen or sixteen years old and dressed all in black. Her dark hair was cropped short, framing a pale heart-shaped face. She wore no makeup at all, save for the bloodred lipstick that slashed across her mouth. A small silver ring dangled from her left eyebrow, complementing the braces that lined her teeth.

I flashed my shield, introduced myself, and asked if her parents were home. "Nope," she replied in an animated voice. "Why are you looking for them? Did Melvin embezzle money from some little old lady's trust account or something?"

"Not as far as I know," I smiled. "Who's Melvin?"

"My stepfather," she said, returning the smile. "You mean you're not here to investigate him?"

"Not tonight."

"That's a pity," she observed. "So why are you here, then?"

I pointed back in the direction of Beverly Thompson's Lexus. "I'm interviewing people along your street about that car over there."

She leaned out of the door and looked around me at the SUV. "So what's going on?" she asked.

"I was wondering if you might have seen the person who parked the car there, or if you might have seen any activity around the car?"

"Nope. Sorry," she said, shaking her head. "I've been up in my room slaving over a term paper about Albert Camus. I hadn't even noticed that car was there, and I don't know who it belongs to."

"You didn't happen to see any other unfamiliar vehicles parked on the street here tonight, did you— maybe when you might have been taking a break from your paper?"

She thought about that for a second, then said, "Yeah, as a matter of fact, I did. I came downstairs a couple of hours ago to get a glass of juice and I noticed that there was a van parked right about where that car is parked now."

"Did you recognize the van?"

"Nope. Never saw it before." She gave a small shrug. "I don't mean to sound snotty or anything, but it didn't look like a car that would belong to someone who lives in this neighborhood. I thought that it probably belonged to a guy who was doing some work for somebody, like a plumber or something, you know?"

"Can you describe it for me?"

She scrunched her face in concentration for a moment, then shook her head. "Not really. It was black and sort of beat-up looking, like it had some miles on it. It didn't have any windows on the sides—or at least not on the side that I could see—and that's why I thought it probably belonged to a workman. It didn't look like the sort of van that somebody would be using to haul her kids from their piano lessons to soccer practice, if you know what I mean."

"Yes, I think I do. Was there any writing on the side of the van that you could see?"

She simply shook her head.

"Any body damage, or anything else about it that would make it easy for someone to recognize it?"

Again she shook her head. "Not really. Like I said, it looked kind of old and dilapidated, but there weren't any major dents that I could see."

"You didn't by any chance get a look at the license plate?"

"No. I didn't see the back of the van, only the passenger's side."

"And you didn't see anyone in the van or hanging around near it?"

"Nope."

"Is there anyone else at home with you, Ms. . . . ?"

"Chasen. And no, there's no one else here. Melvin and Cheryl are over at the club sucking down gin with their lame-ass friends, and I'm here wrestling with Albert."

I handed her a card. "Okay, Ms. Chasen. Thanks for your help. I'll let you get back to your paper. But if you remember anything else about the van, please give me a call, okay?"

"No problem," she responded, taking the card. She looked at it for a moment, then looked back up to me with bright blue eyes. "You don't know anything about existentialism, do you, Detective Richardson?"

"Nope," I smiled. "You're on your own there, Ms. Chasen."

She shook her head. "I was afraid you'd say that."

Chapter Five

Back at the car, I radioed Dispatch and asked them to issue a crime-information bulletin for the van the young woman had described. The chances of finding it were exceedingly slim, especially without a plate number, but this was the only viable lead that we had so far. Maggie and I continued our canvass of the remaining homes along the street but found no one other than the Chasen girl who'd noticed the van or anything else of any consequence.

On the desk in David Thompson's study, we found a studio portrait that one of the neighbors identified as a fairly recent photo of Beverly Thompson. Back at the station, we duplicated the photo and released it to the media, asking anyone who saw the woman to call a special hotline number immediately.

That done, we gave it up for the night a little after two A.M., and twenty minutes later, I finally made it to the nursing home. The night-shift supervisor buzzed me in and said, "Are we really late tonight, Detective, or really early this morning?"

"I'm afraid that we're really late tonight, Mrs. Reilly," I responded. "Unfortunately, it's been one of those days."

She nodded, gave me a sympathetic smile, and returned to her desk. I walked up the stairs to the second floor and pushed through the doors that led to the critical-care unit. Here the lights had been dimmed to the overnight setting, and at the far end of the hall an elderly Hispanic custodian was quietly mopping the floor.

I continued on down the hall and found that, as usual, Julie's door was standing slightly ajar. Her room was illuminated only by a small night-light burning on the table next to the bed and was completely silent, save for the barely audible sound of a car passing on the street below. I went in, closed the door behind me, and stepped over to the bed. I kissed Julie lightly on the top of the head and said, "I'm finally here, babe. Sorry I'm so late."

As had been the case every night for the last eighteen months, she made no reply. I stroked her long blonde hair for a minute and then took her hand and sat down in the chair next to the bed.

Looking back to the bedside table, I noticed that there was one message on the answering machine. I pushed the button to play the message and listened as my mother-in-law said, "Sean, if you find the time to visit Julie tonight, I wanted you to let you know that Denise will be arriving at four thirty tomorrow afternoon. We'll be going directly from the airport to the nursing home and will probably be staying with Julie until seven thirty or so. Denise and I would like to have some private family time alone with Julie and so if you are going to visit tomorrow, it would be best if you could arrange to do so at some other time. There's no point in making this any harder on all of us than it has to be."

Shaking my head in weary frustration, I erased the message, squeezed Julie's hand, and said, not for the first time, "How could that miserable shrew possibly be your mother?"

Julie had been born and raised in a wealthy suburb of Minneapolis. Her father, John, was president of one of the largest banks in Minnesota and a pillar of the community. Her mother, Elizabeth, was the quintessential executive wife–society matron, whose world revolved around a hectic schedule of club meetings, parties, charity functions, shopping, exercise, and spa treatments.

As children, Julie and her sister, Denise, had attended only the finest schools, had vacationed only in the trendiest locales, and had associated only with the "best" people. Denise, who was a year younger than Julie, bought into the program early on and had rapidly become the apple of her mother's eye. Much to Elizabeth's consternation, though, Julie had graduated from high school and then effectively opted out of her mother's master plan.

Julie refused to attend Elizabeth's alma mater, a fairly conservative private college in Connecticut, and insisted on putting some distance between herself and her mother, not to mention the cold, gray, gloomy winters of Minnesota. To her mother's mortification, she enrolled at Arizona State in Tempe and graduated with a degree in business. Much more her father's daughter than her mother's, Julie then remained in Arizona and took a job with a bank in Phoenix.

She'd been working at the bank for little over a year when we met at a party thrown by a mutual friend. While it might not have been exactly love at first sight, it was something very close. Two years younger than I, Julie was bright, warm, and articulate, and she possessed a great sense of humor. We shared many of the same interests and held very similar political views. The fact that she was also one of the most beautiful women I'd ever met was simply an added bonus. After dating for five months we moved in together, and six weeks later, Julie took me home to Minnesota to meet her family.

Her mother was decidedly unimpressed.

Elizabeth had simply taken it for granted that her daughters would follow her example and marry someone in their own social and economic stratosphere. She vehemently refused to accept the possibility that Julie might "settle" for an unsophisticated, middle-class police detective. Julie's father, on the other hand, had supported her decision to go to college in Arizona and took it as an article of faith that she was intelligent enough to make her own decisions when it came to matters of the heart. He was much more supportive of our relationship and welcomed me into his home.

The breach between Julie and her mother was completed at the end of our visit, when Julie informed her family that we would be married the following month—in Arizona in front of our own friends, rather than in Minnesota in front of Elizabeth's. In the end, only Julie's father had attended the ceremony and proudly gave his daughter away, while Elizabeth and Denise stubbornly remained at home.

Five years later, Elizabeth was still waiting for Julie to come to her senses, when a drunk driver who was still on the road despite two previous convictions for DUI ran a red light and smashed broadside into Julie's Acura. The Acura's airbags deployed, and amazingly, Julie had walked away from the crash with no apparent injuries, save for a slight bump on the head. But two days later she collapsed while at work and had never regained consciousness.

For the last eighteen months, she'd remained in what her doctors described as a persistent vegetative state with no cognitive brain function. She was able to breathe on her own, but otherwise was kept alive only by remaining attached to a feeding tube that pumped chemical nutrition and hydration into her stomach.

For the first few months after the accident, the doctors held out some small hope that Julie might eventually regain consciousness, but they warned that there was little hope that she could ever function effectively on her own again. For several critical minutes after she collapsed, her brain had been deprived of oxygen, and the damage done, the doctors argued, was irreparable.

My world completely shattered, I'd taken a leave of absence for three months and had spent virtually every waking moment at Julie's bedside, willing her to regain consciousness. But hard as it was to admit it, I ultimately understood that this was not going to happen. And as a bedside witness to the indignity of what had become Julie's "life," I also knew that she would not want it to.

Shortly after we were married, Julie and I had gone to a lawyer and drawn up our wills. At the lawyer's suggestion, we'd also made living wills, declaring that our deaths should not be postponed by artificial means in the event that either one of us should incur an incurable and irreversible injury, disease, or illness. We'd each also signed a power of attorney for health care, granting each other the authority to make these medical decisions in the event that we were unable to make them for ourselves.

Six months after Julie had been hospitalized, the doctors indicated that they no longer held out any hope that she would ever regain consciousness, and in the most difficult and heartbreaking decision of my life, I instructed them to honor her wishes and remove the feeding tube. Before they could do so, however, Elizabeth obtained a court order preventing it. She then filed a lawsuit attempting to set aside both Julie's living will and the medical power of attorney that Julie had granted me.

While the legal case worked its way through the system, Julie was moved from the hospital to a long-term-care facility. Elizabeth bought a condo in Scottsdale and now spent several days a month in residence, meeting with her lawyers and devoting more time and attention to Julie than she had ever deigned to spare in the five years between our marriage and the accident.

My relationship with Elizabeth was barely civil and was conducted mostly through our respective lawyers.

She tried as much as possible to avoid being at the nursing home when she thought that I might be there. When direct communication between us was unavoidable, we managed it mainly by leaving messages for each other on the answering machine that had been installed on the phone line in Julie's room. My affection for Julie's father notwithstanding, I very much regretted my decision to have offered her family the opportunity to be at her bedside when the feeding tube was to be removed.

I sat there for an hour or so, holding Julie's hand, thinking about all of the things that I would have wanted to share with her at the end of the day, and inevitably giving free reign to the memories that so sweetly haunted my days and nights. Finally, at about three thirty, I got up from the chair, leaned over, and kissed Julie on the cheek. "I love you Jules," I said quietly.

Then I gently laid her hand back at her side, slipped out of the room, and made my way home alone to our empty house.

CHAPTER SIX

Four hours later, I climbed the stairs back up to my office in the Homicide Unit on the third floor of the police headquarters building on Washington Street in downtown Phoenix. The lieutenant's door was standing open, and as I reached the reception area, he looked up from the report on his desk, put down his reading glasses, and waved me in.

The lieutenant, Russ Martin, was a twenty-two-year veteran of the force and had been head of the Homicide Unit for the last five years. His hair, which had once been as thick and dark as my own, was now thinning and flecked with gray. But six mornings a week, he began his day in the gym, and even at fifty-two he remained in excellent physical shape. He pointed me toward a chair in front of his desk, and I said, "What's up?"

Toying with a pencil, he said, "Beverly Thompson's picture hit the airwaves first thing this morning. So far we've had fourteen callers claiming to have seen her within the last twelve hours in locations from Tucson all the way up to Prescott. Patrolmen are following up on all the local reported sightings, and we're coordinating with police and sheriff's departments in the outlying areas. Doubtless, as the day progresses the number of calls will escalate, but we don't have anything that looks solid yet."

With the pencil, he tapped the report he'd been reading. "Ballistics says the bullets we got out of David Thompson match the slugs they recovered from the elderly woman that Pierce and Chickris drew last Friday. It looks like the same shooter did both her and Thompson."

"Any obvious connection between the Thompsons and this other woman?"

"None that I know of," he sighed. "But the report just landed on my desk ten minutes ago. Obviously the cases are related, though, and the four of you will need to work them together. You're senior; I'd prefer that you take the lead."

He paused for a moment, toying with his glasses and staring at the photo of his wife and three kids that sat on the edge of the cluttered desk. Then he looked back to me. "That said, Sean, I'm sorry, but I've got to ask. Are you sure you're up for this?"

I'd been waiting for the question for the last couple of months and was surprised only by the fact that it had taken him this long to ask it. Certainly it was a fair question, especially under the circumstances. The department was now confronted with a complex investigation that would inevitably attract a great deal of attention in the media, and his ass would be on the line much more so than mine. He needed to know—and had every right to demand—that his lead investigator would be tightly focused on the case and capable of performing effectively.

I certainly understood that if I were too distracted to give the case the time and attention it demanded, my record to date would be of absolutely no consequence. The lieutenant would have to assign the overall direction of the investigation to someone else. I waited a moment myself, then looked him in the eye and gave him what I hoped was an honest answer.

"Yeah, Lieutenant, I'm up for it. And I promise to let you know the second I feel that I'm not."

"Okay then," he said. "Doyle is back from vacation tomorrow, but Riggins won't be back from his father's funeral for another few days. So until Bob gets back you can use Doyle as well."

I pretended to think about it for a moment, then said, "I don't know, Lieutenant. Are you sure that's necessary? Why don't we see what McClinton, Pierce, Chickris, and I can do with this thing over the next few days? Then you could evaluate the situation, determine whether you think we need any additional help, and decide at that point who might be the best addition to the team based on where we are."

The lieutenant shook his head. "Look, Sean. I know you have your issues with Doyle, and I'm not suggesting that I don't understand where you're coming from. But you need to set all that bullshit aside. Whether either of us likes it or not, Doyle is still assigned to this unit. Beyond that, you know damned good and well that you're going to need all the manpower you can get on this thing. Certainly you can find some way to use him productively at least for the next few days. In the meantime, you need to get on it."

The lieutenant gave me a copy of the ballistics report, and twenty minutes later, Maggie and I were holed up in the squad's conference room with Elaine Pierce and Greg Chickris, the team that had caught the case of Alma Fletcher.

Chickris was the youngster of the unit. Tall and rail thin, he was a former college golfer who, in spite of the demands of the job and a young family, still somehow maintained a three handicap. Pierce was divorced, in her midforties with two teenage kids—a stocky bottle blonde who'd come into the Homicide Unit about six months after me. Her aggressive nature complemented her partner's more laid-back personality, and the two of them had a very good record of clearing cases. I asked Elaine to bring Maggie and me up to speed on their case.

She flipped open the folder in front of her and without looking at it said, "The vic is Alma Fletcher, sixty-four, a retired third-grade teacher, married to Robert Fletcher, also sixty-four. He works for a small insurance agency in Glendale. He found his wife in the living room when he got home from work about six o'clock on Friday evening. She'd been shot twice—one in the head and one in the heart. Either one would have gotten the job done.

"The ME puts the time of death at about ten thirty that morning. The husband has a concrete alibi—he got to work at eight, and people put him there all day until he left at five. The two had been married for thirty-nine years, and all their friends say that the marriage was rock solid. We found no evidence of any discord, no financial problems, nothing to suggest that the husband might have had any reason to hire the job done.

He's clearly devastated, and we've ruled him out as a possible suspect.

"The victim was not sexually assaulted, and nothing was taken from the home. Neither the husband nor any of the woman's friends could think of anyone who might have been even slightly angry with her, and so we haven't been able to come up with anything that might even remotely resemble a motive. None of the neighbors saw anything unusual the morning of the killing—no strangers in the area, nobody selling magazines door-to-door, or any such thing."

"Did the techs give you anything?" Maggie asked.

"Nada," Greg sighed. "At least not yet. They found no prints that didn't seem to belong there, but they did get some hair and fibers, and if we come up with a suspect maybe we can match them up to him. Of course it's also possible that the guy's had a prior conviction, in which case we may already have his DNA."

"We should get so lucky," Pierce and I said, almost in unison.

Arizona had begun collecting DNA samples from convicted sex offenders in 1993. Gradually, the list of those required to give samples had been expanded, and since January 2004, everyone convicted of a felony in the state had been required to submit a sample. Thus, DNA collected at a crime scene could be compared to the samples on file in the state's database or in CODIS, the FBI's database of DNA samples collected from criminals nationwide.

As Greg suggested, it was possible that our killer was a prior offender and that he might have been required to submit a DNA sample. Unfortunately, in the normal course of things it would still be several days before the tests would be completed and we'd have an answer one way or the other. In the meantime, we'd have to pursue the investigation using more traditional techniques.

Looking to Elaine, I said, "Do we know how Fletcher's killer got in?"

"We're assuming that she let him in. There was no sign of a forced entry, so we figure that he rang the front doorbell. She answered it, and he backed her into the living room and shot her."

"Did anyone report seeing an unfamiliar vehicle in the neighborhood that morning?" Maggie asked. "In particular, did anyone notice a black van?"

Greg shook his head. "Naturally, we asked about strange vehicles, but no one indicated that they saw one."

"Still, you'll want to go back and ask them again," I suggested. "We believe that last night the guy was driving a black van that looks like it might belong to a tradesman of some sort. Maybe one of Fletcher's neighbors saw it but didn't realize the significance. If so, there's at least a chance that we can get a better description."

"Sure," Elaine agreed.

"In the meantime," I said, "we need to dig into this woman's life and see where it intersects with either David or Beverly Thompson. So far, we don't know which of the Thompsons was the killer's real target. Was he after her and the husband blundered into it, or was it the other way around? I'm assuming the killer didn't simply pick these people at random. There must be some connection that ties Fletcher to one or possibly both of the Thompsons."

"How do you want to carve it up?" Greg asked.

"You guys go at it from Fletcher's side; Maggie and I will go at it from the Thompsons'. Assuming that they weren't related in some way by blood or marriage, the most obvious question is, was Fletcher a client of Beverly Thompson's or perhaps a patient of David Thompson's? There's gotta be a link there somewhere. Let's find it."

Greg rose to get out of his chair, but I waved him back down. "There's one other thing," I sighed. "Chris Doyle is back from vacation tomorrow. The lieutenant's going to assign him to work with us until Bob gets back from his father's funeral."

Maggie rolled her eyes. "Oh, that'll be a big fuckin' help. Even if Doyle *is* back in the building tomorrow, he'll still be on vacation, and the lieutenant knows that as well as all the rest of us. The time we'll have to spend babysitting that asshole is time that we could be spending doing something productive."

Pierce and Chickris understood Maggie's history with Doyle almost as well as I did, and none of us was going to dispute her observation. Unfortunately, though, the lieutenant had left us little choice in the matter. I shrugged and said, "Sorry. But whatever the case, that's the situation we're in. So obviously the best thing for all concerned would be for us to get out there, find our killer, and rescue Beverly Thompson before the close of business today. Then we won't have to worry about Doyle."

While Elaine and Greg went off to reinterview Alma Fletcher's husband and friends, Maggie and I decided to start with the staff at David Thompson's office. Maggie said that she wanted to hit the john before we left, and I nodded my acknowledgment. Five minutes later, she returned and said, "Are you ready to roll?"

"Yeah. Who's going to drive?"

"To Scottsdale—at this time of the day? Are you fuckin' kidding? You drive."

I could've pulled rank and insisted that she do it, but I enjoyed driving and found it oddly therapeutic, even in the congestion of the Valley's traffic, and especially on a day as beautiful as this. As we walked out of the station into the dry desert air, the temperature stood somewhere in the high sixties and a brilliant sun punctuated the cobalt sky. Slipping on my sunglasses, it struck me that it was an altogether far-too-perfect day for the task that lay ahead of us.

My department ride was a Chevy Impala, two years newer and a lot more reliable than Maggie's. As the engine sprung to life, so did Angie Stone, singing "Love Junkie" on the CD changer I'd surreptitiously installed in the trunk.

"Hey! Not bad for a middle-aged cracker," Maggie laughed, cranking up the volume.

"Fuck you, Maggs," I responded as I pulled out of the lot and accelerated onto Seventh Avenue.

CHAPTER SEVEN

Beverly Thompson came slowly awake again a little after nine o'clock, Thursday morning, still a bit groggy from the aftereffects of the chloroform. For the briefest moment she thought that she was waking from a horrible nightmare, but then she flashed again on the image of David slumping to the floor of the garage. In the same instant, she felt a sharp twinge of pain between her thighs, and she realized that the nightmare had been all too real.

Her captor had loosened her clothes, pushed them out of his way, and raped her three times during the course of the night, slamming himself into her with an intense anger that he refused to explain. Obviously he knew who she was and expected that she should know him. But he didn't look at all familiar to Beverly, and he refused to tell her his name or to explain why he had kidnapped her and murdered her husband.

She had cried through most of the night—harder

during his assaults—but it failed to move him at all. If anything, the man seemed to take a grim satisfaction in her pain, and in response to her tears, he drove himself into her even harder.

At around four in the morning, he had finally stopped. He unlocked the handcuff that bound her left wrist to the wall at the head of the bed and removed the rope that restrained her left leg. Then he pulled a cheap thin blanket over the two of them and fell asleep on the bed beside her. After that he left her alone.

The bedroom door was cracked open, and she could hear him now, moving around in one of the other rooms. She heard what sounded like a cupboard door closing and the sound of dishes clinking against each other. A minute or so later, she heard footsteps moving back toward the bedroom. She closed her eyes and turned her head away, pretending to be asleep, and praying that the man would not assault her again.

He came into the room and she heard him set two items on the small nightstand next to the bed. Then he sat down on the bed and grabbed Beverly roughly by the shoulder. "Wake up, princess," he said. "Time to rise and shine."

She turned to look at him, feigning that he had awakened her. He waited until she appeared to be fully awake, then said, "Okay, sweetheart, I've got places to go and people to see. You'll have to live without me for a while." Pointing to the nightstand, he said, "Your breakfast is served."

Beverly glanced over and saw a bowl of what appeared to be granola mixed with almonds and raisins, floating in milk; a spoon; a paper towel folded in half, apparently to be used as a napkin; a large glass of orange juice; and two bottles of water. She looked back at her abductor, who was taking a ring of keys from the pocket of his jeans. Stretching over her, he unlocked the handcuff from her right wrist. Then he took her by the hand and pulled her slowly to her feet.

"Time for a quick tour," he said.

Beverly was now tethered only by a cable made of braided wire that had been sheathed in plastic and bolted to the cuff that gripped her right ankle. The cable looked to be about fifteen feet long, and the other end was anchored into the floor near the foot of the bed.

With her free hand, Beverly quickly buttoned the top two buttons on her blouse and pulled her skirt back down, covering herself as best she could while the man led her across the bedroom and into a small bathroom, the cable dragging across the floor behind her. The bathroom, like the bedroom, had been completely insulated, and a piece of plywood had been nailed over what was apparently a small window above the dingy toilet.

The cable was long enough to allow Beverly to reach the toilet and the small stained sink next to it. A washcloth and a bath towel, both of which might once have been white but which were now frayed and gray, had been draped carelessly over a towel bar next to the sink.

Beverly's captor was dressed this morning in a pair of clean blue Levi's and a sleeveless green T-shirt imprinted with the logo of a local gym. As she surveyed the bathroom, he spun her around and grabbed her hard by the shoulders. Once sure that he had her full attention, he said in a harsh voice, "Okay, Beverly, you listen to me now like your life depended on it, because believe me, it does. While I'm gone, you need to be a good girl. Stay calm and quiet, and don't do anything that might attract attention to yourself."

Gesturing at the insulation, he said, "Even if you were to shout yourself hoarse, no one would be able to hear you, besides which, this house is in the middle of one of the city's highest-crime neighborhoods. On the off chance that anybody did hear you, the odds are very good that it wouldn't be somebody whose acquaintance you'd want to make, if you get my drift. And even if you were lucky enough to attract the attention of somebody who might call the cops, you wouldn't want that to happen either."

Pointing back to the bedroom door, he continued, "If you haven't already noticed, that door is the only way in and out of here. What you can't see from the inside of the room is that the door is wired with explosives. I'm going to arm it when I leave. If the cops or anyone else opens that door, this house—and you and them along with it—will be blown to hell and back.

"So believe me when I say that it's in your own best interests for you to just sit here quietly and mind your manners while I'm out. You can reach the john and the sink. There's enough water there to get you through the day, and that should be all you need. We'll have a late lunch when I get back, and then maybe we can think of some way to amuse ourselves through the afternoon."

Tearing up again, Beverly tried to shrink away from him. "Who *are* you?" she pleaded again. "Why are you doing this to me?"

The man shook his head. "You know, Beverly, my feelings are starting to be hurt real bad. I was sure you would have recognized me by now, but I think I'll let the mystery build a little longer. Perhaps it'll come to you."

Still gripping her shoulders, he pulled her close again and forced a hard kiss on her. Releasing her, he stepped back and shook his head. "Jesus, babe, you've got a serious case of morning mouth there. I didn't even think about getting you a toothbrush and some toothpaste. I'll pick some up on the way home."

With that, he turned and walked away, leaving her standing in the bathroom. She watched as he crossed the bedroom to the door. He gave her a small wave, then closed the door behind him. Beverly heard him lock the dead bolt from the other side, and a couple of seconds later, she heard a small metallic click that sounded as if it came from somewhere near the top of the door. Then everything was quiet.

CHAPTER EIGHT

Greater Phoenix stretches some forty-five miles from north to south and sixty miles from east to west, in a valley originally settled by the Hohokam Indians about three hundred years before the birth of Christ. For reasons not entirely clear—perhaps because fourteenth-century air-conditioning units were so notoriously difficult to service and maintain—the Hohokam abandoned the valley early in the fifteenth century, and it then remained largely empty of population until the first white people settled here in the 1860s.

The metro area now includes a couple dozen incorporated cities and towns, Phoenix principal among them, and a number of unincorporated communities. These cities, towns, and villages originated as discrete entities, but over time they've grown and have been fused together into one sprawling urban region that the chamber of commerce markets as the Valley of the Sun.

Maggie and I were on our way to Scottsdale, which lies directly east of Phoenix and which, in the north, is separated from its sister city only by the four- to six-lane concrete expanse of Scottsdale Road. Traffic was surprisingly light for that time of the morning, and thirty minutes after leaving the department, we pulled into the parking lot of a large medical complex near

Shea and Ninety-second, where David Thompson's office was located.

Thompson's office manager was a woman named
Alice Ballentine. By even a charitable estimate, the
woman was probably a hundred pounds overweight,
and she'd stuffed herself into a pair of capri pants that
she'd apparently purchased at least twenty pounds
ago. Her short blonde hair was curled tightly to a perfectly round head, and she was sporting about twice
as much makeup and three times as much cloying per-
fume as a woman twice her size would have needed.
Like the receptionist, she'd obviously been crying, and
her eyes were red and raw.

Maggie and I introduced ourselves, and Ballentine
escorted us back to a small office. She squeezed herself
into a chair behind the desk and invited us to take the
two guest chairs in front of her. Grabbing a couple of
Kleenex from a box on the desk, she blew her nose and
dropped the tissues into the wastebasket.

"This is just so unbelievable," she said. "Why would
someone have done it?"

"That's what we're trying to determine, Ms. Ballentine," Maggie said in a sympathetic voice. "Do you
know of anyone who was upset with Dr. Thompson—
anyone who might have threatened him for some
reason?"

Ballentine shook her head vigorously. "No, no one.
I've been with Doctor for eleven years, and in all that
time I never heard him have a cross word with anyone—
and I mean that literally. He was an absolutely excellent
man to work with—extremely competent, very professional, very personable.

"So many doctors, particularly specialists like Dr.
Thompson, have huge egos and very little time and
patience for other people. But Doctor wasn't like that at
all. He took a genuine interest in his patients and in
his staff. He always had time for others and gave very

generously of himself." She paused long enough to blow her nose again and to swipe at her eyes with the tissues.

"I gather that the doctor had a very successful practice?" I asked.

"Oh, yes. Doctor was very much in demand. He frequently had to turn down new patients because there simply wasn't room in his schedule."

"And none of his patients was unhappy in any way?" Maggie asked. "Or perhaps was there a relative of a patient who might have been upset because he or she felt that Dr. Thompson had not done enough to help someone?"

"No, of course not," Ballentine insisted. "Unfortunately, like any other cardiologist, Dr. Thompson occasionally encountered a patient who was simply beyond help. It was always a very difficult situation for him, but he always did everything humanly possible on that patient's behalf. Doctor worked very closely with the families of his patients and was always very honest with them and very supportive of them. None of them ever blamed him for things that were obviously beyond his control."

"What about in the doctor's private life?" I asked. "Do you know of anyone who might have been upset with him for something that had nothing to do with his medical practice?"

Again she shook her head. "No, at least not that I'm aware of. Certainly he never indicated anything like that."

"I gather that, as Dr. Thompson's office manager, you were responsible for the financial end of his practice?" I said.

"Yes, I am," she answered tentatively.

"Was the doctor in any difficulty financially?"

She shook her head vigorously. "Oh, Lord no. The practice was very successful, and Doctor was fairly conservative financially. He'd owned his home for a number of years. He invested wisely, and he didn't spend lavishly on anything. Of course I wasn't privy to the details of his personal finances, but I know you'll discover that there were no problems in that regard."

"How well do you know Mrs. Thompson?" Maggie asked.

Ballentine stiffened a bit. "A little," she replied. "In the time that she and Doctor have been married, Mrs. Thompson has been in the office a few times. She's attended a couple of Christmas parties and other staff functions. But we don't socialize, if that's what you mean. She's quite busy with her own life. I know her mostly through listening to Doctor talk about her."

"And were she and Dr. Thompson a happy couple?" Maggie asked.

"I guess so," Ballentine conceded. "Of course they'd only been married for a little over two years, but Doctor still seemed very attracted to her. After he married her, he devoted somewhat less time to his practice than he had in the years before so that he would have more free time to spend with her. I guess if he hadn't been happy it would have been the other way around, wouldn't it?"

I nodded. "Ms. Ballentine, one of the problems we're facing in this investigation is that at the moment, we still don't know whether Dr. Thompson's killer might have been targeting him or his wife or perhaps both of them together. Do you know of anyone who might have been angry with Mrs. Thompson? Did the doctor ever hint at anything like that?"

"No," she said slowly. "Doctor never suggested anything to that effect. But then she is a lawyer, isn't she? Wouldn't she be a much more likely target than a respected surgeon?"

Ignoring the question, I said, "Can you tell us about

the families of Dr. and Mrs. Thompson? We understand that neither of them had any children, but what
about parents, siblings, or other relatives?"

Ballentine shook her head. "Doctor was originally
from Cincinnati. I know that he has an older brother
who still lives there and their mother is in a nursing
home in Ohio. Doctor's father died a number of years
ago. Mrs. Thompson is a Phoenix native, but both of
her parents are deceased. She has a brother and a sister, both of whom are older than her. I believe they
both moved away from Arizona some years ago, and I
don't know where either of them lives now."

I made a note, then said, "One last thing, Ms. Ballentine, and then we'll let you get back to work. Can you
tell us if the doctor ever treated a patient named Alma
Fletcher, or perhaps her husband, Robert Fletcher?"

Ballentine shook her head. "Neither of the names
sounds familiar, Detective, but I'll check."

Maggie and I sat quietly while Ballentine worked
with the computer on her desk. After a couple of minutes, she looked up from the monitor and said, "No,
Detective. According to our records, Doctor never
treated a patient with either of those names."

We spent another hour and a half interviewing the
other members of Thompson's staff, but none of them
was able to give us any more information than we'd
gotten from Ballentine. Most of them cried unasham-
edly during our interviews, but they were at a loss to
understand why a killer might have targeted their employer.

As we settled into my Chevy in the parking lot, Maggie shook her head and said, "Why is it that the people
who work in hospitals and doctor's offices always seem
to be in worse physical shape than the people who
work in offices anywhere else? Most of them are overweight, and half of them still seem to smoke. Christ,

most of the people in Thompson's office are in worse shape than those slobs in our department who eat three meals a day at the damned Krispy Kreme. What the hell is up with that?"

"Beats me, Maggs," I replied. "Maybe they figured that when their hearts gave out prematurely from all that bad behavior, 'Doctor' could just build them a new one."

"Maybe," she nodded, buckling her seat belt. "But if it's all the same to you, after spending thirty minutes with that Ballentine woman, I'm gonna skip lunch today."

CHAPTER NINE

Judge Walter Beckman left his condominium complex in Scottsdale at ten fifteen A.M. Carl McClain watched as the judge wheeled his three-year-old Buick through the gates of the complex and out to Seventy-sixth street. Thirty minutes later, Beckman left the Piestewa Freeway at the Glendale Avenue exit, obviously headed in the direction of his country club.

As far as McClain could determine, the retired widower's entire life revolved around the club. On the second day that he'd trailed the judge there, McClain had been bold enough to follow him into the pro shop at a discreet distance. Feigning interest in a display of golf shirts, he watched as Beckman signed in at the desk and then went out to the cart-staging area to meet the other members of his foursome.

Figuring that the round of golf would take at least five hours, McClain had checked back at three P.M. The Buick was still where the judge had left it, and Mc-

Clain found a parking place that would allow him to keep an eye on the car.

At four forty-five that afternoon, he was still watching the Buick when Beckman finally shuffled back through the parking lot. The judge unlocked the car, settled into the driver's seat, and sat there for a few minutes, apparently waiting for his head to clear. Then he started the car and drove very slowly and carefully back home. McClain had followed Beckman back to the condo complex, driving ten miles an hour under the speed limit and twenty miles an hour slower than the rest of the traffic. Sober as a judge, my ass, McClain had thought.

McClain's problem was that, on all of the occasions that he'd followed the judge thus far, the old bastard had never had an unguarded moment. The parking lot at the country club was too exposed, and there were always people around. In addition, the escape routes from the club left a great deal to be desired. If he were to do Beckman there, the chances of making a clean getaway in the Econoline would be slim at best.

When not at the club, the judge seemed to spend virtually all of his time in his condominium, which was located within a gated community. McClain figured that ultimately, if all else failed, he could climb the fence late at night, avoiding the guard at the gate and probably slipping by the advertised video surveillance. He could then make his way to the judge's front door. But that option had drawbacks as well.

It was possible that a camera might catch him going over the fence and that one of the guards might happen to see it on the monitor. Or perhaps one of the other residents might spot him climbing the fence and call the police. Then too, of course, there was always the chance that even if McClain did make it to the judge's condo unobserved, the old coot might refuse to answer the door at that hour of the night.

McClain reasoned that sooner or later Beckman would have to leave himself in a vulnerable position, but watching the judge signal another turn into the country club, he realized that the moment wasn't going to come this morning. Still, Carl McClain was a patient man who'd already waited a long time for an opportunity to set things straight. Although the clock was now ticking, he could afford to be patient for a more few days. And on the bright side, he now had Beverly Thompson to keep him entertained while he counted down those days.

Beverly stood glued to the floor of the grimy bathroom for a good five minutes after her captor had locked the bedroom door and left. Finally, when she was sure that she was alone, she went into the bathroom, used the toilet, and then opened the hot-water faucet in the sink. After a couple of minutes, the water was still only lukewarm, and she concluded that it wasn't going to get any hotter.

She soaked the washcloth and washed herself as best she could. After drying herself with the towel, she pulled the skirt back up, rearranged her bra, buttoned her blouse, and tucked it into the skirt.

Beverly hardly recognized the image that stared back at her from the filthy mirror above the sink. Her hair was in complete disarray. Her eyes were puffy and red, and her left cheek was swollen and bruised from when the man had slapped her after shooting David. Looking at herself, she began crying again. Then she shook off the tears, realizing that she needed to make the best use she could of whatever time she had to herself.

The mirror fronted a small medicine cabinet, and Beverly opened it but found the cabinet empty. A cheap fiberglass shower module had been installed in the corner of the bathroom, and the shower curtain was threaded over a piece of pipe that had been wedged into notched-out two-by-fours bolted into the wall above the module. She pushed the curtain aside to find the shower empty as well. The only implement of any kind in the bathroom was a plunger with a cracked wooden handle that was sitting next to the toilet.

Reaching above the toilet, Beverly ran her hands over the small piece of plywood that had been nailed over the window. Six large nails with flat heads had been driven through the plywood into the window frame. There would be no hope of prying the plywood away from the window without a clawhammer or a crowbar of some sort.

Dragging the cable behind her, she went back into the bedroom. The only pieces of furniture in the bedroom other than the bed itself were a card table, two folding chairs, the small nightstand, and a lamp that sat on the nightstand. Beverly pulled open the three drawers of the nightstand. Like the medicine cabinet, they were all empty.

She sat on the bed for a moment, staring at the glass of juice and at the cereal, which was already getting soggy in the milk. She suddenly realized that she'd had nothing to eat since lunch yesterday, and even though she had no appetite, she knew that if she had any hope of escaping, she would have to maintain her strength.

She forced down the cereal and drank half a glass of the juice. Then she folded her right leg up onto the bed so that she could examine the cable that was bolted to her ankle. The cable appeared to be about a quarter of an inch in diameter and was secured to a metal cuff that was about three inches wide. The cuff was hinged at the back and the two wings were bolted together at the front of her ankle. The short thick bolt was secured with a square nut. There was only an inch of play between the cuff and her ankle—not nearly enough room to allow her to somehow squeeze her foot out of the cuff.

Gripping the head of the bolt with her left thumb and forefinger and the nut with her right, Beverly tried to unscrew the nut, but succeeded only in cutting her finger on the rough edge of the bolt. The man had obviously used wrenches to tighten the nut to the bolt, and without wrenches there would be no way to loosen it.

She got up from the bed and examined the other end of the cable, which was secured to a ring in the floor by another thick bolt. As was the case with the ankle cuff, only someone with a wrench would be able to undo it.

The cable was long enough that Beverly could roam the entire length and width of the small room. Moving around the room, she tentatively pressed her fingers into the pink insulation, testing carefully, and discovered the two bedroom windows. Like the one in the bathroom, they had been sealed with plywood.

She saved the door for last. Careful not to touch it, she examined it carefully. The dead-bolt lock looked new, and from the inside it could be opened only with a key. But even if she had a key, would she dare to open the door? Was it really wired to explode, or had the man threatened her with that only as a means of keeping her from attempting to open it? She remembered the sound of the metallic click after he had closed the door. What had he done? Beverly got down on the floor and looked closely at the tiny gap between the floor and the bottom of the door. But she couldn't see anything on the other side.

Discouraged, she walked back and sat down on the bed. Staring at the door, she thought of David slumping to the floor of the garage and began crying again.

CHAPTER TEN

Neither Maggie nor I had eaten anything since early morning, and dinner was doubtless a long time into the future. So, in spite of Maggie's earlier pledge to pass on lunch, we decided that we should take advantage of the opportunity to eat something while on our way from David Thompson's office to that of his wife.

In Maggie's case, "lunch" consisted of a small garden salad with a simple oil and vinegar dressing on the side, accompanied by a refreshing cup of soy milk. Apparently deciding to live life in the fast lane, she ordered chocolate soy milk rather than vanilla, which was her usual choice. I was less confident than she that we'd be eating again any time soon and so ordered a Coke, a medium-rare hamburger, and a side salad of my own.

Watching the juice drip from my burger, Maggie arched her eyebrows, shook her head, and gave me a look that asked, *How can you possibly eat that shit?*

We'd had the "diet" conversation so many times by now that she really didn't need to say anything at all. I knew her lecture by heart, just as she knew my responses. And the fact that I'd ordered a salad with the burger rather than a large side of fries did little to allay her concerns about my long-term health and well-being.

In an effort to change the subject, I asked what she'd been doing when we'd been called out last night.

She shook her head. "Dinner at my mother's."

"And what's your problem with that?" I countered. "Your mom's a great cook."

"The problem was not the cooking," she sighed. "The problem was the company. Mom's trying to play matchmaker again."

"Oh, God. Who is it this time?"

"The new associate pastor from her church. He's about my age, and divorced with a couple of kids. He just moved here from Memphis with the kids in tow, leaving the ex-wife behind, for reasons that aren't entirely clear—at least to my mother. The two of us have absolutely nothing in common save for the fact that we're both divorced and that we were both in the army. I can't imagine why in the hell Mom would think I'd have any interest in they guy, let alone why he'd have any interest in me."

"Is the guy deaf and blind?"

"No, of course not."

"Then trust me, Maggs, he's interested."

"Right," she snorted. "At least he will be until he discovers that except for weddings and funerals, I haven't been in a church in probably the last ten years and that I have no intention of ever going into one again. I'm sure that, plus the fact that I'm totally incapable of relating to little kids, should pretty well squelch whatever interest he might have in a big fuckin' hurry."

"No doubt," I laughed. "But I'm sure he was captivated by your ladylike language."

I waited while she ate a bite of her salad and then said, "So tell me about him."

She gave a small shrug and jabbed her fork into the salad. "His name is Patrick Abernathy, and he's a good-looking guy. He's bright and seems to be reasonably laid-back for a minister—not that I've ever dated a minister before."

"You gonna date this one?"

"Shit, I don't know, Sean. It's not like my dance card

is especially full at the moment. I got the feeling that he might ask me out, and if and when he does, I'll guess I'll make up my mind then."

"So what's the story with the kids and the ex-wife?"

"I'm not really sure. The two kids are both girls. One's ten; the other's seven. He seemed a bit reluctant to talk about them. I got the feeling that he didn't want to scare me off by going on nonstop about his kids and maybe leaving the impression that he was desperate to find them a new mother.

"Of course Mom asked him a million questions about them and insisted that he show her pictures. They are pretty cute kids—if you're the kind of person who likes kids, I mean—and Patrick claims that they're both extremely smart and that they're doing very well in school.

"As to the former Mrs. Abernathy, I have no idea. He made no mention of her whatsoever, and of course Mom didn't feel compelled to press him on that subject. He and Mom talked about his work at the church, and he and I talked about the Diamondbacks and about how happy we both were to be out of the fuckin' army. Only he didn't describe it that way, of course—at least not in front of my mom."

"Well, it sounds like he must have made a good impression on your mother."

"Oh, yeah, no question," Maggie sighed, reaching for her soy milk. "Shit, maybe he'll ask her out instead."

Just after one o'clock, we walked into the offices of the law firm in downtown Phoenix where Beverly Thompson was a partner. The managing partner, Alan Ducane, was expensively but conservatively dressed in a navy blue suit that hung very well, even on his portly frame. A fringe of gray ringed his otherwise bald head, and a pair of reading glasses was hooked over the breast pocket of his jacket. He showed us into a richly appointed law library, and the three of us took seats at a long mahogany conference table.

"This is such a tragedy," he said. "We're all in shock. Is there any news yet about Beverly?"

"No, sir," I replied. "I'm afraid there isn't. As you might expect, since we released Ms. Thompson's photo this morning, we've had a number of reported sightings, but none of them has led us anywhere yet."

The lawyer shook his head. Absentmindedly toying with his glasses, he said, "What can we do to help?"

"Well, sir," Maggie said. "Obviously, we're very interested in knowing whether you or anyone else here can think of anyone who might have been upset with Ms. Thompson. Is there an angry client or coworker who might have wanted to harm her?"

Again, Ducane shook his head. "Absolutely no one, Detective McClinton. Beverly is well liked and respected by everyone here and, for that matter, by everyone who knows her. She's a very bright woman with a strong social conscience. She's an excellent lawyer and she hasn't got an abrasive bone in her body. I can't think of anyone who would wish her harm."

"Ms. Thompson specializes in medical malpractice?" I asked.

"Yes. The bulk of her clients are people with claims against doctors and insurers, and she has a very good record of winning favorable settlements for them. Like any other attorney, of course, she occasionally loses a case and a client winds up disappointed, but to the best of my knowledge, none of her losing clients has ever been angry enough to do something like this."

"What about the people she sues?" Maggie asked.

Ducane shrugged. "The people she sues are doctors who are insured against malpractice suits, or the insurance companies themselves. Obviously, they don't like to lose the money, but it's hard to imagine that an insurance company would hire someone to kidnap an attorney in a case they're contesting. And even if they did, it wouldn't accomplish anything of course. Another lawyer would simply step in and take over the case."

"How long has Ms. Thompson been with your firm?" I asked.

"A little over sixteen years. After law school, she spent a couple of years working in the public defender's office. That pretty much soured her on the idea of doing criminal law, and then she came to us. She was an associate for three years and then made partner."

"And you know of nothing going on in her life outside the office that might have prompted someone to attack her and her husband?" Maggie asked.

"No, I don't. Beverly and David were a terrific couple, very much in demand socially, and to all appearances, very much in love with each other. As I said, I can't think of anyone who might have wanted to harm either of them."

We spent some time interviewing Thompson's secretary and a number of other people in the office, but none of them knew anything that was of any help. Ducane provided us with addresses for Thompson's brother in Washington, D.C., and for her sister, who lived in Nebraska. With his assistance, we went carefully through Thompson's desk. However, as had been the case with the Thompsons' home offices, we found no threatening notes, no blackmail letters, or anything else suggesting that anyone had posed a threat either to Thompson or to her husband. And according to the files, neither Alma nor Robert Fletcher had ever had any sort of professional association with Beverly Thompson.

At four o'clock, Maggie and I met again in the Homicide Unit's conference room with Pierce and Chickris.

Some other group had used the room since we'd been in it earlier in the day, and they'd left in their wake three donuts that looked to be about as stale and tasteless as the box they were sitting in. Greg poured coffee for himself and Maggie after Pierce and I declined the offer. Then he dropped into a chair, snagged a maple-frosted donut from the box, and pushed the box across the table toward the two women. Maggie gave him a look, then picked the box off the table and pitched it and the last two donuts into the wastebasket. Saying nothing, Greg turned in my direction, arched his eyebrows, and shook his head.

Unfortunately, Pierce and Chickris had made no more progress on their end of the investigation than we had on ours. None of Alma Fletcher's neighbors remembered seeing a black van in the neighborhood on the day of her murder, and none of the people that Elaine and Greg reinterviewed was able to shed any additional light on the killing.

"We're still at a complete dead end with Fletcher," Elaine sighed. "We have no motive, no suspect, and no forensics worth a shit. And neither Mr. Fletcher nor anyone else we talked to had ever heard of either David or Beverly Thompson. It doesn't look like we're going to make a connection from that end."

"But there *has* to be one," Maggie protested. "Why would some cretin just randomly pop a little old lady and then turn around and shoot Thompson and abduct his wife?"

No one had an answer for that, and after a few seconds, Greg said, "What have you guys got from your end?"

"Not a helluva lot more than you have," Maggie replied. "We've contacted the Thompsons' siblings, but neither they nor anyone else has received a ransom demand from whoever took Mrs. Thompson. That, combined with the connection to the Fletcher woman, makes it seem pretty unlikely that she was grabbed so that the kidnapper could extort a payoff out of somebody."

"And I take it we've gotten nothing off the hotline?" Elaine asked.

" 'Nothing' is right," I sighed. "At least nothing solid. We've had reported sightings all over the friggin' state now, and the local authorities are chasing them down as fast as they can. But none of the reports has panned out, and it's hard to imagine that any of them will.

"Thompson was snatched twenty-one hours ago, and her picture's been out there for seventeen. You've got to figure that whoever grabbed her has already killed her and dumped the body. Either that or he's gone to ground with her somewhere. Certainly he's seen the TV coverage long before now, and he's got to know that we're looking everywhere for Thompson. I can't imagine that he'd risk being seen in public with her at this point."

"So what else do we have?" Greg asked.

"Not much," I sighed. "The Thompsons' phone records just came in. I assume you've got Fletcher's?"

Elaine nodded. "Yeah, we've got 'em, but we checked all the calls both in and out for the three months before she was shot. There was nothing out of the ordinary there."

"Okay," I said. "Let's compare Fletcher's records to the Thompsons' and see if there are any numbers in common. Then we can work our way through the Thompsons' calls and see if there's anything that jumps out at us there."

CHAPTER ELEVEN

The first baseman was a tall, rangy blonde with long straight hair, good eyes and hands, and even better foot speed.

Wearing a black cowboy hat pulled down low over his eyes, Carl McClain sat hunched over in the twelfth row directly above first base in the Alberta B. Farrington Softball Stadium, watching the girl intently as he had for each of the last three Arizona State home games.

He was impressed by the girl's natural athletic ability. It was also clear that she'd put in her time in the gym, and on the practice field as well, and the combination of her natural ability and her work ethic had enabled her to make the team as a freshman.

The girl was also extremely attractive, especially compared with the other young women on the field. Most of the other players had the heavy thighs, thick bodies, and butch haircuts typical of all too many female athletes. But the first baseman was a knockout, and McClain speculated that she was probably a real heartbreaker.

There were two outs in the bottom of the third inning, and ASU was leading Stanford 3–1. With the count at two and two, the Stanford batter hit a short pop-up in the direction of ASU's second baseman. The girl moved under the ball, made the catch without difficulty, and retired the side.

McClain watched the first baseman as she loped into the dugout and disappeared. Then he pulled the cowboy hat even lower over his eyes and turned to look at the girl's mother, who was sitting six rows down and about forty feet to his right.

The mother, whose name was Amanda, was a blonde herself. She wore her hair considerably shorter than her daughter's, in a style that was designed to appear casual and carefree. McClain would've bet, though, that she'd probably spent at least a couple hundred bucks to get her hair cut just exactly right and that she probably dedicated at least thirty minutes a day to keeping it that way.

Amanda was thin and lightly tanned, and the diamond set on her left hand sparkled even at this distance. She'd worn a different outfit to each of the three games that McClain had attended, and this afternoon her small, pert breasts were peeking out over the top of a light blue camisole. Below the cami, a pair of brief white shorts left no doubt about the fact that Amanda's legs were still her best feature, hands down.

Being rich agreed with her, McClain decided, and she had aged very well. In fact, closing in on forty, Amanda was even sexier than she'd been at nineteen, which was when Carl McClain had first sweet-talked her into going to bed with him. He promised her that he'd pull out, but then of course he didn't. It was the first in a long line of promises that he'd made to Amanda and then broken, and the result had been Tiffani, the first baseman.

As Stanford took the field, Amanda turned and scanned the crowd behind her—perhaps sensing his eyes on her?

Not very likely, he decided. Besides which, Amanda was, and always had been, a woman who was used to having eyes on her—one of those women who naturally expected it. No, more than likely she was simply anticipating the arrival of Richard, the man who was now her husband and their daughter's stepfather.

McClain looked away, just another spectator casually surveying the crowd on a beautiful afternoon at the ballpark.

He wasn't really worried that Amanda might recognize him after all this time. He was thinner now too—in his case by nearly seventy-five pounds—and he had toned up considerably. He'd never been one of those prison head cases who lived in the weight room, striving to become the Incredible Hulk or some fuckin' thing, and he didn't have the genes for it anyway. But the crappy prison food had finally tamed his insatiable appetite; he'd worked out on a regular basis; and after sixteen years, he'd morphed into a man who looked nothing at all like the Pillsbury Doughboy that Judge Walter Beckman had once sentenced to life for murder in the first degree.

Just then McClain saw Richard, his tie loosened and his suit coat slung over his shoulder, making his way up the stairs to join Amanda. McClain wondered why in the hell the guy didn't just lose the tie altogether and leave the suit coat in his Jag. It wasn't like the temperature was suddenly going to drop thirty-five degrees into the low forties. But the man was conscious of his image, and the coat and tie doubtless made a statement that Richard thought important.

Thirteen years ago, when Amanda married Richard, McClain had wasted a lot of sleepless nights, lying awake in his cell, swearing that if he ever got out of prison, he'd cut Richard's dick off and stuff it down his throat. But McClain was older now and, he hoped, at least a little wiser.

McClain could hardly blame Amanda for divorcing him. He'd given her plenty of cause even before the night of the murder. And he really couldn't blame her either for cutting him off completely, both from herself and from their daughter. He could never have imagined Amanda and Tiffani riding the bus out for visitors' day every other week, and in truth he never would have wanted them to. In the end, he couldn't even blame Amanda for marrying Richard. She saw her chance and she took it, both for herself and for her daughter. What else was the woman supposed to do?

He'd had no direct contact with Amanda or with Tiffani since two days after his arrest, but he had his sources. He understood that Richard loved both his ex-wife and his daughter and that he treated them very well. McClain also knew, in his heart of hearts, that Richard had been a much better father to Tiffani than he ever could have or would have been himself, and he was truly grateful for that. And so in the end, he'd abandoned his dreams of revenge against Richard and focused them on other, more deserving targets.

McClain watched with a profound mixture of longing and regret as Richard settled into his seat next to Amanda. She put her hand on his arm and gave him a small peck on the cheek. Then they both turned to watch as Tiffani moved into the batter's box.

McClain turned to watch too, and with the count at two and one, the pitcher threw one in low and just outside. Tiffani uncoiled and took a smooth, strong cut at the ball, drilling it into left center field. The outfielder bobbled the ball momentarily, and Tiffani whipped around first base and slid safely into second.

McClain jumped to his feet, cheering and clapping with the rest of the home-field crowd. With a lump in his throat, he watched his daughter come to her feet and brush herself off. At least he'd done one goddamn thing in his life that he could be proud of.

CHAPTER TWELVE

Cross-checking Alma and Robert Fletcher's phone records against those of Beverly and David Thompson gave us nothing. There had been no calls from the Fletchers' phones to the Thompsons' and none from the Thompsons' to the Fletchers'. The two couples had made no outgoing calls to the same numbers, nor had they received any incoming calls from the same numbers. That accomplished, Maggie and I left the office at four thirty and returned to the street where Beverly Thompson's Lexus had been abandoned.

We continued to assume that the killer had transferred Thompson from the Lexus to the black van that the Chasen girl had described for me. Given the timing of Thompson's abduction, we further reasoned that the killer had probably parked the van near the Chasen home sometime between five o'clock and six thirty last night. We were hoping to find someone who had not been home while we were canvassing last night but who had been home earlier in the evening and who might thus have seen either the van or perhaps even the killer himself.

Again, Maggie took the south side of the street while I took the north. I began with the house in front of which the van had been parked. Unlike last night, the couple who lived in the house was at home, and a small gray-haired woman opened the door as far as the security chain would allow. I introduced myself and showed her my badge and ID.

The woman took a good long look at both through

the crack in the door, glancing back and forth from me to the photo on my ID. Finally she called to her husband and only when he was standing protectively beside her did she finally loosen the chain and open the door. "I apologize for being such a fraidycat," she said sheepishly. "But after what happened only a couple of blocks away last night, I'm feeing a bit nervous."

The woman, who looked to be in her late sixties, introduced herself as Helen Fulton. I assured her that she needn't apologize for being sensibly cautious and asked if she or her husband had noticed any strange vehicles parked in front of their house on the previous evening.

"I certainly did," she said. "That's why I called the police."

"I'm sorry, ma'am," I said, caught off guard. "You say you called the police?"

"Yes, I did."

Pointing to her husband, she said, "I was waiting for Marvin to get home because we were going to our daughter's for dinner last night. He was late and I was looking out the window for him a little before six o'clock when I saw an old black van pull up in front of the house.

"Well, I wasn't expecting anyone other than Marvin and I didn't know who it might be. I watched a man get out of the van, but instead of coming up to the door, he simply started walking off down the street."

"Which way did he go, Mrs. Fulton?"

"That way," she said, pointing east.

"Okay, just so I understand, the man got out of the van on the driver's side, which would have been the side away from the house?"

"That's right."

"And once he was clear of the van, you watched him walk away?"

"Yes."

"And the man was alone?"

"Yes. That is, unless there was someone who stayed in the back of the van where I couldn't see them."

"How well did you see the man?"

She gave me an apologetic look. "Not all that well, I'm afraid. My eyes aren't what they used to be, and I really only saw the man at a distance from the side and from the back. I didn't get a good look at his face."

"How was the man dressed?"

"In black. He had on a long-sleeve black shirt and a pair of black pants. I remember thinking that was odd, because it was still fairly warm, even at six o'clock last night. I thought that a person walking any distance in that outfit was bound to be hot and uncomfortable."

"How old would you say the man was?"

She shrugged. "I could only guess, Detective. The way he carried himself, he struck me as a young man, probably between twenty and forty, but I didn't see him well enough to make a better guess."

"Was the man wearing a hat?"

"No."

"What color was his hair?"

She thought about it for a moment, then shook her head. "I'm sorry. I don't have any recollection of his hair."

"Why did you call the police, Mrs. Fulton?"

"Well, I was angry because he just parked his van there and walked off. This is a fairly narrow street, and most of the residents are careful to park in their garages and driveways. If the man had been visiting someone nearby, it would have been different. But I thought it was very inconsiderate of him to leave his van in front of our house and then just walk away like that."

I nodded sympathetically, and she continued, a bit sheepishly. "To be honest, I was in a bad mood anyhow, because Marvin wasn't home on time, and so I went out and wrote down the license number of the van and called the police to report it."

"Did you call nine-one-one or your local precinct?"

She gave me a look as if she was questioning my sanity. "Why the local precinct, of course. I'm not silly enough to call the emergency number for something like this."

"No, of course not," I agreed. "And what happened?"

"Well, the person who took my call said that she'd refer it to the traffic division. She said that if the van was still there this morning, I should call again. But of course, it wasn't, and so I didn't think any more about it."

"I understand," I said. "By any chance do you still have the license-plate number?"

"Yes, it's still on my pad in the kitchen."

Mrs. Fulton retrieved the plate number. I thanked her, raced back to the car, and asked Dispatch to run the plate. While they did, I drove up the street and spotted Maggie coming out of a house three doors down. I tapped the horn and waved her over.

Just as she got into the car, the dispatcher returned to the line. "The plate belongs to a 2003 blue Volvo sedan. It's registered to a William Desmond in Scottsdale."

"A Volvo sedan—you're sure?"

"The computer is."

"Well, shit," I replied.

The dispatcher gave me the address, and as we headed in that direction, I brought Maggie up to speed. "For the last nineteen hours, we've had a CIB out on that van, and all the while, the goddamn plate number's been in the system. Some idiot at the precinct level wasn't bright enough to make the connection between the black van that Fulton reported and the one we're looking for in a murder/kidnapping that occurred only three blocks away?"

"What can you say?" Maggie sighed. "As usual, the right hand is paying no fuckin' attention to what the left one is doing."

"No shit," I agreed. "It looks as though the plate that Fulton reported was almost certainly boosted from some unsuspecting citizen and doesn't belong on the van we're looking for. Still, it would have been nice to know that last night. We might have had a slight chance of catching this bastard. By now, he's almost certainly ditched the stolen plate."

CHAPTER THIRTEEN

Carl McClain had, in fact, ditched the license plate that he had "borrowed" for the purpose of abducting Beverly Thompson, and had replaced it with the one that actually belonged on the van.

He'd bought the van for fifteen hundred dollars, cash money, and the seller had given him a bill of sale and the title to the van. Like any good citizen, McClain had dutifully gone to the DMV and registered and licensed his new vehicle. Unlike any good citizen, however, he had done so using a name and address other than his own. A little after five thirty, he pulled the van back into the garage of his rental house.

The insulation in the bedroom and bathroom was effective enough that Beverly failed to realize that McClain had returned until she heard his key in the dead bolt that locked the bedroom door. Sitting on the bed and leaning back against the wall, she watched as he slowly opened the door. He looked in to see her sitting there and then bent over to pick up a medium-size cardboard box. He closed the door behind him and returned the key ring to his pocket. Turning to Beverly, he said, "Dinner time, princess. Did you miss me?"

Without waiting for a response, he carried the box

over and set it on the card table. Reaching into the box, he set out two plates, two forks, two bottles of Diet Coke, and a roll of paper towels. He arranged them on the table, tearing off two paper towels, folding them in half, and setting them next to the plates. He then reached back into the carton and produced a large pizza box. He opened the box, set it in the middle of the table, and pointed Beverly toward the chair opposite him.

"Eat up, Beverly. You must be hungry, and it won't stay hot forever."

Without waiting for her response, he pulled a slice of sausage pizza out of the box, dropped it onto his plate, and attacked it with a fork.

The thought of sitting across the table from the man was repellant, but Beverly had eaten nothing, save for her morning cereal, in over sixteen hours. Reluctantly, she pulled herself off the bed, walked across the room, and sat in the second folding chair.

McClain pointed at the box. "Help yourself. I didn't know what you might like, and so I got half sausage and half pepperoni."

Beverly, who hadn't eaten pizza in at least six months, didn't want either sausage or pepperoni. But opting for the lesser of two evils, she picked up a fork and took a piece of the sausage half. McClain watched her take a bite, then opened one of the Diet Cokes and set it in front of her. "So how was *your* day, honey?"

Beverly stopped chewing for a moment, unsure of how to respond and afraid of provoking the man. Then, her rage and frustration momentarily overwhelming her fear and her grief, she swallowed the pizza. Stabbing the air with her fork, she said, *"How was my day?* How do you think my day was, you despicable asshole? What sort of sick fucking game do you think you're playing at here?"

She held her eyes hard on his, refusing even to give

him the satisfaction of seeing her blink. McClain returned her stare for several long seconds. Then he leaned back in his chair, smiled, and nodded his head. "That's the spirit," he said approvingly. "That's the Beverly we know and love. And as to what sort of 'fucking game' I'm playing at, sweetheart, I'm about to give you another demonstration. Finish your dinner first."

Beverly set the fork down and pushed the plate away, leaving the slice of pizza unfinished. Looking at the center of the table and not at McClain, she pleaded softly, "Who *are* you? Please . . . Why are you doing this to me?"

McClain waited until she raised her eyes to meet his again. Then he said, "You should goddamn well know the answer to that, Beverly. But the good news is that you've got nine more days to figure it out. The bad news is that after that it won't make a damn bit of difference—not to you, at least."

He held her eyes until she looked away again. For the next fifteen minutes she said nothing more as McClain methodically ate several more pieces of pizza and sipped at his Coke. Finally, he pushed his plate away and reached back down into the cardboard box he had set off on the floor next to his chair. He came out with a toothbrush shrink-wrapped in cellophane and a tube of Crest. He set them on the table next to Beverly and said, "Go brush your teeth."

Without looking at him, she shook her head slightly. Again in a soft voice, she said, "No."

McClain gave her a couple of seconds. Then speaking very quietly and deliberately, he said, "Go brush your teeth, Beverly. If you do not, I will tie you down on the bed again and hurt you in ways that you've never imagined, even in your worst nightmares."

He waited patiently as she sat there for another full minute. Finally, and still without looking at him, she reached out and picked up the toothbrush and the Crest. Then she got up from the chair and slowly made her way to the bathroom, the cable snaking across the floor behind her.

CHAPTER FOURTEEN

The address in Scottsdale and the Volvo sedan both belonged to a William Desmond. Shortly after seven, Maggie and I rang his doorbell. From inside the house, we heard what sounded like a small child crying, and a few moments later a young woman with a baby at her shoulder opened the door. A little boy, maybe two or three years old, was wrapped around the woman's right leg, still crying. "Yes?" she said in a voice that indicated clearly that she had no time for small talk.

We let her take a look at our shields and IDs. Then Maggie said, "Mrs. Desmond?"

The woman nodded apprehensively, and Maggie said, "We're very sorry to bother you, ma'am, but is your husband at home?"

At that, the baby started to cry as well. Desmond shifted it to her other shoulder and patted it on the back. "No, he's not. My husband is traveling out of town on business. Why? What's happened?"

Skipping over her question, I said, "When did Mr. Desmond leave on his trip?"

"Sunday night."

Maggie jotted in her notebook, then said, "Your husband owns a 2003 Volvo sedan."

"Yes, why do you ask?"

Again ignoring her question, I said, "And is your husband driving the car on his trip?"

"No," Desmond replied, clearly confused. "He left the car at the airport and flew. That's what he always does."

Maggie sighed. "Do you know where at the airport he might have left the car?"

The woman shifted the baby again. "I assume that it's in the West Economy lot. That's usually where he leaves it when he flies United."

We thanked the woman and left. Forty-five minutes later, we were in an airport patrol car with a Sky Harbor security officer driving up and down the aisles of the West Economy parking lot. Twenty minutes after starting the search, we were looking at a blue Volvo. It had been backed into a parking space, and the rear of the car was shielded by the minivan parked immediately behind it. I got out of the patrol car and walked behind the Volvo. Its license plate was gone.

I took it for granted that the person who'd taken the plate had been careful enough to wear gloves. Still, we stood guard over the car until a Crime Scene Response van arrived. The techs carefully dusted the area around the license-plate holder and raised a few fingerprints. We could only hope that at least a couple of them might belong to our killer.

CHAPTER FIFTEEN

Just before eight o'clock, Carl McClain locked the bedroom door again and went out through the kitchen and into the garage. He carefully backed the van out of the garage. Then he got out, closed the garage door, and locked it securely.

Back in the van, he headed north. The night people

were coming out now, and two young drug dealers stood brazenly on the corner, openly soliciting business. Half a block up the street a rail-thin hooker who was either drunk or high—or maybe both—waved halfheartedly at his passing van. Only a few blocks ahead, the lights of Chase Field, home to the Arizona Diamondbacks, shone brightly against the clear night sky.

McClain cursed softly, even though there was no one else in the van to hear him. He'd forgotten that the damned rodeo was opening tonight, and he hoped that he could be done with the evening's chore and back before the fuckin' cowboys were finished for the night. He really didn't want to have to fight the traffic that would be flooding out in every direction away from the park once the rodeo had ended.

Seventeen years ago, when Carl McClain had accidentally made the mistake of his life, there had been no Arizona Diamondbacks and, of course, no Chase Field. Back then, the area immediately north of McClain's new rental home was still in transition. Historically, the neighborhood had been Phoenix's infamous skid row—home to the transients, alkies, druggies, dealers, hookers, and others, some of whom had been pressed farther south by the urban renewal that had produced the new Civic Plaza, the US Airways Arena, and ultimately, the ballpark.

McClain had driven downtown that night more out of boredom than out of any truly pressing need. Amanda was pregnant for the second time and in absolutely no mood for sex. In consequence, McClain had been mildly horny, but nowhere near desperate. He was cruising down Second Street, a half-finished Budweiser clamped between his thighs, when he saw the two women standing on the corner. Mostly just for laughs, he pulled over and rolled down the window.

The taller of the two women, a thin brunette with a

nice rack, leaned into the car, letting McClain get a good look at her tits. In her best effort at a sultry voice, she said, "You lookin' for a party, honey?"

McClain pretended to think about it for a moment, then figured, what the hell, why not? He smiled at the woman. "Well, I don't know, baby. What sorta party you offering?"

The woman gave him a throaty laugh and laid her hand on his shoulder. "Anything you'd like, sugar. You're the boss."

Again, McClain pretended to think about it. Then he touched the woman's cheek. "How much for a blow job?"

Holding his gaze, she said, "You look like a nice guy, honey. How 'bout I give you the early bird–special price. Fifty dollars?"

McClain sighed. "Fifty dollars sounds a bit steep, baby. But I think I could go forty."

Now the woman pretended to think about it, like maybe Donald Trump might drop out of the sky at any moment, ready and willing to pay the asking price. Finally she looked back to McClain. "Okay, sweetie, why don't you show me the money?"

McClain showed her the forty and she walked around the front of the car exaggerating the natural sway of her hips. She got in on the passenger's side and said, "Why don't you drive on down the street a couple of blocks, sugar, and I'll show you a special place where we can park private like."

He dropped the car into gear and pulled slowly away from the curb, failing to notice that the second woman on the corner was jotting his license-plate number into a little green notebook.

The hooker showed him where to park in an alley behind a small grocery store that had already closed for the night. Then she unrolled a condom onto his erection. He would have rated the blow job about a six on a scale of ten, and when the whore was found dead in the alley the next morning, it was the second hooker and her little green notebook that sent Carl McClain to prison for the rest of his natural life.

Twenty minutes after leaving Beverly naked and sobbing on the bed behind him, McClain braked the van to a stop in the parking lot of a small strip mall on Glendale Avenue. Dodging traffic, he jogged over to a convenience store on the opposite side of the street.

On the off chance that the convenience store might have video cameras that monitored the area in front of the store, he tugged his cowboy hat low over his forehead and trained his eyes on the ground ahead of him. He walked directly up to the pay phone hanging off the outside wall of the store, picked up the receiver, and deposited two coins.

Hunched into the phone, he dialed the number of a high-end furniture store on North Scottsdale Road and asked for Jack Collins. A minute or so later, Collins came to the phone and assured McClain that he'd be at the store until closing and would be happy to show him bedroom suites in a variety of styles and price ranges. But McClain would have to be there by nine o'clock, when the front doors of the store would be locked.

McClain thanked the man and promised to be there no later than eight forty-five. Then he hung up, careful to smudge any fingerprints that he might have left on the phone, and jogged back to the van. Ten minutes later, he pulled to a stop in a quiet residential neighborhood in west-central Phoenix.

He waited for a car to pass, and then the street was clear. Leaving the cowboy hat in the van, McClain got out, locked the vehicle, and began walking west. Two blocks later, he turned a corner and walked another half block north. He paused long enough to pull on a pair of thin latex gloves, then walked up to the front door of the gray stucco house that belonged to Jack Collins and his wife, Karen.

Both Collins and his wife were in their late fifties. Their two children were grown and gone, and after watching the couple on and off for the last two weeks, McClain knew that Karen would be at home alone while her husband pulled his one night shift of the week at the furniture store.

McClain was wearing a jacket that he'd stolen from a Southwest Gas Company truck two weeks earlier. In his left hand he carried a clipboard that he'd also taken from the truck, and in the right pocket of the jacket was his Glock 26 pistol. On account of its compact size, the 26 was nicknamed the "Baby Glock," but it would be more than sufficient for the task at hand.

Standing on the front porch, McClain took a deep breath and pressed the doorbell. A minute or so later, the porch light came on and Karen Collins peered out through the small window in the door.

Seventeen years earlier, she'd been a grade-school teacher—a plain, thin woman with short dark hair. Her figure was all angles and lines, and she had a particularly severe face dominated by a sharp, straight nose. McClain had speculated that her students probably called her Mrs. Hatchet Face, and the second she took her seat in the jury box, he knew that she'd vote guilty on all counts.

Back then, she'd taken at least some care with her hair, clothes, and makeup, but at some point in their years apart, she'd obviously abandoned the effort. She was still rail thin, but her hair had gone completely gray, and she no longer made any effort to make herself look even remotely appealing. She stood on the other side of the door, dressed in a pair of jeans and an oversize T-shirt. A pair of reading glasses dangled from a cord around her neck.

McClain smiled brightly, holding the clipboard away from his chest so that Collins could see both the Southwest Gas logo and the name Dennis, which was stitched just below the logo. Holding the smile, he said through the door, "Gas company, ma'am. We've had a report of a leak in the neighborhood. May I talk to you for a moment?"

Collins nodded, then unlocked the door and opened it a scant six inches. Leaning to her right, she looked out to McClain through the crack in the door and said, "Yes?"

McClain threw his shoulder forward, slamming the door back into the woman's face and knocking her down to the floor. She sat there in the small entryway, momentarily stunned and bleeding from her nose. Before she could gather her wits and let out a scream, McClain closed and bolted the door.

Dropping the clipboard to the floor, he leaned over, grabbed Collins roughly by the hair, and stuck the pistol in her face. "Not a word, Karen," he cautioned. "Not a single fuckin' word."

Continuing to grip the woman by the hair, McClain pulled her to her feet. Still dazed from the blow from the door, Collins nearly toppled over, but McClain held her steady and she slowly got her bearings back. As she did, she began to whimper.

For a moment, McClain toyed with the idea of dragging her off into the bedroom and making his revenge even more complete. But he decided that the woman was simply too unappealing and that it would be unwise to deviate from the plan. As much as he would have liked to prolong the woman's punishment, in this case, short and sweet was best.

He pulled her into the living room and dropped her into a large upholstered chair. A reading lamp cast a bright light over the chair, and on a table beside the chair a John Grisham novel lay open next to an empty coffee cup. Collins started to cry and McClain squeezed into the chair, facing her and straddling her lap.

"Please," she said, sobbing, "I'll do anything you want. I have money I can give you. Just please don't hurt me."

McClain leaned forward, his face scant inches away from the woman's. "You'll do anything I want? You'll give me money? Well, shit, I'm sorry to say that it's a little late for that, Karen. You fucked me over good, and now you've got to pay the price, along with everybody else who helped you do it."

"What do you mean?" she pleaded. "In what way did I harm you?"

McClain leaned back, letting the woman get a better look at him. After a moment he said, "You voted to convict me of first-degree murder, Karen. And of some other assorted bullshit charges that the prosecutor threw into the mix."

Her tears gave way to the shock of recognition. "McClain?" she said.

"In the flesh, you bitch . . . Glad to see me? Anything you wanted to say to me?"

Collins began crying again. In a low halting voice, she whispered, "I'm sorry . . . I saw the news . . . Please, I'm really very sorry."

McClain pulled a small plastic bag from his pocket. He opened the bag and shook it, allowing the contents to fall from the bag onto Collins's T-shirt and onto the chair. Then he pushed himself off the woman's lap and stared down at her. She looked up to meet his eyes, crying harder now. "Please, Mr. McClain," she said again. "Please . . ."

He held her eyes for another few seconds, then shook his head. "Too fuckin' bad, lady, but 'sorry' just doesn't cut it."

He shot her in the heart at close range, and she

crumpled into the chair. The last sound that Karen Collins would ever make was a small, quiet gasp that somehow still sounded surprised, even though she'd seen it coming.

CHAPTER SIXTEEN

On television, when a police detective is assigned to a murder investigation, he always seems to have the luxury of working that case and only that case until it's resolved. But of course, on television the average detective can always clear even the most complicated homicide in no more than sixty minutes tops, with time out for twenty-seven minutes worth of commercials. Thus, even during an abnormally busy week, his caseload will likely never turn into a backlog.

Unfortunately, out here in the real world we're a bit slower than that. And adding insult to injury, the citizens are seldom courteous enough to wait for the police to resolve one homicide before some inconsiderate jerk goes out and commits another one. So, even though Maggie and I were devoting virtually all of our waking hours to the Thompson murder and kidnapping, we were nevertheless back in the on-deck circle when a citizen named Jack Collins came home from work on Thursday night and found his wife shot to death.

Collins called 911. Dispatch alerted the Homicide Unit, and the sergeant rousted Maggie and me. We got to the crime scene a little after ten thirty to find the husband in a state of shock and his wife dead in the living room.

After taking a preliminary look at the victim, the

ME suggested that the woman had probably been shot sometime within the last couple of hours and that she had died instantly. Inevitably, though, he refused to be held to that observation until he had completed the autopsy and had received the results of the various tests he would run.

A check of the house indicated no signs of forced entry. Either a door or a window had been left unlocked or Karen Collins had opened the door to her killer. But then, of course, we couldn't yet rule out the possibility that the killer might have had his own key.

To all outward appearances, Jack Collins was truly shocked and devastated by his wife's murder. But sadly, all too often in cases like this, the grieving spouse turned out to be the one who had pulled the trigger. The victim had been killed in her own home, and by his own admission, her husband had been present in the home shortly thereafter. It was certainly possible that he might have been present in the house at the time.

For me this was always one of the most difficult and painful parts of a homicide investigation. But as much as I hated doing it, I had no choice.

The patrolman who first responded to the call had isolated Jack Collins in the kitchen. Maggie and I found him there, sitting at the kitchen table, staring blankly at a bowl of apples and ripe bananas. The room was small, but intelligently designed to make the best use of the available space. A loaf of bread sat on a wire rack next to the oven, and the faint, yeasty aroma of freshly baked bread lingered in the air.

Collins was still dressed in the suit and tie he'd apparently worn to work, although he'd taken off his glasses and set them on the table in front of him. He looked to be somewhere in his late fifties or early sixties and was carrying twenty or twenty-five pounds of excess weight, most of which had settled around his waist. He'd obviously been crying, and as we took chairs on either side of him, he raised his head and met my eyes with a look of total despair.

We introduced ourselves, and I said sympathetically, "Mr. Collins, please know that we are truly sorry for your loss and that we hate to intrude on you at a time like this. But we're anxious to move as quickly as we possibly can to find the person who committed this terrible crime, and we have some questions that we need to ask."

Collins nodded his understanding, and I said, "When was the last time you saw your wife, sir?"

He swallowed hard. "This noon. We had lunch together here in the kitchen before I went to work."

"Did you speak to Mrs. Collins after that?" Maggie asked.

"Yes. She called me around five o'clock to see how my day was going. We talked for a couple of minutes— just small talk is all. Then I called her about eight thirty to tell her that I might be late getting home. A customer had called to say that he'd be coming in at the last minute before we closed. But then he didn't show. I waited until a few minutes after nine and then came home. I got here about nine thirty and found Karen."

Collins teared up and began crying again. I waited a few moments, then asked, "Who was the customer?"

"I don't know. He called the store and asked for me personally. He said that he was looking for bedroom furniture and that a friend of his had recommended me. He didn't give me his name or his friend's name. I told him I'd be there until nine, and he promised to be there no later than a quarter to."

"You didn't recognize the voice as someone you knew or someone you might have talked to before?"

"No. All I can tell you was that he sounded like a young man and like a legitimate customer. Nothing in his voice or in what he said suggested that he might have been handing me a line of some sort."

He paused for a moment, swiped at his eyes with a handkerchief, and said, "Are you thinking that the man who called me might be the son of a bitch who did this?"

"I don't know, Mr. Collins," I replied. "But it is a suspicious circumstance. A man you don't know calls to make sure that you're at the store and that you're going to be there at least until nine. Then your wife is shot within an hour of the call and the man never shows up at the store. It's certainly possible that he was somehow involved in your wife's death, so obviously if there's anything at all you can remember about the conversation, we'll want to know about it."

He nodded, and Maggie said, "When you last talked to your wife, Mr. Collins, how was her mood? Did she seem worried or angry or upset in any way?"

"No, she was fine. She told me that she was relaxing with her book and that she wouldn't expect to see me until I got here."

"Nothing struck you as being out of the ordinary?" she said. "Even in retrospect?"

"No, not at all. She seemed perfectly normal."

"Can you think of anyone who might have been angry with Mrs. Collins?" I asked.

Collins shook his head. "No. Sitting here, I've been racking my brain trying to imagine who might have done this. There's absolutely no one."

"Have you or your wife received any threatening letters or phone calls?"

"No—at least I haven't. And certainly Karen would have told me if she had."

"Would your wife have opened the door to a stranger at this time of night, Mr. Collins?" Maggie asked.

"I wouldn't have thought so—certainly not without

a very good reason. But I'm assuming that's what she must have done."

The conversation paused for a few seconds, and then I said as sympathetically as I could, "I apologize in advance for even having to say this, sir. But as I hope you can understand, in a case like this our natural first step is to try to eliminate the surviving spouse from suspicion."

Collins blanched slightly and another tear rolled down his cheek. He squeezed his eyes tightly shut, lowered his head to his chest, and began to sob quietly. We gave him a couple of minutes, and finally he composed himself again. Looking to the center of the table rather than at either of us, he said, "I understand, Detective. What do you need me to do?"

"Again, sir, I'm sorry to ask," Maggie said, "but were there any problems in your marriage?"

Collins shook his head. "No, Detective. Like any other couple, Karen and I had our occasional disagreements, but we haven't had a significant argument in years. She was enjoying her retirement, and I was looking forward to mine. We were going to travel and finally have a chance to enjoy life, just the two of us together."

Through his tears, he looked to Maggie and said, "I understand that you have to ask these questions, Detective, but I promise you that I did not kill my wife. I loved her."

"Mr. Collins," I said, "do you own a gun?"

For a second he seemed to come out of his trance and he shot me a withering look. Then he turned his eyes back to the center of the table. "No, Detective, I do not. Karen hated guns and would never allow one in the house."

"Okay, sir," I sighed. "Again, we're very sorry both for what's happened here tonight and for having to put you through this ordeal. If you don't mind, we'd like to have a technician come in and give you a gunshot residue test for the purpose of confirming the fact that you have not fired a gun this evening. After that, we'd like you to walk through the house with us and check to see if anything might be missing."

Collins nodded his assent, and Maggie stepped back out into the living room and asked one of the technicians to administer the test. The tech, whose name was Tom Schaeffer, came into the kitchen and took the seat that Maggie had vacated.

Schaeffer pulled on a fresh pair of latex gloves, then opened an SEM examination kit and removed a small metal disc. He carefully dabbed Collins's right hand with the adhesive side of the disk, then slipped the disc into an evidence bag that he labeled and sealed.

He repeated the procedure on Collins's left hand and sealed the second disc in a separate evidence bag. Back in the lab, Schaeffer would examine the discs using a scanning electron microscope, looking for tiny particles of lead, barium, and antimony. Though not totally conclusive, the presence of significant amounts of these elements would indicate that the tested subject had recently fired a gun.

Once Schaeffer was finished, Collins walked us slowly through the house. But outside of the living room, the place seemed to be in perfect order. Nothing was disturbed, and Collins noted that nothing seemed to be missing.

As we completed the tour back in the kitchen, I explained that he would not be able to remain in the house for the night, and Collins choked up again. Shaking his head, he said, "I doubt that I will ever be able to spend another night in this house, Detective."

There was nothing we could say to that, and so while Maggie went out to check on the results of the neighborhood canvass, I walked Collins back to his bedroom and waited while he packed a few clothes into an overnight bag. He was standing in front of the dresser, staring into a drawer, forcing himself to go through the motions of packing, when I said, "This may seem an odd question, Mr. Collins, but by any chance was your wife acquainted with either David or Beverly Thompson?"

He looked away from the dresser, holding a pair of socks in his hand. "No, I don't think so, Detective. I recognize the names from the news, and Karen and I talked about the abduction, but neither of us knew them. Do you think there might be some connection between that case and my wife's murder?"

"I'm not really sure," I responded. "How about a woman named Alma Fletcher? Does that name mean anything to you?"

Collins shook his head, clearly confused. "No, Detective. I don't think I've ever heard the name. But again, why do you ask?"

"Well, sir, it's just that Mrs. Fletcher was the victim of a similar crime last week. She was a few years older than Mrs. Collins, but she was alone in her home while her husband was at work. She apparently opened the door to someone who then shot her. As in the case here, nothing in the home was disturbed, and nothing was taken. We have reason to suspect that the person who killed Mrs. Fletcher was the same one who killed David Thompson and abducted Mrs. Thompson.

"Naturally, we'll be checking to see if the same weapon was used in this case as well. But the similarities between this crime and the one committed against Mrs. Fletcher are so strong that I naturally wondered if there might have been anything that linked Mrs. Collins and Mrs. Fletcher together."

Still holding the socks, he lowered his head and said in a sad voice, "No. I'm sorry, Detective Richardson, but I've never heard the name before."

CHAPTER SEVENTEEN

I left the Collins home a little after three A.M. and got to the nursing home fifteen minutes later. I kissed Julie hello and dropped, exhausted, into the chair next to her bed. A vase brimming with carnations had materialized on the table next to the bed. The card leaning up against the vase had been signed by Julie's sister, Denise, expressing her love and assuring Julie that she was in her sister's prayers. Shaking my head, I set the card back on the table. Apparently neither Denise nor Elizabeth was aware of the fact that the carnation had been perhaps Julie's least favorite flower.

Sitting there, I thought about the complicated relationship between Julie, her mother, and her sister. I also found myself thinking long and hard about the question the lieutenant had posed earlier in the morning.

I'd wanted to be honest with him, and I didn't want to let him down. Even more important, of course, I didn't want a deranged psychopath running loose in the city, shooting and kidnapping defenseless citizens because I'd been distracted and had missed a vital clue or had failed to make a logical deduction from the little evidence that we had uncovered.

I desperately wanted to believe that even though Julie never left my thoughts, I could successfully compartmentalize the pressure and the pain of my life off duty, and thus prevent them from compromising my ability to lead the investigation effectively. Nonetheless,

in moments like this, alone in my solitude, I sometimes wondered if I *was* up to the job.

And what if I wasn't? Would I ever be able to admit it—even to myself, let alone to the lieutenant?
I felt like I'd aged five years in the last eighteen
months. I was sleeping only fitfully and even then
for only a few hours on most nights. Even though I
continued to exercise on a regular basis, I wasn't eating as well as I should, and that too was beginning
to take a toll.

My social life, which had once been fairly active,
was now nonexistent. Before the accident, my circle of
friends had consisted almost exclusively of other couples that Julie and I had hung out with. For the first
few months after the accident, they had all been genuinely concerned for my well-being, and they continued
to call and to show up at the door with the occasional
casserole.

They also attempted to include me in their activities,
but on the handful of occasions when I accepted an invitation to dinner or to a party, the relationships seemed
increasingly strained and awkward. Beyond expressing their sympathy, no one knew quite what to say,
and I had little or no interest in the topics of conversation that even a few months earlier would have seemed
so normal and compelling. Fairly quickly I began de-
clining virtually every invitation, until the invitations
stopped coming altogether.

The focus of my entire world had now narrowed
down almost exclusively to my responsibilities to Julie
and to my job. And the truth was that, with Julie lost to
me, the job was the only thing keeping me sane. In any
given day it afforded me several hours of relatively
normal human contact. It provided some sense of
structure, logic, and purpose in a world that otherwise
seemed increasingly chaotic and devoid of meaning.

And I was clinging to it like a drowning man. Without it, I would be lost.

By four A.M., I was no closer to a resolution of the question than I had been thirty minutes earlier. And so, reluctantly, I pulled myself out of the chair and kissed Julie good night.

CHAPTER EIGHTEEN

Beverly was sleeping fitfully when the siren came screaming down the street in the middle of the night on Thursday.

McClain snapped awake about ten seconds after she did. As Beverly sat up, he bolted off the bed and stood in the middle of the darkened room, listening as the siren moaned and died, sounding as if it were only a few yards away from the bedroom. McClain turned back, grabbed Beverly by the throat, and threw her down on the mattress. Squeezing the breath out of her, he whispered, "Do not move from this bed, Beverly, and don't make a single fucking sound. If you do, I will kill you in a heartbeat."

With that, he released her and raced from the room, leaving the bedroom door open in his wake. As ordered, Beverly lay quiet and still on the bed, her heart pounding so hard she could almost hear it. Thirty seconds later, McClain stormed back into the room with a pistol in his hand. He grabbed Beverly's arm and jerked her to her feet. Moving behind her, he circled her waist with his left arm, pinning her arms to her sides, and pulled her tightly against his own body. He tapped Beverly's right ear with the pistol and whispered, "Walk with me, Beverly. And keep perfectly quiet."

With that, he began pushing her in the direction of the bedroom door. The cable that was tethered to Beverly's ankle trailed along the floor behind them, and halfway across the room, McClain accidentally stepped on the cable. Beverly nearly tripped to the floor, taking him with her, but at the last second he regained his footing and righted them. Guiding her more carefully now, he took her to the open door, which was as far as the cable would stretch. Still holding Beverly's body tightly to his own, McClain leaned back against the doorframe and listened intently.

From somewhere to their left, Beverly could hear the sounds of footsteps bounding onto what was apparently the front porch, and then the raised voices of at least two people talking to each other. She strained to hear, but could not make out what the voices were saying. Then someone pounded on the door and shouted, "Police! Open up!"

Behind her, Beverly felt her captor tense. He laid the barrel of the pistol against the right side of her head. Into her ear, he whispered, "I don't know what the fuck is going on here, Beverly, but if you make a single sound, or if those assholes attempt to get through that door, I'll blow your goddamn brains out."

Again, someone hammered on the door. Her mind racing nearly as fast as her pulse, Beverly weighed the option of crying out for help. She had no doubt that the man would kill her as he had promised. However, she was fairly certain that he would ultimately kill her anyway, and at least by dying now, she could be sure of the fact that David's death as well as her own would ultimately be avenged.

But, she thought, what if the police did have the house surrounded? Perhaps she still might be rescued and saved. If it ultimately became clear that he had no hope of escape, perhaps her captor would surrender and allow her to live, rather than killing her and making things even worse for himself than they already were. Perhaps she still might survive to see the bastard pay for murdering David, and that was now the sweetest revenge she could possibly imagine.

Desperate to hear what was happening out on the porch, Beverly leaned forward, as though straining to close the distance between herself and her potential saviors by even the slightest couple of inches. For a long thirty seconds, only silence issued from the porch, and then came the sound of a voice saying something about "the wrong address" and "the house next door."

Beverly heard the sound of footsteps shuffling off the porch and she opened her mouth to scream. But as she drew in the breath to do so, McClain clamped his hand over her mouth. Beverly shook her head violently and attempted to bite his fingers, while at the same time she tried to kick back at him. Unfazed, McClain simply tightened his grip on her mouth and slapped the right side of her head with the gun.

McClain listened as the sounds retreated from the porch. Then he dragged Beverly back in the direction of the bed. She fought him every inch of the way, but he was simply too strong, and when they reached the bed, McClain threw her down on her stomach, straddled her back, and pressed her facedown into the pillow.

Leaning forward, he used his chest to keep her trapped in that position, barely able to draw a breath, let alone to cry out. Beverly heard the sound of fabric ripping and a moment later, McClain pulled her head back and stuffed a rag into her mouth. He tied a second strip of cloth around her head, holding the gag in place, then shuffled backward so that he was now straddling her thighs. He grabbed Beverly's left wrist, tied a piece of cloth around it, and then bound her left wrist to her right. He tested the knots and then, apparently satisfied with his work, he leaned forward and said in a low voice, "Stay perfectly still, bitch, or you'll be even deader than your fuckin' husband."

With that, McClain moved off of her and she heard him leave the room and close the door behind him. Despite his threat, Beverly struggled against her bonds, but in doing so succeeded only in making them tighter. Working feverishly, she tried to cup her hands in a way that would allow her fingers to work at the knots that bound her wrists, but it was impossible to do so.

Weeping out of a mixture of anger, fear, and frustration, Beverly inched her way forward on the bed, placed her face against the wall, and attempted to use the pressure of her face against the rough surface of the wall to push the gag away from her mouth. Fifteen minutes later, McClain opened the door and slipped back into the room. He closed the door, walked across the room, and turned on the lamp next to the bed to find Beverly sobbing and still attempting vainly to free herself from the gag.

McClain stood beside the bed and watched her struggle for another thirty seconds or so. Then he touched a hand to her leg, sighed heavily, and said, "Sorry, babe. Close, but no cigar. Fortunately for the both of us, the cops weren't here to rescue you. They were called out to a domestic complaint next door and wound up on the wrong goddamn porch."

McClain removed his hand from Beverly's leg, and a moment later, a knife slashed through the torn pillowcase he had used to bind her hands. "You can finish untying yourself," he said, sighing again. "I need a fuckin' drink."

CHAPTER NINETEEN

At ten o'clock on Friday morning, I got a call from a tech in the crime lab, indicating that the same weapon that had been used to kill Alma Fletcher and David Thompson had also been used in the shooting of Karen Collins. I'd just hung up the phone when Chris Doyle walked through the door, plopped into the chair next to my desk, and said, "Martin says I'm supposed to work with you and the girlfriend on the murders you caught. I know that you're the lead, and I can live with that, even though I was working cases like this while you were still trying to cop your first feel in the back-seat of your daddy's Oldsmobile. But I hope I don't have to tell you that I'm not taking orders from Aunt Jemima."

I looked at him and shook my head, not even trying to hide my disgust.

Doyle was, without question, the unit's premier example of the negative consequences of the protections afforded by civil-service law. He'd rarely ever helped resolve a case of any real complexity, and the few killers he had caught as a member of the Homicide Unit had mostly been poor, stupid mopes that he'd found standing drunk or stoned over the bodies of their spouses, the murder weapon still in their hands, just waiting to confess to the first cop who came walking through the door.

As long as I'd been a member of the unit, Doyle had been skating close to the line of getting his butt kicked out of the department. But he put in just enough hours and did just enough work to avoid crossing over the line. He was eighteen months shy of taking his pension and made absolutely no secret of the fact that getting there was the only thing about the job that still motivated him.

For a number of years Doyle had been teamed with Randy Wandstadt, another troglodyte who shared Doyle's general views about gender, race, politics, and the world as a whole. Wandstadt had finally retired a few months earlier, leaving Doyle as the only single in the squad when Maggie won her transfer into Homicide. The lieutenant paired them together, but their partnership was a disaster from day one, and after the first week, Maggie could have easily filed a complaint accusing Doyle of both racial and sexual harassment.

They were any number of witnesses who could have confirmed Doyle's pattern of behavior and who doubtless would have happily offered evidence against him. Maggie realized, though, that making such a complaint would have branded her forever and would have greatly frustrated, if not destroyed altogether, her ambition to be accepted as a team player and a valued member of the unit. So she stuck it out, giving as good as she got, and demonstrated by her own conduct what a miserable excuse for a human being her "partner" really was.

She endured the situation for nine weeks and then, figuring that she'd proved her mettle, went to see the lieutenant. He granted Maggie a divorce, no questions asked, and given that my partner had just transferred over to Burglary, the lieutenant put us together. I'd admired Maggie's work during her first two months in the unit, and was impressed by the way she'd handled the situation with Doyle. I counted myself lucky to be teamed with her, and we'd settled almost immediately into a very comfortable working relationship. Thus far, we'd also had a very good run of clearing cases, which

certainly seemed to validate the lieutenant's decision
to put us together.

However, while the lieutenant might have been
happy, Doyle was anything but. Perhaps it was because
Maggie was new to the unit. Perhaps it was because
she was a woman. Without question, it had a great deal
to do with the color of her skin. But Doyle had simply
assumed that Maggie would—and should—have been
grateful for the opportunity to break into the squad
under his direction.

The fact that she wasn't was a huge blow to Doyle's
massive ego, and in the wake of their separation, he
pouted like a third grader who'd just been the last kid
chosen for somebody's dodgeball team. He missed no
opportunity to needle Maggie and anyone who defended her. And the fact that virtually every other
member of the unit had invited Doyle to take his opin-
ions and stuff them up his butt had deterred him not
in the slightest.

Since the split with Maggie, Doyle had been partnered with Bob Riggins, a guy so tolerant and easy-
going that, to all appearances, he could have worked
in tandem with virtually anyone. But even Riggins
was losing patience with Doyle, and the rest of us assumed that it would only be a matter of time before
Bob followed Maggie's trail down the hall to the lieutenant's office, asking to be relieved of the burden.

I leaned forward in my chair, waited until Doyle finally met my eyes, and said, "Look, Chris, we've got a
fuckin' maniac out there and a missing woman as well,
and none of us has time for your usual crap. You need
to drop the attitude, pitch in, and do the grunt work
along with the rest us. And if you aren't willing to do
that, then go and tell the lieutenant that you need to be
reassigned. Because if you won't, I will."

He shot me a look but raised his hands in mock surrender. "Hey, no problem, compadre. I'm more than

happy to help out. I just wanted to let you know where I stand."

We spent the rest of the day checking phone records, interviewing Karen Collins's friends and acquaintances, and reinterviewing those of the Thompsons and of Alma Fletcher. But we still found nothing that seemed to connect the growing list of victims in any way.

Meanwhile, the media had gone into warp drive, exploiting the killings for every last possible ratings point and whipping the public into a frenzy. Not surprisingly, an aroused citizenry demanded an immediate arrest of the killer, along with the rescue and safe return of Beverly Thompson, wherever she might be by now. Reported sightings of Thompson continued to pour into the department from across the state and beyond, but none of the leads had panned out.

Since we had not yet found anything to connect the victims, I was beginning to fear that perhaps nothing did connect them, which was a very scary thought. If the victims had simply been chosen at random and murdered by some amoral thrill seeker, the difficulties in catching him would be multiplied exponentially, especially if the killer were as careful as this one appeared to be.

Without some thread winding through the victims' lives that might suggest a direction in which to search for their common killer, we were left working virtually in the dark. We had no idea why the killer had begun this spree, we had no idea where to look for him, and we had no idea where he might strike next. Most important, we had virtually no hope of capturing him unless he made some stupid mistake and got caught in the act, or unless he bragged about his exploits to the wrong person and someone ratted him out. There was still a small chance that the little physical evidence we had collected at the scenes might point us in the direction of a suspect, but I was not holding out a lot of hope for that, either.

The one anomaly in the entire case was the fact that the killer had kidnapped Beverly Thompson. In murdering Alma Fletcher and Karen Collins, the killer had apparently taken pains to ensure that his victim would be home alone at the time of the attack. Why had he not done so in the Thompson case?

Of course we still had no idea which of the Thompsons had been the killer's target. If Mrs. Thompson was the target, why had the killer struck at a time when her husband was obviously at home?

It was entirely possible, of course, that David Thompson had been the target and that his wife had simply arrived home at exactly the wrong moment. But if that was the case, why had the killer kidnapped the woman rather than shooting her as well?

Almost certainly, he had not taken her for the purpose of extorting a ransom out of someone for her safe return. But then, Beverly Thompson was a very attractive woman. It was possible, I suppose, that if she had arrived on the scene unexpectedly, the killer might have made an impulsive decision to abduct her for some sexual purpose. And if that was the case, was he still holding her or had he already killed her and disposed of the body where it had not yet been discovered?

It was all enormously frustrating. But at this point, there was nothing we could do other than to push the investigation in every direction we could think of, hoping that somewhere, somehow, we would finally get the right tip or discover even a small piece of evidence that would point us in the direction of the clever son of a bitch who was now running us around in circles.

At eight o'clock on Saturday morning, I climbed the stairs to the Homicide Unit and found Frank Bohac,

the chief of police, pacing the floor in front of the lieutenant's desk. Bohac had been back on the job for only
two months following a serious heart attack, and the
look on his face suggested that he might be ripe for
another. Holding the editorial page of the morning
paper in his right hand, he waved me into the office
and said, "Have you seen this piece of crap, Richardson?"

I nodded and he said, "Yeah, well so did the mayor
and practically every other asshole who's got his name
on a plaque glued to a door over there at city hall."

Looking from me to the lieutenant, he continued,
"The mayor called to ream my ass about it, and so I'm
over here to ream yours. Where in the hell are we with
this mess?"

"Practically nowhere," Martin sighed, "unless Sean's
come up with something overnight that I don't know
about."

I shook my head. In a voice that conveyed the frustration we were both feeling, the lieutenant said,
"Look, Chief, I know that the media is killing us and
that you're under the gun here. But we're working the
case as hard as we can from every angle we can think
of. The problem is that so far, we can't find anything
that links the victims in any way, save for the fact that
they were all shot with the same gun. We haven't got a
single decent lead to follow, but it sure as hell isn't for
lack of trying."

Bohac stopped pacing and perched on a corner of
the lieutenant's desk. He looked briefly to Martin and
said, "Are we sure about that?" Turning to me, he said,
"Look, Richardson, I understand your personal situation, and I do sympathize. I know you're going through
hell right now. Still, I can't afford to have the lead detective on this case distracted for *any* reason, no matter
how important. I need somebody who can be focused
on the job twenty-four–seven, and given the way the

fucking thing is racing out of control, I'm frankly wondering if you should still be the guy."

I took a deep breath while he stared me down. "With all due respect, sir, my personal situation has not in any way compromised the way in which I've handled this case. The team is working it full out, and it's got everybody's undivided attention—mine included. But as the lieutenant says, there's no discernable pattern to the crimes. There's no apparent connection among any of the victims, and the guy is leaving us nothing to work with.

"The one thing we do have," I said, "is the little physical evidence that we've collected at the crime scenes, including some DNA. It's at least possible that our guy is a prior offender and that his sample will be among the ones that have been analyzed and cataloged into the database. But it isn't helping that we have to wait our turn over at the lab. If you could order those guys to jump our samples to the head of the line, that would be a huge help."

"You think there's a chance in hell?"

I shrugged. "We won't know until we try. But every hour between now and the time the techs get to our samples is one more hour that this asshole is out on the streets."

For a long moment, his eyes bored into mine. Then he sighed. "Yeah, okay. I'll call over there as soon as I get back to the office and tell them that your case takes precedence over everything else they're working on. Then we can all get down on our knees and pray that this cocksucker is on file. But either way, you need to show me something here, and you need to do it soon."

He pitched the paper into the trash can and rose to leave. As he reached the door, he looked back to the lieutenant. "Keep me up to the minute on this, Russ. And for God's sake, bring me some good news soon.

I'm tired of looking like an incompetent idiot every time some fuckin' reporter throws a question at me."

I left the lieutenant's office and walked down the hall to find Maggie sitting at her desk, drinking a cup of coffee and reviewing some paperwork. Theoretically, it was her day off as well as mine, but in the middle of an active investigation, there was no such thing as a day off. She was wearing jeans and sporting a Metallica T-shirt, and to look at her, it seemed pretty clear that she hadn't gotten any more sleep over the last few nights than I had.

Even so, I noticed that her gym bag had been dropped into the corner of the office and that her hair was still slightly damp from the shower. Obviously she'd sacrificed some time this morning that she might otherwise have spent in the sack so that she could go to the gym and put herself through what was always a very demanding workout. As I dropped into the chair next to her desk, she looked up from the report she was studying and wished me a good morning.

"Like hell," I countered. "I just ran into the chief in the lieutenant's office. He's got a burr up his ass about our lack of progress on this case, and he's wondering if the lieutenant shouldn't assign the lead to somebody else."

Maggie sighed heavily and shook her head. "That's what you get for coming up the front stairs, Richardson. How many fuckin' times do I have to remind you that if you'd come up the back way like I do, you wouldn't walk right by the lieutenant's office and you wouldn't keep getting your ass in a sling like that.

"I swear to God, I think you're learning disabled. But for that matter, if that's what he's thinking, then so is the chief. Maybe he could turn the case over to Doyle. Christ, I'll bet that dickhead can't even spell *Beverly Thompson*. And the thought that he might help us find her sometime during this millennium boggles the imagination."

"Yeah, you're no doubt right about that. So what do you have there?"

"The phone records from the furniture store where Jack Collins works. He told us that immediately after the prospective customer called him at the store saying that he wanted to come in and look at bedroom furniture, Collins called his wife to tell her that he might be late getting home. The call from the store's number to the Collins home was made at eight thirty-four. Three minutes before that, there's a call to the store from a number that goes back to a gas station/convenience store on Glendale Avenue. That's gotta be the call from the alleged customer. I was thinking that we should get over there with an evidence tech and have him dust the phone and the area around it. I know the chances are between slim and fuckin' none, but we might just get lucky and raise some useful prints."

An hour later, we were standing outside of a Circle K convenience store as Dick Holmes, the evidence tech, dusted the area around the phone that was attached to the outside wall of the building. "I sure as hell hope you don't have your expectations set too high here," Holmes said. "You know I'm going to raise about forty different sets of prints from this phone, and the chances that we'll be able to identify any of them are around one in a million."

"We know that," Maggie countered. "But even at those odds, it's worth the effort."

I poked Maggie's arm with my elbow and directed her attention to a video camera that was mounted on a light pole in the parking lot and aimed at the front of the store. She looked up at the camera and said, "We couldn't get that lucky, Sean. Keep your fingers crossed."

Leaving Holmes to go about his business, we walked

into the store and asked to see the person in charge. A Middle Eastern man of indeterminate age was on duty behind the counter and indicated that he was the manager. We flashed our shields and asked him how long he kept the tapes from his video surveillance cameras.

"We keep them for a week," he said, with no accent whatsoever. "Then we use them over again."

"Great," I replied. Pointing back at the camera outside, I said, "We'd like to see the tapes from that camera for last Thursday night."

"Should I ask if you have a warrant?"

"No, you shouldn't," I replied. "You should just cooperate like a good citizen and volunteer the tapes. And you should probably also stop wasting so much time watching mindless cop shows on television."

The guy shrugged. "Okay. Watch the counter for a minute. If a customer should accidentally wander in here, tell him I'll be right back."

With that, he locked the register, stepped out from behind the counter, and disappeared through a door at the back of the store. A couple of minutes later, he returned and handed me three videotapes. "These are the tapes from all three cameras from six P.M. last Thursday night to six A.M. on Friday morning. But I don't know what you think you're going to see on them. If I can trust my night manager—which I don't—we sold about six hundred dollars' worth of gas and miscellaneous crap that night, and nothing out of the ordinary happened at all."

We wrote the manager a receipt and promised to see that the videos were returned when we finished with them. The guy handed them over and shot me a look, suggesting that he had little more confidence in that assurance than he apparently did in his night manager.

Back at the department, Maggie grabbed a cup of coffee. I dug a Coke out of the small refrigerator in my office, and we settled into the conference room to look at the tapes, beginning with the one from the outside camera.

The call to the furniture store had been made at 8:32 on Thursday evening. A running clock was embedded in the videotape and I fast-forwarded to 8:25. We started watching the tape at regular speed, and just as the clock hit 8:31, a man in a battered cowboy hat walked directly under the camera's position and stepped up to the phone. He was wearing jeans and a jacket with the collar turned up, but in the black-and-white video, it was impossible to determine the jacket's color, which looked to be somewhere in the neighborhood between black and navy blue.

With his back to the camera, the guy picked up the receiver and plugged two coins into the phone. He dialed a number, then lifted the receiver to his left ear.

For the next two minutes and twelve seconds, Maggie and I stared intently at the screen, willing the man at the phone to turn, even slightly, so as to expose his face to the camera. Ninety seconds into the call, Maggie pounded a fist onto the table. "Come on, you asshole. Give us a look!"

Despite Maggie's encouragement, the guy remained stock-still with his head down, looking in the direction of his feet. He then hung up the phone, pulled a handkerchief from the right-hand pocket of his jacket, and wiped down the receiver. Still using the handkerchief, he returned the receiver to the phone, then turned and walked away from the phone box, staring intently at the ground ahead of him.

Through it all, the guy never once looked in the direction of the camera to allow us even a partial glimpse of his face. The cowboy hat was pulled down low over his eyes, and as he walked away from the phone, we couldn't even see his chin, let alone any other distinguishing features. Without much hope, Maggie and I looked at the other two tapes, but neither of them allowed a view of the phone from inside the store, and so in the end all we knew was that our caller—and prospective killer—was a white male who appeared to be of average height. The bulky jacket he was wearing made it impossible to make an educated guess at his weight; we could tell only that the guy was not obese.

We ran the tape again, in slow motion this time, but saw nothing more than we had at regular speed. As I rewound the tape, Maggie shook her head and said, "Shit! Is this guy that good, or is he just fuckin' lucky? We've got the bastard right there in front of our eyes, but he gives us absolutely nothing. He could be any one of a million guys."

"I know, Maggs," I sighed. "Jesus, you'd think we could catch one decent break in this goddamn case. But we're not gonna get him from this."

I called Dick Holmes and told him that he needn't bother sorting through and trying to identify the prints he'd gotten from the phone. Maggie and I then decided to chase down a couple of leads that had come in on the tip line. We were walking down the hall, headed for the stairs, when Chris Doyle sauntered out of the conference room with a cup of coffee in one hand and a half-eaten sandwich in the other. He grinned at Maggie and pointed his sandwich in the direction of her T-shirt. "Used to a terrific band," he said. "But the last CD was a pale imitation of their earlier work."

Maggie shook her head. "Let me guess, Doyle. The music critic for *Rolling Stone* just died and Jann Wenner was so desperate that he gave *you* the job?"

Doyle laughed. "Believe me, sweetheart, he could do a helluva lot worse." Turning to me, he said, "Where are you whiz kids off to?"

"We're checking out a couple of tips from the hotline," I replied. "How are your interviews coming?"

Doyle took a bite out of the sandwich. Trying to talk around the food in his mouth, he said, "I'm still talking to Collins's friends and neighbors, but none of them knows a fuckin' thing. I'm just spinning my wheels."

"Well, stay on it," I said. "This case is going to break somewhere, and you never know who's going to have the key piece of information that will finally send us in the right direction."

"Oh, don't worry about me," he replied sarcastically. "Once I've finished my lunch, I'll be back out there giving this case a hundred and twenty percent of my time and effort, just like always."

Turning to go, he pointed back at Maggie's chest. "The T-shirt looks great on you, babe. And if you'd like to come over and listen to my record collection some night, just say the word."

Maggie rolled her eyes and gave her best impression of a sweet smile. "Your *record* collection? Jesus, Chris, thanks for the offer, but I'd hate to have to ask you to take your hand off your little tiny dick long enough to crank the handle on the Victrola."

Neither of the tips that Maggie and I were chasing panned out, and at the end of the day we were still no closer to finding our killer than we'd been twelve hours earlier. Unfortunately, none of the other members of the team had enjoyed any better luck than we had, and a little after seven P.M., Maggie and I called it a day, hoping that a good night's sleep might leave us in better shape to get at it again in the morning.

Once home after visiting Julie, I sorted through the mail and changed into a sweatshirt and jeans. Then I poured a couple fingers of Jameson into an old-fashioned glass and went out to the patio that opened off the kitchen and living room. I dropped into a chair and dragged another around to face me. Propping my feet up in the second chair, I took a large sip of the whiskey.

Although the temperature had dropped into the middle fifties, it had been another gorgeous day with bright blue skies and the daytime temperature reaching into the middle seventies. However, as was so often the case lately, my mood contrasted sharply with the beautiful weather. It struck me—not for the first time—that these days I probably would have been much more at home psychologically in some dingy northern city where the snow, the cold, and the gray gloomy skies would better match my spirit.

From my days as a rookie cop I'd been dismayed by the violence that people so casually inflict on each other, and the responsibilities of the job had always weighed heavily on me. But they'd felt especially burdensome during the last few months when I'd been without Julie's presence to serve as a counterbalancing force.

On my third day as a member of the department, I'd been the first patrolman to respond to the homicide of a nineteen-year-old woman named Maria Gonzalez, who'd been bound, gagged, raped, and then knifed to death in the tiny apartment she had shared with her mother and her younger sister. The sister, Rosalita, was twelve. She'd discovered the crime when she came home from school, and called 911, screaming and crying into the phone. I'd been on the scene only long enough to survey the situation and call for backup, when the mother arrived home from work and walked in on the tragedy.

Even though I was eight inches taller and at least sixty pounds heavier than Mrs. Gonzalez, I could barely restrain her as she attempted to reach her daughter. Desperate to safeguard whatever evidence might remain in the bedroom where the assault had occurred,

I wrestled her away from the door. She struggled tenaciously against me, scratching, biting, and kicking, all the while pleading desperately with God to undo the catastrophe, until finally the paramedics arrived and gave her an injection that mercifully put her to sleep.

Two days later, homicide detectives arrested the twenty-five-year-old son of a woman who lived across the hall from the victim, and charged him with the crime. The man had been out on parole for three months, and had two prior convictions, one for burglary and another for statutory rape. He'd used a condom in the assault in an apparent effort to avoid leaving any seminal fluids at the scene that might assist the investigators in identifying him. But then, inexplicably, he'd left two bloody fingerprints on the bedroom doorframe that left no doubt as to his identity.

The experience had changed my life. I'd joined the force fresh out of college because I couldn't afford to go directly to law school. My plan was to work hard, save some money, perhaps take a few night-school law courses, and then ultimately go back to school and complete the degree. But I'd been awed by the tenacity, skill, and reverence with which the lead detective had worked the Gonzalez case. Watching him, I understood, in a way that my academy courses had never conveyed, the critical importance—the sanctity even—of the work that he did.

Within days of the killer's arrest, I'd abandoned any thoughts of law school and had set my sights on joining the Homicide Unit. I realized, certainly, that there could never be justice for Maria Gonzalez or for her mother and sister. But I also understood more clearly than ever before the fact that someone had to fight for them and for others like them. Someone had to make the effort, however vain it might be, to bring the scales back closer to even.

That was my job now, as it had been for the last

seven years. During that time, I'd worked scores of cases, and friends—often well-meaning but at other times just morbidly curious—asked how anyone could do it. In particular, they wondered how I could avoid being slowly but inevitably consumed by the depravity and the brutality that were central to my every working day.

There was, really, no way to respond. I could try to describe the satisfaction I took in clearing a case. I could talk earnestly about the importance of getting a killer off the streets before he could claim another victim. I could respond glibly that it was a nasty job but that somebody had to do it. But I could never begin to explain the hold that Maria Gonzalez still exercised over me.

Twelve years after the fact, the memory of that afternoon haunts me still. Late at night, deep in my dreams, I see her lying there on the bed in that pitiful apartment, so horribly abused. My heart breaks again as I listen to her mother, sobbing and begging God to bring her daughter back.

I feel Mrs. Gonzalez's indescribable pain even more sharply now than I did on that terrible day so many years ago. But then, I now understand something myself about the futility of attempting to bargain with God.

CHAPTER TWENTY

Carl McClain spent most of the weekend away from the house, and for that, at least, Beverly was grateful. She was also thankful for the fact that the frequency and intensity of his sexual assaults had diminished, at least for the time being.

After viciously raping her three times within hours of her abduction, McClain had taken her only once or twice a night in the time since. And after the first night, he had not been nearly as brutal with her. As a result, the physical damage she suffered as a result of the attacks had declined somewhat.

The psychological damage was another matter altogether.

Save for her outburst during the pizza "dinner" on the second evening, Beverly had spent the first three and a half days of her ordeal in a virtual stupor. The shock of the abduction, her confinement, and the repeated sexual assaults was exceeded only by the trauma of having watched David die so violently in front of her. And the sudden onslaught of these horrors had literally overwhelmed her, shutting down her senses as though some psychological circuit breaker was protectively tripping switches in a desperate effort to head off a total emotional and intellectual meltdown.

She finally hit rock bottom around midmorning on Sunday. McClain left the house a little before eight, telling her that he would be gone until late that evening. The next thing Beverly knew, it was ten thirty. She returned to consciousness to find herself naked and shivering on the bed, even though the temperature in the house had to be somewhere in the midseventies. She realized that she hadn't been asleep exactly. Rather, she'd been drifting in a state of suspended animation, her eyes open, staring blankly at the door that McClain had closed and locked behind him two and a half hours earlier.

The hopelessness of her situation was suddenly too great to bear, and she burst into tears. Weeping uncontrollably, she crawled across the bed and found her skirt, which had wound up on the floor beside the bed. She pulled the narrow leather belt out of the loops and let the skirt fall back to the floor.

Dragging the cable behind her, she grabbed one of the folding chairs from the card table, carried it into the bathroom, and set it in the shower stall. In her mind's eye, again she saw David falling to the floor of the garage as if in slow motion.

Shaking and a bit unsteady, she climbed up onto the chair and fed the belt through the buckle, creating a small loop. She tied the end of the belt around the shower-curtain rod and said a silent, desperate prayer that both the belt and the rod would be strong enough. She cinched the knot tight and spread the loop in the belt as wide as it would go. Then she forced the loop over her head and leaned forward slightly, taking the slack out of the loop.

Crying harder now, she thought of her mother and father. And one last time, she thought of David. Beverly did not believe in God or in Heaven, and she had no vain hope of seeing David again in a glorious afterlife of some sort. But she did believe in hell—of this she could offer witness. And death would be a blessed release from its dreadful grip.

She wrapped her hands around the shower rod and pulled herself up, raising her knees and lifting her weight off of the chair. A wave of relief, totally unbidden and completely unexpected, suddenly swept through her. "I love you, David," she said aloud.

She lowered her right leg, preparing to kick the chair away. But then, as suddenly as the wave of calm had materialized, it receded, only to be followed by a sense of rage and anger that Beverly had never before experienced.

She closed her eyes and swallowed hard. For a few more seconds, she clung to the rod. Then, reluctantly, she set her feet back down on the chair and slowly let her legs take her weight again. "I love you, David," she whispered.

CHAPTER TWENTY-ONE

On Friday and Saturday, Chris Doyle made a half-hearted effort to assist the rest of the team in interviewing the relatives, friends, and coworkers of the victims in our continuing quest to find something—anything—that would link the victims together. Having apparently exhausted himself in the process, he insisted on taking his regular day off on Sunday, leaving Maggie, Pierce, Chickris, and me to continue the effort without his assistance. The fact that we had to do so was certainly no great handicap, and we all fervently hoped that Bob Riggins would be back to work ASAP, relieving the four of us of Doyle's company. Maggie and I were on our way to an interview early Sunday afternoon, and I asked her if she'd heard anything from Abernathy, the minister.

"Yeah. He took me to the Rhythm Room last night to hear Bad Sneakers, the Steely Dan tribute group."

"That sounds like a good time. Those guys are on my short list of local faves."

She nodded her agreement. "Yeah, well, the music was very good. We danced and had a few drinks. Actually, I had a couple of glasses of wine. He had one gin and tonic and then switched to club soda, so that he could preach with a clear head this morning."

"Did he say anything more about the ex-wife?"

"Yeah. He asked me what had happened with me and Timothy, and so I gave him chapter and verse. More than anything else, I did it to impress upon him the thousand and one ways this job can fuck up an otherwise pretty good relationship, even if there aren't any kids involved.

"Anyhow, once I showed him mine, he figured he had to show me his. Apparently, while he was overseas in the army, the missus had a torrid affair with a sexy jazz musician who lived down the street. Once Patrick got back, she confessed her sins and begged his forgiveness, promising that nothing like that would ever happen again.

"It obviously hit him pretty hard, but he sucked it up, did the Christian thing, and took her back. He says he did it partly because of the kids, and partly because he still loved her in spite of what she'd done. Then, ten months ago, the jazz musician left Tennessee for a gig in Chicago, and Mrs. Abernathy went right along with him. She left a note for Patrick and didn't even say good-bye to the girls."

"Jesus, that's not too cold, is it?"

"No shit. Anyhow, Patrick and the kids were all pretty devastated. He filed on the bitch, asking for custody with no visitation rights for her, and she didn't even contest it. A judge granted the divorce and Patrick decided that the best thing for all concerned would be to get the hell out of Memphis. The job at my mom's church came up and he applied. The church board offered him the job, and he 'accepted the call.' I wanted to ask him what sort of god would put some poor son of a bitch through a hell like that just to 'call' him to a new ministry, but I managed to hold my tongue."

"There's a first," I laughed. "So, you gonna see him again?"

Maggie shook her head. "Hell, Sean, I don't know. On the plus side, he *is* a nice guy. He's attractive. We like the same music, and he's got a good sense of humor. If it weren't for all the baggage he's carrying, there might be a chance that something could happen between us. But he's obviously been badly wounded, and I really don't want to be the woman who catches him on the rebound, and then breaks his heart again when it doesn't work out.

"On top of that, of course, there's the kids. I tried to make it clear that I don't relate very well to children and that unlike my mother, I'm not a churchgoing kind of woman. I also told him that I loved my job and that it would never allow me to take on the responsibility of a couple of kids in addition to a husband."

"How'd he react to that?"

"He said that he wasn't expecting me to make a lifetime commitment on the basis of a couple of dates and that he understood that my job would make it hard to have a family. But he insisted that lots of cops do have families and successful relationships and that I shouldn't rule out the possibility that it could happen for me. He said he'd like it if we could continue to see each other without any pressure or expectations and just see where things might go."

"So how'd you leave it?"

"I told him that I'd enjoyed the evening, and that if he wanted to go out again sometime I would. But I also told him straight out that I wasn't interested in anything beyond that, and that if he was, then he needed to be looking for some other woman. He said he understood and insisted that he wasn't going to put any pressure on me. Then he took me home, walked me to the door, and left me with a very chaste kiss. I don't know if I'll be hearing from him again or not."

I signaled a turn and said, "I know you're trying to be fair to the guy, Maggie, but do you think there's a chance here that you're not being fair to yourself?"

"How do you mean?"

"Well, maybe you're so concerned about making sure that his feelings aren't hurt that you're not willing to give this thing a fighting chance. I confess I have a hard time imagining you keeping company with a minister. But if you like the guy—and it seems that you do—why not chill out a bit and see where it goes? Maybe it works and maybe it doesn't. But the guy's an adult. I'm sure he knows the emotional risks as well as you do."

She sat quietly for a minute or so, staring out the window at the traffic passing in the opposite lane. Then she turned to look at me. "How in the hell did you manage it, Sean—you and Julie, I mean? Do you mind my asking?"

I shook my head. "No, it's okay. How do you mean?"

She gave a small shrug and went back to looking out the window. "This job. The hours. The things you see. How did the two of you build such a solid relationship around it? God knows Timothy and I couldn't do it."

"I'm not sure I really know, Maggs," I sighed. "Thankfully, it wasn't something that we ever had to work at. For openers, Julie respected the job. Unlike her mother, she never thought that being a homicide detective was beneath me—that I should aspire to something 'better,' or more socially respectable. I think it also helped a lot that I was already working homicide when Julie and I met and so she knew exactly what she was getting into from the start."

Smiling at the recollection, I said, "Second date. I'm trying to make a good impression, right? I made a reservation at Vocé—dinner, then Khani Cole and her band in the lounge after. Julie's dressed to kill. It's gonna be a great night, and two minutes after the waiter puts the salads in front of us, I get called out to a murder-suicide."

"Oh, Christ," Maggie laughed. "I'll bet that made the big impression you were after."

"Yeah, well . . . I put Julie in a cab and fell all over myself apologizing. But she took it right in stride. *She's* apologizing to *me* because the evening got ruined, and that's when I knew she was a keeper. She always understood that the hours were unpredictable, and she knew that in the middle of a case like this, there's precious little time in your life for anything but the case. She gave me the space I needed to do the work, and she never worried that I didn't love her or that maybe the job was more important to me than she was.

"Certainly it also helped that Julie was a very independent woman—comfortable not just in her own skin, but in her own company. On those nights when I couldn't make it home for dinner on time, or when she had to spend the occasional evening alone, it wasn't a major crisis; there wasn't ever any drama. She was content to lose herself in a book or a movie, knowing that we'd make up the time together later."

"Yeah, well, that damned sure doesn't sound like Timothy. He didn't mind that I was a cop. Hell, to tell the truth, I think the fact that I was a woman in a uniform with a gun and a pair of handcuffs really turned him on. But the man liked his dinner, his sex, and his social life to be right on schedule. And once I made detective and the hours became increasingly unpredictable, it upset the balance of his whole world. He thought that cops and robbers should work a sensible nine-to-five schedule just like everybody else. And when it became clear that they didn't, things started to go downhill in a huge fuckin' hurry."

She hesitated for a moment, then said, "Is it hard for you to talk about her? Would you rather I didn't ask?"

I shook my head. "No, Maggs, it's okay."

She nodded. "It's just that every once in a while you suddenly disappear into yourself for a few minutes. I'm pretty sure I know where you're going when that happens, but I never quite know how to react. My sense is that you'd really rather not talk about it, and so I usually just shut up and wait for you to come back into the moment. But I hope you know that even though I might not say so very often, I really do care about the situation you're in.

"I wouldn't begin to pretend that I can understand the kind of pain you must be feeling, but if you do want to talk about it, or if there's ever anything I can do to help somehow . . ."

"Thanks, Maggie," I sighed. "I do know that you care, and that means a lot to me."

Shaking my head, I said, "I just keep thinking about all the thousands of little things that would have made a difference. If the system hadn't let that fuckin' drunk back out on the road . . . If Julie hadn't left work to run an errand . . . If she'd have left thirty seconds earlier or twenty seconds later . . . If the traffic had been heavier or lighter . . .

"I'd give my life if I could just go back and change any one of those things. But I can't. Nobody can. And unfortunately, at this point, there's really nothing else that could be of any help."

The time and effort we put in on Sunday got us no closer to our killer than we'd been on Saturday night. At midmorning on Monday, I was sitting at my desk reviewing some notes from the Collins case when the phone rang. I answered it to find Tony Anderson from the crime lab on the other end of the line. We exchanged hellos, and he said, "You owe me a big one, Richardson. I'm about to make your day."

"God, I hope so," I sighed. "I could sure as hell use some good news for a change. What've you got for me?"

"We have a DNA match for hair samples that were taken from Beverly Thompson's Lexus and from the chair in which Karen Collins was killed."

I dropped my feet from the desk to the floor and sat bolt upright in my chair. "Jesus, Tony, you've got to be kidding. I can't believe we got that lucky. Who's the match?"

"His name is Richard Petrovich, a white male, now forty-two years of age. He submitted the sample while a guest of the state six years ago. I'm faxing you the results as we speak."

"Thanks, Tony. And you're right—I do owe you a big one."

I hung up the phone and practically sprinted down the hall to the fax machine. For a minute or so I stood there, anxiously drumming my fingers on the table. After what seemed like an eternity, the machine began humming and Anderson's fax spooled out into my hand. I took a quick glance and then ran back up the hall to Maggie's office.

"We've got the bastard," I said. "Come on over. I'm running him now."

Maggie followed me back to my office. Too excited to sit, she stood behind me as I dropped into my chair and called up the state-prison records on my computer. Glancing at the fax, I typed Petrovich's name and Social Security number into the appropriate spaces and hit ENTER.

A moment later, the screen refreshed. Six and a half years ago Richard Petrovich had pled out on charges of burglary and attempted rape. Under the plea arrangement, he'd done six years in the Lewis complex of the state-prison system in Buckeye and had been released last September.

According to the records, Petrovich had been assigned to report to the parole office in south Phoenix. I grabbed the phone and called the office. After waiting on hold for several minutes, I was finally connected to Petrovich's parole officer, whose name was Nina Ellis.

Ellis had a deep, no-nonsense voice and sounded like a woman that you didn't want to screw around with. I asked her if Petrovich had reported as ordered. Apparently without even having to consult her records, Ellis said, "Yes he did, Detective, right on time. And he's reported in on time as scheduled ever since. If the rest of my clients were as conscientious as Petrovich, this job would be a cakewalk. Why're you asking?"

"We just need to have a chat with him on a couple of matters. Do you know if he's found a job?"

"Yeah. The day he first reported he told me that he'd landed a job as a welder at a small manufacturing plant on East Buckeye Road. The owner is a righteous citizen named Fred Bourquin who's hired a number of ex-cons and given them the chance at a fresh start. The guy rides them like a mother hen, both on and off the job, making sure they have the help they need and that they keep their noses clean. Please don't tell me that Petrovich's screwed up again."

"I can't say for sure, Ms. Ellis, but we do need to talk to him."

She sighed heavily. "Well, I don't know what this might be about, Detective, but I've seen a lot of scumbags come and go through this office, and I've gotten to be a pretty good judge of character. Petrovich is a guy who screwed up and made a stupid mistake. But he pled to it and by all accounts was a model prisoner. He did his time, and I've rarely known an ex-con to work hard as he has to put his life back in order.

"I've seen him every two weeks since his release, and at least as of last Friday, he's stayed clean and sober. His employer is very happy with him, and by all appearances, he's a model ex-con. I'd be very surprised to hear that he'd gone off the rails."

"Well, I don't know that he has, Ms. Ellis. As I said, for the moment we simply want to talk to the guy."

Ellis gave me Petrovich's home and work addresses, and Maggie and I hurried down the hall to the lieutenant's office, where we found him on the phone. He took one look at the expressions on our faces and said, "I'll have to get back to you on that, Rusty."

He hung up the phone, looked from Maggie to me, and said, "What?"

I gave him the news and he thought about it for a moment. "You're assuming that Petrovich will be at work?"

"Yeah," I said. "And I think that the best approach would be to go in relatively low key. This place employs a number of ex-cons, and so they're probably accustomed to periodic visits from the police. If we go in full bore, we may well start a riot. But if we do it quietly, Maggie and I can probably waltz right in, grab Petrovich, and get him out of there without turning it into a major incident."

Martin nodded. "Okay. But take enough backup to surround the place and make sure he has absolutely no chance to escape."

The place where Petrovich worked was in a light industrial area in the southeast corner of the city. While the uniforms and the Crime Scene Response team waited in the parking lot of a Jack in the Box a quarter of a mile away, Maggie and I made a reconnaissance loop around the block where the shop was located.

It was a stand-alone operation doing business in a white cinder-block building that desperately needed a fresh coat of paint. The place was surrounded by a tall chain-link fence that was topped by concertina wire, and the lot outside of the building was littered with refuse. Off to one side of the yard, a number of pallets stood sealed in plastic and stacked ten or twelve feet high. There was no way of telling if the pallets held raw materials or finished product.

The other side of the yard was apparently the employee parking lot, and half a dozen aging vehicles were lined up haphazardly, butting up against a driveway that led to a garage door on the north side of the building. There was no black van among them. A door marked OFFICE in faded red letters stood squarely in the middle of the building, facing the street.

I turned the corner and drove down the street along the east side of the building. About ten feet of space separated the shop from the fence behind it. Most of the space was filled with junk that looked like it might have been abandoned and left rusting there for years. As was the case in front, all of the windows in the building were open, and as I drove slowly down the street, the whine of a high-pressure drill and the loud rapid thudding of an air hammer assaulted our ears.

After circling the block, we drove back up the street and rejoined the uniforms and the techs. I propped a legal pad on the hood of my car and drew a rough sketch of the building. Looking to Jon Beers, the ranking patrolman, I said, "Unless he tries to go over the fence, the only way out is through the open gate in front of the place. You can put a couple of guys along the fence at the rear of the building to make sure he doesn't try to get out the back. Then you and the other two guys can take the front. Maggie and I will drive right up to the office door and bring him out that way."

Beers nodded and we took a couple of minutes to check our equipment. Everybody took one last good look at Petrovich's mug shot. Then Maggie and I got into my Chevy and led the uniforms back down the street while the techs waited for our call.

Beers dropped two of his men at the fence at the back of the building. Then I drove up to the front of the building, pulled into the yard, and stopped in front of the office door. Beers pulled his squad across the entrance, effectively sealing the gate, then he and the other two members of his squad got out and took up their positions. Maggie and I waited a moment at the door, then opened it and walked into the building.

The door opened into a small, cluttered office. Two

metal desks had been pushed together, facing each other in the center of the room, and at one of them a heavy bleached blonde sat smoking a cigarette and sorting through what looked like a stack of invoices.

The door to the shop was closed, and the office must have been heavily insulated. The racket of the industrial equipment, which was so loud outside of the building, was considerably muffled in here. The blonde was wearing an Arizona Cardinals T-shirt and a pair of faded blue jeans. She looked up at our entrance and said in a raspy voice, "Can I help you?"

Maggie and I walked over to the woman's desk and gave her a look at our shields and IDs. "Phoenix PD, ma'am," I said. "We need to have a word with Richard Petrovich."

The woman seemed unfazed by the request, as if it were a fairly routine experience. She set her cigarette down in an ashtray next to a bottle of Mountain Dew, got up from the desk, and said, "Wait just a minute. I'll get Fred."

Maggie touched the woman on the arm and said, "No, ma'am. Please just take us back into the shop and show us where we can find Mr. Petrovich."

For a moment, the blonde hesitated. Then she looked from Maggie to me, sighed, and said, "Follow me."

She led us out into the shop, closing the office door behind us. I counted five men working at various tasks, one of whom was a welder. He had his mask down over his face and his torch in his hand and was kneeling in front of the project he was working on. As we stepped through the door, everyone except the welder stopped working and turned to stare at us.

Every man in the place looked like a hardened con. All of them sported what appeared to be jailhouse tats, and several of them wore earrings. Out here the temperature was at least twenty degrees hotter than it had been in the office, and the uniform of the day consisted of ripped jeans and muscle shirts. Most of the men were perspiring, and the testosterone level in the room was doubtless somewhere off the scale.

While the welder remained oblivious, four sets of decidedly hostile eyes followed our approach across the floor. Most of them were focused tightly on Maggie, mentally undressing her without even attempting to disguise their interest. Then a sixth man appeared from the far corner of the shop, older, heavier, and obviously the boss. Wiping his hands on a red rag, he interrupted our progress halfway across the floor and said, "Help you?"

The welder finally realized that something unusual was under way. He turned off his torch, set it on the floor beside him, and raised his mask. I showed my hands to the heavyset man and said, "Mr. Bourquin?"

He nodded his head. Maggie pointed in the direction of the welder and said, "No problem, sir. We just need to have a few words with Mr. Petrovich here."

Yielding no ground, Bourquin said, "About what?"

"About nothing that's any concern of yours," I replied. "We're not here to cause problems for you or for anyone else, but we do need to talk with Mr. Petrovich out front. Please step out of the way, sir."

Bourquin glared at me for a long moment, then stepped aside, saying nothing more. While Maggie kept an eye on him and on the other four men, who had gathered behind him, I stepped over to Petrovich.

He was easily the smallest man in the room, perhaps five-eight and a hundred and fifty pounds. His dark hair was plastered to the top and sides of his head, and he stood holding the welding helmet at his side with a mixture of what seemed to be confusion and fear written all over his face. I touched him lightly on the arm and said, "Mr. Petrovich, would you please step out front with us?"

He nodded and together we walked across the room.

Suddenly remembering the welding helmet, he handed it to his boss. Bourquin took it, nodded at him, and said, "Let me know if you need anything, Richard."

Maggie led us through the office and out into the yard, closing the office door behind us. We took Petrovich over to the car and I told him to assume the position. He did so, and I patted him down, finding nothing in his pockets other than a set of keys, some loose change, and a worn, thin wallet that held a driver's license, a Social Security card, a yellowed snapshot of a small girl, and twenty-seven dollars. "He's clean," I said.

Turning back to Petrovich, I said, "Okay, Mr. Petrovich, we have some questions for you downtown." I read him his rights, and then, nodding in the direction of the uniforms, I said, "Let's not make this any harder on each other than we have to."

He shook his head. "I'm not gonna resist, but I haven't done anything. Why do you wanna talk to me?"

"That can wait until we get downtown," I replied. Gesturing in the direction of the parked vehicles, I said, "Does one of these belong to you?"

"That one," he replied, pointing at an aging Chrysler sedan.

I held his key ring out in front of him. "These are the keys?"

"Yeah. The round one is the ignition."

"All right. We'll take good care of it. But what now I need is for you to put your hands behind your back."

He did as instructed, and I cuffed him and put him into the backseat of the Chevy. Then Maggie and I got into the car and I backed out into the yard. A patrolman pulled the squad away from the exit and as I reached it, I rolled down the window and handed Petrovich's keys to Jon Beers. "It's the green beater Chrysler," I said. "Have the techs load it up and get it over to the garage."

Chapter Twenty-two

After taking the weekend off to watch his daughter play in a softball tournament, Carl McClain was back on the job at midmorning on Monday with five days left to wrap up his business in Phoenix. A few minutes after ten, he watched Judge Walter Beckman leave his condominium and head north up Seventy-sixth Street.

McClain assumed that Beckman was leading him back to the country club again, and thus was surprised when only a couple of minutes later, the judge signaled a right turn into a complex of medical offices just off of Thompson Peak Parkway. McClain made the turn behind him and watched as Beckman carefully parked the Buick in a spot at the back of one of the buildings. The old man locked the car and then shuffled off toward the rear entrance of the building.

McClain slowly drove a circuit around the perimeter of the complex. While the parking lot on the south side of the buildings was virtually full, only a handful of cars were parked on the east side near Beckman's Buick. McClain pulled into the spot on the left of the judge's car and shut off the van's ignition.

Hunching down in the seat, he used the large rearview mirrors on both sides of the van to scan the building behind him. It looked like the blinds were closed on virtually all of the windows on this side of the building, shielding the offices against the glare and the heat of the midmorning sun.

Patience *is* a virtue, McClain thought, smiling to himself.

He cranked down the windows on the driver's and passenger's doors in the hope of getting some air to circulate through the van while he waited. Then he slipped on a lightweight blue nylon jacket and retrieved the Baby Glock from its hidey-hole under the dash. He checked the gun and slipped it into the pocket of the jacket. He then adjusted the rearview mirror on the driver's side so that it was focused on the door leading out of the building, and settled in to wait.

Over the next hour, five more cars parked in the rear lot and their occupants disappeared into the building. Finally, the door to the building opened and McClain watched Beckman come out and make his way slowly in the direction of the Buick. McClain waited until the old man was about twenty feet away, then opened the door and got out of the van.

He walked around behind the van, letting Beckman squeeze in between the van and the driver's side of the Buick. Once the judge was effectively corralled there, McClain slipped in behind him and said, "Excuse me, sir?"

The old man turned back to look at him. McClain slipped the Glock out of his jacket pocket, holding it low so that no one but the two of them could see it. The judge's eyes widened and in a quiet voice, McClain said, "Don't do anything stupid, buddy. Just do exactly what I tell you to do, and you'll be home safe and sound in time for lunch."

Beckman reached toward his hip pocket, apparently going for his wallet. "I'm sorry. I only have a few dollars on me," he said in a frightened voice.

"Don't worry about that for now," McClain responded.

With his left hand, McClain reached out and slid back the side door of the van. Gesturing with the pistol, he said, "Get in."

The old man, clearly confused, took a tentative step

in the direction of the van, then paused, apparently pondering the high step up into the vehicle.

"That's right, sir," McClain said, patiently.

He transferred the gun to his left hand. With his right hand, he reached out, took the judge's elbow, and guided him into the van. "Up we go, Your Honor."

As the judge disappeared into the van, McClain took a quick look around and saw no one else in the parking lot. He scanned the windows in the building behind him, but the blinds in virtually all of the windows remained closed, and he saw no one looking out. He stepped up into the van behind Beckman and slid the door shut.

The old man crouched, stooped over in the middle of the van, and McClain waved the gun at him again. In a distinctly harsher voice, he said, "Lie down on the floor."

Beckman shook his head in confusion. "What do you want?"

McClain slapped the old man sharply across the face. "Shut the fuck up and lie down."

The judge did as instructed, slowly sinking to the floor of the van and lying on his back.

"Roll over," McClain said.

Again, Beckman followed the order, and McClain squatted down, straddling Beckman's back. He stuck the Glock in his pocket, reached under the passenger's seat, and came out with a roll of duct tape. He unrolled a piece of the tape and tore it off. Then he roughly grabbed Beckman's arms and taped them together behind his back.

McClain tore off another piece of the tape, leaned forward, and slapped it over the judge's mouth. As the old man began struggling helplessly beneath him, McClain ripped off a third strip of tape, turned around, and bound Beckman's ankles together. Then he got up off the old man's back.

"You just lie still now for a while, Your Honor. We're going for a little ride."

McClain unfolded his painter's tarp and draped it over the judge. Then he slipped into the driver's seat and cranked the ignition. Less than three minutes after he had first walked up behind Beckman, Mc-Clain drove slowly and carefully out of the parking lot and turned west onto Thompson Peak Parkway. Two blocks later, he headed south down Scottsdale Road.

Chapter Twenty-three

In the small interview room, Richard Petrovich smelled of a man who'd been working hard in the heat of the day—and of fear.

I took off the handcuffs and pointed him in the direction of a chair. He sat nervously, his brown eyes darting from Maggie to me and then back to Maggie again before finally focusing at a spot on the table between us. His nose looked as if it had been broken at some point and not reset quite properly, and his skin seemed exceptionally pale for someone who'd lived in Arizona all his life. But I chalked that up to the fact that the guy was doubtless scared shitless.

Unlike the interview rooms on the sets of most TV cop shows, there was no one-way mirror that would allow people to watch our exchange directly, but video cameras would capture the interview and send it to a recorder and a monitor in a control room nearby. The lieutenant, Pierce, and Chickris would be watching us there.

Maggie and I took chairs on the opposite side of the table and I began by identifying for the record the three of us present in the interview room. I noted the date and time and formally advised Petrovich that the interview was being recorded on audio and video.

He displayed no macho, tough-guy bravado; rather he looked genuinely scared and confused. I leaned forward in my chair and said, "Mr. Petrovich, we apologize for dragging you in here like this, but as I said, we've got a few questions for you."

He nodded, saying nothing.

"Can you tell us how you spent last Wednesday night?" I asked.

He looked away, apparently thinking about it. Then he turned back to me. "I got home from work about six. I made myself some dinner and then watched television for a while. I went to bed a little after ten."

"Can anybody verify that?" Maggie asked.

"No. I live alone, and I didn't see or talk to anyone that night after I got home."

"What did you watch on television?" I asked.

He shrugged. "I dunno. Nothing for very long, I guess. I was channel-flipping the way you do. I watched the Suns game for a while, but otherwise I was just bouncing around the channels until I got tired and went to bed."

"How about Thursday night?" Maggie asked.

"About the same. The job leaves me pretty well exhausted, and by the end of the day, I don't have energy enough to do anything besides go home and collapse in front of the tube. I'm trying to stay sober, and so I don't go out to the bars. I sometimes go to a movie on the weekends, but except for that I stay pretty much to home. Why do you want to know what I was doing on Wednesday and Thursday nights?"

Ignoring the question, I leaned in closer and said, "How well did you know Karen Collins?"

Vigorously shaking his head, he said, "I don't. I never heard the name before."

"How about Beverly Thompson?" Maggie asked.

Again he shook his head. Then, looking completely astonished, he said, "Wait a minute! You mean the woman who's been in the news—the one who was kidnapped?"

"Yeah," Maggie said. "That woman."

Petrovich jumped up out of the chair, looked at Maggie, and said, "Jesus Christ, you can't be serious! You think I had something to do with that?"

"Didn't you?" I asked.

"No! Absolutely not! No fucking way! Who the hell says I did?"

"Sit down, Mr. Petrovich," I said.

Reluctantly, he took his chair again and clasped his hands together on the table in front of him. Trembling in anger or fear, or perhaps a combination of both, he said in a desperate voice, "Please, you've got to believe me. I *was* home all night both Wednesday and Thursday. I never heard either of those names, except for hearing the Thompson woman's name on the news. And I had nothing to do with her going missing."

"You did six years for robbery and attempted rape, is that right?" Maggie asked.

Petrovich nodded. In a distinctly less animated tone, he said, "Yes I did. And I paid the price."

"How did that happen?" I asked.

He sighed heavily. Speaking slowly in a defeated voice, he said, "Seven years ago, I was a drunk and out of work because of it. I was out drinking one night and ran through what little money I had. I was stumbling home around midnight and I walked past this house. It was a hot night and I could see that a window on the side of the house was open.

"I don't know how in the hell I could have been so stupid, except for the fact that I was drunk. But I figured I might find a few bucks so that I could go back to the bar and do some more drinking. Anyway, I pulled the screen off and climbed in the window. A woman was in bed and I woke her up. She jumped out of bed and started screaming. I went after her and grabbed her."

Shaking his head, he continued, "I wasn't trying to rape her. I just wanted to shut her up so that I could get back out the window and get away. But we were tussling and her nightgown got torn partway off. The noise woke up the woman's sister and brother-in-law, who were sleeping down the hall. He ran in and pulled me off of her. Then he punched my lights out and called the cops."

Petrovich paused for a few seconds, then looked at us earnestly and said, "I'm not a violent man, not even when I was drunk. Up until that night, my closest brush with the law was a couple of traffic tickets. I terrified that poor woman. I shamed myself and lost my family as a result. But I took my medicine and promised myself that I'd never touch a drink again. Since I got out of Lewis, I've been straight down the line."

"Do you own a gun, Mr. Petrovich?" Maggie asked.

"No, of course not! That would violate my parole."

"And you don't know Beverly Thompson?" I said.

"No."

"You were never in her car?"

"No!"

"You don't know Karen Collins?"

"No!"

"You were never in her home?"

"No!"

"Well, then, Mr. Petrovich," Maggie said, "how do you account for the fact that hair taken from Ms. Thompson's car and from Ms. Collins's home matches up to your DNA?"

Looking totally confused, he shook his head. "I can't . . . It doesn't . . . I was never there!"

His eyes finally settled on mine, and I said, "Six

years ago, while you were at Lewis, you were required to submit a DNA sample for the state's criminal database?"

"Yes."

I threw up my hands. "Well, our forensics team found hair samples at both crime scenes. And when the lab analyzed them and checked them against the database, they matched up to the sample you gave."

Petrovich's eyes widened, and for a moment he looked like a man who'd just received the shock of his life. Then he began vigorously shaking his head again. In an anguished voice, he said, "No way. It's got to be some sort of mistake. Please . . . I *wasn't* there. I don't know anything about either woman."

He held my eyes with his, as if begging me to believe his denials. I gave him a few seconds, then leaned across the table and sighed. "Look, Mr. Petrovich. This isn't a stupid television program you're in here. We're not going to play some lame good cop/bad cop routine with you, and I'm not going to go ballistic and beat the hell out of you to make you tell us what you know. The truth is that we don't need to do any of that crap. We've got you dead to rights with the DNA evidence, and believe me when I say that you'll be a lot better off cooperating with us, rather than giving us these bullshit answers that plainly contradict the evidence."

I closed the distance between us and said in a quiet voice, "You can still help yourself here, Richard. At least tell us what you did with Beverly Thompson. If she's still alive and if you help us save her, you can go a long way toward saving yourself. But if you stonewall us here, you're gonna to go down hard.

"Right now your car's in our garage and our technicians will be going through it with a fine-tooth comb. While they're doing that, my partner and I will be searching every square inch of your apartment. And if there's anything in your car or in your apartment to connect you to either of these women—and I do mean *anything*—we're going to find it. And by then it'll be way too late for you to do yourself any good. You need to believe me when I say that things will go a lot easier for you if you're straight with us now."

"But I *am* being straight with you," he pleaded. "I didn't do *anything.*"

We kept at it for another twenty minutes or so, but Petrovich continued to insist that he did not know either Beverly Thompson or Karen Collins, or Alma Fletcher for that matter. He continued to claim that he was home at the time Thompson was kidnapped and again when Collins was shot. He told us that he'd been at work the morning that Fletcher was shot. That alibi we would check, of course, but the DNA evidence had not put Petrovich at the scene of Fletcher's murder. The only thing tying that crime to the other two was the ballistics evidence.

I left the interview room feeling totally conflicted. There was no question about the fact that the physical evidence put Petrovich at two of our three crime scenes. But the guy had seemed genuinely confused by our questions and by the DNA evidence against him. He had also appeared sincere in protesting his innocence. Either he was an outstanding actor or something was totally out of whack here. We put him in a holding cell and went to search his apartment for the weapon that had been used in the three killings and for any other evidence that might tie him to any of the victims.

CHAPTER TWENTY-FOUR

McClain appeared to be in an excellent mood when he got back to the house a little after one o'clock. Beverly listened as he unlocked the door, then watched as it swung open into the bedroom. He was carrying two large McDonald's bags, and Beverly could smell the burgers and fries from across the room. Behind him, she could see the backpack sitting on the floor out in the hall.

Since climbing down from the chair in the shower twenty-six hours earlier, Beverly had been trying to focus as tightly as she could on even the smallest details of her surroundings. When McClain went out this morning, the backpack had been laying on its side. Now it was standing up, resting on its bottom end. She assumed, then, that he must have taken the backpack with him and set it back on the floor before unlocking the door.

Without being obvious about it, she tried to look carefully at the outside of the door, looking again for some sign that it either was or was not wired with explosives.

She reasoned that if McClain was telling the truth, the device would not be so obvious as to alert any unsuspecting person who might try to open the door. It would have to be concealed, probably above the door, where someone entering the room would be least likely to notice it. When she had watched him walk out through the door this morning, Beverly had spotted what looked like a metal ring attached to the door only an inch or so down from the top.

As usual, before leaving for the day, McClain had set out Beverly's breakfast—the same meal of orange juice and cereal that he'd served her every morning of her captivity. This morning, she'd asked him if he'd please leave her the box of cereal as well. He was often gone all day, she explained, and the one bowl of cereal was not enough to keep her from getting very hungry by the middle of the afternoon. Couldn't he at least allow her the opportunity to have a bowl of dry cereal to tide her over if she needed it?

McClain decided that he could. He went out to the kitchen, returned with the box of Kellogg's Low Fat Granola, and set it on the card table. "Bon appetit!" he said, smiling. "Enjoy your day, darling."

Once he'd gone, Beverly drank the juice and ate the cereal. Then she rinsed off the bowl and spoon in the bathroom sink and set them on the card table to dry in the air.

Up until this morning, she'd spent the bulk of the daytime hours sitting on the bed, leaning up against the wall opposite the door, because this was the most comfortable position she had found. But after finishing breakfast, she moved the card table and the two chairs closer to the door, near the foot of the bed. She sat down in a chair facing the door, poured another cup or so of cereal into the bowl, and settled in to wait.

When she finally heard McClain's key in the door, she spooned some of the dry cereal into her mouth and began chewing it slowly. He walked through the door to find her apparently eating the cereal for lunch. From this new vantage point, she could see that what she'd thought was a metal ring near the top of the door was actually a hook that had been screwed into the door.

She looked immediately back to McClain, who closed the door behind him and then slipped the key ring into the right front pocket of his jeans. He stood for a moment just inside the room, watching Beverly chew her cereal. Stating the obvious, he said, "You moved the furniture?"

Beverly set her spoon down in the bowl. "Do you mind?" she asked in a quiet voice. "It's just that where you had it before, it was right between the bed and the bathroom. Every time I walked back and forth to the bathroom, I kept getting the cable tangled up in the table and chairs. So I moved them."

He looked at her for a long moment as if trying to gauge the honesty of her response. Beverly returned the look with what she hoped he'd read as an expression of supplication on her face. Then he gave a small shrug. "Fine by me, princess. Anything to make you more comfortable." He set the McDonald's bags on the table between them and said, "Let's eat."

McClain took the chair on the opposite side of the table and pulled two medium Diet Cokes and a pile of paper napkins out of the first bag. From the second, he produced two Quarter Pounders with Cheese and two large fries. He set one of each in front of her. "I know you're probably getting tired of the junk food," he said. "Believe me, so am I. I'll bet I've gained five pounds eating this shit over the last few days. But tonight I'll cook at home—something reasonably healthy like a salad and some chicken or something."

"Thank you," she replied.

As McClain dove into his food, Beverly slowly ate a couple of fries and then unwrapped the burger. She *was* hungry, and even the lukewarm fast food tasted good. McClain swallowed a bite of the hamburger and said, "I had a very good day at the office, in case you're interested. Things are suddenly coming together very well."

Beverly paused, a French fry halfway to her mouth.

Carefully, she set it down on the hamburger wrapper in front of her. Looking up at McClain, she said, "Can't you please tell me what this is all about? What do you mean when you say that things are coming together? And what's my part in all of this? Why are you holding me here?"

Toying with a French fry of his own, McClain said, "Your role is evolving, Beverly. For the moment, your part in this little drama is to keep me entertained while I attend to some other pressing business. But I promise that you have a much more important role ahead of you, and I won't keep you in the dark much longer. I can tell you, though, that I met an old friend of yours today. I'm sure that if he were able, he'd want to send along his regards."

Shaking her head, she said, "What old friend? Who?"

He laughed. "Nobody you have to worry about now, sweetheart. Just finish your lunch."

McClain ate his burger and polished off the last of his fries. Then he sat back and slowly sipped at his Coke while he watched Beverly finish her lunch. She ate the last of her fries, wiped her mouth with a paper napkin, and took a drink of the Coke. She set the paper cup back on the table and McClain said, "Stand up, Beverly."

For a long moment, she looked down at the center of the table. Then she swallowed hard and stood up, backing a couple of feet away from her chair. He looked at her for a couple of seconds, then said, "Take off your blouse."

Saying nothing, she slowly unbuttoned the blouse and set it over the back of the chair in front of her.

"Now your bra," he said.

She did as instructed, laying the bra over the blouse. Nearly a minute passed as McClain stared at her, looking from her eyes to her breasts and finally back to her eyes again. Holding her eyes with his, he picked up the cup and took a long sip of Coke. Then he gestured with the cup in the direction of her skirt.

Again, Beverly swallowed hard. Looking away from him toward the door, she released the clasp of her belt and unbuttoned the wraparound skirt. Reluctantly, she drew the skirt away and held it at her side.

McClain had torn off her panties the first night, and thus she now stood before him completely naked. Again, he stared at her body. Then he said quietly, "Go lie down on the bed, Beverly."

She dropped the skirt on the seat of the chair and did as she was told. McClain walked over to the side of the bed and stripped off his own clothes, watching her expression as he did. He was already hard and he forced himself into her with no preliminaries whatsoever. Beverly lay below him, gritting her teeth, but making no effort to resist as he thrust himself into her with a mounting intensity.

As she felt McClain building to a climax, Beverly said a silent prayer to David, begging his understanding and forgiveness for what she was about to do. Then she reached up and grabbed McClain's arms, digging her fingernails into his biceps. Arching her back slightly, she squeezed her thighs together and gave a small shudder. Then she quickly dropped her hands from his arms and let her legs go slack. Shaking her head, she began to cry. "No," she said through the tears. "No."

McClain thrust himself into her twice more, then froze and moaned at his release. He held his position for a long minute, then withdrew and dropped down to Beverly's side. She turned her face away from him, sobbing harder now.

McClain lay beside her for a couple of minutes, listening to her cry. Then he reached over and took her by the chin, forcing her to look at him. "Well, what do you know about that?" he said. "What do you know about that?"

CHAPTER TWENTY-FIVE

Richard Petrovich lived in a small, cheap apartment on the city's south side, about two miles from the shop where he worked. The neighborhood was a mixture of residences and small businesses, and at least half of the signage in the area was in Spanish. Most of the people out on the street were Hispanic, and several homeless men were camped out with their shopping carts in a tiny park a block from the building where Petrovich lived.

The apartment was above a small neighborhood grocery store that looked more like a miniature fortress. The few tiny windows were secured with thick iron bars, and a heavy wrought-iron gate protected the front door. As we pulled to a stop in front of the store, a tall, emaciated blonde stumbled out the door with an open beer in one hand and the balance of a six-pack dangling from the other. Paying no attention to us whatsoever, she wandered uncertainly down the middle of the street for half a block or so and then crossed into the yard of a tiny house on the other side of the street.

Maggie and I watched her go into the house, then walked into the dimly lighted store. A heavyset clerk behind the counter took a brief look at our shields and IDs, then went into the back room and returned with the owner-manager. We showed him our search warrant for Petrovich's apartment, and he led us out and around the side of the building to a rickety set of stairs. We followed him up to the second-floor landing, and he used one key to open the metal gate that guarded the apartment door and a second to open the door itself. Then he stood aside and gestured us in.

The temperature outside was in the low eighties; inside the small apartment it had to be well over a hundred degrees. We quickly opened the windows and I turned on one small window air conditioner in the living room and another in the bedroom. Listening to them clatter to life, I sincerely doubted that they were up to the job.

We began by making a brief tour through the place. In addition to the living room and bedroom, Petrovich's living space consisted of a tiny kitchen and an even smaller bathroom. All the rooms appeared clean and tidy. A few magazines and newspapers were stacked neatly on a table in the living room, which also contained a well-worn couch and a matching easy chair. A small Panasonic television set rested on an aluminum stand opposite the chair. On top of the television set was a framed photo of the little girl whose picture I had seen in Petrovich's wallet.

The kitchen appliances and counters had been wiped down. A bowl, a glass, and a spoon had been washed and left in a dish drainer next to the sink. The bed had been made. The clothes that constituted Petrovich's limited wardrobe had been folded and put away or hung in the closet. In the bathroom, the tub and the sink had been scrubbed clean, and a few toiletries were lined up neatly in the medicine cabinet above the sink. And Beverly Thompson was obviously not in residence.

We spent an hour searching the sweltering apartment to no avail. Petrovich had created a small hiding place behind a baseboard in the bedroom, and in it I found a few photographs and papers that he apparently was attempting to protect in case a burglar targeted the apartment. I also found a small .22-caliber revolver. But the weapon that had been used in our killings was a nine-millimeter pistol, not a .22, and we found nothing that tied Petrovich in any way to any of our victims.

Careful to preserve any fingerprints that might be on the gun, I slipped it into an evidence bag. Then we locked up the apartment and returned the keys to the owner. Once back in the car, Maggie and I both pitched our jackets into the backseat and I cranked the AC to high. As the cool air rushed over us, I turned to Maggie and said, "Thoughts?"

"Jesus, Sean, I don't know," she sighed. "The DNA match aside, this guy just doesn't look or feel at all right to me. He gives every impression of being exactly as his parole officer described him."

"I know," I agreed. "That's my sense too. I think he was genuinely surprised when we asked him about Thompson and Collins. I'd swear he never heard of either woman except on the news, and on the basis of what we've seen so far, I'll bet you a dinner at the Zinc Bistro that the lab guys are not going to find anything in his car, either."

"No bet," she replied.

Back at the department, I left Maggie in her office and walked down to the holding cell where we'd left Richard Petrovich. He eyed me warily as I entered the cell, and I told him to sit down. He sank onto a bench built into the back wall of the cell.

"Okay, Mr. Petrovich," I said. "The technicians are still going through your car, but I have no idea what's going on with that. My partner and I have been through your apartment. We didn't find anything there to tie you to our killings."

He looked up at me expectantly. "So as soon as they discover there's nothing in my car, I can go?"

I slowly shook my head. "No, I'm afraid you can't.

We didn't see any evidence in your apartment linking you to Collins and Thompson, but we did find your hidey-hole. I've got your gun. It's down in the trunk of my car. And as you pointed out this morning, that violates your parole."

Petrovich paled, then gave me a look of despair. "Jesus Christ, Detective, you saw that neighborhood. Would you live down there without a gun?"

"No, probably not," I admitted. "But then I'm not fresh out on parole."

Petrovich looked away, staring off into space, and the silence built for a long minute. Finally I said in a quiet voice, "Look, Mr. Petrovich, there's two ways you can play this. You can demand a lawyer, and assuming that we don't come up with anything in your car, a judge will probably rule that we can't hold you on the DNA evidence alone. But if that's the way you want to go, we'll have to report the weapons violation to your parole officer and you'll be on your way back to Lewis."

He looked down at the floor and began slowly shaking his head. "On the other hand," I continued, "we might hold you as a material witness for a few days while we try to figure out what your DNA is doing at our crime scenes. If you went along with that and didn't jump up and down asking for a lawyer to get you out right away . . . well, my car's got a big trunk. There's a lot of junk in it. You never know, your gun might accidentally get lost in there."

Petrovich looked back up at me and swallowed hard. Then, with a resigned look on his face, he nodded his head.

Chapter Twenty-six

A little after four o'clock, I called the duty officer and told him that I was taking a couple of hours of personal time. Then I locked up my desk and walked down the stairs and out the door into another beautiful late afternoon. The temperature stood somewhere in the mid-seventies and only a few scattered wisps of clouds were anywhere to be seen in a bright blue sky.

It was exactly the sort of day that convinced thousands of visitors every year to chuck their lives in the Midwest and relocate to the Valley of the Sun, and it struck me that it would have been a perfect evening to sit out in the backyard with Julie, sipping margaritas and cooking dinner on the grill while we talked through the events of the day. Instead, I got into the car and drove to north Scottsdale to be deposed by Philip Loiselle, the lawyer who was determined to prevent her from finally finding peace.

The deposition was a part of his—and Elizabeth's—ongoing effort to invalidate Julie's living will and the medical power of attorney that she'd signed. They were attempting to establish that Julie had never really intended that the living will should be invoked under circumstances such as her current condition.

Elizabeth, who'd barely spoken to Julie in five years, and who'd certainly never discussed these sorts of matters with her, had testified in a deposition of her own that her daughter had always been a fighter and that she would never willingly surrender her life, even under the most extreme circumstances. She insisted, on the basis of her own religious faith, that it would be morally wrong for the doctors to terminate Julie's life. And contrary to the testimony of Julie's doctors, she insisted that as long as Julie remained alive there was always the chance, no matter how slight, that she might regain consciousness and perhaps even go on to lead a normal life.

Julie's father had remained aloof from the debate. On the one hand, he respected Julie's wishes and her right to make her own decisions. On the other, he couldn't imagine the prospect of watching his daughter die, even though in every meaningful sense of the word, she already had. He came out to Arizona occasionally, grieving for a day or two at Julie's bedside, and then retreated to Minneapolis, neither actively supporting nor opposing his wife's activities.

His pain and confusion mirrored my own, and I understood and identified with his heartache instinctively. He adored Julie. He had loved and supported her at every turn, and he too had been devastated by her loss. In life or death, Julie had always been his daughter, whereas in Elizabeth's case, and for whatever reason, Julie had become another cause.

Over the course of an hour and a half, guided by my own lawyer, Steve Nelson, I testified as patiently as possible. I swore again that Julie was of sound mind and that she had clearly understood what she was doing when she signed her living will and the medical power of attorney. I described in great detail how active she had been, both physically and intellectually, and I repeated the details of several conversations in which she had clearly insisted that she would rather be allowed to die than be forced to live with an injury or an illness that would leave her physically or mentally incapacitated. I testified that, her mother's religious faith notwithstanding, Julie had long ago stopped attending church and had abandoned any belief in God or in a life after this one.

The ordeal left me totally drained and completely depressed. Living every day with the loss of Julie and of the life we'd had together was almost more than I could bear. But having to share so many of our most personal moments for the benefit of her mother and the legal process was inexplicably painful. It seemed a violation of Julie's privacy, and I found little consolation in the fact that I had no choice in the matter if I was going to fulfill the trust that she had placed in me.

I left the lawyer's office, made my way to the freeway, and drove slowly back to the department, fighting the rush-hour traffic all the way. As a partial compensation, though, Mother Nature provided a spectacular sunset to help offset the frustration of the drive.

As the sun slipped from the sky, the McDowell range stood out in sharp relief to the east, the mountains a deep purple in the advancing dusk. Above me, the sky faded slowly from a cobalt blue to a pale gray. To the west a bank of clouds gradually dissolved from a light pink to a brighter orange and then to a blazing crimson before finally draining out to a gunmetal gray and then disappearing altogether as the darkness descended over the Valley.

Back at the office, I devoted a couple of hours to catching up on my paperwork, and that accomplished, I drove over to the nursing home. Thankfully, my mother-in-law had left no messages for me on the answering machine.

I kissed Julie hello and dropped into the chair next to her bed. The nurses had washed and brushed her hair, and dressed her in what had been her favorite pale blue pajamas. She looked for all the world as if she were just sleeping peacefully in our own bedroom, waiting for me to get home at the end of my shift so that she could draw me gently into her arms and exorcise the demons of another horrible day.

I found it impossibly hard to accept the fact that she would never be able to do so again, and as I took her hand, the pain of losing her nearly overwhelmed me yet again. Exhausted, I hunched forward and said quietly, "I'm lost, Jules, and I miss you so much. I've got some asshole out here shooting people right and left. I've got a woman missing and probably dead, and I can't figure out what more I could or should be doing to catch the bastard and stop him. And it's killing me that I can't at least have the comfort of talking my troubles through with you."

Sighing, I sat back in the chair and mentally replayed the events of the day, trying to imagine what we might have done differently—what we might have done better. I wanted to believe that Richard Petrovich was our killer and that by arresting him we had brought an end to the string of shootings. But I also knew that if he was the killer, we now had virtually no hope of finding Beverly Thompson alive. If Petrovich wasn't willing to trade her location for a chance at making things easier on himself, then almost certainly he had already killed her and disposed of the body.

But despite the DNA evidence, my gut told me that Petrovich was not the guy, and absent the DNA, we had absolutely no evidence against him and not even a hint of a motive. Why in the hell would he have decided to target Fletcher, Collins, and the Thompsons? We still had no connection among any of the victims and no connection between any of them and Richard Petrovich. It was possible that one would still surface, but for the life of me I couldn't imagine what it might be.

If Petrovich was not the guy, the bad news, of course, was that the killings might continue. The good news, if there was any, was that Beverly Thompson might still be alive somewhere. But if so, where? And what more could we be doing to find her? If Petrovich wasn't the guy, who was? And what more could we be doing to stop him?

After an hour of wrestling with the various permutations of the problem, I kissed Julie good night and headed home. In the kitchen I stripped off my coat and tie and draped them over the back of a chair. I spent a couple of minutes at the counter, sorting through the day's mail while I tried to decide what to do about dinner. I really wasn't at all hungry, but I hadn't eaten anything since lunch and knew that I needed to get something into my system.

I opened the refrigerator door and scanned the contents. The most appealing thing staring back at me was a take-home box containing some leftover tortellini that I'd started at Tutti Santi the night before Beverly Thompson was kidnapped. I put it in a bowl and gave it a minute and a half in the microwave—just enough to take the chill off—and ate it standing at the counter.

Not quite ready to surrender to bed, I wandered into the living room and poured three fingers of Jameson into a heavy old-fashioned glass. Then I put Lil' Debbie & Blue Plate Special into the CD player, slipped on my headphones, and stretched out on the couch, balancing the whiskey on my chest. By the time Lil' Debbie was halfway through "Stormy Monday," I'd already fallen fast asleep thinking about Julie, about Beverly Thompson, and about the random accidents and inexplicable injustices that constituted life early in the twenty-first century.

CHAPTER TWENTY-SEVEN

True to his word, Carl McClain spent the late afternoon in the kitchen. After forcing himself on Beverly, he lay beside her for fifteen or twenty minutes, puzzling over what had just transpired and listening to her sob. Finally, he touched her lightly on the hip. Then he got up from the bed, gathered up his clothes, and walked out of the room, closing the door behind him.

Beverly lay there, weeping softly for another few minutes, until her despair was trumped by the compulsion to scrub her body clean of McClain's touch. With the cable trailing behind her, she made her way to the bathroom. She closed the door as far as the cable would permit, then used the toilet and stepped into the shower.

As always, the water temperature was only a little north of lukewarm, but at least the pressure was reasonably decent. Beverly let the water course over her body, then picked the bar of cheap soap out of its plastic container. She scrubbed herself vigorously and stood under the showerhead, rinsing herself until the water turned cold.

She shut off the water, and a second later she heard a light tap on the bathroom door. She peered around the shower curtain to see McClain dressed in a fresh pair of jeans and a new T-shirt. He stepped tentatively through the door, looking as though he might be somehow embarrassed, and held out a clean bath towel. "Here," he said.

Beverly reached a hand out from behind the curtain

and took the towel. As she did, McClain pointed back at the bed. "I left you one of my shirts. Your blouse and bra are in the washing machine. You can wear the shirt until they're dry. It's clean," he added.

Beverly nodded slightly. "Thank you."

McClain returned the nod and then backed out of the room, pulling the door closed behind him again, as far as the cable would allow. Beverly stared at the door for a few seconds, then dropped the shower curtain back into place and began drying herself. Suddenly she found herself weeping again, grateful for the simple relief of something as basic as a freshly laundered towel. Catching herself, she pounded a fist into her thigh. "Stop it," she whispered. "Do not let him do this to you."

She finished drying herself and spread the towel out over the shower rod to dry. Back in the bedroom, she slipped into the blue long-sleeve shirt that McClain had left on the bed and buttoned it up. It was way too large for her, but she was thankful for that as well.

For a moment, she flashed back to the Sunday mornings when she had often worn one of David's shirts while they relaxed in bed with the *Arizona Republic* and the *New York Times*. Catching a sob in her throat, she forced the thought from her mind and belted her skirt around her, letting the shirt hang out over it.

McClain had left the bedroom door slightly ajar— only an inch or so—but enough so that she could hear him puttering around in the kitchen. The aroma of something roasting in the oven drifted down the hall, infused with an underlying scent of rosemary. McClain was apparently a "classic rock" guy, and on the radio in the background, Beverly could hear Sammy Hagar lamenting the fact that he couldn't drive fifty-five.

She debated the wisdom of trying to sneak a look out into the hall. If she stretched the cable as far as it would go, she could just reach the bedroom door. She had no way of knowing what the floor plan of the house was outside of the bedroom and bathroom. She knew that the bedroom door swung quietly on its hinges. If she opened it a bit farther, would McClain see or hear her from the kitchen?

She took two steps in the direction of the door and then stopped. In the past, McClain had always closed the door when he left the room. Why had he left it slightly open now? Was he testing her, waiting to see if she would attempt to take advantage of the opportunity? And what would he do if he caught her?

She took another small step toward the door and reached tentatively out to the knob. On the radio, Sammy gave way to Creedence Clearwater Revival, and Beverly suddenly realized that McClain was no longer making noises in the kitchen.

She turned, walked quickly back to the bed, and sat down. Just as she did, he walked through the door carrying silverware and napkins. Handing them to her, he said, "Dinner's almost ready. You can set the table. Your beverage choices this evening are water and beer—or both, if you'd prefer."

"Both, please," she replied.

Ten minutes later, he returned carrying two glasses of water and clutching two longneck bottles of Miller Genuine Draft between his arm and his chest. He set the drinks on the table and said, "Have a seat."

Beverly took her chair while McClain made another trip to the kitchen. He returned with two salads, set one of them in front of Beverly, and took the chair on the other side of the table.

The salad consisted of a variety of fresh mixed greens—romaine, endive, and red-leaf lettuce—along with some diced cucumber and some thinly sliced red onions. It had been lightly tossed with balsamic vinai-grette, and in truth, it was an excellent salad. Beverly ate a few bites, then looked up to McClain. "Thank you for the salad. It's very good."

He flashed her a look of self-deprecation. "Sorry about all the junk food so far. Normally I don't eat that kind of crap—not any more at least. But I've just been too busy too cook."

She hesitated for a few seconds, calculating how best to play him, and wondering how far she should press her luck. Then she swallowed another bite of the salad and said, "I don't want to make you angry, but can I ask what you've been busy doing?"

McClain set down his fork and looked at her for a moment as if trying to decide how to respond. Finally he gave a small shrug. Looking away from Beverly, he said in a soft voice, "My daughter was in a softball tournament this weekend. Most of the time I was gone, I was watching her play."

Beverly was genuinely dumfounded. It had never occurred to her that this sadistic rapist—this fucking *murderer*—might have a family, let alone that he might care about them. The bastard had shot and killed David without giving it even a second thought. He had destroyed the only family she had, and then the cocksucker had nerve enough—balls enough—to have a family of his own?

The thought of it—the rank injustice of it—infuriated her beyond anything that McClain had done to her thus far. It took every ounce of self-discipline she possessed to prevent herself from flipping the table into his lap and cursing him to hell. She took a deep breath, nodded slightly, and looked up at the rotten son of a bitch. "How old is your daughter?" she asked.

"Nineteen."

"She's in college?"

"Yeah, ASU. She plays first base."

Beverly nodded again. "She must be pretty good if she's playing at that level."

The asshole actually blushed. "Yeah. She was a high school all-star and won a full athletic scholarship."

"You must be very proud."

Again, he seemed embarrassed. "Yeah. Whatever. She's a good kid."

He set his napkin on the table. "Keep your salad if you want, but the chicken should be ready now."

He got up from the table and left the room, taking his empty salad plate with him. Watching him go, Beverly curled her fingers into her hands and pressed her nails into her palms. She took a few deep breaths, then slowly exhaled and took a long pull on her beer. Attempting to channel her rage as productively as possible, she finished the salad.

After a few minutes, McClain returned with two plates. He'd roasted a small chicken and divided it in half. He'd also prepared oven-browned potatoes and fresh green beans, seasoned with lemon. He set Beverly's plate in front of her.

"It looks very good," she observed.

He shrugged. "One way to find out."

They ate quietly for the next twenty minutes, and in fact the food was excellent. Beverly wondered where someone like McClain had learned to cook, but she couldn't bring herself to ask him. He finished a few minutes ahead of her and waited patiently while she finished. Finally, she pushed the plate away, leaving only a little bit of the food uneaten.

McClain made two trips taking the dirty dishes out to the kitchen. Then he came back into the bedroom. "I have to go out for a while," he said. "Would you like another beer before I go?"

"Yes, please. Thank you."

He returned with the beer in one hand and her blouse and bra in the other. The blouse was on a hanger and it was obvious he had ironed it. He gave her the beer and then, somewhat self-consciously, handed her the clothes. "These are ready, but you can hang onto the shirt if you want."

"Thank you."

McClain nodded and, saying nothing more, turned and walked out the door. Beverly listened as he locked it. Then she heard again the small metallic click that followed. She waited a couple of minutes to be sure that he was actually gone, then stripped off his shirt and put her own clothes back on again. She put McClain's shirt on the empty hanger and hung it on the doorknob. Then she walked into the bathroom and poured the beer down the sink.

CHAPTER TWENTY-EIGHT

McClain picked up the backpack and walked out through the kitchen feeling decidedly out of sorts. Today, for the first time, he'd actually found himself feeling some sympathy for the woman. And flashing back to the resigned, defeated look on her face as he'd handed her the clean towel in the shower, he even experienced a small twinge of guilt about the way in which he was treating her.

Thinking about it, he was pissed off—both at her and at himself. So she came while he was screwing her this afternoon. So what?

It was a normal human reaction, and he'd expected that it would probably happen at some point. Every woman he'd ever been with had always insisted that he was great in bed and that he had a huge dick. Sooner or later, Beverly was bound to get off, whether she liked it or not.

Obviously, she hadn't liked it. She'd been upset with

herself when it had finally happened, and that he could understand. He knew that he probably wasn't her favorite person in the world right at the moment. What he could not understand, though, was his own reaction to the fact that it had happened. He'd felt a tenderness for her that led him to wonder whether he was being entirely fair to the woman. Suddenly he's doing her laundry and cooking her a goddamn dinner like he'd invited her over for a fucking *date* or something. She'd even gotten him talking to her about Tiffani, for chrissake.

What the hell was he thinking? The woman had conspired to screw him over. She'd help cost him both Tiffani and Amanda, not to mention seventeen years of his fuckin' life.

Shaking his head at the thought of it, he opened the door from the kitchen and stepped out into the garage. Once he'd dealt with the judge, he decided, he'd take the bitch back to bed and show her something about sympathy.

McClain flipped on the light in the garage, then unlocked the garage door and lifted it open. It was another beautiful night in the desert, the air crisp and clean, and he inhaled a deep breath. God, it felt good to be free.

He checked to make sure that no one was loitering about, watching him, then opened the door to the van and climbed in. "Hey, Your Honor," he said. "I hope you didn't mind waiting. I had a little lady who needed my attention more than you did. Anyhow, it's better that we do our business together now, rather than out in the broad daylight."

His arrival produced no reaction from the judge, who lay completely still under the painter's tarp. McClain waited for a moment, expecting Beckman to shift his position at least slightly, but the tarp didn't move even an inch in any direction.

McClain got out of the driver's seat and squeezed his way into the back of the van. Squatting down, he picked up a corner of the tarp to see Beckman's lifeless eyes staring back at him vacantly. "Oh, shit, Judge!" he protested. "What the fuck did you go and do to me now?"

He pulled the tarp down farther and checked Beckman for a pulse, knowing that he wasn't going to find one. Had the old bastard not been able to breathe with the duct tape over his mouth? Did the shock of being grabbed cause him to have a heart attack? Had the afternoon heat been too intense in the close confines of the garage and the van?

Shaking his head in disappointment, McClain concluded that whatever it was really didn't much matter at this point. He certainly wasn't sorry that the old man was dead, but he very much regretted having missed the opportunity to talk with him before he died. McClain had wanted Beckman to know why he was going to die and who was going to do it to him. He hoped that the old goat had suffered like hell before it happened.

Working in the cramped quarters of the van, McClain rolled the judge's body up in the tarp and secured it with duct tape. Then he backed the van out of the garage, locked the garage behind him, and headed west.

He drove a couple of miles before finding the sort of place he was looking for, then pulled into an alley behind a row of darkened buildings. Halfway down the alley, he stopped next to a large Dumpster with its lid hanging open. He got out of the van and checked to make sure that there was no one else around. Then, moving as quickly as he could, he slid open the side door of the van and pulled the judge's body out.

The old man probably didn't weigh even a hundred and fifty pounds. In one fluid motion, McClain hoisted the package up to his shoulder and pitched it into the Dumpster. Then he got back into the van and drove carefully back home to deal with Beverly Thompson.

CHAPTER TWENTY-NINE

On Tuesday morning, Tony Anderson called to report that the crime lab had taken an inordinate amount of hair, fibers, and other physical evidence out of Richard Petrovich's Chrysler.

"I've never seen a car that filthy," he complained. "I'll bet the damned thing literally hadn't been washed or vacuumed in a year. We've probably taken samples from half the population of the greater metro area out of that car. Unfortunately, though, so far we've got nothing that matches up to any of your victims. I'm sorry, Sean. I'll fax over the preliminary report."

I thanked him and hung up the phone. Frankly, I wasn't surprised by the news, but it left us in a very difficult position. Maggie and I both agreed that Petrovich just didn't feel at all right for the crimes we were investigating, and we had absolutely nothing to tie him to any of them, save for the DNA evidence that put him in Beverly Thompson's Lexus and in Karen Collins's home. But if he wasn't the guy, how in the hell did his hair get there?

I was thinking about all of this when the phone rang again and the receptionist announced that Jack Collins was downstairs asking to see me. I put on my suit coat, went down to meet him, and escorted him back up to my office. He dropped into my visitor's chair looking like he hadn't slept in a month. "How are you doing, Mr. Collins?" I asked.

He shook his head sadly. "I don't really know, Detective Richardson. I'm still basically in a state of shock. The medical examiner has released Karen's body, and her funeral is tomorrow morning. But between your investigation and the preparations for the funeral, it's like I haven't had any time to begin grieving yet."

"Again, I'm sorry, sir," I said. "I know how difficult this must be. What can I do for you this morning?"

"Well," he replied, "the reason I'm here is because on the night of the murder you asked me about a woman named Alma Fletcher."

"Yes, sir?"

He shifted in the chair a bit. "Well, as I said that night, the name meant nothing to me. I didn't think I'd ever heard it before."

Leaning forward, I said, "And now?"

"Well, I've been going through some of Karen's stuff, looking for photos and things like that to display at the visitation and the funeral? This morning I was looking at one of her old scrapbooks and found a newspaper clipping that she'd saved."

I nodded my encouragement and he continued. "Seventeen years ago, Karen served as a juror in a murder trial. The clipping was about the trial, and the article quoted the jury foreman—or forewoman, I guess it would be. Her name was Alma Fletcher."

Collins reached into the pocket of his shirt and came out with a yellowed news clipping. Scarcely able to contain my surprise, I took it from him, carefully unfolded it, and quickly read the story. Fletcher and Collins had served together on a jury that had convicted a defendant named Carl McClain on a charge of first-degree murder.

According to the article, McClain had been charged with the strangulation death of a prostitute named

Gloria Kelly. The presiding judge was someone named Walter Beckman and the prosecuting attorney was Harold Roe. Interestingly, the lead detective in the case was Mike Miller, a longtime veteran of the department who'd been my first partner when I joined the Homicide Unit, nine years after the trial. As Collins indicated, the jury forewoman had been Alma Fletcher. And McClain's court-appointed public defender had been a woman named Beverly Deschamps.

With Collins still sitting in my visitor's chair, I grabbed the phone and called Beverly Thompson's office. Her administrative assistant confirmed the fact that prior to Beverly's marriage to David Thompson, her last name had been Deschamps.

I thanked the woman, hung up, and called Tom Meagher, an assistant county attorney and my occasional opponent on the tennis courts. Thankfully, he was at his desk and he answered the phone on the second ring.

"Tom?" I said. "It's Sean. Seventeen years ago your office convicted a guy named Carl McClain of first-degree murder."

"Yes, we did," he replied. "And three months ago we turned him loose."

"Why in God's name did you do that? The guy was sentenced to life without the possibility of parole."

"Yes, he was," Meagher sighed. "Then, inconvenient as it was for all concerned, especially for Mr. McClain, it turned out that he was innocent."

"And we know this how?"

"DNA evidence," he replied. "Plus, the real killer confessed. The victim was a hooker, and McClain was with her just before she was killed. There was semen in the body that matched his blood type, and of course back then, they couldn't get any more precise than that. McClain apparently changed his story a couple of times and was not a very effective witness on his own behalf. As a result of all of that, he got himself convicted and sent to Lewis for the rest of his life.

"That was the end of the story. Except that four months ago the common-law wife of the victim's former pimp ratted her husband out for the killing. Initially he denied it of course, but a DNA test proved that the semen from the vic was his, not McClain's. He finally gave it up and admitted that he'd killed the woman because she'd been holding back money on him."

"And what became of McClain?"

"I haven't the slightest idea," Tom replied. "The state apologized profusely and let him go. He's a free man, and we had no right to keep tabs on him. I imagine that by now he's probably out shopping for a lawyer so that he can sue the hell out of us. What's your interest in all of this anyhow?"

"My interest is that, within the last two weeks, two of the jurors at McClain's trial have been shot to death. The attorney who defended him has been abducted and her husband was killed as well."

"You've gotta be kidding," Meagher exclaimed. "This is the Thompson case?"

"Yeah. After she graduated law school, Thompson spent two and a half years in the PD's office. One of her clients was Carl McClain."

"Jesus Christ, Sean, I don't know what to say. McClain was clearly innocent of the hooker's murder, and he'd never been charged with any other crime. Obviously, we had no cause to hang on to him or to track his movements once he left Lewis."

"I know that, Tom," I replied. "And I'm certainly not blaming you guys. But it looks like McClain may be looking to settle scores for the time he lost."

"Jesus," he said again.

I thanked Collins for coming in and hustled him back downstairs. Then I sprinted back up to the third floor and found Maggie coming out of the women's john. I grabbed her by the hand and said, "Come with me."

"What the hell's going on?" she asked as I hurried her down the hall.

"We've got the wrong guy, Maggie. It's not Petrovich. It's somebody named Carl McClain."

"Tell me," she said, picking up her pace to match mine.

The door to the lieutenant's office was standing open, but the lights were off and he was nowhere in evidence. Turning to his secretary, I said, "Where is he?"

"In a meeting with the chief," she answered. "He should be back in about an hour."

"Make sure he is," I insisted. "Interrupt him if you have to, and I don't care if he is with the chief. Tell him we'll be back in an hour or less and that we have to see him about the Thompson case immediately. Get Pierce and Chickris in here too."

"Okay," she said. "I'll tell him."

I headed Maggie in the direction of the stairs, and as we made our way over to the county jail, I described my conversations with Jack Collins and Tom Meagher. Fifteen minutes later, a guard brought Richard Petrovich into an interview room. He dropped into a chair and I said, "Carl McClain."

Petrovich shrugged. "What about him?"

"You tell me."

Again he shrugged. "We were in Lewis together—we both worked in the shop for a while. McClain was in for murder. Like most everybody else in the joint, of course, he claimed that he was innocent. Only in his case, it turned out that he really was. Some other guy confessed to doing the murder and they turned Carl loose."

"Have you seen him since?"

"Yeah. When he got out he spent a few days sleeping on my couch while he was looking for a place to stay."

"When was the last time you saw him?"

Petrovich scratched his head. "Jesus, I dunno . . . Probably the end of November or early December. He rented a house somewhere and left my place. He said he'd stay in touch, but I haven't seen or heard from him since."

"Did he have a job?" Maggie asked.

"Not that I know of. But I don't think he was looking for one. He said he had some money coming to him and that he wouldn't be needing to work for a while."

I nodded. "Do you know where the money was coming from?"

"No, he didn't tell me."

"Did he say where the house he rented was?" Maggie asked.

Petrovich shook his head. "No. He just said that once he was settled, we should get together so that he could repay me for my hospitality."

"Did he talk at all about his plans?" I asked. "If he wasn't looking for work, what did he intend to do with his time?"

Again, he shook his head. "He didn't say. He was really pissed about the fact that he'd spent seventeen years in the can for something he didn't do. He said he was going to get a lawyer and sue everybody in sight. I told him that's what I'd sure as hell do."

"Yeah, I suppose," Maggie said. "You're sure you haven't seen or heard anything of him since?"

"I told you, no."

"McClain didn't come out of Lewis itching to get back at the people who put him there and ask you to help him?" she asked.

"No," he insisted. "Like I said, he told me he was going to sue the bastards for millions, but he didn't say he was going to be sharing it. Besides, what the hell help could I give him? I'm a welder, not a fuckin' lawyer."

"Well, then, Mr. Petrovich," I said, "we've got a

problem, because two of the people who put McClain in Lewis are dead. Another one is missing, and your hair was found at two of the three crime scenes."

Petrovich's eyes widened. "That's what this is about? The Thompson woman and the others you were asking me about—they're tied in with Carl?"

"Not anymore, they're not," I replied, "except for maybe Thompson."

"Well, Jesus," he said, agitated. "I sure as hell didn't have nothin' to do with any of that. Like I said, the guy bunked with me for a couple of nights and I haven't seen or talked to him since. I have no damn idea where he is or what he might be doing. And whatever it is, I sure as hell haven't been helping him."

"But you see our problem, Mr. Petrovich," Maggie said. "You and McClain are pals in the joint and he looks you up the first thing he gets out. You give him a place to stay and tell him what a raw deal he got. Then the next thing you know, the people who sent him to the pen start turning up dead and we're finding your hair at the crime scenes. What are we supposed to think?"

Petrovich slumped in his chair and a tear welled up in his eye. "I don't know, Detective," he said, plaintively. "I don't fuckin' know. But I swear to God, I didn't have anything to do with any of it."

CHAPTER THIRTY

Even though it was still only February, and even though it was still only ten o'clock in the morning, the temperature was already in the high seventies. And even though he'd only walked a block and a half,

McClain was sweating like hell in his gas-company jacket. Jesus, he thought, wiping the perspiration off his brow. Maybe there is something to this global warming bullshit after all.

Yesterday he'd called the law offices of Kutsunis, Trumbull, and Roe only to learn that Mr. Roe was on vacation this week. "Lucky guy," McClain had observed. "Did he get to go someplace exotic?"

Roe's secretary laughed. "Not this time," she volunteered. "He's just taking some time at home to relax. Did you want to leave a message?"

"No, thank you, ma'am," McClain responded politely. "It's a minor matter. I'll try him again next week."

At nine fifteen this morning, McClain had called the Roe home from a pay phone and asked for Mrs. Roe. Mr. Roe interrupted his vacation long enough to answer the phone and explain that his wife was out for the morning and that she'd be back by the middle of the afternoon. Again, McClain declined the offer to leave a message, and at five after ten, clipboard in hand, he punched Roe's doorbell.

Roe answered the door almost immediately, and McClain explained that a gas leak had been reported in the neighborhood. Had Mr. Roe smelled any gas?

"No, I haven't," Roe responded.

McClain made a note on the clipboard. "I'm really sorry to bother you, sir, but could I take a quick look at your furnace and water heater?"

"I suppose so," Roe said.

McClain stepped into the foyer of the expensive home, and Roe closed the door behind him. Then he turned and said, "This way."

McClain knew that Roe had abandoned the prosecutor's office two years after his trial for the more lucrative rewards of private practice, and looking around the house, it seemed clear that the move had paid off. The place had obviously been decorated by a professional, and everything—the furniture and all the accessories—fit perfectly together. The artwork was contemporary and looked expensive, although McClain realized that he didn't know shit about art.

He did know that Harold Roe was now somewhere in his fifties, but it looked like the guy had aged twenty-five years rather than only seventeen. He was thick around the middle and had lost most of his hair. He wore aviator-type glasses with thick bifocal lenses, and he shuffled ahead of McClain like an old man. As they passed Roe's home study, Roe looked over his shoulder to McClain and said, "The utility room is right down here."

Roe turned back to face ahead, and McClain grabbed him by the shirt collar with his left hand. Dropping the clipboard, he pulled the Glock from his jacket pocket and jammed it up against Roe's neck. "Oh, that's all right, Harold," he said. "In here will do just fine."

He pushed the lawyer into the study and practically threw him into a large easy chair that faced a mahogany desk. "What the hell?" Roe blustered.

McClain brushed a pile of papers and a couple of framed photos off the corner of the desk onto the floor. Then he perched on the desk and faced the older man. "Well, Harold," he said, "it looks like you've done well by yourself."

Roe sat trembling in the chair, but made a game effort to pretend that he wasn't intimidated. "Who the hell are you?" he asked. "And what do you think you're doing?"

"I'm the Spirit of Christmas Past," McClain said, smiling. "And I have a score to settle with you."

"What score? What the hell are you talking about?"

McClain leaned forward, invading the lawyer's personal space. "I'm Carl McClain, you fat prick."

Roe seemed genuinely surprised. Shaking his head,

he said, "McClain? My God, I never would have recognized you."

"Yeah," McClain laughed, leaning back again. "I'm hearing that a lot these days."

"And you want to settle a score with me? Why?"

Now McClain was surprised. "Why do you think, you stupid fuck? You sent me to prison for life for a crime I didn't do!"

Roe came half out of the chair, then sat down quickly again when McClain gestured at him with the gun. "Jesus, McClain, I was just doing my job! And it's not like there wasn't any evidence against you. You admitted to being with the woman. The semen that was found in her matched your blood type. A jury found you guilty, and the judge agreed with them. It's not like it was all my fault!"

McClain shook his head. "Oh, Harold, for chrissake, I'm not blaming you all by yourself. I know that you aren't the only one who's guilty here, and the other people involved are paying the price as well. It's just that this morning it's your turn."

"But this is insane," Roe pleaded. "The state admitted its mistake, McClain. You're a free man."

"Yeah, Harold, but you know what they say in the old song. 'Freedom's just another word for nothin' left to lose.' My wife is long gone, and my daughter along with her. Once I was arrested, my wife aborted my other kid. My mamma died while I was in the can, so I've got no family to welcome me back. And on top of all that, I've lost what should have been the seventeen most productive years of my life. So what the hell do you expect me to do, Harold—shake hands all around and say, 'Hey, that's all right, guys. We all make mistakes'?"

"No, of course not," Roe protested. "I expect you to be good and pissed. Christ, I sure as hell would be. But it *was* a mistake. Nobody deliberately tried to frame you for something you didn't do."

McClain slammed his fist onto the desk. "Bullshit, Harold! None of you cared whether you had the right guy or not. The cops simply wanted to clear the goddamn case. The judge was anxious to get me off his docket as fast as he could so he could get back to the fuckin' golf course. You wanted another notch on your belt for sending a cold-blooded killer away for life, and those mindless assholes on the jury just nodded their heads and swallowed all the crap you fed them. And the attorney that the county so generously provided for me was so goddamn young and green that she didn't have the slightest idea what to do about it all. Shit, by the time you were done, you had *her* convinced I was guilty."

Roe sunk back into the chair and McClain shook his head. In a much softer voice, he continued, "I told you pricks that you had the wrong man, Harold. I told you that I didn't do it. But none of you gave a shit. I was a convenient scapegoat—somebody you could pin the rap on. And none of you could spare the time to make sure that I really was guilty. I didn't get the chance to watch you preen on the TV at the end of the trial, but I read what you said in the paper the next day. You were pretty full of yourself, Harold."

Roe twisted in the chair, sweating and begging now. "But I thought I'd done a good job. I thought I'd sent a guilty man to jail. You can't believe how awful I felt when I read that you really were innocent. And besides," he pleaded, "all I did was present the evidence that the police had gathered in the case. If you're going to be angry with someone, you should be angry with them."

"Oh, don't worry about that," McClain assured him. "The cops will pay as well. But you didn't just 'present' the evidence, Harold. You jammed it down the jury's throat, and you *enjoyed* doing it. For that week, you were a star, Harold. And don't tell me you weren't getting off on it—remember, I was there every goddamn day."

"I do remember," Roe said, starting to tear up. "And I am sorry. But killing me won't bring back your family or give you back the time that you lost."

"No, you're right about that, Harold," McClain conceded. "But at least I'll have the satisfaction of knowing that the people who took those things away from me have paid the price for doing it."

McClain raised the pistol, and Roe began to sob in earnest. "Please, Mr. McClain. Please don't to this."

McClain let him cry for a minute, then shook his head. "Jesus Christ, Harold," he said disgustedly. "Don't be such a pussy. At least take it like a man."

Roe looked up at him. "Please," he said again through the tears. "Please."

"Oh, fuck it," McClain said, raising the Glock.

He shot Roe through the left eye and then, just for good measure, put a bullet in his heart as well. The shots caused the lawyer's body to jerk, and then he slumped forward in the chair. McClain slipped the pistol into the right pocket of his jacket. From the left pocket he pulled a small Ziploc bag with a few of Richard Petrovich's hairs in it—the last of the three bags that he'd collected.

McClain had never known a guy with that much body hair—Christ, the guy shed like an Old English sheepdog. McClain had carefully collected the hair from Petrovich's bed one day while his host was at work.

He opened the bag and shook the hairs out over Roe's body. It was a lousy way to repay the guy for his hospitality, but McClain figured that Petrovich wouldn't suffer all that much as a result. He assumed that the cops would match the hair up to Petrovich and that they'd hassle him for a while, long enough at least for Petrovich to be a convenient distraction while McClain attended to business. But sooner or later, they'd finally figure out what was really happening and turn Petrovich loose. McClain only hoped that it would be later rather than sooner.

CHAPTER THIRTY-ONE

Just after eleven thirty, Maggie and I climbed the stairs back up to the Homicide Unit to find the lieutenant waiting for us. We collected Pierce and Chickris and adjourned to the conference room, where we brought them up to date with respect to the morning's developments.

"I don't know what role, if any, Petrovich is playing in all of this," I said. "But clearly the guy we need to be looking for is Carl McClain. And obviously, we need to warn all the other people who were involved in his arrest and conviction that they may be in danger as well."

"Okay," Martin agreed. "Issue a crime-information bulletin on McClain, noting that he may be driving a black van, license plate unknown, and that he should be considered armed and dangerous. Get his last prison mug shot and we'll release it to the media, asking anyone who may have seen him to come forward. Then start tracking the son of a bitch."

Turning to Elaine and Greg, he said, "You two get into the records. Get names and addresses for the judge, the rest of the jurors, and anybody else who was involved in the case. Then let them know what's going on."

Chickris nodded. "Of course the first thing they're

gonna do is demand police protection. What do we tell 'em?"

Martin shook his head. "Unfortunately, there's just no way. We have no idea how many people this jerk might actually be targeting, but even if there are only twenty people or so directly connected with McClain's trial, that still gives him about twenty potential targets. We know from what he's done already that he may well strike at any time of the day or night, and to put even a loose net around that many people twenty-four–seven would require more bodies than we can possibly manage.

"Tell people to be careful; tell them not to open their doors to strangers, and tell them to let us know immediately if anyone seems to be paying them undue attention. But for the moment, we can't offer anyone around-the-clock bodyguards."

The meeting broke up and Maggie called Dispatch to issue the CIB while I phoned the Department of Corrections and told them to pull McClain's complete file. I asked Maggie to start checking with the local utilities to see if McClain had recently applied for new electric, gas, water, phone, or cable service, while I went over to the DOC offices on Jefferson Street.

Thirty minutes later, I was back at my desk looking at a copy of Carl McClain's prison records. He'd done just under seventeen years by the time the mistake was discovered, and at least according to the file, he'd kept his nose clean. Through the years, he'd worked in the prison library, in the kitchen, and in the shop, which is where he'd met Richard Petrovich. He'd apparently stayed clear of the prison gangs and had been written up for only a few minor infractions of the prison rules. In all that time, the only visitor he'd ever had was his mother, and according to the file, she had died two years ago.

The file said that on arriving at the prison, McClain had been five feet eleven inches tall and had weighed two hundred and sixty-five pounds. The most recent photo in the file was seven months old and showed a man with wavy dark hair and a prominent nose, wearing a pair of glasses that looked as if they might once have belonged to Buddy Holly. In the picture, he was still a little pudgy, although it didn't look like the head and shoulders belonged on a guy who weighed two sixty-five.

I walked the photo down the stairs and gave it to the sergeant in charge of media relations. He promised to get it out in a hurry. "Make sure they tell people not to approach him," I cautioned. "Tell them just to find the nearest phone and call nine-one-one."

Back upstairs, I walked over to Maggie's office. "Anything?" I asked.

"No phone, and no cable," she replied. "I'm still working on the other."

I nodded, crossed the hall to my own office, and grabbed the phone book. Mike Miller was still listed, and apparently still in the same house he'd owned when we were partnered together. I dialed the number and listened to it ring on the other end. I was just about to hang up when Miller answered, sounding as if he was out of breath.

"Mike? Sean Richardson. Did I catch you at a bad time?"

"Sean? Jesus. It's been a while," he replied. "And no, you didn't catch me at a bad time, I was just out in the garage puttering around. What's up?"

"I've got a problem and I need to talk to you about it. Can I come out?"

"Sure. What sorta problem you got?"

"Let me tell you when I get there. I'll see you in about thirty minutes if that's okay."

"That's fine," he said. "You still drinkin' ten Cokes a day?"

"Probably not quite that many," I laughed.

"Well, I think I got one around here someplace. I'll try to find it while I'm waiting for you."

Mike Miller was a tough detective from the old school who could have come straight out of Jack Webb's *Dragnet*. I was twenty-nine when we were first partnered together; he was fifty-five and in the middle of his second divorce. We'd been teamed together for a year when he finally took his pension and went to work as a consultant for a home-security company.

I pulled into the driveway of his home in northeast Phoenix and found him in his garage, waxing the red '65 Mustang convertible that he'd spent years restoring in his spare time. The last time I'd seen the car, it hadn't amounted to much more than a mass of loose parts scattered around the garage. Now it sat on the tiled garage floor, gleaming no doubt even brighter than it had the day it was first driven off the showroom floor more than forty years ago.

Mike had weathered well. At sixty-two, he still looked to be in pretty good shape, save for the slight paunch he was developing. Never one to ape the latest styles, he'd always worn his hair in a brush cut, not much longer that it had been when he was a young marine. The hair was completely gray now, and he stood quietly, wiping his hands on a shop rag, as I stepped into the garage and walked slowly around the Mustang. "Beautiful," I said, smiling.

His pride in the car and in the job he'd done with it was written all over his face. Sticking out his hand, he said, "Thanks, Sean. It's good to see you. How the hell are you?"

His grip was as strong as ever, and once I'd extracted

my hand, I shrugged and said, "Good, Mike. And you?"

"Great. So how's the job treating you?"

"Well, actually, Mike, that's what I needed to talk to you about."

He nodded. "Okay, why don't we take ourselves out of this heat and into the air-conditioned kitchen?"

He led me into the house, punching the button to close the garage door as he did. The house, like the garage, was spotless and everything was in its proper place, even down to the salt and pepper shakers that were aligned precisely in the middle of the kitchen table. Mike had always been a bit compulsive in that regard, and thus far three wives had tried but failed to live up to his standards of cleanliness and organization. He offered me a chair at the table and said, "I assume that you probably don't want a beer at this point in your day?"

"You'd assume wrong," I said. "I'd love one. But I'd better just have a glass of water instead."

Opening the refrigerator door, he said, "I actually do have a Coke."

"Great. A Coke then, please."

He came out of the refrigerator with a Coke and a Bud Light. He dropped a few ice cubes into a glass, handed me the glass and the Coke, and saluted me with the beer. "Old times."

"Old times," I agreed.

I poured some Coke into the glass and we each took a long swallow of our drinks. Then Mike put down his glass and said, "So what's the problem?"

I looked at him across the table. "The problem is Carl McClain."

He sighed heavily. "Oh, shit."

A few seconds passed while he contemplated his beer. Then he looked up to meet my eyes. "Don't tell me that somebody's decided to open an investigation to see how we fucked up the case?"

"No, that's not it at all, Mike, although in reality that might be more welcome news. Unfortunately, it looks like McClain has decided to settle scores with the people who sent him to the pen. So far, two of the jurors from his trial have turned up shot to death. The woman who was his PD has been kidnapped, and her husband was killed in the process."

"You're shitting me," he said. "The dumb fuck gets out of jail a free man and goes on a rampage that's going to put him right back in there?"

"Looks like it."

He stared off out the window for a minute, then shook his head and took a long pull on the Bud.

"Tell me about the case," I said.

"You seen the paperwork?"

"No, I haven't dug it out yet. I only just discovered what was happening a couple of hours ago, and I wanted to talk to you first. I figured I'd get a lot better sense of the situation hearing it directly from you."

Miller nodded. He took a moment to collect his thoughts, then said, "The victim was a pross named Gloria Kelly—twenty-three, as I recall. She'd been strangled with a piece of clothesline rope and dumped in an alley immediately after giving somebody a blow job. A grocery store owner discovered the body when he came to open up the next morning. Kelly was still wearing the clothesline, and the ME figured she'd been dead for five to eight hours by then. Ed Quigly and I caught the case—Jesus, there's a guy I haven't thought of in a long time."

He paused for another sip of beer, apparently thinking about his old partner, then continued. "Vice told us that Kelly was in the stable of a pimp named Charlie Woolsey—a white guy who had a string of seven or eight girls that he was running. We rousted Woolsey, who told us that the vic had been working the previous night with another girl, whose street name was Bambi.

"I forget what her real name was—not that it matters—but we found her. She told us that Kelly had gone off with a trick a little after ten the night before, and that was the last she saw of her.

"Anyhow, the girls had a system where they wrote down the license numbers of each other's johns. The idea was that if a party started to get rough, the girl could warn the guy that her friend had copied down his number. Bambi gave us the plate number of Kelly's last customer and it ran back to Carl McClain's five-year-old Pontiac.

"We got a warrant for the Pontiac and found McClain at work. His first story was that he was nowhere near downtown that night—that he'd just gone out for a ride. He claimed that he'd stopped in a biker bar somewhere on Cave Creek Road for a drink. But he couldn't remember the name of the bar and he said he didn't see anybody that he knew in there anyway.

"We tossed the car of course, and we found one of Kelly's earrings. She was wearing one when the body was found; the other had rolled under the front seat of McClain's Pontiac."

I nodded, saying nothing, drinking my Coke and letting Mike tell the tale his own way. He drained the beer and got another one out of the refrigerator. He popped the top, threw the cap in the garbage can under the sink, and sat back down at the table. Without breaking stride in his story, he continued.

"We hauled him in and gave him what passed for the third degree back in those days. His second story was that he *had* been with Kelly. He said he hadn't been straight with us at first because he didn't want to get dragged into a murder investigation. Even more important, he didn't want his old lady to find out that he'd been with a hooker—he said she'd of cut his balls off.

"He admitted that he paid Kelly forty bucks for a blow job, and claimed that she'd put a rubber on him before she did it. When it was over, he said, he pitched the rubber out the window into the alley. Then he took Kelly back to the corner where he picked her up. He claimed that everything was copacetic. Kelly told him to be sure and come again. He said he would. He said that when they got back to the corner, Bambi was nowhere in sight. Afterward, he said, he drove straight home and went to bed.

"Naturally, we checked the alley, and we found about ten used rubbers. Apparently both Kelly and Bambi took johns down there on a regular basis. It was possible that Kelly might have used one of the rubbers on McClain, but who could tell?"

"Sure," I agreed.

"McClain gave us a blood sample. He was a type A secretor and so was the guy who'd left the semen in Kelly's throat. In addition, McClain's blood had an enzyme profile that matched only about ten percent of the adult male population. The semen had the same profile. Of course back then, we couldn't do anything more sophisticated than that—we didn't have any of this DNA and CSI shit that makes the job so easy for you kids today."

"In your fuckin' dreams," I snorted.

He laughed at that and went on. "Anyhow, we got a warrant for McClain's house, looking to see maybe did he have any clothesline lying around somewhere. And would you believe that when we got to the place we found his old lady hanging out the wash on the clothesline in the backyard?"

"No shit?"

"No shit," he answered, taking another hit on the

beer. "And there's about ten more feet of it coiled up in his storage shed.

"Of course, clothesline being clothesline, we couldn't make a solid match between the rope around the hooker's neck and the stuff that was strung across McClain's backyard. All we could tell was that the piece that had been used in the murder looked to be about the same age as McClain's.

"Anyhow, by the end of the day McClain had admitted to being on the scene at about the time Kelly was killed. He admitted to having oral sex with her, and the semen in her throat matched up to his blood type. We had her earring in his Pontiac. We had the testimony of the second pross, and then, of course, there was the clothesline.

"Taken separately, none of the pieces would have been enough to hang him for it, but all of it together was enough—especially considering that his PD was completely wet behind the ears. Harold Roe was the prosecutor and he steamrollered the poor girl—and McClain along with her, of course. The jury came back with murder in the first. The judge gave him life, and then it turns out that he didn't do it."

As tactfully as I could, I said, "There was no reason after to think that the conviction might have been a mistake?"

He shook his head. Looking me straight in the eye, he said, "None. At least not until last fall. Shit, you know how it is, Sean. By the time McClain finally came to trial, Quigly and I were already several cases down the line with new ones comin' in every week. We stopped long enough to accept the pats on the back we thought we deserved and then went on to other business and forgot all about Carl McClain."

"I can sure as hell understand that," I conceded.

"Damn right," he said, somewhat defensively. Shaking his head, he said, "Ever since I read about the pimp confessing, I've been waiting for the shit to start raining down, but we did it by the book, Sean.

"At the time, two or three people alibied Woolsey. His other girls claimed that they didn't know anybody who would have had a reason to kill Kelly, and none of them suggested that there was any trouble between her and the pimp. Apparently, even Bambi didn't know that Kelly was holding out on him—or at least she didn't admit to knowing it, and so we had no reason to look at him."

"Doesn't sound like it," I agreed.

The conversation paused and I said, "Do you have any idea where Quigly is these days?"

Miller pointed north. "Montana somewhere, that is if he's not dead by now. He took his pension three or four years after the McClain case and got the hell out of the desert. Said he'd rather shovel snow and freeze his ass off than spend another summer frying down here. Why do you ask—you gonna talk to him too?"

"No point." I shrugged. "We're warning everybody who was associated with the McClain case that he's out, apparently looking for revenge. But if Quigly's hidden away somewhere in Montana, he's probably not a likely target."

"And I am, I suppose?"

"I'd certainly think so, Mike," I sighed. "I can't believe that the guy intends to stop with a couple of jurors and his defense attorney. If he blames her for what happened, you gotta think he's pretty pissed at you too."

"No doubt," he agreed.

He thought about that for a few minutes, then said, "You got a recent photo?"

"About seven months old. We've given it to the media. I'd imagine it's on the air by now."

"I'll take a look," he said. "In the meantime, I've still got a permit to carry, so if he does come after me, I'll be ready."

Miller walked me back out through the garage, and again I admired the Mustang. As we stood in the driveway, he said, "So what's it like, workin' with a girl?"

"Shit, Mike," I laughed, "if Maggie heard you say that, she'd hand you your fuckin' lunch. The woman's tougher than you are, and the mouth on her would make you sound like an altar boy."

He arched his eyebrows, and I said, "Seriously, Mike, she's a damn good detective and she more than holds her own in the unit. It's not like the old days, working with you, of course, but it's a helluva big improvement over being saddled with Snyder."

"Yeah, well, working with Homer Simpson would be an improvement over Snyder," he conceded. "So, you gonna catch this bastard, Sean?"

"I hope so," I said, getting into my Chevy. "But in the meantime, be careful Mike—I mean it. This cocksucker is serious."

"I get the message," he replied. "So you and your tough new partner get out there and find him."

Leaning on the door of my car, he looked up and down the street as if evaluating his defensive perimeter. Then, looking back to me, he said, "What the hell do you suppose the bastard did with Thompson?"

"God only knows," I sighed. "On the plus side, we haven't found her body yet, which may mean that she's still alive. But if she is, that may not be so good, either."

"Yeah, I get your meaning."

He tapped the roof of the car a couple of times and then said, "Okay, Richardson, get on it, just like I showed you how. And don't be such a stranger."

CHAPTER THIRTY-TWO

Beverly was lying awake on the bed when she heard McClain's key in the lock a little after noon. She sat up and watched apprehensively as he opened the door, wondering what sort of mood he'd be in. After seeming to soften a bit during dinner the night before, he'd left the house and returned an hour later, apparently furious.

Beverly had no idea what might have set him off. She was sure that she hadn't done anything to upset him, but he'd burst into the room and slammed the door shut behind him. Without saying a word, he'd stripped off his clothes and dropped them onto the floor. Then, moving very deliberately, he had picked Beverly up from the chair where she'd been sitting at the card table and thrown her onto the bed.

She'd pleaded with him, begging him to tell her what was wrong, but he'd refused to make any response. Straddling her on the bed, he ripped her blouse off, sending the buttons scattering across the floor of the room. Then he tore off her bra and her skirt and raped her more violently than at any time since the night he'd abducted her. When he was finished, he'd left her sobbing on the bed, snatched up his clothes, and left the room again, slamming the door behind him. Through the entire ordeal, he'd not spoken a single word.

A couple of hours later, he'd come back into the room, obviously drunk. It was the first time Beverly had known him to drink anything, save for the beer he'd consumed with the chicken dinner. He fell onto the bed beside her, then reached out to pull her to him. She pushed herself away and got off of the bed. Mc-Clain reached out in her direction, then let his arm fall limply onto the bed. "Aw, fuck it," he said, and then passed out.

Beverly lay awake through most of the night watching him sleep, speculating about what might have caused his behavior to change so dramatically from the early evening and trying to calculate how she should react to it. Finally, she'd fallen asleep herself, and when she'd awakened about seven thirty in the morning, McClain was no longer in the room.

He returned a little after eight, still quiet, but apparently no longer angry. Avoiding any eye contact with Beverly, he set her breakfast on the card table, leaving the box of granola along with it. He left the room for a minute again, then returned with a clean white long-sleeve shirt. He draped the shirt over the back of one of the chairs. Without looking at Beverly, he pointed at the box of cereal. "I should be back with lunch a little after noon, but if you get hungry . . ."

Leaving the sentence unfinished, he had turned, left the room, and locked the door behind him. Beverly watched him go, unable to fathom what he might be thinking. Finally, she got up from the bed and showered. Her own clothes were completely ruined, and so she'd put on the shirt he had left and then had eaten her breakfast.

Now, as she watched him come into the room, she sensed that the fury of last night had passed, at least for the moment. McClain set two Subway bags on the card table and looked directly at her for the first time today. Then, looking quickly away again, he said, "Lunch is ready if you are."

She watched as he set two sandwiches and two drinks on the card table. Then he crumpled up the bags and set them on the floor beside him. Saying nothing, Beverly got up from the bed and sat down across from him.

"There's one tuna salad and one turkey," he said. "You can take your pick."

She looked at him, waiting until he raised his eyes to meet hers. "Either's fine with me," she replied. "Really. If you have a preference, take it."

McClain shrugged and reached for the tuna salad. They unwrapped their sandwiches and ate quietly for several minutes. McClain seemed lost in thought. There was almost a contrite air about him, and he continued to look practically anywhere except directly at Beverly. Finally, she set down her sandwich and broke the silence. In a quiet voice, she said, "I'm sorry, but could I ask a favor?"

McClain set his sandwich on the table and picked up his soft drink. Looking at her across the top of the cup, he said, "What?"

"Well, it's just . . . I was wondering if you'd mind bringing me something to wear? My own clothes . . ."

Looking away, she hesitated for a couple of seconds and then looked back at him. "If you could get me a couple of T-shirts, and maybe a pair of sweatpants or something—just so that I'd have something to put on. It doesn't have to be anything fancy. You could just go to a Target or someplace like that . . ."

McClain sat quietly for a moment, apparently mulling it over. Then he sighed and got up. "I'll see what I can do," he said. He turned and walked out of the room, abandoning his sandwich, half-eaten on the table behind him.

Chapter Thirty-three

Leaving Mike Miller, I drove through an In-N-Out Burger store and picked up a late lunch. I was eating at my desk and sorting through my message slips when Elaine walked through the door, wearing a new black pants suit. She'd colored her hair again within the last couple of days, and it looked as though this time she'd had the job done professionally.

It suddenly struck me that she'd recently lost a little weight as well, and I wondered if there was a new man in her life that I hadn't heard about yet. She perched on the desk and helped herself to a French fry.

"Better not let McClinton see you do that," I cautioned.

"Why?" she taunted. "Would she be upset because I was eating a French fry, or because I was eating one of *your* French fries?"

"Oh, bite me, Elaine."

"Don't tempt me," she laughed.

Quickly changing the subject, I said, "So how are you and Greg coming with your list?"

She finished the French fry and said, "We've put together a basic list that includes the judge, the prosecutor, the principal witnesses who testified against McClain, and all of the jurors who served at the trial—or at least the ones who've survived so far. And you've already talked to the lead detective. So the first thing I came in here to ask you is, how far do we go with this? Who else should we be thinking of here?"

I took a sip of my Coke. "Jesus, Elaine, I'm not sure.

We've got no way of knowing who in the hell the guy might have decided to target. It sounds to me like you've listed the most obvious possibilities, but to be on the safe side, we should probably have Media Relations amplify their original press release.

"When we gave them McClain's picture this morning, we simply indicated that he was wanted for questioning in the Fletcher and Collins killings. I guess we'd better go ahead and announce that new information leads us to believe that McClain is trying to settle scores with the people who sent him to prison. That way anybody who was even remotely related to the case will at least have fair warning. I'll run it by the lieutenant."

She nodded, swallowing another French fry. "Okay. The second thing I wanted to ask you is, Chickie and I thought it would be better to see as many of the people on the list as we can in person rather than just talking to them over the phone. We'll want to know if they've noticed anyone watching them, if they've been getting weird phone calls, and shit like that. Plus, they'll probably need some hand-holding."

"Makes sense," I agreed.

"So do you and McClinton want to take part of the list?"

"Sure. We'll want to get to these people as quickly as possible, preferably before they hear it on the news and panic."

"Okay," she said.

She pulled a sheet of paper out of a file folder she'd brought in with her and handed it to me. "Here's half the list. There were three jurors and one minor witness who disappeared from the local records while McClain was in Lewis. We're assuming that they simply moved away, but so far at least we've got no forwarding addresses.

"Presumably, if we can't find 'em, McClain can't

either, but maybe they'll hear a newscast or read about it in the papers. Otherwise," she said, pointing to the list, "the addresses and phone numbers are current."

Taking the sheet of paper, I said, "We'll get right on it."

Elaine grabbed the last of the fries, hopped down from the desk, and headed out the door. "Thanks for lunch," she said.

I walked down the hall and found Maggie at her desk, sorting through her own message slips and eating an apple. I explained the plan of attack and she collected her purse and jacket. After a typically beautiful spring morning, it had turned into a cloudy afternoon, and as we walked out into the parking lot, the sky began spitting rain.

"Oops," Maggie observed sarcastically. "Rain during the peak of the tourist season. The chamber of commerce will be pissed about that."

"No doubt," I agreed.

We had seven names on our list, and I mentally sorted their addresses into an order that would allow us to get to them most efficiently. Doubtless, some of them would be at work or whatever, and we'd have to get back to them in the evening, but this seemed the most logical approach.

Accordingly, the first person we attempted to contact was Byron Patterson. On the list she gave me, Elaine had identified Patterson as an expert witness, but there was no indication as to what he might have testified about.

We arrived at his home to find him taking a set of golf clubs out of the back of an SUV. I parked in the driveway behind him, and Maggie and I hurried out of the rain and into the shelter of the open garage. As we did, Patterson hung the golf bag on a rack that also held a couple of tennis racquets, a serious backpack, and two expensive mountain bikes. Not surprisingly,

Patterson was thin and fit even though he was obviously somewhere in his middle sixties.

Maggie and I introduced ourselves and I told Patterson that we understood that he'd testified at the murder trial of Carl McClain.

"Right," he said, nodding his head. "I was the one who made the blood-type match between McClain and the semen that was found in the victim's throat. And," he said a bit defensively, "even though it now turns out that McClain was innocent, the blood types *did* match."

"Yes, sir," Maggie said. "We all understand that the technology back then wasn't what it is today."

"No, ma'am," Patterson agreed, "it certainly wasn't. But we did the best we could with what we had. So why are you asking about McClain's trial at this late date? I saw the article in the *Republic*. I know that the mistake was corrected and that McClain was set free."

"Yes, he was," I said. "And while he should have been released, of course, unfortunately it looks like he's come out of the system determined to revenge himself on the people who put him there. Since his release, two of the jurors from his trial have been shot to death, and the woman who served as his public defender has been kidnapped."

Patterson's eyes widened. "You're serious?"

"Deadly serious," Maggie said. "We're warning everyone who was associated with McClain's conviction to be on guard."

"You think he's coming after me?" Patterson asked anxiously.

"We have no way of knowing that, Mr. Patterson," I answered. "We only know what he's apparently done so far, not what he intends to do. We don't know who else might be on his list."

"But what am I supposed to do?"

"Well, at a minimum," I said, "be alert to what's

going on around you. Don't open your door to anyone that you don't recognize. Keep an eye out for unfamiliar vehicles parked in the neighborhood. We think that McClain is driving an older black van, but we don't know if that's the only vehicle he's using. Be alert to anyone who might seem to be following you. Let us know if you get any hang-ups or other odd phone calls. Do you have caller ID?"

"Yes."

"Okay. I'd suggest that you make a list of calls that come from numbers you don't recognize. We presume that McClain must be scouting his targets. If he is watching you, perhaps we can catch him in the act."

Patterson shook his head. "Jesus, Detective, I don't know . . ."

"As an alternative, Mr. Patterson," Maggie interjected, "if it's at all possible, you might want to think about leaving town for a few days without letting anyone other than us know where you're going. We're mounting an intensive public manhunt for McClain. With any luck, we'll run him to ground shortly and eliminate the potential threat."

Patterson nodded slowly. "Well, I suppose we could go visit my brother up in Payson for a couple of days . . ."

"That might be the safest bet," I agreed. "But again, if you do notice anyone who seems to be taking an undue interest in you before you can get away, be sure to let us know."

I gave Patterson one of my business cards, and he promised to call if he noticed anything out of the ordinary in the next thirty minutes or so. "After that," he said, "I expect to be packed up and on the road. I just hope that you can catch this guy quickly, though. My wife and my sister-in-law don't get along all that well."

The next name on our list was a juror named Brenda Dulles. Nobody answered the door at her apartment, so I wrote a message on the back of one of my cards, asking her to call me as soon as possible, and wedged the card between the door and the jamb.

The third name was that of Harold Roe, the prosecutor who'd won McClain's conviction. We arrived at his home about three thirty, by which time the rain had stopped falling. The clouds had scudded away, and it had turned into a beautiful afternoon. As had been the case at our last stop, no one answered the door. Again I left a card, and Maggie and I were walking back to the car when a Buick sedan pulled into the driveway and the garage door began rolling up.

The Buick braked to a stop in the garage, and a well-coiffed woman in her middle fifties got out of the car carrying a couple of large shopping bags from Nordstrom's and Neiman Marcus. She identified herself as Roe's wife, Rachel, and expressed surprise at the fact that her husband hadn't answered the door. Pointing back at a Lincoln Town Car sitting in the garage next to her Buick, she said, "As you can see, his car's right there, so he *must* be here. Probably he just didn't hear you."

Roe led us into the garage and opened a door that took us through a mudroom and into the kitchen. She dropped her keys and the shopping bags on the counter and called her husband's name. But the house was completely silent, and no one responded. Looking perplexed, Roe said, "That's odd. Harold won't even walk down to the mailbox. If his car is here, then he's got to be here too."

We followed her out of the kitchen and into a hallway that led toward the back of the house. "Harold?" she called again.

A moment later, she let out a sharp scream. I stepped up beside her and saw the body of a man, presumably her husband, slumped over in a chair in the study. He'd been shot at least twice and was obviously dead.

Mrs. Roe screamed again and then collapsed. Maggie and I caught her before she hit the floor and carried her over to a couch in the living room. Then I pulled out my cell phone and called for backup.

While Maggie stayed with Mrs. Roe, I drew my weapon and moved carefully through the house. The rest of the rooms appeared to be undisturbed, and the shooter was obviously long gone. I holstered my weapon and went back to the living room to let Maggie know that the place was clear. Then I walked over to the study and stood in the doorway, taking in the scene.

Some papers and a couple of pictures were lying on the floor next to the body, and it looked as if they'd been swept off a corner of the desk. Except for that—and for the body, of course—the room appeared to be in good order. If the killer had been looking for something in the study or somewhere else in the house, he or she had looked very carefully. But I was fairly certain of the fact that Roe had not surprised a burglar.

For the next several hours, we worked the scene along with the Crime Scene Response team, the ME, and the rest of the usual cast. We canvassed the neighborhood, but found no one who had seen or heard anything out of the ordinary. No one reported seeing a black van anywhere near Roe's home.

Inevitably, the shooting had drawn a swarm of local media. By the time Maggie and I were ready to leave, two news-channel helicopters were hovering over the scene, and I counted vans from four different television stations parked haphazardly in the street with their satellite dishes pointed skyward, ready to dispatch the latest bloody horrors to the greater metro area just before bedtime. The reporters pressed against the crime-scene barriers, and a patrolman was struggling to keep them in check.

As Maggie and I made our way to the car, several of the reporters shouted my name, and I reluctantly turned and walked over to the barricade. Six or seven reporters shouted questions simultaneously and then thrust their microphones in front of my face.

By now, of course, the reporters had discovered and announced the victim's identity; there would be no courteous withholding of the information until family members could be notified. Several of the reporters demanded to know if Roe had been killed by Carl McClain.

I held up my hands and waited until things were as quiet as they were likely to get. Then I said, "I'll make a brief statement now, but will take no questions. Media Relations will probably hold a press conference later and will answer your questions then. For the moment all I can tell you is that we have a shooting victim whom you've already identified as Mr. Harold Roe, a local attorney.

"As most of you know by now, Mr. Roe was the attorney who prosecuted Carl McClain for the murder of Gloria Kelly. As you also know, we are looking for Mr. McClain in connection with the deaths of two other people who were involved in his trial. At this time, however, we have no conclusive evidence to suggest that Mr. McClain was involved in this crime.

"As we did earlier today, we would ask anyone who has information regarding Mr. McClain's whereabouts to contact the police. But again, we would warn any such person not to make direct contact with Mr. McClain, whom we believe to be armed and extremely dangerous."

I turned and headed toward the car, ignoring the questions shouted at my back. The patrolmen parted the crowd, and Maggie and I made our way back to the department, where we found the lieutenant still in his office, waiting for us. We dropped into chairs in front of the desk and gave him the details of the latest shooting.

I finished the update and asked him what Pierce and Chickris had accomplished.

Leaning back in his chair, he said, "They've contacted all of the people on their list, either in person or over the phone. The only exception is the judge who presided over the case. He's a widower named Walter Beckman who lives alone in a condominium complex in Scottsdale, and he seems to be missing.

"Beckman failed to show up for his usual golf game this morning, and he didn't call the club or anyone else to say that he'd be late or that he'd be unable to come for some reason. Apparently that was totally out of character, and so his playing partners were worried that something might have happened to him.

"One of the guys that Beckman plays with has a key to Beckman's condo and went over to check up on him. Beckman wasn't home. His car wasn't in the garage, and this morning's *Republic* was still lying in the driveway. Yesterday's paper was lying open on the kitchen table next to a box of cereal and a bowl that had a couple flakes of cereal and a little milk dried in the bottom. It looked like Beckman had started reading the paper during his breakfast yesterday and then hadn't gotten back to it.

"The guy—whose name is Tom Matthews—called the golf club, and Beckman still hadn't shown up. Matthews was getting increasingly concerned, and he remembered that Beckman had said that he had an appointment with his ophthalmologist yesterday morning. The office is only a couple of blocks away from Beckman's condo, and so Matthews went over to see if Beckman had kept the appointment. He spotted Beckman's car in the parking lot, and the receptionist in the ophthalmologist's office told him that Beckman had been there yesterday and that he'd left a little after eleven. Apparently that was the last time anybody saw him. Matthews called and reported Beckman missing at noon today."

"Oh, shit," I sighed. "That doesn't sound good."

"No, it doesn't," Martin agreed. "It's possible, of course, that Beckman's gone missing for some reason that has nothing to do with Carl McClain. But more than likely, either McClain's got him somewhere or has already killed him and dumped the body someplace."

"What about the rest of the people that were on our list?" Maggie asked.

"I gave the names to Riggins and Doyle, and they touched base with the ones you didn't get to. Everybody's scared shitless, and some of them are leaving town in a hurry, but so far they're all alive and well."

"What'd you do with the media?" I asked.

"As you suggested, we released a statement indicating our belief that McClain might be targeting anyone who was associated with his arrest and conviction. It was the lead story on all of the early-evening newscasts and, given Roe's murder, will for sure lead the ten o'clock news."

"Anything from the hotline?" Maggie asked.

"Oh, yeah," he sighed, running a hand through what was left of his hair. "Since we released McClain's picture at noon we've had several calls from people who swear that they've seen him, and scores more from people who've seen mysterious black vans. We're tracking down the reports as fast as we can, but we've got nothing solid yet. I tell you, this whole damn thing is turning into one gigantic cluster fuck."

CHAPTER THIRTY-FOUR

Just after five o'clock, McClain walked into the bedroom. Saying nothing, he handed Beverly a shopping bag with Target's bull's-eye logo emblazoned on it. She opened the bag to find three T-shirts, two pairs of sweatpants, and a three-pack of black bikini panties. Looking up at McClain, she said, "Thank you."

He shrugged, obviously embarrassed. "About the . . . uh . . . I didn't know what size. I just got medium."

"That's fine," she nodded. "Thank you."

He turned to leave, and as he reached the door, Beverly said, "Uh, excuse me . . ."

McClain turned back to face her. "What?"

She pulled a pair of the sweatpants out of the bag. "I'm sorry," she said. "It's just that with this cable around my ankle, I won't be able to get these on."

He stood there for a moment and then shook his head. "Jesus, what an idiot. I didn't even think about that."

Beverly decided to press her luck. In a soft voice, she said, "Is the cable really necessary? I mean, you lock the door every time you leave the room. I can't get out of here anyway. Isn't it sort of redundant?"

McClain looked at her for a long moment. Then he looked at the sweatpants she was holding in her hand and sighed. "Hold on a minute."

He left the room and returned with two wrenches. "Sit on the bed," he said.

Beverly did as instructed, and McClain crouched down in front of her. He set the wrenches on the bed and grabbed her roughly by the shoulders, showing her that he was still the boss. "Now listen carefully, Beverly," he said in a firm voice. "I'll trust you to this extent: As long as I'm here in the house, I'll leave the cable off. But when I leave the house it goes back on."

Beverly nodded. "Okay. Thank you."

McClain squeezed her shoulders hard. "Don't fuck with me now, Beverly—I'm warning you. If you try anything cute, the cable goes back on and stays on. And believe me, I'll make you regret it."

"I understand," she replied meekly. "I promise I won't try anything."

"Okay," he said.

Releasing her, he picked up the wrenches, unscrewed the bolt, and removed the cable. Her ankle was red and chafed, and she began massaging it. McClain reached out, pulled her hands away, and looked at the ankle. "Wait," he said.

He briefly left the room again, then came back and handed her a small plastic bottle of hand lotion. "Here. Try some of this on it."

Beverly nodded. "Thank you," she said again.

And saying nothing more, McClain turned and left the room.

Beverly watched him go and, for the first time in nearly a week, she allowed herself a tiny smile. Somehow, someway, she would beat this bastard yet.

She rubbed some of the lotion into her ankle. Then she took off the shirt he had loaned her and pulled on a pair of the panties, a San Francisco 49ers T-shirt, and a pair of blue sweatpants. Two hours later, she heard McClain's key in the door again.

This time he handed her two beers, some silverware, and the roll of paper towels. "I'll be right back," he said.

Beverly set the table, folding a couple of the paper towels into napkins. McClain returned with a pizza on a cooking sheet and two plates. He set the pizza in the middle of the table and handed her one of the plates. "Sorry we're temporarily back to junk food," he said. "I was going to get to the grocery store, but then some problems came up late this afternoon and I couldn't get out of the house again. So we'll have to make do with a frozen pizza tonight."

Beverly took a sip of her beer, then said tentatively, "Can I ask what sort of problems?"

McClain sat back in his chair, took a pull on his own beer, and said, "You still don't know who I am, do you, Beverly?"

She slowly shook her head. "No, I'm sorry, but I don't. I know you think that I should recognize you, but I'm sure I've never seen you before."

"Well, that's probably a good thing," he sighed. "So far nobody else has recognized me either, which means that you and I will probably be safe and sound here for the next four days."

"I'm sorry, but I don't understand."

McClain set down his beer and waited until she looked up to meet his eyes. He waited another couple of beats and then said, "You let them send me to prison, Beverly. For something I didn't do. And for the rest of my fucking life."

She was thunderstruck. "Carl McClain?" she said, incredulously. "You're telling me that you're Carl Mc-Clain?"

"In the flesh," he nodded.

She paused for several moments, taking in the enormity of it, trying to comprehend something that was clearly incomprehensible. "But how . . . Are you telling me that they paroled you?"

He flashed her a lazy smile. "Even better than that," he said. "They pardoned me."

"Pardoned you? But when? How?"

"Three months ago. The real killer finally confessed, and the DNA proved that it was him and not me."

Three months ago.

Beverly shook her head again. Three months ago, she and David had been in Tuscany on an extended vacation. It had been the best three weeks of her life, and in the middle of it all, some idiot had decided to turn Carl McClain loose on the world?

"But I didn't hear anything about it," she said.

McClain gave her the smile again, broader this time, as if he was very pleased with himself. "Yeah, I know. Most of these stupid bastards, they get cleared after being inside for ten or twenty years, and the first thing they want to do is hold a fuckin' news conference and get their faces splashed all over the front page of the newspapers.

"Well, not me. I had very definite plans for if I ever got out, and I didn't want anybody to see me coming. Fortunately, after you failed me so miserably, a couple of years ago I was able to hire a real attorney to try to get my case reopened. When the other guy confessed, I told the attorney no publicity and definitely no pictures."

McClain laughed. "The poor bastard couldn't understand that at all. 'You're an innocent man,' he kept saying. 'Why don't you want everybody to know it? They sure as hell plastered your picture all over the place when they convicted you.' But I told him just to let it go—that I wanted to slip back into the world on my own terms. In the end, there was just a brief story in the *Republic*, and so here we are."

Beverly started to cry. "But Carl, I don't understand. Why me? I defended you. I did the best I could for you . . ."

He leaned forward across the table and pulled her hands away from her face. "Well, your best wasn't very damn good, now, was it Beverly? There I was, an innocent man, but you let them convict me anyhow."

"I did everything I could," she said again. "I worked day and night for you. And after all, it wasn't my fault that the evidence was stacked against you so heavily. Don't you think that you bear at least some of the responsibility for what happened to you?"

McClain released her hands. "How do you figure that?" he asked.

She picked up her "napkin" and swiped at her tears.

"Well, for openers," she said, "you chose to have sex with a prostitute. Obviously, if you hadn't done that, you would never have been arrested in the first place. Then when you were initially questioned about the killing, you lied to the police. If you'd been truthful with them right from the start, perhaps they would have been more willing to believe you. Certainly the jury would have been more inclined to do so."

He sighed and shifted in his chair. Looking at the pizza rather than at Beverly, he said, "Yeah, well, the last I heard, getting a blow job from a hooker isn't a capital offense in this state—at least not yet. And neither is lying to the cops. I told them the truth fast enough once they found her earring in my car. A decent lawyer wouldn't of let them send me down for that."

"So why didn't you hire a 'decent' lawyer in the first place?" she asked bitterly.

Rising to the bait, McClain answered, "Because, as you know damn good and well, I couldn't afford one. So I got stuck with you."

Beverly threw up her hands. "And you expected what—that you'd get Perry Mason out of the Public Defender's Office? You're smarter than that, Carl. What sort of lawyer do you think is going to work for the salaries they can afford to pay? Hell, if you're looking to lay the blame somewhere, why don't you just start with the damned county commissioners?"

McClain gave her a hard laugh. "Yeah, well, now that you mention it, maybe I should add those fuckers to my list."

"I don't know what you expect me to say here," she said in a defeated voice. "Yes, I was young. And yes, I was relatively inexperienced. But I *did* do everything I could for you. Where do you think I went wrong? What else do you think I could have done?"

She stared at him, waiting for an answer, but he simply turned away. Nearly a minute passed before finally he looked back to her. In a resigned voice, he said, "Christ, Beverly, I don't know. You're the lawyer, not me. I just keep thinking about all that bullshit we learned in civics class about how our justice system is set up to protect the innocent—about how everybody's presumed innocent until proven guilty beyond a reasonable doubt. Jesus, what a crock . . ."

"I can understand how angry you must be," she said, "and I don't blame you for that. And I know that you can never get back the time you lost, but you're still a young man. Why throw away the rest of your life? What does that accomplish?"

"*You* understand how angry I am?" he said, mocking her. "Jesus Christ, Beverly, you couldn't *begin* to understand. You haven't been there. When you let them send me away, I lost everything that mattered to me—my wife, my child, my freedom, even my poor mother. And the *only* thing I had to hold on to for all those endless days and nights was the dream that some day I might have a chance to even the score. That's all I have left now."

"And so you killed my husband," she said quietly. "You've kidnapped me and raped me repeatedly. What else are you going to do to 'even the score'?"

McClain looked away. "I am sorry about your husband," he said. "I had no ax to grind with him and I had no intention of shooting him. I only wanted you. If you hadn't laid on the fuckin' horn and attracted his attention, he'd still be alive tonight.

"As to what else I'm going to do . . . well, so far I've settled up with the judge, your old friend Harold Roe, and two of the jurors."

Beverly stared at him. "They're dead?"

"God damn right. And in the end, they were all extremely sorry for what they'd done to me."

She swallowed hard, trying to comprehend the depth of his madness. "And you expect to get away with this?"

"To be honest," he sighed, "I don't know. I *hope* to get away with it, but it's more important that I finish what I came out to do. And I still have a few more people to see before I'm ready to ride off into the sunset."

"You're going to kill me too, aren't you." She said it as a matter of fact, not as a question.

For a long moment, McClain stared at the cold pizza sitting on the table between them. Then finally he looked up to meet her eyes. "The jury's still out on that, Beverly," he said.

Chapter Thirty-five

At ten o'clock, McClain sat down to watch the evening news. The lead story was the same as it had been at six. A tall blonde model posing as a "reporter" stood in front of Harold Roe's house and breathlessly updated the situation. What it amounted to was this: Harold was still dead, and McClain was still the prime suspect.

On the television screen was a picture of the old, fat McClain with his glasses and a full head of hair. As long as the cops had everybody looking for that poor stupid mope, the sleek new McClain figured that he should be able to wander the streets in relative safety.

The prison authorities could tell them that he'd lost the weight. So could his old buddy Richard Petrovich, for that matter. But none of them knew about the contact lenses, and none of them realized that he'd shaved every single hair off of his body. Only Beverly could tell them that. But then, of course, in spite of what he'd suggested over dinner, she wouldn't be getting the chance.

Thinking about their conversation over dinner, he wondered if he'd made a mistake in going after her. The rest of them, no question. But Beverly?

Lying in his prison bunk, he'd been convinced that she deserved it more than anybody else on his list. Christ, he would have done better defending himself.

Or maybe not.

The new hotshot attorney that he'd finally been able to hire had gone through the motions of appealing the conviction on the grounds that McClain had not been adequately represented by counsel. But every court that heard the argument had thrown it out. On the record, at least, it appeared that Beverly had done the best she could with what she had to work with.

But what the printed record didn't show was that she'd seemed tentative in her presentations to the court and in her examinations of the witnesses—unsure of herself and of her client as well. Just his luck to be the first person she'd ever defended on a murder rap.

She *had* worked hard during his trial; McClain would have to give her that. She'd come into court every day looking haggard and drawn. He remembered her saying that she wasn't sleeping much, both as a result of the hours she was putting in and on account of the anxiety of it all. But in consequence she'd stood before the court looking and acting exactly like the rookie she was. Her inexperience was apparent to everyone—to the judge, to the jurors, and to McClain himself.

On the other side of all that was the sex appeal. Tired as she might have been, Beverly still had a fantastic face and an even better figure. Even the bags under her eyes and her tasteful, conservative suits couldn't hide that. Every man in the courtroom had been glued to her every move, and McClain had hoped that if nothing else, the five males on the jury would be seduced by Beverly's body, if not by her arguments on his behalf.

Unfortunately it hadn't worked out that way, and fairly or not, McClain blamed her for that too. Lying awake, listening to the night sounds of the cell block and plotting his revenge, he'd always put Beverly's name at the top of the list, convinced that she deserved the number-one slot for being so inept, and fantasizing about the ways in which he'd like to repay her for that ineptitude.

Thinking about it now, he wondered if he'd been entirely fair to the woman. For seventeen long, hard years he'd been consumed by the idea of having his way with her. But in truth, was it really because she had failed him, or simply because he wanted her? Had he simply been looking for an excuse to take her?

And what of her argument that he might have attempted to make something of himself?

In theory, of course, that was his other option. He could have walked out of prison and hired a top gun as his new attorney. Instead of eliminating the people who had conspired to steal seventeen years of his life, he could have sued the hell out of them. Doubtless, the county attorney's office and the other agencies involved would have been tripping all over themselves offering a settlement of some sort. And that, combined with the money he'd inherited from his mother, would have been more than sufficient to give him a start at a new life. But by the time society's mistake had been discovered and "corrected," McClain was burning with a rage that had been smoldering for all those years, and there was simply no way that he could lead anything approaching a normal life until that rage had been extinguished.

And anyway, what sort of a life could it have been?

With his mother dead, the only two people he cared about were irretrievably lost to him. In spite of the fact that the state had now declared him to be an "innocent" man, he could not begin to fathom a scenario in which Amanda and Tiffani would welcome him back into their lives, even in the most marginal way. Nor could he imagine that employers would be lining up to offer top-level jobs to a guy who'd spent nearly half of his life in the system, no matter the fact that his conviction and imprisonment had turned out to be a lamentable and tragic mistake.

Even had he not opted for his present course of action, McClain well understood that, like that poor jerk Richard Petrovich, he would have spent the rest of his life on the margins of society, working at jobs that commanded little if any respect, that offered very little money, and that allowed a man virtually no sense of pride or satisfaction. Having chosen his current path, McClain would at least have that—the satisfaction of knowing that the bastards who had combined to steal his life were getting their just reward.

And that included Beverly.

She "understood," she said, how angry he must have been. Shit, in a thousand years, she would never—*could* never—understand that, no matter how diligently he tried to reason with her or how harshly he might punish her. No one could.

McClain's first few months in the joint had been an indescribable nightmare. And even seventeen years after the fact, he sometimes snapped awake in the middle of the night, startled out of his sleep by a memory so sharp and so immediate as to convince him that he was living it all again.

He had been so young and so green, tossed into a sea of hardened, bitter, and sadistic men who lived by their own rules in a prison system that was overcrowded, underfunded, and totally unconcerned with such quaint ideas as rehabilitation and humane treatment. He had quickly discovered that the inmates truly *did* run the asylum, and his initiation into the system had been hellishly brutal.

After four months of physical and psychological abuse that no one on the outside could ever begin to imagine, he had finally surrendered and made an "arrangement" with an older, stronger longtime con who offered Carl protection and taught him how to survive in the system. But Carl had paid dearly for that knowledge and protection, and that too had fired his determination to one day avenge himself against the system and the individuals who had consigned him to that hellish nightmare.

Perhaps Beverly *had* done her best. And maybe, in retrospect, he should have thought harder about including her on the list of his targets. But that was water under the bridge. The die was cast. And no matter what he might think about Beverly now, that was the cold, hard fact of the situation.

McClain returned his attention back to the television set as the blonde interrupted her spiel and raced over to join a group of reporters pressing up against the police barricade. The camera swung away from the woman to show a man with a detective's shield hanging over the pocket of his suit coat approaching the reporters. As the detective came within range, the reporters shouted questions at him, and McClain heard his own name mentioned in several of the questions.

The detective appeared to be in his middle thirties, tall and a bit on the thin side, like a runner maybe. The suit looked expensive and was well tailored; McClain wondered if it was Italian. The camera zoomed in close to show dark, wavy hair cut to a medium length, with the first touch of gray showing at the sides. Strong features filled out a face highlighted by eyes that might have been blue or gray; from the television, you couldn't really tell. McClain thought he saw a profound sadness in the eyes, but maybe the guy was just tired.

The detective told the reporters that McClain was wanted for questioning but that there was no evidence yet to link him to the tragic death of Harold Roe. He advised anyone seeing McClain to be cautious, warning them that McClain was considered to be armed and dangerous. Then he turned away and left the reporters clamoring behind him.

The camera swung back to the blonde, who identified the detective as Sean Richardson of the Phoenix Homicide Unit, who was "leading the hunt for suspected killer Carl McClain." For a moment, a picture of the "old Carl" flashed on the screen again, and then the camera cut back to show Richardson getting into his car with his partner, a black woman who looked to have a pretty good body herself.

McClain made a pistol with his thumb and forefinger and pointed it at the detective. "Boom!" he said. Then, more quietly, "Happy hunting, pal."

CHAPTER THIRTY-SIX

For an hour after dinner was over, Beverly remained rooted to her chair at the card table, her mind spinning. Carl McClain had haunted her dreams for months following the trial, and she found it impossible to imagine that the doughy, irresponsible kid she'd defended so many years ago had somehow morphed into the toned, determined, self-confident man who was now at the epicenter of her nightmares.

She could readily understand that, given the circumstances, McClain would be outraged. Anyone would be. He'd lost seventeen years of his life, branded as a killer and locked away in the company of society's foulest rejects. Who wouldn't be furious? And who wouldn't feel some fundamental impulse to strike out at those he deemed responsible?

Still, that couldn't possibly justify the actions he had taken. Unfortunately, the system was not perfect, and certainly Carl McClain was not the only innocent victim to be wrongly judged and punished by it. That such a thing could happen was more than a regrettable tragedy. It was unforgivable.

But it was also understandable. Justice depended upon the actions and the good intentions of fallible human beings who, sadly, could and did make mistakes. But for the most part, they were just that—mistakes—and nothing more. In McClain's case as in others, well-intentioned policemen, prosecutors, witnesses, jurors, and a judge had screwed up, plain and simple. Not to mention McClain's public defender.

As she'd told him, Beverly had done her best for him. And from the beginning she had feared that, as McClain had responded, her best had not been very good.

Beverly had been the youngest student in her law-school class, an idealist with the naive expectation that she could make a difference in the world. On graduating, she had rejected offers from several good law firms, opting instead for the Maricopa County Public Defender's Office. She'd envisioned herself fighting on behalf of society's downtrodden, impoverished, and innocent victims, only to find herself assigned to de-

fend the interests of a bewildering variety of sleaze-
bags and genuinely terrifying amoral monsters, 90
percent of whom were guilty as hell of the charges
levied against them and, doubtless, of much more.

Carl McClain had fallen somewhere into the middle
of that range. Beverly had been assigned the case when
a more seasoned attorney had abruptly left the office
to go into private practice and when no one else was
available to shoulder the responsibility.

She'd never found McClain to be particularly fright-
ening. Rather, he'd always impressed her as an overweight, self-indulgent jerk who'd managed, by virtue
of his own ineptitude, to get caught up in the system.
He'd insisted, naturally, that he was innocent. But of
course that's what they all said. Beverly had never
known whether to believe him or not, but that was
beside the point. Even if McClain was the stone-cold
killer that the prosecution described for the jury, the
law still mandated that he was entitled to the best defense that she could provide for him.

In truth, Beverly was already beginning to question
the merits of a system that insisted that wife beaters,
drug dealers, burglars, rapists, and killers were entitled
to the best defense that the Maricopa County taxpay-
ers were willing to pay for. But she'd taken on McClain's
case with all the enthusiasm she could still muster for
the job, and she'd worked as long and as hard as she
could to win his acquittal.

She had begun second-guessing her efforts even before the jury delivered its verdict. And for months
after McClain was delivered into the system, she was
haunted by the fact that she might have allowed an innocent man to go to prison for a crime he had not committed. The evidence against McClain was strong, but
it was not open-and-shut. And Beverly wondered
whether, absent any eyewitness evidence beyond that
of the second hooker, a more skilled attorney might

have been able to raise enough reasonable doubt in the minds of the jurors to have changed the outcome.

For weeks, she'd lain awake at night thinking about different approaches she might have taken and about the alternate arguments that she might have made. She mentally replayed her cross-examinations of the prosecution's witnesses, now formulating questions that she might have asked but didn't. And three months after the case ended—three more months in which she had defended the interests of mostly undeserving miscreants and worse—she'd thrown in the towel and accepted an offer to become a medical-malpractice specialist for the firm of Ballman, Nicholson, and Wyffels.

As the years passed, she immersed herself in the job, which she found to be more rewarding and intellectually challenging than she ever could have imagined. And in the process, finally, Carl McClain faded from her consciousness until he had become nothing more than a dim, distant, and regrettable memory.

CHAPTER THIRTY-SEVEN

When the news ended at ten thirty, McClain clicked off the television and pulled himself out of the living-room chair. He thought about putting the cable back on Beverly's ankle, but decided against it. Moving quietly, he checked to make sure that the door to the bedroom was securely locked and then went out to the garage. He pulled on a pair of thin latex gloves and spent twenty minutes wiping down every surface on the van that he might have touched. Then he backed the van out of the garage, locked the garage door behind him, and headed south and east toward the Sky Harbor Airport.

The cops were looking for a black van now, and even though they didn't have a plate number, McClain decided that the van had already served its purpose and that it was probably time to dump it for safety's sake.

He stuck to the side streets until he reached the airport, which was only a couple of miles from the house. Once there, he grabbed a ticket from the automated dispenser at the entrance to the parking garage immediately across the street from terminal 2. He drove up the ramp to the exposed upper level and parked the van in the middle of the lot.

On the way down the stairs, McClain stripped off the gloves then he threw them along with the key and the parking ticket into a trash barrel at the bottom of the stairs. Then he walked across the street to the terminal and grabbed a cab. He instructed the driver to drop him at a bar seven blocks away from the house, and he stayed in the bar long enough for one quick drink. Then he walked on home, watching carefully and keeping his hand on the pistol in his jacket pocket all the way there. As he'd warned Beverly, it wasn't the best of neighborhoods.

It was just after midnight when McClain got back to the house. He put the gun into the backpack in the hall and stood in the living room for a couple of minutes thinking about drinking a beer and watching some late-night television. Then he thought back to Beverly and the way she'd looked, sitting at the card table in her oversized T-shirt while he told her who he was and what he was doing.

He quietly unlocked the door to the bedroom and stepped in. The lights were on, and Beverly had fallen asleep on top of the bed, still wearing the clothes he had given her this afternoon. McClain locked the door behind him and slipped the key ring back into his pocket. Silently he undressed and lay down on the bed beside her.

She came awake slowly as he slipped his hand under the T-shirt and cupped her breast.

"No," she said. "Please, Carl, no."

She tried to push him away, but he threw a knee over her leg, pinning her down. He peeled off the sweat-pants and the panties, careful not to tear them this time, and forced himself into her. For a few more seconds she tried to push him off, but then she gave up and lay still beneath him, letting him have his way.

McClain built to his climax slowly and deliberately, and then, when he was nearly there, Beverly arched up into him and shuddered. "No," she cried again. "Please no."

He finished a few seconds later and rolled off beside her. Beverly turned her back to him and began sob-bing into her pillow.

CHAPTER THIRTY-EIGHT

Valentine's Day fell on a Wednesday.

I was already awake when the alarm began buzzing at five A.M. I punched it off, snapped on the light, and sat on the edge of the bed for a minute or two, contem-plating the picture of Julie that faced me from the nightstand. Sighing heavily, I got up, quickly made the bed, then brushed my teeth and made a pass at comb-ing my hair.

I pulled on a T-shirt, a pair of running shorts, and my Asics and did five miles through the neighborhood in just under forty minutes. The temperature was somewhere in the high forties, and at that time of the morning, traffic was still fairly light. A good portion of my route paralleled the Kierland Golf Club, and as I ran along the broad sidewalk that bordered the course, the city around me slowly came back to life for another day.

By the time I'd gone to bed a little after one A.M., we'd had scores of calls from people who reported seeing Carl McClain or a black van matching the description we'd released. We'd follow up on any tip that looked even remotely promising of course, but I knew that it would be mostly busywork that would not get us any closer to catching the guy.

My gut instinct told me that we wouldn't find him anytime soon, unless we got incredibly lucky. McClain had been out of prison for a little over three months before beginning his killing spree, which convinced me that he was not acting impulsively. Obviously, he'd taken the time to scout his victims and was working carefully from a plan of some sort.

I assumed that he'd used the time between his release and the murder of Alma Fletcher to create a base of operations somewhere and to lay the groundwork for the actions that were now unfolding. I wondered if he had also used the time to alter his appearance, and if so, in what way.

I found it interesting that he had abducted Beverly Thompson and Walter Beckman, rather than simply killing them in their homes, as he had the other victims. What had been his purpose in doing so, and was he still holding them for some reason or had he killed them and hidden the bodies?

And where did Richard Petrovich fit into the scheme of things? Why had we found his DNA at the scene of the crimes and not McClain's? Was Petrovich assisting McClain, or had McClain somehow engaged in a bit of clever misdirection?

Was McClain still driving the black van, and if so, would we have any chance of finding it among the hundreds of similar vehicles in the greater metro area? Most important, how many more names did McClain have on his list, and who would he be going after next?

Heading north toward home again, I dropped down into the pedestrian tunnel that would take me under Greenway Parkway, and my thoughts flashed back to Julie.

This was the second Valentine's Day since the accident. Three years ago tonight, I'd taken her to dinner at Mary Elaine's at the Phoenician—an extravagance, but well worth it, especially in hindsight.

The dinner had been excellent in every respect, and Julie had looked especially beautiful in a black cocktail dress with thin spaghetti straps. She'd worn her hair up that night, something that she did only rarely, and usually only when she was wearing the diamond earrings that I'd given her for her thirtieth birthday.

After dinner, we'd gone out to the patio off the Thirsty Camel bar for a Cognac. The stars sparkled overhead, and directly below us the waters of the resort's sprawling pool complex shimmered bright and blue. The landscape lighting threw the palm trees into shadowed relief, and off in the distance, planes glided soundlessly into the Sky Harbor Airport. I remember draping my suit coat over Julie's bare shoulders as the temperature turned cooler and kissing her softly as we waited for the valet to bring the car at the end of the evening.

It had been a perfect Valentine's Day celebration, and as I let myself back into the house at the end of my run, I knew that I'd never have another to approach it again.

I got into the office, showered, and shaved at seven thirty and checked my messages. Then I opened my first Coke of the day and pulled out a gray legal pad. Twenty minutes later, Maggie walked in, dressed in a navy blue suit with a skirt that reached her knees, a taupe blouse, and dark blue pumps with a medium heel. She shook her head and said, "How can you possibly be drinking that crap at this time of the day?"

"It's the pause that refreshes," I countered. "Besides, it can't be any worse for a person than that coffee you're drinking."

"Richardson," she sighed, "you are fuckin' hopeless."

Pointing at the chart I'd drawn on the legal pad, she said, "What've you got there?"

"So far, nothing at all," I replied. "I'm putting all of the people we identified as McClain's possible targets onto a grid along with their addresses, their roles in his apprehension and prosecution, and whatever other information seems to be relevant. I'm trying to see if there's any pattern that emerges out of the victims he's attacked already. If so, it might point us in the direction of whomever he's going after next."

"And?"

"And nothing," I sighed. "At least not so far. If there is a pattern here, I'm sure as hell not getting it. Why don't we go see Petrovich again?"

Twenty minutes later, a guard brought Petrovich into an interview room at the jail. He took a chair across the table from us and said, "I hear on the news that the guy who prosecuted McClain got himself shot yesterday while I was sitting here in the can. You still think I'm tied up with McClain in all of this?"

"Are you?" Maggie asked.

Petrovich shook his head. "Fuck no. Jesus, what do I have to do to convince you people of that?"

"Well," I said, "you could start by explaining how your hair wound up at two of the crime scenes."

"I wish to God I could," he answered.

I dropped McClain's photo on the table between us. "When you last saw McClain, did he still look like this?"

Petrovich studied the photo for a few moments and then said, "Yeah, only a little thinner." Tapping the picture with his finger, he continued, "He was really heavy when I first met him in the can, but over the last couple of years he dropped a lot of pounds and toned up a bit."

"Did he lose weight in his face?"

"Yeah, his face is definitely thinner now."

"What about the glasses and the hair?" I asked.

Petrovich shrugged. "The same as in the picture, I guess. When he was at my place after he got out, his hair might have been a little longer than it is here, but it's still jet-black, and he's still wearing the same geeky glasses."

"Okay," I said, putting the photo back in its envelope. "We're going to send a police artist over here later this morning. I want you to work with him—help him do some sketches showing what McClain looks like now, with his thinner face."

"And then you'll let me out of here?"

"No," I said as Maggie and I got up from the table. "At least not right away. But you'll be doing a favor for yourself as well as for us, because the sooner we can catch McClain, the sooner we'll have a chance to ask him whether you've been helping him out or not."

CHAPTER THIRTY-NINE

Valentine's Day fell on a Wednesday.

Beverly woke up wearing only the T-shirt. Her panties and the sweatpants were still on the floor where McClain had dropped them the night before. McClain was not in the room, but he hadn't put the cable back on her ankle, and so she assumed that he was still in the house somewhere. She got up and used the bathroom, then dressed again and sat on the bed. Only then did she stop to realize what the date was.

She thought of David and began crying softly. Pushing aside the image of him falling to the floor in the garage, she thought about how sentimental he had always been.

Before meeting David, Beverly had never really cared much about Valentine's Day one way or the other. To her way of thinking, it was just another of those manufactured holidays—like Grandparents Day, or Secretary's Day—that the greeting-card companies, the restaurateurs, and the chocolate makers had invented to pump up their bottom lines.

But for David, it was the real deal. Their first Valentine's Day together had been their fourth date, three years ago now. He'd sent two dozen beautiful red roses to her office, making her the envy of every woman in the place.

Her first reaction was to be a bit put off by it, thinking that he was making a grand gesture just for the sake of impressing her. And in truth, she was a bit disappointed both in him and in herself, because she hadn't judged him to be a guy who would feel compelled to do something like that. That night he had taken her to T. Cook's for dinner, and she'd been all prepared to be cool and distant. But it was immediately apparent that he was completely sincere.

Over cocktails, he'd told her that he hoped he wasn't coming on too strong. The last thing he wanted to do, he said, was to scare her off. But the truth of the matter was that he'd never looked forward so much to a Valentine's Day before. Preparing for the trial, watching her in court, he'd been totally overwhelmed, he told her. He couldn't wait for the trial to end so that he could ask her out, and he was terrified at the prospect that she might say no. He was falling in love with her, he said.

They had slept together for the first time that night. And on each of the next two Valentine's Days, David had sent two dozen red roses to her office and had taken her to dinner at T. Cook's.

Just after nine o'clock, McClain came into the room to find Beverly sitting on the bed, crying. He stood in the doorway for a moment, holding a tray of food in his hands and watching her. Then he looked away and pushed the door nearly closed with his elbow. He set the tray on the table. In addition to the cereal, milk, and orange juice, there was an apple, a banana, and a box of raisins.

Beverly continued to cry, and he handed her the roll of paper towels. She pulled a sheet off the roll, wiped her eyes, and blew her nose. Then she looked up at McClain.

"I have to go out," he said. "I could be gone much of the day, so I left some fruit with your breakfast."

She looked away, refusing even to acknowledge him. He gave her a minute or so and then said, "Come sit on the edge of the bed."

Saying nothing, she turned and dropped her feet to the floor. McClain took the two wrenches out of his back pocket and set them on the floor. From the other back pocket, he produced a white athletic sock. He pulled it onto Beverly's foot then picked up the cable and bolted it around her ankle. He put the tools back in his pocket and looked up to see Beverly staring into her lap, refusing to meet his eyes.

He hesitated for a moment, then said, "I'll see you when I see you."

McClain left the room, bolting the door behind him.

Beverly remained sitting on the bed, clutching the wadded-up paper towel, staring into her lap, and ignoring the breakfast that McClain had set out on the table. Two hours later, it was still sitting there.

CHAPTER FORTY

At eleven o'clock, Maggie and I rang the doorbell at the home of Carl McClain's ex-wife in Fountain Hills. The house was probably worth at least a million five, even given the depressed state of the Valley's current real-estate market. Taking in the view of the surrounding neighborhood, Maggie said, "It looks like the lady did pretty well for herself after she dumped McClain."

"The lady" answered the door wearing sandals, designer jeans and a form-fitting white top. The first thought that crossed my mind was that the guy who'd replaced Carl McClain in her affections was doing pretty well himself. The second thought that crossed my mind was that Carl McClain must have been a total fucking idiot to be out consorting with hookers.

"Mrs. Randolph?" I asked.

The woman acknowledged that she was Mrs. Randolph, and Maggie and I showed her our IDs and badges. Randolph sighed heavily. "Please come in," she said. "I saw the news last night and figured that sooner or later someone would be coming to see me."

Randolph led us into comfortable living room and offered us seats on the couch. She sat on a love seat at a right angle to the couch and leaned forward, resting her forearms on her thighs. Cutting right to the chase, she said, "I assume you're here to talk to me about Carl."

"Yes, ma'am, we are," Maggie responded.

"Well," Randolph said, "all I can tell you is that I haven't seen the guy in seventeen years. And in all that time, I've never heard a word from him, which is fine by me. I wish to hell they'd just left him in prison."

"Well, Mrs. Randolph," I said, "it turns out that he *was* innocent, after all."

She pushed a stray hair back into place and fixed me with deep blue eyes. "Innocent?" she said. "Well, now, that's a relative term, isn't it, Detective Richardson? Carl may not have killed that woman, but he did screw her, if you'll pardon my French. And it's not like she was the first."

She looked away and focused on a spot somewhere in the middle distance. "I was twenty-one years old at the time, with an eighteen-month-old daughter and another baby on the way. We were dirt-poor, living in a ramshackle trailer park like a couple of derelicts, and Carl was working only sporadically, mostly when he felt like it. But he still had money for whiskey and hookers. Christ . . ." she said, her voice trailing away.

"So what did you do, Mrs. Randolph?" Maggie asked sympathetically.

The woman gave a hard, self-deprecating laugh. "I did the only thing I could do, Detective. I scraped up enough money for an abortion. Then I swallowed my pride, packed up my daughter, and went home to my mother. Every day for the next two years, I ate a boatload of crap, listening to my mother say, 'I told you so,' while I went to a community college and tried to save myself.

"I worked hard, got the degree, and managed to get a reasonably decent job. Then I moved myself and my daughter into an apartment of our own and reclaimed my life. Shortly after that, I was lucky enough to meet a man who was the polar opposite of Carl McClain. He married me, adopted my daughter, and has been an absolutely fantastic husband and father in every way. My life was perfect. And then one day I picked up the paper and read that Carl had been released from prison—that he was an 'innocent' man."

"I imagine that must have been quite a shock," I said.

Randolph laughed ruefully. "That's the understatement of the year, Detective."

"And I gather that McClain has not attempted to contact you since his release?"

She shook her head. "No, he hasn't. But then I doubt that he'd know how to find me. My mother was the last link to my former life, and she died eight years ago. I have no friends or acquaintances from the days when I was married to Carl, and I haven't used his name since I divorced him. I went back to my maiden name then, but I haven't used that in the last thirteen years, either."

"Well, still," Maggie said, "if he wanted to find you, it wouldn't be all that hard. Your divorce is a matter of public record, and of course, so is your marriage to Mr. Randolph. We had no difficulty finding you and, I'm sorry to say, neither would McClain."

"I suppose," she sighed. "And my husband and I did discuss the possibility after we saw the news last night. Do you think that we're in danger?"

"We honestly don't know the answer to that, ma'am," Maggie replied. "We have no way of knowing what your former husband is thinking or what he might be planning to do next. But of course, it is possible that he might be angry with you for divorcing him and for cutting off any contact between him and his daughter. You should take precautions just in case."

Randolph nodded wearily. "Yes, I know," she said in a resigned voice. "My husband and I talked about it last night. Our daughter plays softball for ASU and they're on a road trip to Palm Springs starting today.

We decided that we'd fly over and be with her there. My husband had a couple of things to do in his office this morning, and then we'll be going to the airport at noon. We don't plan to be back until Monday. Do you think you can catch Carl between now and then?"

"Well, we're certainly trying our best, Mrs. Randolph," I said. "In all honesty, though, it just depends on what he does over the next few days. If he's out on the streets, someone may recognize him, and we may get him. But if he goes to ground after all the publicity, he may be able to hide indefinitely. Needless to say, though, if he should contact you in any way, be sure to let us know immediately."

"Of course I will," she sighed.

Randolph stared at the floor for another few seconds, then looked back up to meet my eyes. "I know now that Carl didn't kill that woman," she said. "All the same, I sure as hell wish you could have left him right where he was."

CHAPTER FORTY-ONE

McClain left his rented house and headed in the general direction of the Civic Plaza. It was a beautiful morning, sunny and in the low sixties, and he decided that he should be getting out more often at this hour of the day, taking advantage of his freedom and of the great climate at this time of the year.

From Tonto Street, he went left onto First Avenue and then walked ten blocks north to the Wells Fargo bank where he had rented a large safe-deposit box. At the service counter, he signed the ledger as Alan Fischer and wrote in the date, February 14. Only then did he realize that it was Valentine's Day, and only then did he understand the probable reason why Beverly had been so depressed this morning. He shook his head, now feeling a bit depressed himself, and followed the attractive customer-service representative down the hall to the elevators.

The woman escorted him downstairs to the vault. There he handed her his key and waited patiently as she inserted it and the master key into the door fronting his box. The woman stood aside and asked McClain if he'd like to take the box to a private booth. He indicated that he would, and pulled the box out of its slot. The woman led him to an unoccupied booth and left him, saying, "Just let me know when you're ready to put the box back, Mr. Fischer."

"Mr. Fischer" assured her that he would and closed the door of the small cubicle behind him. He then opened the box, which held two additional sets of fake IDs, a handful of keepsakes, and $101,300 in cash.

The money represented the proceeds from the sale of his mother's house. His father had abandoned the two of them when Carl was five, and neither he nor his mother had ever seen or heard from the son of a bitch again. After that, his mother had raised him alone, sometimes working two jobs to make ends meet. She'd managed somehow to hang on to the house in Glendale, and it was the only real home that Carl had ever known.

In his father's absence, Carl became his mother's "little man," and she was the only one who had steadfastly believed in his innocence. Upon his conviction, she'd insisted on taking out a second mortgage on the house to hire a new lawyer and fund an appeal, but Carl had refused. His mother had sacrificed enough on his behalf already, and she'd had precious little to show for it, even before he was arrested and charged with homicide.

When his mother died of a heart attack two years ago, McClain had inherited the house. Through his mother's attorney, he arranged for its sale, and was fortunate enough to sell the house at the peak of the real-estate boom, netting McClain a little over $140,000. He'd used up about $25,000 of the money funding his own appeals before Charlie Woolsey finally copped to the murder of Gloria Kelly and McClain was set free.

Once out of prison, McClain had converted the balance of his inheritance to cash and hidden it from any sort of scrutiny in the safe-deposit box. Using contacts from his prison days, he'd purchased three sets of excellent fake IDs, including that of "Alan Fischer," the one that he'd used to rent the safe-deposit box as well as the house where he was now holding Beverly Thompson. A portion of the remaining money would fund his revenge, and after that, he planned to use the last of the fake IDs and the balance of the cash to start a new life somewhere far from Arizona.

McClain counted out three thousand dollars, figuring that should be enough, and stuffed it into his pocket. Then he dug down into the box and retrieved a small photo of Amanda and Tiffani that had been taken at a studio in a JCPenney store when Tiffani was eight months old.

It had changed him, having a daughter and another child on the way. While he might not have become a model citizen overnight, he had felt a growing sense of responsibility. He'd also developed a newfound appreciation and respect for Amanda, who was now the mother of his daughter and not just some stupid, if attractive, girl he had once conned into bed. He'd understood that it was time for him to get his shit together and face up to his responsibilities. And then something totally stupid like random recreational sex had brought it all to a dismal end.

He spent a couple of minutes studying the picture, then said quietly, "Happy Valentine's Day, girls."

Then he closed up the box, summoned the customer-service representative, and returned the box to the vault.

Three blocks from the bank, McClain stopped in front of a coffee shop, dropped fifty cents into a sidewalk vending machine, and bought a copy of the morning's *Arizona Republic*. Inside, he got a cup of black coffee and took the coffee and the paper to a table in front of the window. He took a sip of the coffee, then opened the *Republic* and read with interest the articles relating to the murder of Harold Roe and the hunt for his suspected killer. Fortunately, the photo of the "suspected killer" looked nothing at all like the current edition of Carl McClain, and satisfied that the police were no closer to finding him than they'd been a week ago, McClain nonchalantly turned to the classifieds and found AUTOMOBILES FOR SALE.

He'd bought the van expressly for the purpose of abducting Beverly Thompson, and it had come in unexpectedly handy when he had no other way to get at the judge. But he figured that he'd have no further use of such a vehicle and so decided to go in an entirely different direction, especially since the cops were now expecting to find him driving a van.

While drinking his coffee, he circled several possibilities. Then he got some change from the girl at the counter and took the paper to a pay phone in the back of the shop. The second call he made was to a woman who'd advertised a seven-year-old Ford Taurus for sale. The woman insisted that the car was in very good shape and explained that she was selling it only so that she could buy a nearly new Mustang convertible from her brother-in-law, who was going into the air force. McClain wrote down the address and told the woman that he'd come by to look at the car in thirty minutes or so.

He found a cab and took it to the address, which was just across the city limits in Glendale. The woman who answered the door was a chunky blonde, twenty-three or four maybe, wearing low-rise jeans and spilling out of a blue halter top. The Taurus was parked at the street—a tired, gray, nondescript car that would vanish perfectly into the sea of vehicles that flooded the Valley's streets and freeways every day.

McClain walked around the car examining it with a critical eye that was intended to suggest that he wasn't all that knocked out by what he was seeing. He noted a couple of dings and scratches, then squatted down and examined the tires, sighing and shaking his head as he ran his fingers over the remaining tread. He stood up, turned to the woman, and said, "How many miles did you say it had on it?"

"Seventy-two thousand," she replied brightly. "Here, you can see for yourself."

She opened the door and leaned into the car, inserting the key into the ignition while exposing a butterfly tattoo at the small of her back and the top of the hot pink thong-style panties that she was wearing under the jeans. Backing out of the car, she invited McClain to sit behind the wheel and start up the engine.

He did so, noting that the mileage was as advertised. The engine ran quietly and smoothly, and McClain observed that the interior, while worn, was still in pretty good shape for a car of its age. The blonde leaned into the window, offering McClain a generous look at her breasts, and said, "So what do you think?"

"Well, it seems okay," he replied. "Can we take it for a test spin?"

The woman readily agreed and jumped in on the passenger's side. McClain drove the car several blocks down the street and back, noting a little play in the steering but detecting no serious problems. He parked back in front of the woman's house and pulled the lever to pop the hood. He stepped around to the front of the car, raised the hood, and pulled out the dipstick. He held it out for the woman to see and said, "Looks like it's been a while since you changed the oil."

She shrugged as if embarrassed. "I've been meaning to, you know, but since I decided to sell it . . ."

She let the sentence hang in the air while McClain replaced the dipstick and dropped the hood. Turning to the woman, he said, "You have a clean title?"

She nodded. "Right in the house, all ready to go. All I have to do is sign it."

"And you're asking twenty-nine hundred?"

"Right."

McClain pulled the roll of bills from his pocket, letting her get a good look. "What would you say to twenty-five hundred, cash on the spot?"

The blonde thought about it for a moment while biting her lower lip. Then she looked up at him and said tentatively, "Could you go twenty-seven?"

McClain shook his head. "I would, except that I'm going to have to replace those tires right away."

She shoved her hands into the back pockets of her jeans, thrusting her chest out and letting him think about it for a minute. Then, when he said nothing more, she shrugged and said, "Okay, twenty-five hundred would be acceptable."

They went into the house and the blonde signed over the title. McClain had her write him a bill of sale as well, and then he counted out the twenty-five hundred. She walked him back out to the Taurus and let him get another good look at her boobs and ass as she collected a few personal belongings from the trunk and the glove box. Then they thanked each other and McClain drove his new car away.

CHAPTER FORTY-TWO

At midmorning on Wednesday, a homeless man who was scavenging in a Dumpster behind a small strip mall discovered the body of an elderly man, wrapped in a canvas tarp. Thankfully, Bob Riggins had returned to work the previous day, and he and Chris Doyle were now working together again. The two of them caught the call, and when they dug the wallet out of the victim's back pocket, Judge Walter Beckman was no longer a missing person. Riggins phoned the news to the lieutenant, and he in turn sent Maggie and me out to join them.

We got to the scene and found the body lying on what appeared to be a painter's tarp next to a large green Dumpster. Bob was questioning the homeless man who'd made the gruesome recovery. The ME was engrossed in his initial examination of the body, and Chris Doyle was leaning his fat lazy ass against the fender of his car, watching the Crime Scene Response team sort through the trash from the Dumpster.

As we walked past Doyle, Maggie said, "Another hard day at the office, huh, Chris?"

Doyle slowly looked her up and down and then said, "Fuck you, McClinton. You still have no idea what being a *real* detective is all about, and there's no way in hell I need to justify my work habits to a rookie like you."

Maggie wisely ignored the jab, and we walked over to join Riggins. Doyle continued to lean against the car, his eyes focused tightly on Maggie's butt as we passed him. I asked Bob what he had, and he sighed. "Not much yet."

Riggins introduced us to Devon Smith, the small black man who'd discovered the body. Smith stood nervously by a shopping cart that he or someone else had liberated from a Basha's supermarket, and which apparently contained all of his earthly possessions. A garbage bag tied to the side of the cart appeared to be about half full of aluminum cans and plastic bottles. Although the temperature was now well up into the seventies, Smith was wearing a blue watch cap, jeans, and a jacket over what appeared to be two or three shirts. He was missing the majority of his teeth, but he appeared to be sane and sober.

Maggie and I acknowledged the introduction, and Riggins said, "Mr. Smith found the body about ninety minutes ago. He checks this Dumpster every other day or so, looking for recyclables. He was last here on Monday about this time, and the Dumpster was only about a quarter full. When he got here this morning, the thing was virtually full, and he found the body about in the middle of the trash. He banged on the back door of one of the shops and told them to call the police."

Smith listened to Riggins's summary and nodded his head. "I pulled that tarp open, 'bout took ten years offa mah damn life. You never seen a man move so fast as me gettin' outta that thing."

Smith had nothing else to offer, and so we turned to the ME, Matt Welser, who estimated that Beckman had been dead for forty to sixty hours. "That's only a rough guess, though," he cautioned. "The fact that the body was wrapped tightly in that tarp, plus the fact that it's been sitting in that Dumpster for some time at least, will raise hell with our effort to determine the precise time of death. But once we get him into the morgue, I'll be able to pin it down a bit more closely for you."

"Any thoughts on the cause of death yet?" I asked.

"No, not yet," he replied. "There's no obvious signs of any trauma—no gunshot wounds, stab wounds, blows to the head, or anything like that. So for the moment, at least, your guess is as good as mine."

Welser signaled the ambulance attendants that they could go ahead and remove the body, and I walked over to Gary Barnett, the lead tech. Talking around the two sticks of gum that substituted for his Marlboros while he was working a crime scene, he said, "The old man who found the body had rearranged the garbage that was on top of it, but we've separated it out and sorted through it.

"We'll be talking to the storekeepers once we've finished, but on the basis of what we've seen so far, it looks like all the garbage that was on top of the body went in starting yesterday morning. The stuff immediately under the body went in late Monday afternoon. So judging by that, it would appear that the body was put into the Dumpster sometime Monday evening."

"That fits with what we've got so far," Maggie sighed. "Beckman was last seen about eleven o'clock on Monday morning. We're assuming that McClain grabbed him as he was leaving the ophthalmologist's office, so he must've killed him sometime that afternoon or early evening, then dumped him here that night."

"That's what it looks like to us," Barnett agreed. "If we find any reason to think otherwise, I'll let you know."

We spent the next couple of hours interviewing the staffs of the stores leasing space in the strip mall where the Dumpster was located, but we learned nothing that was of any help. Only one of the stores stayed open as late as eight o'clock, and no one reported seeing or hearing any abnormal activity in the alley two nights earlier. None of the people we interviewed recognized the photo of Carl McClain, save for having seen it on the news, and none of them remembered seeing a black van in the neighborhood on the night in question.

The alley behind the strip mall butted up against a residential area, and an eight-foot-high cinder-block wall separated the commercial area from the houses. In an effort to cover all the bases, we interviewed the residents who lived immediately on the other side of the wall, but none of them was able to be of any help either. By three o'clock in the afternoon, we were back in the office, no closer to finding Carl McClain than we'd been first thing in the morning.

CHAPTER FORTY-THREE

While serving on the jury that had convicted Carl Mc-Clain, Larry Cullen had made his living selling Chevys. In the seventeen years since, he'd graduated to Cadillacs, and he was now the assistant sales manager at a dealership located in the giant luxury-auto mall on North Scottsdale Road, out near the 101.

Cullen had been more than a little unnerved when detectives Pierce and Chickris dropped by the dealership on Tuesday to tell him that McClain had apparently killed two of the other jurors who'd voted to convict him and that he might have Cullen in his sights as well. The detectives suggested that Cullen think about taking a short vacation. But what with a huge new mortgage, plus the fact that he was paying alimony to two ex-wives, Cullen could hardly afford to take his scheduled one and a half days a week off, let alone think about going on any damn vacation.

He'd asked Pierce and Chickris if the police couldn't

provide him with some sort of protection until they managed to corral McClain, but the detectives explained that, regrettably, that wouldn't be possible. They urged Cullen to be alert to anyone who might be taking an undue interest in his activities, told him to be careful about opening his door to strangers, and wished him good luck.

At two o'clock on Wednesday afternoon, Cullen was sitting at his desk at the dealership, thinking about Carl McClain, when the receptionist buzzed his phone and told him that a customer was asking to see him. Cullen slipped into his sport coat and walked out to the showroom floor. The receptionist pointed him at a tall, well-built man who was examining the sticker in the window of an Escalade.

The customer was wearing sunglasses and a blue blazer over a polo shirt and a pair of gray slacks. A thin mustache echoed the color of his longish gray hair, and Cullen judged the guy to be somewhere in his late forties or early fifties. As Cullen approached, the man turned and extended his hand.

"Mr. Cullen, how are you, sir?"

Cullen couldn't place the guy, but flashed him a well-practiced smile and shook his hand.

"You don't remember me, do you?" the man asked.

"I'm sorry, I don't," Cullen admitted. "Your face is very familiar, though. I know that we've met."

"Don't worry about it," the man said, waving it off. "It's been a while, and I know that in your position you must meet scores of new people all the time. Believe me, I could never remember them all. I'm Dave Lewis. You sold me a Buick four years ago, back when you were still working at the place down on Camelback Road."

"Of course," Cullen said brightly. "I remember now. How are you, Dave?"

"Fine," the man replied. "But I'm in the market for a new car, and I was thinking about moving up to an

STS. I heard that you were up here now, and so I thought I'd come in and see what sort of a deal you might be able to make me."

"Great," Cullen replied, positively beaming. "I really appreciate your thinking of me, Dave. Will you be trading in the Buick?"

The prospect shook his head. "No, Larry, I won't. My youngest daughter is off at college now and she's moving out of the dorm and into an apartment. I'm passing the Buick along to her, which is why I'm in the market. I was hoping maybe you could give me a test drive and then we could talk some numbers."

"I'd love to," Cullen insisted. He pointed to a car immediately outside of the showroom window. "Why don't we take that black one right there? You can put it through its paces and see what you think."

"That'd be great, Larry," the customer said, nodding.

Cullen excused himself long enough to get the keys and a set of dealer plates, then led the guy outside and put him in the driver's seat. Cullen walked around, took the passenger's seat, and spent a few minutes running through the basic features of the STS. Then he said, "Why don't we take her out and see how she feels?"

The prospect started the car and eased it through the lot and out onto Scottsdale Road. "If it's okay with you, Larry," he said, "why don't we take it down the 101 a bit and then make a loop back?"

"That'd be fine," Cullen assured him.

A half mile north of the dealership, the customer turned east onto the 101 and merged into traffic at eighty miles per hour. He complimented the Caddy's acceleration and handling, and Cullen reiterated his earlier observation that the STS was a great road car. He also reminded the prospect that, regrettably, the city of Scottsdale had installed photo radar equipment along this section of the 101 that would trap anyone going more than ten miles an hour over the posted 65 mph speed limit.

The man sighed heavily and backed off to just under seventy-five, muttering about the approach of the total police state in which no one would ever be able to enjoy a moment of privacy again.

"Amen to that." Cullen nodded sympathetically.

The customer took the Pima Road exit and headed south, apparently looking for a through street that would take him back in the general direction of the dealership. Traffic on Pima was relatively light, and a half mile south of the freeway, the customer turned right onto a side street that had been cut in for a future subdivision.

"Oops, I'm sorry, Dave," Cullen said, "but this street doesn't go through."

"So it doesn't," the prospect conceded. "I'll just turn around up here and head on back."

A block later, the street dead-ended in front of a large saguaro cactus, and the customer swung the Caddy into a broad turn, heading east again. Twenty yards back up the street, he pulled in behind a gray Ford Taurus that somebody'd left parked out here in the middle of nowhere. Two hundred yards away, traffic moved up and down Pima Road, and overhead a small corporate jet descended in the direction of Scottsdale Airport. Otherwise, the two cars were surrounded by a small patch of desert that was a year away from being Scottsdale's latest exclusive gated community.

"Is something wrong, Dave?" Cullen asked, suddenly concerned.

"No, not at all, Larry," the prospect assured him. "In fact, everything's just about perfect." The man reached into the left pocket of his blazer and came out with a small pistol.

"What the hell is this?" Cullen blustered. "Are you planning to steal this car?"

"You should be so lucky, Larry," the man laughed.

As Cullen watched, his heart suddenly pounding, the "customer" slowly peeled off his mustache and lifted away the hairpiece he was wearing.

"What the fuck?" Cullen blustered, no longer the eager-beaver salesman.

"What sort of a bullshit artist are you, Larry?" the man asked, as though disappointed. "You never sold me any fuckin' Buick."

"McClain?" Cullen asked tentatively, praying desperately that it wasn't.

"Right you are, Larry," McClain said, smiling.

Cullen flung open the door of the Caddy and swung his legs out to the ground—as if he thought he could outrun a nine-millimeter bullet. McClain fired once, popping the salesman in the back of the head.

Cullen slumped to the ground outside of the car, and McClain got out and checked to make sure that he was dead. Using a handkerchief, he carefully wiped down all of the surfaces that he'd touched on the Caddy. Then he gently closed the passenger's-side door, walked ahead to his Taurus, and drove away, leaving Larry Cullen alone in the desert behind him.

Two cyclists discovered Larry Cullen's body baking in the desert sun beside the STS at four thirty that afternoon. Given that the victim was found within the Scottsdale city limits, the initial investigation fell to the Scottsdale PD. Only when they announced the identity of the victim later that evening did we realize that Carl McClain had apparently settled up with another of the jurors who had sent him to prison.

As the lead investigator for our team, I acted as the liaison with Scottsdale. Their lab sent over the bullet that the ME had recovered from Cullen's body, and our techs quickly confirmed that the slug had been fired from the same weapon used to kill the other victims that we were attributing to Carl McClain. Otherwise, McClain had left the Scottsdale detectives no more evidence to work with than he'd left us.

The receptionist at the auto dealership described the customer who'd driven away with Cullen as a well-dressed middle-aged man with gray hair and a thin mustache. Otherwise, she remembered nothing about him and had paid no attention to him once Cullen had come out to the showroom floor to take the man in hand. The Scottsdale crime-scene techs dusted the car and collected a number of fingerprints. But they reported that most of the area around the driver's seat had been wiped down, and so we assumed that none of the remaining prints would confirm that McClain had actually been in the vehicle.

Counting Beverly Thompson, McClain's list of victims had now grown to seven, and we were no closer to catching the guy than we'd been the night that Robert Fletcher arrived home from work and discovered his wife's body. Using every departmental resource we could spare, we continued to track down all of the reported McClain sightings that had been pouring in from all over the Valley ever since we released his prison mug shot. But none of the reports had panned out.

Given all of that, the mood was decidedly somber when Maggie, Elaine, Greg, and I met with the lieutenant, Riggins, and Doyle in the conference room at eight o'clock that night. Maggie had copied our list of McClain's potential targets onto an erasable board, and as she drew a black line through Larry Cullen's name, we were left with nine jurors, four witnesses, and the two police detectives—Mike Miller and Ed Quigly—who were still alive.

We'd still been unable to locate three of the jurors and one of the witnesses, all of whom had disappeared from the local records. Those names were circled on

Maggie's list, and we hoped that if we couldn't find them, McClain couldn't either. Also on the list were the names of Amanda and Richard Randolph. Maggie had put a question mark after each of their names, given that we weren't certain whether McClain intended to target them or not.

We were all frustrated as hell, and the lieutenant was feeling even more heat from the brass and the politicos higher up the food chain. But as a practical matter we were, for the moment at least, powerless. We knew with some certainty who our killer was and we assumed that we understood his motive. Richard Petrovich had worked with the sketch artist to update McClain's photo, and we'd plastered both McClain's most recent photo and the new sketches all over the newspapers and the airwaves. The local Silent Witness program had offered a generous reward for information leading to McClain's arrest. But until someone actually spotted the guy and gave us a chance to grab him, there was little or nothing more that we could do.

The meeting broke up a little after nine. The lieutenant, Maggie, and Chickris all drifted back to their respective offices, leaving Elaine, Riggins, Doyle, and me in the conference room. While the three of them were finishing their coffees, I continued to contemplate the list Maggie had written on the whiteboard, hoping that some inspiration might magically jump out at me.

Standing next to me, Doyle saw me staring at the list and said, "You know, Richardson, if you'd had a *real* partner when all this shit hit the fan, instead of being saddled with Little Miss Affirmative Action, you might not still be sitting here with your thumb up your ass and this McClain guy running circles around you."

I was simply too damned tired and frustrated to argue with the stupid shit, but I turned, looked up at him, and said, "What—you mean a real partner like you, maybe? Christ, Doyle, if you were responsible for this case, we still wouldn't have the slightest damn clue what was going on here, and probably never would. As for McClinton—hell, she's only been in the squad for seven months and already she's four times the homicide detective you ever were or ever will be."

"Well, naturally you would say that," he sneered. "Tell me, Richardson—are you even gonna wait for them to take your old lady off life support before you take a shot at McClinton? Or are you banging her already?"

I was out of the chair before I could even stop to think, and an instant later my right fist smashed into Doyle's face. He dropped to the floor, hemorrhaging blood from his nose. After a couple of moments, he shook his head as if trying to clear the cobwebs and stammered, "What the fuck?"

I stepped over him, still seething, and said, "Listen, you contemptible son of a bitch. If you *ever* say anything like that to me again, I'll beat you within an inch of your worthless fuckin' life. And if you're man enough to want to do anything about this, we can go down to the parking lot right now."

Stunned, Chickris, Pierce, and Riggins stood frozen in place, looking back and forth from Doyle to me and back to Doyle again. Doyle made no effort to get up off the floor, and finally Elaine moved over, took me gently by the elbow, and guided me out of the room. "It'd probably be a good idea for you to go on home now, Sean," she said. "Riggins, Chickie, and I will clean up the mess."

Chapter Forty-four

Beverly was sitting on the bed when McClain unlocked the door a little after six o'clock and walked into the room carrying a shopping bag and his two wrenches. He set the shopping bag on the floor and Beverly turned, swinging her legs off the bed. McClain squatted in front of her and unbolted the hinge, releasing her from the cable. He gently pulled off the athletic sock, and cupping her heel in his hand, he examined her ankle. "That's looking better," he observed, "but you'll want to put some more lotion on it."

Releasing her foot, he picked up the shopping bag and held it out to her. "It occurred to me that you maybe might like something to read, and so while I was out this afternoon, I stopped by a Borders and picked up a few things."

"Thank you," she replied. "I appreciate it."

McClain stood by the bed and watched as she opened the bag and pulled out several books and magazines. He'd bought a *Newsweek* and an *Atlantic Monthly*, as well as paperback novels by Lawrence Block, Robert B. Parker, Sue Grafton, and Nick Hornby. "I didn't know what you might like," he said tentatively, "but I hope there's something in there that will appeal to you. If not, you can give me some ideas for the next time I'm out."

"These look fine," she said. "I've read a couple of these authors before, and I've enjoyed them. Thanks."

"You're welcome," he said. "I'll go get to work on dinner."

McClain walked toward the door. As he reached it, he turned back to Beverly. "I got a bottle of wine to go with dinner. Would you like a glass while you're waiting?"

"Yes, please," she replied.

McClain drew the door closed behind him without locking it. A couple of minutes later, he returned with the bottle of lotion and a glass of chilled white wine. "It's a Pinot Grigio," he said. "To be honest, I don't know a lot about wine, but the guy at the store said that it should go well with the dinner."

Beverly nodded. "Thank you, Carl. Actually, Pinot Grigio is one of my favorite wines."

"Good," he said, smiling almost shyly. "Dinner'll be ready in about thirty minutes."

With that he left the room again, leaving the door ajar about six inches. Beverly waited until she heard him moving about in the kitchen, then got up from the bed, went quietly into the bathroom, and poured three-quarters of the wine down the sink. Then she sat back down on the edge of the bed, shaking her head in amazement.

He picked today, of all days, to bring her presents and wine? Did the despicable bastard really think that they were going to celebrate Valentine's Day together? Was he completely deranged?

But this, after all, was what she'd been aiming for—some sort of reverse Stockholm syndrome in which her captor developed an emotional attachment to his hostage.

After her outburst on the second night of the ordeal, Beverly had forced herself to be pleasant, submissive, and nonconfrontational, and the effort had required virtually every last ounce of strength and self-discipline that she possessed.

She'd now faked three orgasms during his sexual

assaults, hoping to convince McClain that she was bonding to him against her will. That, of course, had been the most difficult and most disgusting part of her battle. She hated herself for betraying David and for allowing an animal like McClain to think that he could conquer her and that he could make her respond to him in such an intimate way.

Rationally, she knew that she had no choice, and she also knew that David would have understood—that he would have expected and encouraged her to do everything in her power to survive and to see McClain punished. Still, she felt as if she were conspiring with McClain in her own violation and in her own diminution as a human being. And she realized that if her ordeal lasted too much longer, McClain *would* win his revenge no matter how it ended. Even if she did somehow manage to survive, she would have debased herself to such an extent that any life she might have in the wake of the experience would be worthless.

On the positive side, though, McClain seemed to be buying into the illusion she was attempting to create. He had definitely softened in his treatment of her, as evidenced by the new clothes, her occasional freedom from the cable, the lotion, and now the books, magazines, and wine. But how far had he really come?

Beverly was certain that McClain's initial plan had been that he would ultimately kill her, and she had little doubt that he still intended to do so. When she'd braced him with it the other night, he'd been evasive, insisting that was still to be determined. But realistically, she couldn't imagine a scenario in which he would leave her alive to identify him and testify to his crimes.

She could only hope that she might be able to soften him enough to make him vulnerable somehow—that he might get careless and make even a small mistake that would allow her a chance to survive and see him punished. And that slim, desperate hope was the only thing now keeping her alive.

Beverly could no longer imagine what sort of life, if any, might exist for her even if she were to survive this horrible nightmare. And she realized that in an odd sense, she and McClain were now united in an unlikely communion: each of them was now willing to sacrifice everything to avenge an injustice that life had dealt to them. In the end, only one of them could succeed, and Beverly was now more determined than ever that it would not be Carl McClain.

She picked up the Lawrence Block novel and the glass of wine, moved over, and took her usual seat at the card table, facing the door. McClain was still making noises out in the kitchen. Could he see the bedroom door from there?

Beverly set the paperback and the wine on the table. Listening carefully, she got up and moved toward the door. She stood for a moment, her hand on the doorknob, then tentatively peeked around the door and out into the hall.

McClain's backpack was sitting on the floor again, and the kitchen noises were coming from down the hall to Beverly's right. Without opening the door any farther, she looked up at the hook that was screwed into the outside of the door. A two-foot length of cable, like the one McClain used to tether her to the floor, hung from the top of the doorframe. The cable had a small loop in the end and was long enough to reach the hook in the door itself. But the cable was simply screwed into the top of the doorframe; it was not attached to any explosive device. The clicking she heard when McClain locked the bedroom door each day was nothing more than a sound effect.

From the kitchen, Beverly heard the radio playing

softly, tuned again to a classic-rock station. Above the
music, something suddenly began to sizzle as McClain
apparently dropped a piece of meat into a sauté pan.
Cautiously, she pulled the door open a bit farther and
looked out into the hallway. Beverly could hear Mc-
Clain working in the kitchen, but from this vantage
point, she could not actually see into the room. Beyond
the kitchen, at far the end of the hallway to her right,
was a closed door that might lead to—what?—a utility
room, or perhaps a garage?

Beverly held her breath and stepped out into the
hall, praying that in her bare feet, she would not make
any noise that McClain might hear above the sounds
he was making in the kitchen. A few feet down the hall
on her left, a door opened into a second, smaller bedroom. The room was empty of furniture, save for a
dresser and a chair. McClain had tossed a pair of jeans
over the back of the chair, and several T-shirts were
folded and neatly stacked on top of the dresser.

Across the hall from the second bedroom was the
bathroom that McClain was using for himself. A razor
and a variety of toiletries were organized around the
sink, and a number of magazines were stacked on top
of the toilet tank. Beverly stepped into the bathroom
and took a quick inventory, but she saw nothing that
might serve as a weapon.

In the kitchen a small hand mixer whined into action. Hoping desperately that McClain would be oc-
cupied for another couple of minutes, Beverly stepped
out of the bathroom and looked to her right, where
the hallway led into the living room. From the hallway, she could see a tattered couch and an easy chair
that faced out into the room.

She realized that, logically, there should be a door
leading out of the house somewhere at this end of the
structure, most likely from the living room itself. But
did she dare try to reach it? If she did, would the door

be locked? If it wasn't, could she open the door quietly enough so that McClain would not hear her? And if she could get through the door, would she have any realistic chance of making good her escape before McClain discovered her missing and came tearing after her in hot pursuit?

Beverly well understood that if McClain caught her outside of the bedroom, every effort she had made and every indignity that she had endured in her campaign to soften him up would have been for naught. He would tie her to the cable for good, and she had no doubt that he would punish her brutally. But she also understood that this might well be the only opportunity she would ever have to effect an escape.

In the kitchen, the mixer continued to whine. Beverly took a deep breath, then took three steps into the living room. A small television set sat on the wall opposite the easy chair, and ten feet away, at the other end of the living room, was the front door.

It looked like McClain was preparing for a siege. He'd nailed a two-by-four across the door, effectively sealing it shut. Four feet back from the door, he'd nailed another two-by-four into the floor, and he'd jammed a third piece on an angle between the door and the board on the floor, bracing the door. Beverly realized that it would be impossible for anyone to push the door open from the outside. From the inside, you'd have to have a pry bar and a hammer to disassemble the defenses that McClain had constructed.

Beverly's heart sank as she realized that McClain must be entering and leaving the house through a door at the back or on the side of the house. But where was that door in relationship to the kitchen? Could she have any chance of reaching it without him seeing her? And if so, would she find it locked and barricaded as well?

In the kitchen, the mixer suddenly stopped and Beverly heard the sound of McClain's footsteps walking out of the kitchen and into the hall. Her heart suddenly racing, she looked desperately around the small living room but saw no place to hide. As McClain's footsteps drew closer, she pressed herself back against the wall next to the television set. Cursing herself for having been so foolish, she waited for the inevitable explosion when McClain walked into the bedroom to serve dinner and discovered that she wasn't there.

McClain had discarded a couple of empty beer bottles in a wastebasket next to the television set. Moving as quietly as she could, Beverly reached down and picked one of the bottles out of the basket. Gripping the bottle by the neck, she held it behind her back in her right hand, hoping that when McClain tore into the living room looking for her, she might be able to get in one miraculously lucky blow that would disable him at least momentarily.

The house fell suddenly quiet, save for the sound of the radio in the kitchen, and Beverly imagined McClain standing in the door of the bedroom, perhaps holding their dinners in his hands, and suddenly realizing that she wasn't in the room. She swallowed hard and braced herself so that she could push away from the wall and spring at McClain the moment he rushed into the living room. But then she heard the door to the second bathroom screech on a protesting hinge before bumping closed.

Beverly held her position for another couple of seconds, every nerve in her body pulsing in fear. Then she forced herself to step away from the wall and peek out into the hall. The bathroom door was tightly closed and from inside the small room, Beverly could hear water running into the sink. She gently set the beer bottle back into the wastebasket and took a deep breath. Then, again on her tiptoes, she raced down the hall past the bathroom and into the bedroom. When McClain walked through the bedroom door two and a half minutes later, he found Beverly sitting at the card table, the glass of wine in her hand, as she read the opening pages of the Lawrence Block novel.

Tonight's dinner was chicken again. McClain had sautéed chicken breasts and seasoned them lightly with lemon and herbs. He'd mashed Yukon Gold potatoes and steamed some fresh green beans. This was apparently his favorite vegetable, but they were done perfectly tender-crisp and seasoned with lemon and butter.

He brought in the bottle of wine and filled Beverly's glass to a third full. He then poured himself a few ounces and set the bottle on the table. "I intended to make another salad," he said, "but the lettuce had started to fade on me. I'm sorry. I should have checked it before I left. I made extra potatoes and beans to make up for the lack of a salad."

"That's fine," Beverly said. "You needn't apologize. It looks great."

She cut a small piece of her chicken breast and ate it. It was done exactly right—moist, tender, and seasoned perfectly. "Again," she said, truthfully, "this is really very good. Can I ask where you learned to cook so well?"

McClain flushed. "In the joint," he said in a self-deprecating tone. "My mom was a great cook—one of those people who never used a recipe and who could create a fantastic meal out of whatever she happened to have on hand at the time. I never really paid much attention to how she did it. I guess I just assumed that all women cooked like that. Then I got married and found out that all women *didn't* cook like that. At least Amanda sure as hell didn't."

Toying with his wine glass, he seemed lost in reverie for a moment. Then he gave Beverly a small, sad smile. "God knows, the girl was fun to hang out with, and she was great in the sack. But put her in the kitchen and she didn't know shit from Shinola.

"The food was even worse in the joint, of course—lots of starches, mystery meat, and canned vegetables. In Lewis most of us had jobs, and after a while, I wound up working in the kitchen. Four years ago we got a new warden, and he had the bright idea of introducing a culinary program. He figured that teaching cons how to cook would give them a marketable skill when they went back out into the world. He also hoped it might improve the quality of the food in the prison mess and reduce at least some of the bitching about the meals.

"Of course, what the warden didn't realize is that seventy-five percent of good cooking is shopping. And as long as we were getting lousy raw ingredients, the end result wasn't all that much better. But at least some of us who enrolled in the program learned a few basic principles."

Beverly swallowed some potatoes. "I hope you don't think I'm saying this just to humor you, Carl, but you do seem to have a real knack for this. Obviously you must have inherited a considerable amount of your mother's natural talent. Once you learned you were going to be freed, didn't you ever think about the prospect of trying to find a job in a restaurant somewhere and creating a new life for yourself?"

McClain took a sip of wine and looked over the top of his glass to meet her eyes. "Easier said than done, Beverly," he sighed. "And as I said, I had other plans."

He hesitated for a moment, toying with the wineglass. "Perhaps after what I've put you through over the last week or so, you can begin to get some small, tiny glimmer of understanding of what I went through in prison. Imagine this last week stretching out for the next sixteen years and thirty-three weeks. As angry as you are right now, imagine the rage you'd feel at the end of that time.

"You think you're an innocent woman. You think that you don't remotely begin to deserve what's happened to you here. Some sick bastard's murdered your husband, kidnapped you, and has forced you to have sex with him repeatedly. You probably figure that you're going to die here in this room.

"Well, goddammit," he said, warming to the topic, "that's exactly how I felt. *I* was an innocent man, Beverly. The system sent me to prison for something I didn't do. I lost my wife, and although she didn't physically die, she was sure as hell dead to me. She gave up on me the second I was arrested, and I haven't heard a word from her since. And yeah, she probably had some cause to do it, but in spite of the way I behaved, I loved her."

He hesitated for a long moment, staring at the floor. Then, still without looking up at Beverly, he said, "She took my daughter away from me and she killed my baby . . . She was pregnant when I was arrested, and she got an abortion . . . For some reason, I always think of it as a boy. He'd be sixteen now, and I used to lie awake nights thinking about the things we might have done together, playing ball, going to the games, all that sort of father-and-son shit . . .

"As for the rest of it . . . well . . . you knew me when, Beverly. I went into the pen a fat, pudgy boy who had no idea how to fend for himself in the system. I was new meat, and it wasn't pretty."

Again he paused, pushing a couple of green beans around on his plate. Finally he looked up at her, his eyes harder now. "So like I say, Beverly, imagine the prospect of spending the rest of your life in here—in this room, with me. Then imagine that one day after seventeen years have passed, I walk in and say, 'Jesus, Beverly, I'm really sorry. I made a terrible mistake, and I'm letting you go . . .' You're telling me you could just shake hands and walk away—forgive and forget? Let bygones be bygones, and all that shit?"

"No, of course not," she said, tearing up. "And I truly am sorry for what you went through. And whether you believe it or not, I'm especially sorry that I didn't do a better job for you. You didn't deserve what happened to you, and I can only say again that I tried as hard as I could for you."

Looking up to meet his eyes, she said, "But there is a fundamental difference in our situations, Carl. You *know* that I'm an innocent person, as were the judge, the prosecuting attorney and the jurors who combined to send you to prison. You *know* that while we participated in what ultimately proved to be a gross miscarriage of justice, we did not do so deliberately. We were all doing the best that we could.

"I will tell you honestly that at the time of the trial I didn't know whether you were innocent or not. I *hoped* that you were, but irrespective of that, I believed that like anyone else accused of a crime, you had a constitutional right to the best representation you could get. And whether you believe it or not, that's what I honestly tried to give you.

"As for the others—the prosecutor, the judge, and the jurors—they had no way of knowing whether you were innocent or not. They could only go where the evidence led them. And in fairness, certainly, you have to concede that there was a considerable amount of evidence against you. If they had known absolutely that you were innocent, as you know that they were—if they'd even had a reasonable doubt—then they would have never condemned you to that hell."

A long moment passed. Then, still toying with his wine glass, McClain offered her a remorseful smile. "You know, Beverly," he said sadly, "you're a much better lawyer today than you were seventeen years ago. If I'd of had a lawyer that good back then, I doubt very much that we'd be sitting here having this conversation tonight."

CHAPTER FORTY-FIVE

Leaving Doyle still lying on the floor behind me, I left the building immediately, pausing only long enough to grab my suit coat from my office and lock the door.

I knew that I was going to be in deep shit for punching out Doyle—almost certainly I was facing a suspension and disciplinary action. I deeply regretted the former, and could only hope that whatever punishment I'd face would at least be delayed until after the McClain case was resolved. But I did not for a moment regret reacting as I had in response to Doyle's crude remark. The bastard had gotten exactly what he deserved, and no matter the consequences, I'd never apologize for giving it to him.

I sat in my car for a couple of minutes, taking deep breaths in an effort to get my emotions back under control. Then I started the car and drove over to the florist's shop, arriving only minutes before they closed. I'd placed an order for a dozen yellow roses, and the shop had created a beautiful arrangement. I paid the bill gratefully and continued on to the nursing home.

Given the holiday, the place was a bit more active than it usually was at this time of night. I nodded at a couple of familiar faces, went through the doors and on up to the second floor. The receptionist on duty smiled with a hint of sadness and said, "That's a very nice arrangement, Detective."

I thanked her and continued on down the hall to Julie's room. Someone had left the overhead lights on and the room was almost painfully bright. Julie lay on the bed, dressed in a long blue gown, covered only by a thin white sheet that was folded back just above her waist. As they did every day, one of the nurses had carefully brushed Julie's hair, which was parted in the middle and arranged down over her shoulders, framing her face.

In this light, I was always struck by how pale she'd become. Julie had always been very active and had spent a great deal of time outdoors, running, hiking, and golfing. Although she used sunscreen religiously, for as long as I had known her she'd always had a fairly deep tan. But in the months since the accident, her tan had gradually faded and had given way to the complexion I now imagined that she'd possessed as a young girl in Minnesota.

I turned off the overhead lights and set the roses on the dresser at the foot of the bed. I kissed Julie's cheek, quietly wished her a happy Valentine's Day, and then settled into the chair next to the bed. I sat there for the next hour, softly stroking Julie's hand and thinking about the holidays we'd spent together in happier times.

I was lost in my reverie when the overhead light suddenly snapped on again. I turned, blinking my eyes against the harsh light, and saw my mother-in-law standing in the doorway, conservatively dressed and meticulously made up as always, with a floral arrangement of her own—carnations again.

"I didn't see your car in the lot," she said in the tone of voice she seemed to reserve exclusively for me. "I didn't know if you were coming up today or not."

I gently laid Julie's hand back on the bed, dropped my head into my hands, and massaged my eyes. Then I turned back to Elizabeth and said, "You didn't know if I was coming up today or not? Jesus Christ, Elizabeth, I've been here at some point every day for the last eighteen months. Why in the hell would you think that I would ever miss a day—especially this day?"

"Well, I know that you're very busy with your investigations and all. I have no idea what your schedule is like these days."

"Elizabeth, you know damn good and well that no matter how full my schedule might be, it would never prevent me from being here."

"Well, I wouldn't know about that," she replied stiffly. "I only know that if you had your way, you wouldn't have to come here at all."

Several months ago, when she'd first made a remark of that sort, I'd come very close to punching her lights out. But I realized that as satisfying as it might have been to do so on some primitive level, it would have solved nothing. And I also realized that there was no point in rising to her bait. I stood from the chair and said, "Elizabeth, you're welcome to your pathetic delusions, but I refuse to fight with you in front of Julie."

I turned back to the bed, kissed Julie's cheek, then straightened and turned to leave. But Elizabeth stood in the door, effectively blocking my path. "I'd prefer not to have to fight with you in front of my daughter either," she said. "And on that note, I have something that I wanted to discuss with you—something that I've been thinking about for the last several weeks."

"And what would that be?"

She paused for a long moment and then steeled her eyes on mine. "I'd like to move Julie to a facility back home in Minnesota."

I was thunderstruck. As audacious and combative as the woman had been in the last eighteen months, nothing that she'd done or said could possibly have prepared me for this. Shaking my head, I returned her stare and said, "Elizabeth, I'll say this very slowly and clearly, so that even you can understand it. No. Fucking. Way."

She sighed impatiently and shook her head. "Honestly, Sean, you surprise me."

Gesturing toward the machine that was "feeding" Julie, she said, "You're so anxious to end all of this that I would think you'd welcome the idea. The responsibility would be lifted from your shoulders. You wouldn't have to feel obligated to come in here every day, and Julie would receive much better care at home than she could ever get here."

"Elizabeth, you are so full of crap that I don't even know how to begin to reply. You know perfectly well that the only reason I want to 'end all of this' is because that's what Julie would have wanted. And if you'd spent any time at all with your daughter in the last five years, you would also understand that. As hard as it might be, I am determined to honor her wishes. And if you were any kind of a mother, you'd drop this stupid lawsuit, which you know you'll never win, and honor her wishes as well.

"Even so, if I thought for a moment that there was even the smallest chance that Julie would be better cared for in Minnesota—or anywhere else, for that matter—I would move her there in a heartbeat. But that is not the case and I won't even consider the idea, let alone consent to it."

She pursed her lips and nodded. "Well, Sean, I'm sorry you feel that way, but you may not have a choice in the matter."

Struggling to maintain control, I took a deep breath and said, "I have every choice in the matter, Elizabeth. No matter how much you might hate the idea, I am still Julie's husband, and no court in Arizona will ever allow you to move her without my consent."

"Perhaps not," she admitted. "But how long will you be able to afford to keep Julie in this facility if her family withdraws its financial support? And when you can't afford to do so, where will she go—to a ward in some county facility, where she'll be tended—or more likely, largely ignored—by a staff that's barely trained, underpaid, and completely unmotivated? Is that where you want to see her end up?"

"Look, Elizabeth," I sighed. "As I've said repeatedly, in spite of all our other differences, I am truly grateful for the assistance that you and John have provided in that regard. That said, none of this would be necessary if you had not ignored Julie's clearly expressed wishes about living under these conditions. Beyond that, I have to say that I honestly cannot believe that a woman who is as devoted as you are to her social standing would ever allow her daughter to languish in circumstances like the ones you've just described. Christ, what would all the society matrons back in Minneapolis ever think about you if you did?

"However, if you wish to withdraw your financial support, so be it. I'll sell the house. I'll borrow money. I'll do *whatever* it takes to see that Julie is cared for in circumstances that are as dignified and as comfortable as possible until the courts finish stuffing this ridiculous lawsuit up your tight, bony ass and Julie can finally rest in peace."

Elizabeth's mouth dropped open and she struggled to formulate a response. But before she could, I stepped around her and left the room without another word.

CHAPTER FORTY-SIX

It was seven minutes after midnight when Natasha Williamson stepped into the elevator on the third floor of the Hayden Memorial Hospital. Natasha hated working the three-to-eleven-o'clock shift, and she hated it even more when she had to put in an extra hour of overtime because the nurse who was supposed to relieve her showed up late for the second time in the last two weeks.

The woman always had an excuse at the ready—her babysitter didn't get there on time, her car wouldn't start, or some other damned thing. But Natasha was fairly certain that the attractive young woman had more than likely just been an hour late getting out of some brother's bed again.

Natasha hadn't been decently laid herself in longer than she cared to remember. And even the fact that she got time and a half for working the overtime wasn't compensation enough to offset the fact that she had to spend an extra hour on her tired, aching feet so that some horny little girl could spend an extra hour on her back somewhere.

Natasha leaned heavily against the side wall of the elevator and pushed *P*. The doors were nearly closed when a man stuck his hand in between them, tripping the sensor and forcing the doors to open again. He slipped into the elevator, gave Natasha a slight smile, and said, "Thanks."

The man was around six feet tall and fairly well muscled, wearing jeans, running shoes, and a navy blue T-shirt. He settled against the back wall of the elevator and made no move toward the control panel, simply watching as Natasha pressed *P* for the second time.

The elevator doors closed with a soft hiss, and Natasha turned to face the front of the car. Keenly aware of the man's presence behind her, she watched the indicator above the doors as the elevator dropped slowly from the third floor down through the second and then through the first before settling to a stop in the parking garage in the basement of the building.

Natasha stepped out of the elevator, clutching her purse in front of her. The man waited a couple of seconds and then stepped off behind her. The elevator doors hissed closed again, and the two of them were alone in the half-empty garage.

The floor of the garage was littered with fast food bags, coffee cups, cigarette butts, and other assorted debris that people apparently couldn't hang on to long enough to deposit in the trash can near the elevator doors, and the low ceiling and the dim yellow lights made the subterranean structure feel decidedly claustrophobic. Quickening her pace a bit, Natasha turned left toward the employees' parking area, where she'd left her battered Ford. Over her shoulder, she saw the man turn to follow her.

Her heart racing, Natasha looked left and right, trying to appear casual about it, but she couldn't see anyone else in the garage. A hundred feet ahead of her, the security guard's post stood dark and empty, another casualty of the hospital's ongoing budget crisis.

Seventeen years ago, when Natasha was called for jury duty, she'd been a twenty-four-year-old welfare mother with no legitimate excuse for failing to report. Fearful that she might lose her benefits if she didn't show up, she'd spent two days sitting in the jury pool at the courthouse before being selected to serve in the murder trial of Carl McClain.

Natasha had never seen a dead person before, except for going to her grandma's funeral, and the crime-scene photos of Gloria Kelly, the clothesline still tight around her throat, her eyes bugging out, and her face contorted in horror, had made Natasha physically ill. She'd had no problem whatsoever voting to convict McClain, and for years after the trial, the face of that poor dead woman had haunted her sleep.

All of that was behind her now, or so she'd thought until detectives Riggins and Doyle had interrupted her in the middle of her shift on Tuesday. They'd shown her a photo and some artist's sketches and warned her to be careful. And now, barely twenty-four hours later, a man looking a lot like the one in the sketches was matching her pace, step for step, through the empty parking garage.

On the street above the garage, a vehicle squealed by. Natasha begged God that a car would drive down the ramp ahead of her or that someone else would appear from the bank of elevators behind her. Thirty-five feet away from her car and still holding the large purse in front of her body, she opened the purse and began fumbling for her keys.

Twenty feet short of the Ford, she chanced a look over her shoulder and saw that the man was moving faster now, closing the distance between them. Her heart racing, she found the keys and broke into a trot. From behind her, she heard the man say, "Excuse me, ma'am?"

Panicked, Natasha dropped the keys back into the bottom of the purse and wrapped her hand around the grip of the small .22-caliber revolver that she carried because it made her feel safer when she had to drive home alone at this hour of the night. Her hand shaking, she somehow managed to cock the gun and draw it out of the purse.

The man was less than five feet behind her when Natasha turned and shot him twice in the abdomen.

CHAPTER FORTY-SEVEN

The lieutenant woke me out of a fitful sleep just after one A.M. to tell me that a man tentatively identified as Carl McClain had been shot and was in the emergency room at Hayden Memorial. I dressed quickly, slammed the bubble light onto the dashboard of my Chevy, and raced to the hospital. Fifteen minutes after getting the call, I left my car in a no-parking zone near the ambulance entrance to the emergency room and ran inside.

The victim was still in surgery. The nurse at the desk could tell me nothing about his condition and had no idea how long the surgery might last. Two hospital security guards were on duty at the door to the room where the victim was being treated. I instructed them not to leave the post under any circumstances, except that one of them should come and find me the instant there was any news about the patient's condition.

The city patrolman who'd originally responded to the call had isolated the shooter in a room on the first floor. "A doctor and a nurse are in there with her," he said, pointing at the closed door. "She was pretty shook-up."

"What the hell happened?"

"I'm not for sure myself. The lady was basically incoherent when I talked to her. She's a nurse who'd just gotten off of work. A couple of minutes after she left, she came running back into the building, screaming that Carl McClain had followed her down the elevator and into the parking garage and that she'd shot him. She still had the gun in her hand. She gave it to the ER security guard, and he called nine-one-one. I was the first to respond, and the guard gave the gun to me. I called for backup. Two more squads arrived and sealed the scene down in the parking garage."

"Where's the gun now?"

"Here," he said, handing me a white paper bag that might once have contained somebody's lunch. "I didn't touch the gun myself. I dropped it into the bag using a pen in the barrel. But the stupid security guard had his paws all over it before I could tell him not to. Sorry."

"Not your fault," I said, shaking my head. "Don't leave this spot until I tell you to do so."

The patrolman nodded and I tapped once on the door, then opened it and walked into a conventional hospital room with two twin beds and the usual accompanying furniture. A black woman wearing blue nurse's scrubs lay on the bed closest to the door. She was fortyish, a little overweight, and shaking as if she were freezing to death. A nurse sat on the far side of the bed, using a soothing voice in an effort to calm the woman.

A young man in green hospital scrubs, whom I assumed to be a resident, was taking the woman's pulse. He finished, laid her arm down on the bed, and walked over to the door. I showed him my badge and said, "Doctor, what's her condition?"

"She's terrified, but otherwise unhurt. She seems to be calming down a bit, but I may have to give her a sedative. The patrolman asked me to hold off until a detective could arrive, but I need to stay here and monitor her condition while you talk to her. If she gets too upset, I'll have to insist on sedating her."

I nodded and walked over to the bed. The woman watched my approach with wide eyes and gripped the hand of the nurse who was sitting beside her. The woman was still wearing her employee's badge, and using my most sympathetic voice, I said, "Can you tell me what happened tonight, Ms. Williamson?"

Tears began rolling down her cheeks. She looked at me, swallowed hard, and said, "I served on the jury that convicted Carl McClain. When I got off work tonight, he followed me down into the garage. I tried to get into my car to get away, but he was too fast. I didn't have time. All I could do was shoot him."

She began crying harder. I waited for a moment and then said, "How did you know it was McClain, Ms. Williamson?"

The woman sniffled, blinking her eyes to stem the tears. "Two detectives came by yesterday and showed me a picture and some drawings. I recognized him off of one of the drawings."

"You say he followed you into the garage. Did he have a weapon?"

She shook her head. "I don't know . . . Not that I could see."

"What did he say—did he threaten you?"

Again she shook her head and then nodded yes. "He followed me out of the elevator toward my car. When I tried to walk faster, he walked faster too, getting closer to me. When I got to my car, he tried to stop me."

"Stop you how, ma'am?"

"I don't remember how exactly. He said, 'Wait a minute,' or something like that. I turned and he was right behind me, getting ready to grab me. That's when I shot him. It was all I could do."

Williamson shook her head and began sobbing harder. The nurse squeezed her hand, promising that everything would be all right, and at that point the young doctor stepped in. "I'm sorry, Detective, but I think that's all she can stand for the moment. I'm going to sedate her and you can talk to her again in the morning."

I nodded. "Okay, Doctor, but we'll be posting a guard at her door and she won't be able to leave until we've had a chance to talk with her further."

I walked back down to the emergency room and found Maggie racing through the lobby door. She was dressed in jeans and had thrown a blue blazer on over a white T-shirt. She'd not taken the time to apply any makeup, and her hair was a bit more tousled than usual. But as was almost always the case, she still somehow managed to be the most attractive woman in the room, even fresh out of bed at one forty-five in the morning.

I caught her up, and just as I finished, a doctor in bloody scrubs emerged from the hall leading to the operating room. We identified ourselves, and I asked him how the patient was doing.

"Better than expected, I would say," the doctor sighed. "Fortunately, he was shot with a small-caliber gun that didn't do nearly as much damage as a larger weapon would have done. Also, miraculously, neither of the bullets hit any major arteries or seriously damaged any vital organs. He's sedated of course, and he's going to hurt like hell for a while, but he should eventually make a full recovery."

"Can we at least take a look at him?" Maggie asked.

"Not at the moment, Detective. As I say, he's sedated and he's not going to have anything to say for a while. You can see him in the morning."

Glancing at the nameplate on the guy's left breast pocket, I said, "Look, Dr. Nauman, the man you're treating in there has been identified as a suspect in six homicides and a kidnapping. The kidnapping victim is still missing, and obviously, time is of the essence here. We understand that we can't talk to the man now, but we need to begin the process of establishing his identity immediately.

"If this is our suspect, we'll need to question him at the earliest opportunity. If he isn't, then we've got to know that immediately too so that we're not sitting here twiddling our thumbs while the real killer is still out there at large in the community."

Nauman nodded and said, "Okay, you can take a quick look, but that's all I can allow at this point."

He led us through the door and down the hall to the recovery room. He pulled back a curtain to reveal a man lying on a bed, attached to a variety of monitors and to a drip line that was pumping some sort of clear solution into his system. The victim appeared to be in his early forties and in good physical shape, save of course for the two bullets he'd just taken in the gut.

I guessed him to be about six feet and perhaps a

hundred and ninety pounds. He had dark wavy hair that fell down across his forehead like a reverse comma and a fading tattoo on his arm that read SEMPER FI.

I turned to Nauman and said, "Where are his clothes and personal effects?"

"In there," he answered, pointing to a large black plastic bag under the bed. "Everything's there except for the T-shirt he was wearing. We had to cut it off, and we simply threw it away."

I retrieved the bag and carried it over to a chair at the foot of the bed. I opened the bag and found myself looking at a pile of bloody clothes. Lying on top of the clothes was a pair of glasses with dark brown frames.

I asked Nauman for a pair of surgical gloves and another bag. I laid the glasses on top of the second bag and then pulled a pair of jeans out of the first. The front of the jeans was drenched in blood and I turned them around and retrieved a wallet from the back pocket. I dropped the jeans back into the bag and opened the wallet.

According to the driver's license, which had been issued two years earlier, the man lying on the bed behind me was Daniel Foster, a forty-two-year-old resident of Cave Creek. The photo on the license matched the guy in the bed, and so did the photo on the card behind the driver's license that identified Foster as an employee of the hospital since October 18 of the previous year.

I showed the ID to Nauman. "Do you know him?"

The doctor shook his head. "No, but I know someone who will."

Nauman led us through the labyrinth of hospital hallways until we arrived at the custodial department. The supervisor on duty identified Foster's picture and confirmed that he'd been working for the hospital since a month before Carl McClain was released from Lewis.

According to his time card, Foster had clocked out at midnight, and the supervisor speculated that, like Williamson, he had simply been headed to his car in the employee's parking area of the garage. "Dan's a helluva nice guy," the supervisor insisted. "He'd never hurt a flea. Is this woman fuckin' nuts or what?"

Maggie and I turned the shooting over to a team of night-shift detectives and left the hospital a little after three. We were both still wired, and neither of us was going to be getting back to sleep any time soon, so we decided to get some breakfast. I followed her to a Denny's a few blocks from the hospital, and we slid into a booth at the back of the nearly empty restaurant.

A waitress who seemed far too chipper for that hour of the morning brought a cup of coffee for Maggie and a large orange juice for me. As the young woman walked back toward the kitchen, Maggie gave me a look of mock amazement.

"You're drinking something that might actually be good for you? What the hell happened—did the Coca-Cola Company go out of business overnight?"

"Jesus, I hope not," I countered. "I can't begin to imagine how horrible the withdrawal pains would be."

She shot me a look, then blew across the top of her cup and took a tentative sip of the steaming coffee. Setting the cup back down on the table, she said, "So, can you believe this shit tonight? This woman guns down some poor schmuck just because she thinks he looks like McClain?"

"I don't know, Maggs," I sighed. "The guy *does* vaguely resemble the sketches we've been circulating, and I can imagine that the poor woman was terrified. She had to be scared to death just at the thought that McClain might be out there somewhere gunning for her. And then to see somebody who looked like him following her through that empty garage . . ."

"I suppose," she conceded. "God, I just hope that the rest of the people on the list don't get that trigger-happy. It'll look like the friggin' O.K. Corral around here."

I took a sip of the orange juice, set the glass back down on the table, and shook my head. "For a few minutes there tonight, I actually thought that we might have our hands on this bastard."

"Me too," she sighed. "It would have been nice to have a hold of the cocksucker, in a world of pain, but still conscious enough to tell us about Thompson."

"Yeah, shit. Speaking of poor women . . ."

I drained a third of my orange juice, then said, "I know it makes no rational sense, but for some reason, that's the part of all this that angers me the most. I mean the guy's shot and killed six innocent people, and yet the thing that's got me the most pissed off is that he's holding Thompson out there somewhere and we can't fuckin' find her."

Maggie let out a long sigh. "Well, yeah, I *hope* that he's holding her out there somewhere and that we can still get to her in time. But you know as well as I do there's an excellent chance that Thompson's already dead and buried out in the freakin' desert someplace where we'll never find her."

The waitress served our breakfasts and we ate in silence for a few minutes as the tension of the last couple of hours slowly dissipated. Maggie pushed some scrambled eggs around on her plate and then, without looking up at me, she said, "While I was walking out to my car tonight, I bumped into Elaine. She said that Riggins had just taken Doyle to the hospital."

I put my fork down, leaned back in the booth, and sighed. "I thought you'd left before all of that happened."

"And you weren't going to say anything about it?"

"Not at the moment. I figured it could wait until morning."

She nodded and pushed her eggs around some more. "The fat prick really called me Little Miss Affirmative Action?"

"The hell with him, Maggs. The guy's a cretin. Don't give it another thought."

She nodded. "I understand that wasn't all he said . . ."

"No, it wasn't," I sighed. "But again, don't worry about it. Nobody pays any attention to anything that moron says."

Finally she looked up to meet my eyes. "You don't have to defend me, you know."

"Yeah, Maggie, I do. You're my partner and I have your back, just as I know that you have mine. That said, I understand perfectly well that you don't need my help or anyone else's defending yourself against a clown like Chris Doyle. In that matchup, he's the one who needs all the help he can get. And if it makes you feel any better, I wasn't defending you tonight. I was defending myself."

For a long moment, she said nothing more. Then she gave the slightest of smiles. "Jesus, I'll bet that felt good, even in spite of all the shit you're gonna be in. God only knows how many times I've wanted to do it myself."

"Yeah, maybe. But as you say, there will be a price to pay . . ."

She nodded, saying nothing more. Finally, after another couple of minutes had passed, she pushed her plate away and said, "So, on an entirely different subject, how are you doing otherwise—aside from all this shit, I mean. You've been pretty quiet the last couple of days."

I pushed my own plate away, balled up my napkin, and dropped it on the table. "I know," I said. "I'm sorry."

She shook her head sympathetically. "Jesus, Sean, you don't have to be *sorry*. I know you're going through hell. I just was wondering if anything else had gone wrong."

I turned away for a moment, then looked back to her. "Yes . . . No . . . Shit, I don't know, Maggie. My lawyer called yesterday morning. We have a trial date in April."

Her face softened. "I'm sorry, Sean. I really am. I guess I just don't know what to say."

I shook my head and gave her a weak smile. "Thanks, Maggs, but there's really nothing to be said. I have such horribly mixed emotions about it all that I don't know what to say or think myself. Telling the doctors to remove Julie's feeding tube was the hardest thing I've ever had to do in my life. But then having to spend the last ten months fighting to let her go . . . I know that I have to do this, and I know that it's what Julie would have wanted me to do. But it's so incredibly hard."

"I understand, and again I'm so sorry, Sean. I wish there was something I could do or say that would help . . ."

"I know you do. And I hope you know that I really do appreciate the thought, Maggs. Unfortunately, as I've said before, there's just not much that anybody can do."

We paid the check and walked back out into the parking lot. The temperature had dropped into the high thirties, and Maggie crossed her arms, hugging herself to stay warm. I walked her to her car and waited as she unlocked the door. We stood quietly for a moment watching the traffic pass by on the street. Then Maggie brought her eyes back to mine.

"I wish I could have known her."

"Me too, Maggs. You would have liked each other."

She nodded, and then, saying nothing more, she squeezed my arm and got into the car. I watched as she drove out of the parking lot, then got into my own car and headed home.

CHAPTER FORTY-EIGHT

"So, how would you like to be a staked goat?"

It was nine o'clock Thursday morning. After getting three hours' sleep, I was sitting in Mike Miller's kitchen, drinking a bottle of water. Across the table, Mike took a sip of coffee, set down his mug, and said, "What did you have in mind?"

"We're getting absolutely nowhere trying to flush this bastard out," I sighed. "We've had his name and his picture out there for two days now, and we've had no credible sightings of the guy. Meanwhile, he continues to waltz around the Valley, picking off his victims one by one while we sit here with our collective thumb up our ass.

"To hear the receptionist tell it, McClain had absolutely no problem conning Larry Cullen into walking happily out of the Cadillac dealership with him yesterday, even though we'd warned Cullen that McClain was coming. Clearly he's disguised his appearance somehow, which means that almost certainly he's not going to get recognized off the pictures we've put out there."

"No, probably not," Miller agreed. "So where do I fit in?"

I took another sip of the water. "Look, Mike, given the people McClain has targeted so far, you've got to figure that your name is his list. I mean, if he's going to go after the jurors who voted to send him to prison, then sure as hell he's not going to ignore the lead detective who developed the evidence that convinced those jurors."

"You wouldn't think so," he admitted.

"So, knowing that he's almost certainly going to be coming after you sooner or later, I was thinking maybe we could accelerate the process a bit, which might give us a chance to nail him."

"And you'd do this how?"

"I'm thinking I could put a bug in the ear of a sympathetic reporter, maybe like Ellie Davis over at Channel 12, who might have a few questions for the cop who put Carl McClain in the pen in the first place. You know, where is he now? How does he feel about McClain and his rampage? That sort of crap. You could make some disparaging remarks about McClain's manhood—call him a sick chickenshit who only attacks defenseless old women or whatever. I'm hoping that McClain would see it, or at least read about it, and maybe he'd get all pissed off and decide to deal with you sooner rather than later.

"It's apparent that the guy spends at least some time scouting his victims—he knows their patterns, when they're likely to be at home alone, and so on. I'm figuring that you could stay close to home for a while. We'd put a very loose net around you, and hope that McClain would walk right into it."

"So you spot some guy casing my house, figure that it must be McClain in whatever disguise he's using to escape being spotted, and grab him up?"

"Well, it's not quite that simple," I sighed. "What complicates things is Beverly Thompson. Her body hasn't turned up yet, and so there's some small chance that she's still alive and that McClain is holding her somewhere. We don't want to snatch McClain—or worse, kill him in a shootout if he resists arrest—before we have a chance to find her. So what I'd hope to do is to spot McClain scouting you and then tail him back to wherever he's holding Thompson."

Mike nodded. "You realize, of course, that even if you should get lucky enough to spot him, and even if he should lead you back to wherever he's hiding out, and even if he is holding the woman there, your chances of getting her out alive are still pretty damn slim. Once this asshole realizes that you've got him bottled up, he might very well kill her and himself rather than go back to the pen for the rest of his life. At the very least, he'll try to use her as a negotiating tool."

"I know," I said. "And we'll cross that bridge when we get to it. But for the moment, I don't have any better ideas. Do you?"

"No, not really," he said, shaking his head. "And I'm certainly game for my end of it. I'd much rather have the bastard coming after me now, when I'm expecting it, as opposed to waiting indefinitely, wondering when he's going to show up. I assume you've run this grand scheme by your lieutenant?"

"Actually, no I haven't," I admitted. "I didn't want to take it to him until I'd had a chance to talk to you about it first."

Mike drained the last of his coffee and set the mug back on the table. "Well, go see what the man has to say, then let me know. And," he said, smiling, "you'd also better pray that McClain doesn't somehow get to me before you can get your troops into place."

Back downtown, I followed Maggie's advice and slipped up the rear stairs to the third floor, avoiding the lieu-tenant's office and trying to postpone for at least a few more minutes the inevitable conversation about my confrontation with Chris Doyle. On my desk, I found a message, asking me to call Tony Anderson over at the crime lab. I got him on the phone, and he said, "You'll find this interesting."

"Oh? What've you got?"

"Richard Petrovich apparently got out of jail long enough on Tuesday to visit the scene of Harold Roe's murder."

"Say what?"

"The Crime Scene Response team brought back hairs from the chair where Roe was sitting that match up to Petrovich's."

"But, Jesus, Tony. We both know that he wasn't there. What the hell is going on here?"

"Well," he sighed, "we both know that *Petrovich* wasn't there, but his hair definitely was. My best guess is that McClain somehow collected some of Petrovich's hair and planted it in Roe's chair as a diversion, knowing it would go back to Petrovich and hoping to send you off on a wild-goose chase."

I hung up the phone and, no longer able to delay the inevitable, walked down the hall to the lieutenant's office, ready to face the music. I found him polishing his reading glasses. He looked up for a moment, waved me in, and directed me to a chair in front of his desk. Before I could open my mouth, he went back to polishing the glasses.

"I don't know if you heard or not," he said, "but Doyle slipped in the conference room last night, fell against the table, and broke his nose.

"The stupid shit thought he might try to make something out of it, like maybe suing the department for not properly mopping the floor or some damn thing, but I told him not even to think about it. I also told him to take a week off and give some serious thought to the question of how long he really wanted to remain a member of the Homicide Unit."

He finished with the glasses, held them up to the light for a second to make sure they were clean, and then set them on his desk. That done, he finally looked up at me and said, "So, what's up with you this morning?"

I swallowed hard, more relieved and grateful than I ever could have imagined, and then relayed the news from the crime lab. Shaking his head, the lieutenant said, "So McClain gets out of the can and spends a few days with his old buddy Petrovich while he's looking to get settled someplace. Then, to repay Petrovich for his hospitality, he gathers up a few samples of Petrovich's hair and sprinkles them around the crime scenes?"

"Yeah, it looks that way," I replied. "Petrovich just never felt right to either Maggie or me from the beginning, and the only thing we had to tie him to any of this business was the DNA evidence. But we know that he couldn't have been in Harold Roe's house on Tuesday, and so I think we can safely assume that he was never in Beverly Thompson's Lexus or in Karen Collins's home either. McClain's been jerking us around and using Petrovich to do it. We need to kick Petrovich."

"Okay," he sighed. "What else have you got?"

I briefly outlined my plan to use Mike Miller to bait a trap for McClain. Martin clasped his hands behind his head, leaned back in his chair, and thought about it for a minute or so.

"You don't think McClain will see you coming?"

"There's always that chance," I conceded. "But if we play it right with the reporter, it should look like it was her idea, not ours. In fact I'm surprised somebody hasn't thought to interview Miller already. It would certainly seem like a logical thing to do."

"Yeah, you'd think so," Martin agreed. "Okay, call your reporter and get the ball rolling. And let's figure on meeting at four this afternoon to plan out how we're going to cover Miller."

Ellie Davis was a rarity in local television news circles—a reporter who was actually even brighter than she looked—which, all in all, was pretty damned good. We'd first met a couple of years ago when she did a series of stories on an investigation that I'd led, and since that time, we'd been somewhere on the border with each other—more than simply acquaintances, but not quite friends. She'd interviewed me several times since our initial meeting, always treating me fairly, and in return I'd tipped her to a couple of stories, allowing her a head start on the competition. She was at her desk when I called, and after exchanging preliminary pleasantries, I said, "How'd you like to do us both a favor?"

She gave a throaty laugh. "What sort of favor did you have in mind, Sean—something professional or something personal?"

"Well actually," I said, returning the laugh, "I was thinking along the lines of something professional. But as far as anybody else was concerned—like your boss, for example—they'd have to think that this was your idea."

"Okay, what idea did I just have?"

"I saw your piece last night on the McClain manhunt. I was thinking that you might find it interesting to interview Mike Miller, the detective who led the investigation that sent McClain to the pen originally. He's been retired for several years, but he's still here in the Valley. He's a very interesting guy, and I'm sure that an interview with him would make for a great sidebar to the stories you're doing about McClain's current activities."

"Is there anything in particular Mr. Miller would want to talk to me about?"

"Not that I know of," I said. "But I'm sure that he'd have a perspective on Miller that your viewers would find enlightening."

"And just out of curiosity, how did I happen to have this bright idea?"

"I would imagine that, being the enterprising journalist that you are, you probably called me with a couple of questions about the current investigation. I would further imagine that in the course of our conversation, you inquired as to whether any of the detectives who were involved in the original McClain case were still around. In answer to your question, I would have suggested Mike."

"You said that I'd be doing both of us a favor. What do you get out of this?"

"Nothing more than the satisfaction of seeing that the local public is further enlightened about this vital investigation. But again, you need to make sure that I'm not connected with this idea in any way."

"Right . . . Okay, it actually does sound like a good idea, and it's one I probably should have had myself. I'm willing to be your cat's-paw here, but if there are any important new developments in this case, I hope you'll remember who your friends are."

"I certainly will," I promised.

"Good. And when you have a chance, let's get together for a drink and catch up. It's been a while."

"Will do," I said. "And thanks, Ellie."

CHAPTER FORTY-NINE

Just after nine o'clock on Thursday morning, McClain brought Beverly her breakfast along with a couple of pieces of fruit. He left the food on the table while he attached the cable to Beverly's right ankle and then explained that he'd be gone for much of the day. Once out of the house, he drove the Taurus to the Burton Barr branch of the Phoenix Public Library on Central and parked in the lot on the north side of the building.

McClain had been amazed when he first saw the new central library. The futuristic combination of glass, concrete, and steel looked like something out of a futuristic film, and totally unlike any other structure in Phoenix. McClain still hadn't decided what he thought about the building, but he did like the high ceilings in the reading rooms and the well-designed workspaces. It certainly didn't look or feel like the libraries he had known as a child, but the place was definitely a huge improvement over the prison library he'd been using for most of his adult life.

It was snowbird season in the Valley, and as happened every winter, the sunshine and the moderate temperatures had attracted a considerable number of homeless men and women to the Phoenix area along with their more conventional counterparts. A number of them were gathered on the sidewalk in front of the library along with their meager possessions, and McClain dodged past them as he made his way to the entrance.

Inside, the library appeared to be moderately busy for a Thursday. Patrons, many of whom were Hispanic, were working in the reference room and in the computer area, or browsing through the stacks. A few of the homeless people had made their way into the building and a couple of them had dozed off in chairs. A number of school-aged children, apparently on field trips, were involved in various projects.

McClain took the stairs to the second floor and scanned Alan Fischer's library card into a reader, requesting to use a computer. Fortunately, there was an open station, and the printer spit out a ticket assigning McClain to a computer in the middle of the room. He found the machine and sat down to work.

On leaving prison, he'd had seventeen names on his

list—the twelve jurors, Judge Walter Beckman, Prosecutor Harold Roe, Detectives Ed Quigly and Mike
Miller, and, of course, his PD, Beverly Thompson.

The list could have been longer. It might have included, for example, the four technical experts who
had testified against him. But to McClain's way of
thinking, they were less culpable than the others. Unlike the detectives, who'd built the case against him;
the prosecutor, who'd so eagerly turned a few pieces of
circumstantial evidence into an indictment and a conviction; the judge, who'd consistently ruled against
him; his own attorney, who'd failed him so miserably;
and the jurors, who'd refused to give him even the
benefit of a reasonable doubt, the technical experts
were actually just doing their jobs, guided by the cops
and the prosecutor, who had pointed them at McClain
and then pulled the trigger.

The list also might have included Barbara Clausen—
the infamous "Bambi"—who had set the whole chain
of events into motion with her goddamn little green
notebook. But immediately after the trial, Clausen had
disappeared back into the netherworld of the low-rent
streetwalker, and McClain assumed that she might
well have been dead for years. In any event, he figured,
Bambi would be impossible to find at this late date.

The list certainly would have included Charlie Woolsey, the motherfucker who'd actually committed the
crime for which McClain had been convicted. Woolsey
was now in the system himself, of course, which certainly did not put him beyond McClain's reach. After
nearly seventeen years inside, McClain well understood
that for a tenth of the price of his "new" Ford Taurus, he
could easily find someone to deal with Woolsey on his
behalf. But after seventeen years inside, McClain also
realized that Woolsey would pay a much dearer price
for his sins if McClain simply left him alone to do the
time.

McClain had managed to keep tabs on several of his targets through the vehicle of his recent appeal. His new lawyer had tracked down several of the people involved in McClain's conviction, and McClain left the prison system with their current addresses in the materials that his attorney had collected and given him for review. Upon his release, McClain had begun the process of tracking down the others.

His problem was complicated by the fact that Arizona was a "closed records" state, meaning that most vital records were not open to the public. But he was able to utilize a number of public-access databases as well as more traditional sources—phone books, city directories, and the like—to trace most of his targets.

Three of the jurors no longer had local addresses and phone numbers. McClain's research disclosed that two of the three had died, cheating him of his revenge. He was still trying to track down the third. He had also discovered that Detective Ed Quigly, whom he remembered as a particularly obnoxious son of a bitch, had retired and moved to Montana. He was still trying to track Quigly as well.

In the meantime, he'd begun to work his way through the list, patiently scouting his targets and taking them as the opportunities presented themselves. McClain assumed that the opportunities would not be presenting themselves nearly as readily now that the police had announced that McClain was likely hunting them. But this was a development that he had anticipated.

He had allotted himself a period of two weeks for what he thought of as his first offensive. During that time, he'd hoped to settle with his principal targets, which included Walter Beckman, Harold Roe, Mike Miller, Ed Quigly, and of course, Beverly Thompson. He'd also hoped to deal with at least a few of the jurors during that period, before the police figured out the connection between his targets and began to alert them.

Once the cops had made the connection, McClain's task would be significantly more difficult, but he still assumed that he could remain safely in Phoenix for the full two weeks. He would then finish with Beverly Thompson and make a strategic retreat for three months or so while he began to establish a new life with a new name, far from Arizona. He figured that after some time had passed, his remaining targets would inevitably settle back into their old routines and would once again be vulnerable. He could then return briefly to Phoenix, take as many of the remaining targets as he could in a quick second offensive, and then ride off into the sunset, satisfied and never to return.

Ed Quigly had complicated matters somewhat by disappearing from the state, and Beverly and the judge had been more difficult to get at than McClain had anticipated. Still, he was very happy with the overall progress of his campaign to date. And he was confident that when his initial two weeks expired roughly forty-eight hours from now, he would leave the city pleased with a job well done.

On the computer, McClain went to the Yahoo home page and called up the People Search form. He filled in the appropriate spaces, indicating that he was looking for an E. Quigly in the state of Montana. The computer spent a few seconds searching the relevant databases, and then the screen refreshed. The machine reported a phone number and an address for an E. Quigly in Missoula, and for an E. P. Quigly in Lakeside, wherever the hell that was.

McClain logged off the computer and walked up the stairs to the fifth floor. There were two pay phones near the restrooms, but a woman was using one of them, and so while he waited for her to clear out, McClain wandered through the stacks to the north end of the building.

Through the large windows that made up the north wall of the library, he could see several of the high-rise office buildings that lined the Central Avenue corridor. To the north and east, the Phoenix Mountains and Camelback Mountain rose out of the desert, and beyond them the McDowell Mountain Range. Although it was an otherwise beautiful sunny day with bright blue skies, a curtain of ugly brown smog hung in front of the mountains, obscuring the view.

For the second day in a row, there was a high-pollution advisory in effect, and McClain silently cursed the fucking developers who were largely responsible for the problem. Relentlessly plowing up the desert to throw up one cookie-cutter subdivision after another, the builders day after day threw huge clouds of dust into the air. That, combined with the emissions of tens of thousands of vehicles, industrial plants, and who-could-possibly-guess-how-many goddamned gas-powered leaf blowers, meant that Phoenix residents were now forced to endure some of the worst air-quality problems in the United States.

Normally, the prevailing winds would carry at least some of the foul air out of the Valley, drawing fresh air into the Valley in the process. But over the last several days, a combination of cooler temperatures, a stable atmosphere, and light winds had left Phoenix's infamous Brown Cloud hanging over the metro area, destroying the views and making life miserable for everyone, but especially for those prone to respiratory diseases.

Federal, state, and local agencies seemed powerless to deal with the problem in any meaningful way. They levied token fines against builders who routinely violated ordinances designed to minimize the dust raised by construction and who simply wrote off the fines as a cost of doing business. Mass-transit initiatives that might help reduce vehicle emissions were largely nonexistent or ineffective. And certainly no one in any position of authority was about to suggest that it was time to rein in the Valley's explosive growth.

As a result, people simply shook their heads and wrung their hands while the Valley went to hell in a handbasket. McClain was thoroughly pissed about the whole situation and was damned glad to be on his way out of town. After standing at the windows mourning the situation for several minutes, he returned to the pay phones and found that the woman had finished her call and left. He dug a handful of change out of his pocket and piled it on the phone in front of him.

He picked up the receiver, dialed the 406 area code and the number in Missoula for E. Quigly, and then deposited the coins demanded by the automated "operator." The phone rang twice before an answering machine kicked in. A bright female voice that sounded like it belonged to a woman in her late teens or early twenties said, "Hi! This is Ellen. Either I'm not here right now or I'm doing something much more interesting than answering the phone. Leave me a message and I'll get back to you whenever. Ciao!"

McClain declined to leave a message and crossed "E. Quigly" off his list. Then he dialed the number in Lakeside for E. P. Quigly. This time the phone rang four times before again defaulting to an answering machine. A whiskey-edged voice that McClain recognized immediately, even after seventeen years, said, "You've reached Ed Quigly. Leave your name and number and I'll return your call when I get home."

Smiling, McClain circled Quigly's phone number and address in Lakeside and added a triumphant exclamation point to the note. Feeling like he was on a roll, he decided to move on to Jean Drummond, the one juror whom he had not yet been able to locate.

He had absolutely no recollection of the woman at

all and knew from his files only that Drummond would now be seventy-two years old, assuming that she was still alive. For nine years after the trial, the *Phoenix City Directory* showed Drummond still at the address where she'd been living at the time she voted to convict McClain, but he'd been unable to find any trace of her since. A check of the Social Security Death Index, ObitsArchive.com, and Ancestry.com produced no record of her death, and so, on a hunch, McClain decided to check marriage certificates.

Fortunately, this information was open to the public; unfortunately, it was not available online. Thus McClain left the library, got back in his car, and drove over to the Arizona Vital Records Department.

The agency was housed in an ugly concrete fortress on Jackson Street, in the middle of what looked like a no-man's-land. McClain circled the building three times before finding a parking place that looked relatively safe and made sure to lock the Taurus behind him. In the lobby, a guard pointed him to the records department downstairs, and a clerk showed him how to use the public-access computers to search for the record of a marriage license.

McClain typed in Drummond's name and hit ENTER. The screen refreshed, indicating that eight years earlier, a woman named Jean Drummond had taken out a marriage license with a groom named Herbert Wentworth. His anticipation building, McClain hurriedly filled out a form to request an uncertified copy of the marriage license. He then stood impatiently in line until finally he got to the counter, where a clerk charged him fifty cents for a copy of the certificate.

And there she was. At the ripe old age of sixty-four, Jean Drummond of the same address as McClain's juror had married Herbert Wentworth, age sixty-one. Well, Jean, you sly old cradle robber, McClain thought, smiling.

In a phone booth in the lobby upstairs, he found a Herbert Wentworth listed in Mesa. He dug thirty-five cents out of his pocket and dialed the number. The phone rang four times before handing him over to an answering machine. McClain listened as an elderly male voice said, "You've reached Jean and Herbert. We're sorry but we can't come to the phone right now. Please leave your name and number and we'll call you back just as soon as we can."

Pleased with the results of a very good morning's work, McClain hung up the phone, made a note of the address, and decided to take a ride down to Mesa.

CHAPTER FIFTY

Jean and Herbert Wentworth lived in a small one-story brick home on Belfast Street in Mesa. When McClain drove slowly past, an elderly man was mowing the small patch of lawn in front of the house, stooped over behind an ancient power mower that looked to be about as old as the man himself. McClain assumed that the man was Drummond's husband, Herbert Wentworth, and he watched as Wentworth maneuvered the mower around a yard sign urging the reelection of the incumbent mayor.

An aging Ford Taurus, not unlike McClain's own, save for the fact that it was a faded blue, sat alone in the carport. McClain wondered if this was one of those elderly couples that had only one car and that went virtually everywhere together, going to church, doing the shopping, and running their other errands as a team.

To test the hypothesis, he pulled into the parking lot

of a Circle K convenience store a few blocks away from the home. At a pay phone on the edge of the parking lot, he dialed the Wentworths' number again. This time the phone was answered by an elderly female voice. Leaning into the kiosk, trying to shield the phone from the street noise, McClain said, "Is this Mrs. Jean Wentworth?"

The woman answered in the affirmative, and McClain said, "Mrs. Wentworth, I'm Andrew Hardy from the Committee to Reelect Mayor Broder. I was wondering if you could spare a few moments of your time to respond to a survey that we're conducting?"

"Just a minute, please," the woman said.

McClain heard the sound as the woman set the phone down. For two or three minutes, he heard nothing more. Then, finally, someone picked up the phone again and an elderly male voice said, "Hello?"

McClain again repeated his lie and asked if Mr. Wentworth could spare a few moments for his survey.

"I suppose so," Wentworth said somewhat tentatively.

"Great," McClain said. "I promise that I'll be brief. Our records indicate that you and your wife, Mrs. Herbert Wentworth, are both registered to vote in the city of Mesa. Is that correct?"

"Yes, it is."

"And are you planning to vote in the upcoming primary elections?"

"Yes, we are."

"And are you and Mrs. Wentworth happy with the progress that the city has made under the current mayoral administration?"

"Yes, I guess so."

"Mr. Wentworth, what would you think are the three most important issues facing the city government at this time?"

The man hesitated for several seconds, then said,

"Well . . . of course we're very concerned about keeping property taxes down. For those of us living on a fixed income, it's very difficult when the cost of everything seems to keep going up so rapidly."

"I certainly understand that, sir," McClain said soothingly. "And I hope you know that the current city administration is working diligently to keep expenses down so that we can hold the line and prevent any increase in city taxes and fees."

"Yes, we do appreciate that," Wentworth replied, although his tone of voice suggested that he might be hard-pressed to cite any city initiatives designed to accomplish this laudable objective.

Without giving Wentworth the opportunity to list his other two priorities, McClain pressed on. "May I ask, Mr. Wentworth, are either you or your wife currently employed?"

"No, we've both been retired for the last few years."

"I envy you that, Mr. Wentworth. It must be nice to have the time to travel and pursue your other interests. May I ask if either you or Mrs. Wentworth would be willing to volunteer some time to work on the mayor's behalf in this important campaign?"

"Well . . . I don't know if we'd have the time for that or not. What would that involve?"

"Well, we could use assistance with a variety of things," McClain said, "depending upon what your schedule would permit and what you might be interested in doing. Do you and your wife both drive?"

"No. I drive, but my wife has macular degeneration and so she doesn't drive anymore. And unfortunately she's in the early stages of Alzheimer's. I spend most of my time caring for her, and so realistically, it would be difficult for me to volunteer much time."

"I see," McClain said, sympathetically. "In that case, it would probably be unreasonable for us to impose on you, Mr. Wentworth. But I do appreciate your taking the time to talk with me, and we will appreciate your support on election day. Thank you very much."

"You're welcome," Wentworth assured him, and then hung up.

McClain got back into the Taurus and drove slowly back past the Wentworths' house. Herbert Wentworth was back outside on the lawn in front of the house, talking to a small, frail-looking woman. The woman had short frizzy white hair and was wearing sunglasses and a print housedress that looked like something that McClain's grandmother might have worn.

McClain pulled over to the side of the street for a moment and watched the couple. After another minute or so of conversation, Wentworth gently laid a hand on his wife's shoulder. Then she turned and walked carefully back through the carport and into the house, while her husband returned to his yard work. McClain waited, watching for another few moments, and then drove away, shaking his head and mentally striking Jean Drummond Wentworth from his list.

McClain was four blocks away from the Wentworth house when KSLX segued from John Hiatt's "Memphis in the Meantime" into a block of commercials.

Sleep America was in the middle of another spectacular clearance sale with fantastic bargains to be found on mattresses of every size and brand imaginable. Debbie the Mattress Lady then gave way to the crew from Channel 12, which was hyping the news, weather, and sports reports they'd be featuring at six o'clock. James Quiñones suggested that there might be rain in the Valley's immediate future, Kevin Hunt promised a report on the Diamondback's spring training camp, and Ellie Davis touted an exclusive interview "you won't want to miss!" with Detective Mike Miller, "the homicide cop who first tracked down suspected serial killer Carl McClain seventeen years ago."

The commercials finally finished, the DJ announced the time and temperature over the opening bars of Bonnie Raitt's cover of John Hiatt's "Thing Called Love." McClain wondered whether the choice was intentional or simply an accident. Then he checked his watch and recalculated his schedule for the rest of the afternoon, thinking that it might be nice to be home in time for the news.

CHAPTER FIFTY-ONE

A few minutes before four, I wandered past Maggie's office on my way to the conference room. I found her sitting at her desk, staring off into space, apparently oblivious to anything that might be going on around her. I tapped on the door, walked into the office, and said, "Are we taking a brief mental vacation?"

She snapped out of her trance and looked over at me. "What? Oh, sorry. I slipped away for a moment."

I shot her a look and she let out a heavy sigh. "Patrick Abernathy just called and invited me to go to a Suns game with him and his kids on Saturday afternoon. I don't know what in the hell ever possessed me, but I lost my senses for a moment and said that I would."

"And what's so bad about that?" I laughed. "Jesus, Maggie, it's only a basketball game."

"Like hell it is," she snorted. "You know damned good and well that what he's looking for is an opportunity to see how the four of us might get along together."

"Oh, Maggie, for God's sake. The guy apparently likes basketball. *You* like basketball. Probably his girls like basketball. Don't make such a big deal out of it. Go to the fuckin' game. Eat a couple of hot dogs. Root for the home team, and have a nice afternoon."

"Right, there's an image for you," she laughed. "Me, eating a hot dog."

"Well, it wouldn't kill you, Maggs."

"Maybe not the hot dog," she conceded. "But the rest of the afternoon just might." She hesitated for a moment and then shook her head. "Shit, maybe with a little luck, we'll catch a nice triple homicide that morning and I can beg off."

Maggie and I walked down the hall together and joined Pierce, Chickris, Riggins, and the lieutenant to plan the strategy for covering Mike Miller. "This was your idea, Sean," Martin said. "How do you propose to implement it?"

Looking around the table, I replied, "As you know, Ellie Davis will air an interview with Mike on the six o'clock news tonight. They'll run excerpts from the interview again at ten. The station is hyping the interview in its teases for the newscasts this afternoon and evening, and we're hoping that McClain will see or hear one of the teases and tune in to the broadcast. Failing that, we hope that the print journalists will follow up, interview Mike themselves, and that McClain will see something in the paper.

"I suggested to Mike that he should taunt McClain in the interview, and my hope is that this will cause McClain to go after Mike sooner, rather than later. I want to put a net around Mike starting as soon as we're done here, and hope that we can spot McClain scouting him. Mike's agreed to stay pretty close to home for the time being, so most of the surveillance will be at his house, but we'll cover him with a couple of teams when he leaves the house.

"I assume that we'll use the Special Assignments Unit for most of the surveillance, although we all may have to pitch in occasionally to help out. The house across the street from Miller's is up for sale and is currently unoccupied. I've talked to the listing agent, who in turn has talked to the owner, and they've agreed that we can use the house to watch Mike's, at least for the time being. There's a sale pending on the property, so the realtor isn't showing it any more. We can set up in there with a good view up and down the street."

The others nodded their understanding, and Bob said, "What's behind Miller's house?"

"The back of another house," I answered. "Mike has a privacy fence around his place and so does the neighbor behind him. They share the section of the fence that runs along the property line. It would be virtually impossible for McClain to scout Miller's activity from the back of the house."

"But he could get through the neighbor's yard, over the fence, and into Miller's backyard without us seeing him?" Elaine asked.

"Yeah, he could do that," I conceded. "But the sliding glass door at the back of Mike's house and all of the windows back there are wired into the alarm system. Mike assures me that the system is state-of-the-art and that there's no way Miller could defeat it. If he tried to break in that way, Mike would hear him coming in plenty of time to deal with him himself."

"Sounds like a plan to me," Bob sighed. "I just hope the asshole is watching the news."

An hour later, I was sitting in the second-floor bedroom of the house across the street from Miller's with Brenda Perkins and Dale Johnson, two members of the Special Assignments Unit. The room, like the rest of the house, was empty of furniture, and we'd brought in a card table, four folding chairs, and the rest of our surveillance equipment. Through the lace curtains that hung in front of the bedroom window we had a clear view of the front of Mike's house and of the street between the two homes for a couple of blocks either way.

I handed Perkins a cell phone and said, "If Mike decides to leave the house for any reason, he'll call this phone and let you know. He'll also call downtown so that another team can pick him up as he leaves the house and shadow him wherever he might be going. We'll be manning this room around the clock in four six-hour shifts. You guys need to be alert. We may only get one chance at this asshole."

Perkins and Johnson insisted that they'd be vigilant, and when they had no questions, I left them to the job.

CHAPTER FIFTY-TWO

The six o'clock newscast opened with helicopter footage from a three-car fatal accident that had turned the Loop 101 into a parking lot for miles in either direction of Shea Boulevard. With that out of the way, Lin Sue Cooney introduced Ellie Davis's special report on the hunt for Carl McClain. McClain hitched his leg over the arm of the chair, punched the remote to turn up the volume a bit, and took a pull on his Miller Genuine Draft.

Davis was a petite, attractive blonde, and the opening shot framed her in front of a one-story house that McClain recognized immediately as Miller's. She quickly summarized the investigation into the recent killings in which McClain was a "suspect," and described the intensive and thus-far-unsuccessful manhunt that the police had launched to find him.

Pointing to the house behind her, Davis said, "Seventeen years ago, Detective Mike Miller, now retired and living here in this quiet Phoenix neighborhood, led the investigation that culminated in the arrest and conviction of Carl McClain for the brutal murder of a local prostitute. This afternoon I spoke with Detective Miller to get his reaction to the current manhunt."

The scene shifted, now showing Davis sitting with the retired detective at a table, apparently in the back-yard of Miller's home. Miller was dressed in a black T-shirt, and at least from the waist up, he appeared to be trim and in very good shape for a man of his age. He sat looking at the reporter as though oblivious to the video camera that was hovering just off his left shoulder.

"I remember Carl McClain as a fat, pudgy kid," Miller was saying. "He wasn't particularly bright. He seemed to be one of those guys who just drifts along, living in the moment, trying to gratify whatever impulse might be driving him at that particular instant— drugs, women, liquor, whatever. The night he got into trouble, of course, it was a woman."

Davis: "Were you surprised when it turned out that he was actually innocent?"

Miller: "Definitely. Given the technology available to us at the time, we put together a good, solid case. McClain admitted to having sex with the woman. We found her earring in his vehicle. The clothesline that the victim was strangled with matched clothesline that we found in McClain's possession. And of course, McClain's blood type matched up to what we found in the victim."

On the screen, Miller looked away for a moment, then back to the reporter. "Of course you have to understand that McClain didn't help himself a lot. The guy's apparently a congenital liar, and as the evidence against him piled up, he changed his story several times, trying to invent some lie that he thought we'd buy into. The only result was that in the end, nobody believed him, including the jury."

Davis: "And were you surprised to learn that McClain might be attacking the people who were involved in sending him to prison?"

Miller, sneering: "Astonished would be more like it. I wouldn't have thought that he'd have the nerve to do something like that, let alone the brains to carry it out. But then so far, of course, he hasn't actually killed anyone who was in a position to defend himself. I imagine that any gutless moron can shoot a couple of seventy-year-old women if he's of a mind to."

Davis: "Detective Miller, do you worry that McClain might be targeting you, since you were so instrumental in sending him to prison?"

Miller leaned back in the chair and gave her a small, satisfied smile. "Not for a moment, Ellie. In the first place, I have every confidence in the detectives who are working this case, and I'm sure that very shortly, Carl McClain is going to be back behind bars again for the rest of his life, which is exactly where the little rodent belongs. And if he's crazy enough to knock on my front door, he'll discover in a damn big hurry that *I'm* not a seventy-year-old woman."

Davis flashed him a bright smile. "Retired Phoenix Detective Mike Miller, thanks for insights into the suspect who's at the center of the most intensive manhunt in recent Valley history." Then, turning to the camera: "This is Ellie Davis in Phoenix. Now back to you, Lin Sue."

Cooney nodded, thanked Davis for her "timely report," and then segued into an alarming story about the health department's discovery of mice droppings found in the kitchen of one of the city's most popular upscale restaurants. McClain picked up the remote, clicked off the television, and took another pull on his beer.

Chapter Fifty-three

Two hours after the newscast, I was back at the stakeout across from Mike Miller's house when a pizza delivery guy pulled into Miller's driveway. Brenda Perkins watched the car's brake lights flash and said, "You don't suppose he ordered enough for us too? It's been a long time since lunch."

Through a pair of night-vision binoculars, I watched the kid get out of his car and walk up to Mike's front door, carrying an insulated bag. He rang the bell, and a minute or so later, Mike cracked open the door. He and the deliveryman stood in the doorway talking for another minute or so, and then finally Mike reached into his pocket, dug out a bill, handed it to the kid, and took the pizza from him.

Mike closed the door, and the kid walked back to his car and drove away. Two minutes later the cell phone rang. When I answered it, Mike said, "Sean? You'd better walk across the street and have a slice of pizza."

Miller opened the door as I walked up the sidewalk and then led me into the kitchen. The pizza box was sitting open on the table. Next to the box were an envelope and a piece of notepaper. Miller gestured in the direction of the paper and said, "Take a look, but be careful how you handle it."

I picked up the paper, holding it only by the top corner. The message was printed in block letters, and read,

BANG, YOU'RE DEAD!!!
I SAW YOUR LITTLE PERFORMANCE ON THE TUBE

TONIGHT, MIKE. EVEN AFTER ALL THESE YEARS, YOU'RE STILL PRETTY COCKY, AREN'T YOU? BUT YOU'RE NOT NEARLY AS SMART OR AS TOUGH AS YOU THINK YOU ARE. I COULD HAVE BEEN THE PIZZA DELIVERY GUY AND YOU'D BE ON THE WAY TO THE MORGUE RIGHT NOW. BUT I WANT YOU TO THINK ABOUT IT FOR A WHILE, MIKE. I'LL COME FOR YOU IN MY OWN GOOD TIME, AND WHEN I DO, YOU'LL ONLY WISH TO GOD THAT YOU COULD GET OFF AS EASILY AS ONE OF THOSE 70-YEAR-OLD WOMEN. SEE YOU THEN. MEANWHILE, ENJOY THE PIZZA. C.M.

I looked up at Mike and raised my eyebrows. "You know he could have been the pizza delivery guy."

"No, he couldn't," Mike insisted, smiling. "Not unless he's figured out a way to morph himself into the body of a pimply-faced, twenty-year-old kid."

He reached behind his back and came out with a .38-caliber Smith and Wesson that he'd apparently been wearing under the T-shirt that was hanging out over his jeans. "Besides which," he said, "when I opened the door with my left hand, I had this in my right, hanging at my side. If the guy would've come out of that bag with anything except a pizza, he'd have been dead without ever knowing what hit him."

The receipt indicated that the pizza had come from a Domino's a mile and a half from Mike's house. The young woman at the counter told me that a man had walked into the store and ordered a large sausage and pepperoni pizza to be delivered to a friend. The man paid for the pizza, gave the woman Miller's address, and handed her a note to go into the box along with the pizza.

"He told me he had lost a bet to his friend and was paying it off," the woman explained.

The description she gave me of the man coincided with that provided by the receptionist at the Cadillac dealership where Larry Cullen had worked: He was an "older man," probably in his late forties or early fifties, with longish gray hair and a gray mustache. He was wearing a T-shirt and a pair of jeans. No, the woman said, she hadn't seen the vehicle that the man was driving, but yes, she thought that she would recognize the man if she ever saw him again.

CHAPTER FIFTY-FOUR

That same evening, the ninth of Beverly's captivity, McClain walked through the bedroom door carrying a Domino's pizza box. He dropped the box on the card table and looked at Beverly, who was sitting on the bed in her sweatpants and an Arizona Cardinals T-shirt, reading the Lawrence Block novel he'd bought her. Throwing up his hands defensively, he said, "I know, I know. I'm sorry about the fuckin' pizza. But it's been a long day, and I had to stop by the Domino's place anyway."

Beverly shrugged and set the book down on the nightstand. "It's all right. I'll survive."

He gave her a quick look, then turned away. "Yeah, whatever. You want a beer?"

"Please."

McClain turned and left the room without releasing Beverly from the cable, so she got up from the bed and walked over to her place at the table, dragging the cable behind her. She *would* survive the pizza, she knew, but she was increasingly sure of the fact that she would not survive Carl McClain.

He had definitely softened, but Beverly remained convinced that McClain had planned all along to kill her in the end. And try as she might, putting herself in

McClain's place, she couldn't see any way that he might change his mind, not if he had any hope of getting away with the murders he'd already committed.

He had a plan; she was sure of that. And realistically, he couldn't have that much time left in which to complete it. If in fact he had killed Harold Roe, Walter Beckman, and a couple of jurors, in addition to killing David and abducting her, the police certainly would have made the connection by now. They had to know whom they were looking for, and no matter the change in McClain's appearance, he could not expect to stay ahead of them for all that much longer.

She'd played the waiting game as long as she possibly could. If she was going to capitalize on whatever small advantage she might have created for herself, she would have to move at the next opportunity.

McClain returned with a couple of beers and the roll of paper towels. He seemed lost in his thoughts, practically oblivious to Beverly, and they ate the pizza in silence. Finally, he pushed his plate away and waited for a couple of minutes while Beverly finished eating. She wiped her mouth and laid her "napkin" on the table. McClain said, "I have to go out for a while. We're out of beer, but there is a little of that Pinot Grigio left. Would you like it?"

"Yes, please," she replied.

McClain picked up the dirty dishes and the pizza box and went out to the kitchen. He returned a minute later with a glass and the last quarter bottle of wine. He set them on the table and looked briefly at Beverly. "I'll be back in a couple of hours."

Saying nothing more, he turned and left, locking the bedroom door behind him.

Beverly poured a couple of drops of wine into the glass. Ten minutes later, when she was sure that Mc-

Clain was gone, she got up from the table, walked into the bathroom, and poured the rest of the wine down the drain.

She dropped the wine bottle into the wastebasket next to the sink. Then, for a long couple of minutes, she stood staring into the eyes of a woman she barely recognized, who was staring back at her from the dirty mirror above the sink.

Her hair was a tangled mess. Devoid of makeup, and having now spent well over a week indoors, her face was pale and gaunt. Beverly had no way of knowing how much weight she might have lost over the last several days, but it was clearly showing. She slowly shook her head at the image in the mirror, then lowered her eyes and looked away. She turned to leave the bathroom, then stopped and turned back to look at the plunger that was standing on the floor next to the toilet.

The plunger looked as if it was at least as old as the house itself. The suction cup at the business end might once have been red, but was now faded to a mottled pink. Most of the paint had flaked off the cracked wooden handle, which was about twenty inches long. She picked up the plunger and carefully examined the crack. It was roughly five inches in length, starting about two inches from the bottom of the handle and rising diagonally from the outer edge to the middle of the handle.

Beverly tried to test the crack by bending the handle, but it would only give a little. She picked the wine bottle out of the wastebasket and set it on its side on the floor. Then she laid the plunger across the bottle and anchored the top of the handle to the floor with her left foot.

Grabbing the sink with both hands to brace herself, she stepped on the other end of the plunger with her right foot, gently at first, then gradually increasing the pressure. The wood made a small cracking sound as the fissure in the handle slowly spread from one side to the other. An instant before the break was complete, Beverly eased the pressure, stepped back, and retrieved the plunger.

The top of the handle was now attached only very tenuously to the bottom. The slightest pressure would complete the break, leaving about eighteen inches of the top of the handle tapering down to a jagged point.

Satisfied, Beverly nodded to herself and set the plunger back beside the toilet, turning the crack so that it faced away from the door. Then she picked up the wine bottle, dropped it back into the wastebasket, and returned to her novel.

CHAPTER FIFTY-FIVE

It was the middle of Friday morning when Mike Miller called. "I just got off the phone with Jason Barnes. I assume you want me to give him the same basic interview I gave Davis?"

I put down the Coke I was drinking for breakfast and said, "Who in the hell is Jason Barnes?"

"The reporter from *New Times*. Didn't you tell him to call me?"

"No, I've never heard of the guy, Mike."

"Well, he called here fifteen minutes ago. Said he'd seen the piece on Channel 12 last night and could he do an interview to cover the topic in greater depth than the TV people could do? I told him sure. He's supposed to be here at four this afternoon."

"Well again, I never heard of him. I suppose it's possible that he did see the interview and decided to follow up, which is fine if it will help flush McClain out of his hole. Let me call the paper and double-check the guy."

Fifteen minutes later, I called Mike back.

"I told you I'd never heard of Jason Barnes? Well, the editor of *New Times* never heard of him either."

"No shit?"

"No shit. So what else did 'Jason Barnes' have to say?"

"Nothing more than what I told you before."

I asked Mike if he had the guy's number on his caller ID. He read off the number and I promised to get back to him. Thirty minutes later, he answered his phone again and I said, "The number goes back to a pay phone in the Civic Plaza. I think your old buddy Carl McClain wants to come have a chat with you this afternoon."

We spent the next four hours placing an elaborate net around Mike Miller's home. If McClain did show up at Miller's front door, he'd find a note apologizing for the fact that Mike had been called away at the last minute, and asking "Jason Barnes" to call him and reschedule the interview. When McClain left the house, eight unmarked vehicles would be ready to trail him wherever he might lead us, alternating in and out of the surveillance.

A little after three, Mike taped the note to his front door, walked across the street, and joined Maggie, me, and two members of the Special Assignments Unit in the stakeout house. I introduced Mike to Maggie and the others, and he spent the next forty-five minutes regaling Maggie with exaggerated tales of my early days in the Homicide Unit. But by three fifty, everyone had fallen silent and the tension in the room was thick enough to cut with the proverbial knife.

At two minutes before four, a gray Ford Taurus came rolling up the street and pulled into Mike's driveway. I read the plate number through my binoculars and

Maggie relayed it and the car's description to the team outside.

The man who got out of the car looked to be somewhere in his late thirties, tall and well muscled with medium-length blond hair. He was dressed casually in a pair of tan slacks and a blue oxford shirt with the sleeves rolled up to his elbows. He wore a pair of horn-rimmed glasses and was carrying a briefcase that looked like it should have belonged to a lawyer on his way to court.

Listening to the earphone connected to her radio, Maggie said quietly, "The plate on the car actually belongs on a two-year-old Ford Explorer registered in the name of Janelle Beck of Scottsdale."

Without looking away from the window, I said, "Get somebody to Beck's address right now. Find out where the hell she and her Explorer are."

Maggie moved to the back of the room, dug out her cell phone, called Greg Chickris, and relayed the instructions.

The man across the street looked nothing like the images of Carl McClain that we'd been circulating in the media. He might have been the guy that Maggie and I had watched on the video from the convenience store, but it was impossible to tell. As we watched him walk up to Mike's door, Brenda Perkins snapped off a number of pictures, using a good telephoto lens. The guy picked the note off the door and stood on the porch for a minute or two, reading the note and shaking his head.

Through the binoculars, "Jason Barnes" gave a very good impression of someone who'd just been seriously inconvenienced. Then he took a look at his watch, shook his head again, and set his briefcase down on the porch. He opened the briefcase, came out with a pen, and stepped up to the door. Holding the paper against the door, he wrote something beneath Mike's note. Then he taped the note to the door again, returned the pen to his briefcase, walked back to his car, and drove away.

"He's moving," Maggie said into her radio. "Heading west on Evans."

The surveillance-team leader said, "Copy that. We're on him."

Our objective was to keep a net around the subject car with vehicles ahead of it, behind it, and running parallel on the streets on either side of it. While the team fell into place, I walked across the street and retrieved the note. The man, who we all hoped was Carl McClain, had written at the bottom of Mike's message, "Sorry I missed you, Detective. I'll call this evening to try to reschedule." He'd signed the note "J. Barnes."

While Mike went back home, Maggie and I joined the pursuit, leaving the stakeout team in place in the house across the street from Mike's, just to be on the safe side. The driver of the Taurus appeared to be in no particular hurry and did nothing, even inadvertently, that might have made it difficult for us to tail him. Maggie and I rode silently in the wake of the surveillance team, listening to the chatter on the radio.

The Taurus led us generally south and west. Twenty minutes after leaving Mike's, it pulled into the parking lot of an AJ's grocery store. One of the pursuit vehicles pulled in behind the Taurus, while the others took up positions around the strip mall in which the store was located, ready to resume the chase. Over the radio, one of the surveillance detectives said, "He's out of the car and headed toward the market. Janie and I are on him."

"Stick close," I warned. "Don't let him go into the goddamn john and come out disguised as somebody else. And be sure that he's not dropping the Taurus and picking up another ride."

In response, Al Harris, the surveillance-team leader

said, "Don't worry, the bastard won't get away from us that easily."

We listened as Harris deployed a couple of men to watch the back exits from the store and then moved a couple of people into place to monitor the main entrances in the front. One of the two detectives who had followed the target into the store said quietly into her radio, "He's at the meat counter at the back of the store, looking at steaks."

With McClain safely out of sight of the Taurus, Harris ordered one of his team to approach the car and tag it with a radio transponder that would enable us to track the car even if we lost sight of it. A minute later, the job was done, and the detectives in the store reported that McClain had picked out a couple of steaks and was now talking to the manager of the liquor department, apparently asking about a bottle of wine.

We listened as McClain made his way through the produce section, selecting a couple of baking potatoes and a bunch of carrots. "Steaks, wine, and carrots?" Maggie complained. "Who the fuck is this guy, Wolfgang Puck?"

Whoever the guy was, five minutes later he'd made his way through the checkout line, paying cash for his purchases, and was back in his car, again heading south and west. Again the surveillance team took up their positions around him, now aided by the radio transponder that pinpointed his position exactly.

Just after five o'clock, the Taurus drove past Chase Field, heading south down Seventh Street into one of the city's seedier neighborhoods. The transponder tracked the car as it turned west onto Grant, then south onto Montezuma, and finally west again onto Tonto. At five seventeen, the Taurus pulled into the driveway of a small house on the north side of Tonto. The driver got out of the car, manually raised the door of the attached garage, and drove the car into the garage. He then got out of the Taurus, pulled the door back down again, and disappeared from view.

The surveillance team radioed the address and I pulled over to the side of the street three blocks away. I called Elaine Pierce, who was standing by in the office, and gave her the address. "Get me everything on the house ASAP, Elaine—the owner, the phone number, current tenant if it's not the owner, when they moved in, when they got utilities—everything."

She promised that she would, and the surveillance team began closing up around the house.

By then, we had a little less than an hour of daylight left. One of the surveillance vans took up a position half a block away from the subject house, enabling the team inside the van to watch both the garage and the front door of the house. We circled the rest of the wagons on a two-block perimeter out of sight of the house and set up a command post in a truck disguised as a U-Haul moving van.

Before moving into the command post, Maggie and I drove slowly by the house. It was a small, nondescript, one-story residence built of tan concrete block with a red tile roof. Like the rest of the neighborhood, it had clearly seen better days. The tiles on the roof had faded; some were cracked, and a few were missing altogether. The yard had been sadly neglected and consisted mostly of weeds, litter, and a couple of pathetic-looking bushes.

Like many of the other homes along the street, the house was surrounded by a chain-link fence, and all the windows were protected by iron burglar bars. Looking north, you could see the lights of the Civic Plaza, Chase Field, and the US Airways Arena. But here, only eight or nine blocks away, we were in another world altogether, especially with the darkness closing in.

We parked behind the command truck, tapped on the door, and were greeted by Al Harris, dressed in what I thought of as his combat outfit. Fifteen minutes later, my cell phone buzzed. I answered the call, and Elaine said, "The house belongs to a Walter Kovick of Tempe. He rents it out, and the current tenant is a guy named Alan Fischer. Fischer moved in three months ago, paying a security deposit and the first month's rent with a check drawn on a Wells Fargo bank account.

"Fischer paid the second and third month's rent with a check from the same account, and all of the checks cleared. Power, water, and cable are in Fischer's name. Neither the landlord nor the utilities have a previous address for him. I'm trying to raise someone from Wells Fargo who can tell me how long the checking account's been open, but I'm having trouble getting through to anyone this late in the day.

"Chickie says that Janelle Beck is a department head at Nordstrom's. At the moment, she's in Seattle for a meeting, and her Explorer is supposed to be parked someplace at the airport. Meanwhile, the lieutenant is wearing a path in the tile pacing back and forth between his office and mine. Call him and let him know what's going on."

I thanked her and told her to keep digging into Alan Fischer. I also told her to have a patrolman gather up Kovick, the landlord, and bring him to the command truck. Then I disconnected, called the lieutenant, and brought him up to date.

"What's your plan?" he asked.

"So far, it's looking increasingly like this is our guy," I told him. "We'll keep trying to find out if 'Alan Fischer' has any history prior to three months ago when he rented the house and which is just after McClain got out of Lewis. But we know that he showed up at Miller's door and that he's not Jason Barnes from *New Times* as he claimed to be. We know that he's driving a car with a stolen plate, and we also know that the plate was taken from a car left at the airport, just like the one on the van that McClain was driving when he snatched Beverly Thompson.

"Now that it's getting dark, we'll tighten the net around the house and make sure there's no way he can get out, even on foot, without us seeing him. Let's get a warrant for the house immediately. The next time he leaves, we'll let the team follow him away and keep tabs on him. Then we'll go into the house and see if he's holding Beverly Thompson in there."

"You don't want to go in right away?"

"No," I replied, shaking my head, even though he obviously couldn't see me. "There's really no point. He's not going to hurt anybody else as long as he's in the house, and it'll be a lot easier to grab him in his car away from the place. It'll also be safer for Thompson, on the off chance that she is still alive. We don't want him barricading himself in there and using her for a hostage. And if he hasn't got her in the house, maybe he'll lead us to her."

"Okay," he sighed. "Keep me updated on a regular basis."

Chapter Fifty-six

Carl McClain rolled the garage door down behind the Taurus, walked from the garage into the kitchen, and set his groceries, briefcase, and backpack on the counter. He returned the gun from the briefcase to the backpack, then put the steaks and the carrots into the refrigerator, grabbing a beer in the process.

He dropped the backpack on the floor in the small bathroom off the hallway, then removed the wig and glasses he'd worn on his outing. He returned them to the box that also contained the gray wig and mustache that he thought of as his "middle-age" disguise and stuck the box back on the shelf above the toilet.

That done, he wandered into the small living room, plopped into the easy chair, and put his feet up on the ottoman. He twisted the cap off of the beer, took a long pull, and wondered why in the hell Mike Miller hadn't been home for his interview with "Jason Barnes."

The note had said Miller had to leave at the last moment because of a "family emergency." He was sorry that he hadn't been able to call and reschedule the interview but "you didn't give me your number."

McClain had claimed to be an investigative reporter for *New Times*, the small weekly alternative newspaper, rather than pretending to be from the *Republic* or from one of the television stations, figuring that would make it easier to carry off the deception. Was it possible that Miller had nevertheless sniffed out his plan? But if that was the case, why hadn't the cops been all over him when he got to Miller's door?

Driving home, he was seized by the conviction that he'd missed his chance at Miller, at least for the time being. He couldn't risk pretending to be Jason Barnes or any other reporter again, in case Miller had tumbled to the ruse. And he didn't think that the former detective was likely to fall for something as rudimentary as the gas-company trick. By the time he was five blocks away from Miller's house, McClain had concluded that it was time for a break in the action—a vacation to Montana, maybe—while things in Arizona settled down a bit.

He regretted the fact that he would have to postpone his revenge against Mike Miller. He remembered Miller as a smug, self-confident son of a bitch who was too lazy to do any real detective work. Once Miller and his idiot partner had found the hooker's earring in McClain's Pontiac, they'd taken the easy way out and refused even to consider the possibility that there still might be another explanation for the murder.

Sitting in the cramped interrogation room, sweating like a pig and knowing that the rest of his life was hanging in the balance by the slimmest of threads, McClain had begged the two detectives to believe his story, swearing on his daughter's life that he had not killed Gloria Kelly. But McClain had been a quick and convenient solution to their case, and once Miller and Quigly had sunk their teeth into him, there was no getting loose of them.

Sixteen years after the fact, McClain still became enraged every time he thought of Miller, preening on the witness stand like he'd just fitted the glove to O. J. Simpson and solved the goddamn crime of the century. McClain had particularly looked forward to settling that score, and all other things being equal, he would have nailed Miller right out of the box.

But of course, all other things were not equal.

McClain understood that if Miller had been one of his first targets, the cops would've immediately gone back into the records, checking to see which of Miller's arrests had recently gotten out of the joint, perhaps looking to get even. That would have brought his own name up on the radar a lot earlier in the game and would have made it that much harder for him to get at his other targets. Accordingly, McClain had decided to delay his gratification, put Miller farther down the list, and hope that the detectives investigating the killings would not make the connection among the victims before McClain could get to the retired detective.

Unfortunately, it hadn't worked out that way. But regardless of his hatred for Mike Miller, McClain understood that the smart thing to do now was to stick to the original plan. The two weeks he had allotted himself for this phase of the operation would be up tomorrow, and there was nothing to be gained by being stupid and greedy. Miller and the last couple of jurors could wait on hold for a couple of months, but for the moment, all of McClain's instincts were screaming that it was time to be packed up and gone.

Which also meant that it was finally time to deal permanently with Beverly.

He found, much to his surprise, that he was increasingly reluctant to do so. By the night he'd finally grabbed her, his fury against the woman had been building for seventeen long, hopeless, and hellish years. Virtually every night in prison, he'd drifted in and out of a fitful sleep, fantasizing about the ways in which he might punish her for the mistakes that had consigned him to that godforsaken hole. And on that Wednesday night, with the opportunity finally at hand, he had brutally exorcised those demons. At the time, killing Beverly's husband was simply frosting on the cake because of the obvious additional pain it had inflicted upon her.

In the nine days since, though, he'd begun to second-guess himself. The judge, the prosecutor, and the cops all deserved what they were getting—of that he had no doubt. And so did the jurors. Watching them during the trial, he concluded that he'd never seen twelve dumber, lazier, more closed-minded people assembled together in one small space.

Four old retired farts, three housewives, two completely ignorant welfare mothers, a school teacher on her summer break, a car salesman, and an assembly-line worker who obviously saw the trial as an interesting and restful diversion from the boring routine of his everyday existence. Only one of them was under thirty. And this was supposed to be a jury of his fucking peers?

For four and a half days, they'd sat on their fat lazy asses in the jury box, mesmerized by the case that Harold Roe was building up against him and totally unimpressed by the faltering defense offered by Mc-

Clain's young and inexperienced PD. And in the end, anxious to get home for the weekend, they'd deliberated for only five and a half hours before finding Mc-Clain guilty of all of the charges against him.

McClain was still consumed by a burning hatred for the lot of them, but he was less certain now that Beverly was equally culpable. Maybe she had done her best. Maybe no one else would have done any better. And maybe he had punished her enough already.

It would be simple enough to pack up and get out of Dodge, leaving Beverly tethered to the cable in the bedroom. He could start south, in the direction of the Mexican border, and get twenty or thirty miles away from town. He could call the cops from a pay phone, tell them where to find Beverly, then double back north and take Highway 93 all the way up to Lakeside, Montana, for a brief but rewarding reunion with Ed Quigly.

But could he really afford to do that?

Beverly couldn't tell the police much of anything that they didn't already know, but she could give them a much better description of him than anything they were working with now, and that was the real danger. Leaving her alive to collaborate with a talented police sketch artist would almost certainly be a fatal mistake. And no matter the second thoughts he might be having now, that was one mistake he could not afford to make.

As the light slowly faded from the sky, McClain sat in the darkened living room for another twenty minutes or so, pondering his dilemma. Finally, he drained the last of the beer, went back to the kitchen, and dropped the bottle into the garbage can under the sink. Then he walked down the hall and retrieved his wrenches from the side pocket of the backpack.

Chapter Fifty-seven

Beverly was sitting on the bed, leaning back against the wall and reading the Sara Paretsky novel, when she heard McClain's key in the door a little after six o'clock. He walked into the room wearing a long-sleeve shirt and a pair of tan dress slacks rather than the jeans and T-shirt that constituted his usual uniform. He had his wrenches in one hand and was returning his keys to his right pants pocket with the other.

Beverly put down the novel and scooted over to the edge of the bed. McClain looked at the book.

"You finished *When the Sacred Gin Mill Closes*?"

She nodded. "Earlier this afternoon."

"Did you like it?"

"Yes, I did. The only other Block novel I've ever read was one in the series about the burglar. This one was a lot darker, but I thought it was a much better book."

McClain squatted on the floor in front of her and propped her foot on his knee. "Yeah, I agree. Especially once I got to Lewis, I discovered that I much preferred lying in my bunk with a book to hanging out in the TV room listening to the morons argue over which mindless fuckin' programs they wanted to waste their lives watching."

Setting to work with the wrenches, he continued, "Anyhow, I discovered Block pretty early on and managed to read just about everything he ever wrote. And while I like all his stuff, I agree that the Scudder series is far and away his best work. I love the complexity of the character and the way he's evolved over time."

He finished removing the cable and set her foot on the floor. "So anyhow, I guess that's something I got out of all of this—at least it reinforced my love of reading."

Beverly nodded. In a soft voice, she said, "Well, I'm sorry that's what it took, and again, I'm sorry for my part in putting you there."

McClain rose to his feet and looked away to the wall at the head of the bed. "Yeah, well . . ."

He turned back to Beverly. "I bought a couple of nice rib eyes for dinner. How would you like yours cooked?"

"Medium-rare please."

"I've got a bottle of Cabernet to go with the steaks. Do you want a glass while you're waiting?"

She shook her head. "No thank you, Carl. I'm fine for the moment, and I think I'd like to anticipate having the wine with dinner."

"Okay," he nodded. "I'll go get things started. Let me know if you change your mind."

McClain walked out of the room, leaving the door open about a quarter of the way. A few moments later, the radio in the kitchen came to life in the middle of a Van Morrison song. *Moondance* had been one of David's favorite albums, and Beverly winced at the memory.

She grabbed the Paretsky novel and moved to her seat at the card table from which she had the best view out into the hallway. For a few minutes, she listened to the sounds of McClain puttering around in the kitchen. Then the noises suddenly stopped.

Pretending to read, Beverly watched over the top of the book as McClain walked past the door, headed toward the other end of the hall. Five minutes later, he walked back toward the kitchen, now dressed in a pair of jeans and a black T-shirt and carrying a book of his own. She heard a few more minutes of noise from the kitchen and then nothing, save for the classic rock playing softly on the radio.

She debated for a few minutes the idea of going to the bedroom door and trying to sneak another look up and down the hall. But based on what she'd seen before, she was sure that there was no way that she could get out of the house without having to get past McClain, and she was also certain of what his reaction would be if he were to catch her outside of the bedroom. If she was to have any chance to escape, it was critically important that she contrive a way to remain free of the cable for the next several hours. For now, that had to be her priority.

CHAPTER FIFTY-EIGHT

At six forty-five, a patrolman delivered Walter Kovick to the truck we were using as our command post. The landlord was somewhere in his late fifties, a heart attack waiting to happen. A white XXL T-shirt strained against his stomach, which in turn hung precariously over a pair of chinos that were cinched up a good several inches below what would have been his natural waistline. The guy smelled of beer and cheap cigars, and he'd slopped portions of what looked like several meals onto the front of the T-shirt.

Maggie and I climbed out of the truck and walked Kovick over to the patrolman's squad, where we'd have more room to talk and where we wouldn't have to compete with the distraction of the communications chatter. We put Kovick in the passenger's seat, and Maggie took the back.

"I put a classified ad in the *Republic*, and I posted it on Craigslist," Kovick said. "I don't know which of the ads Fischer saw, but he called me on November fifth and asked to see the house. I showed it to him that afternoon. I remember that he asked a lot of questions about the neighbors."

Maggie leaned forward from the backseat. "What sort of questions, Mr. Kovick?"

The landlord turned back to look at her and shrugged. "He wanted to know if it was a quiet neighborhood. He asked did the neighbors mind their own business— that kinda thing.

"Hell, looking at the fences and the security bars on these houses should have told him the answer to that, but I told him that they did, and he agreed to take the house starting right then. He didn't even haggle about the rent; he just wrote me a check for the security deposit and another to cover the rent for the rest of the month. On the twenty-fifth, he mailed me a check for the December rent."

I handed him one of the photos that Brenda Perkins had taken of "Jason Barnes" earlier in the afternoon. "Is this Fischer, Mr. Kovick?"

Kovick held the picture under the dome light and squinted at it. "Well, it sorta looks like Fischer, only younger. Fischer has gray hair and a mustache. And he doesn't wear glasses."

"Is Fischer about the same height and weight as this guy?" I asked.

"Yeah, I'd say so," he nodded. "But this guy still looks younger to me." He handed the picture back to Maggie. "Of course"—he shrugged—"I only saw the guy the one time."

"So you haven't been in the house since the day you rented it to him?" Maggie asked.

"Nope. Haven't had any reason to, as long as he pays the rent on time and doesn't call to bitch about the fact that the stove's stopped workin' or some damn thing."

I nodded. "And there are secure bars over all the windows?"

"Yeah," Kovick sighed. "It makes the tenants feel better. In case you hadn't noticed, this isn't one of the city's more prestigious neighborhoods."

I handed him a pencil and a yellow legal pad. "Why don't you draw us a rough sketch of the house, Mr. Kovick? Give us the general floor plan and show us where all the exterior doors are."

We sat in silence for the next several minutes as Kovick hunched over the pad under the dome light and worked on his sketch. "There's really not much to it," he said, handing the pad back to me. "A kitchen with an eating area, the living room, two bedrooms, and two bathrooms."

I looked at the sketch. "And the only two ways in and out would be either through the front door in the living room or through the kitchen into the garage and out from there?"

"Right." He pointed to the sketch with the pencil. "You could go through the door here on the side of the garage, or of course you could open the main garage door to the driveway and go out that way."

He handed me the pencil and looked from me to Maggie. "So are you telling me that I rented my house to some damned crook?"

"Right now we don't know the answer to that, sir," Maggie replied. "We've just got some questions for the guy."

"Well, shit," the fat man sighed. "I sure as hell hope not. This goddamn house is a pain in the ass to rent. I swear it's more trouble than it's worth."

We sent Kovick back home with the patrolman, warning the landlord not to discuss our interest in his renter with anyone, and threatening him with dire consequences should he ignore the warning. Now that the darkness had settled in completely, we tightened the circle around the small house, and Maggie and I slipped into the surveillance van that was parked closest to it.

Light showed around the edges of the blinds that were drawn tightly closed over the windows in the rooms at the front of the house and which Kovick had identified as the kitchen and the living room. Greg Chickris had joined the Special Assignments team that was watching the back of the house where the two bedrooms were located. He reported that that the back of the house was completely dark.

I grabbed my radio, called Al Harris back in the command truck, and asked him if we had a microphone that we could surreptitiously attach to the outside wall of the house.

"We've got one," he replied, "but I'm not sure it would be worth the risk of trying to use it. Depending on how thick the exterior walls of the house are, and depending on how well they're insulated, I don't know that we'd be able to hear that much. And almost for sure, we wouldn't be able to hear anything more than noises from the one room where the mic was attached.

"Besides that, we'd have to send a guy over that damned fence with the thing. What with the streetlights and the occasional car driving by, there's enough light out here that if McClain should look out the window at the wrong moment, he'd probably see our guy climbing over the fence."

"Well, shit, Al," I countered. "Chickris says that the back of the house is completely dark. What if your guy snuck over the fence at the back corner of the garage? If he were dressed in dark clothes, he could press up against the house and move from room to room, starting in the back and testing to see if he could pick up anything. If he stays crouched down below the level of the windows, the chances of McClain seeing him would have to be pretty small."

"Okay," he conceded. "It's your party. But I wouldn't get my hopes up."

Ten minutes later, from his position at the back of the house, Chickris reported that Harris's man, dressed all in black, had successfully negotiated his way over the fence and was moving up to the side of the house. Over the next ten minutes, the tech, whose name was Curt Hesler, slowly made his way along the back of the house, stopping every few feet to hold a microphone up against the outside of the house and listen for any sounds coming from within through a set of headphones. Whispering through the lapel mic pinned to his jacket, he reported that he could hear no sounds coming from either of the bedrooms.

Through my night-vision binoculars, I watched Hesler move slowly around to the front of the house. Crouching well below the windows and squeezing himself tightly against the building, he stopped every ten feet or so and pressed the microphone up to the wall. Again, he reported no sound coming from the living room.

Detaching the microphone from his last position under the living-room wall, he crab-walked his way to a spot under the kitchen window and placed the microphone just under the window. A minute or so later, he whispered, "Somebody's moving around in the kitchen. And there's a radio on in here. I'm not hearing any conversation, though."

Five minutes later, Hesler reported that the radio in the kitchen had been turned off and that he could no longer hear any sounds coming from within the house. He made another circuit around the house and reported that he could now hear muffled voices from the larger of the two bedrooms. But he couldn't tell if the voices were those of people conversing in the room or if, perhaps, someone had turned on a radio or a television in the room, which remained dark.

At seven fifty, Elaine knocked on the door of the van and handed me a search warrant for the house. Glancing toward the house, she said, "I finally got through to Wells Fargo. Their records indicate that Alan Fischer opened his checking account three days before he rented the house. The initial deposit was five thousand dollars in cash. There haven't been any other deposits, and the only checks written against the account have been for rent and utilities. The woman told me that the balance in the account is down to a little over eight hundred bucks."

"Have you come up with any other record of Fischer before that week?"

She shook her head. "Not a trace. Riggins is still checking databases. We've come up with a few other Fischers, but we can account for all of them, and none of them is our guy here."

I thanked Elaine, who left to go back to help Riggins chase through the records. Thirty minutes later, Maggie took off her headphones and shook her head in exasperation. "Do you suppose the bastard will be considerate enough to go out for dinner?"

"I don't know, Maggs," I sighed. "I hope to hell he decides to go somewhere before the evening is out. Otherwise we're in for a long night."

Over the next hour, Al Harris worked out a schedule for rotating fresh personnel into the teams watching the house in the event that the stakeout should go on through the night and into the next morning. While none of us was excited about the prospect of maintaining the surveillance throughout the night, we were even less enthused about the idea of confronting McClain in the house and creating a possible standoff and/or hostage situation.

Curt Hesler had insisted on sticking to his post next to the house. He'd now made several circuits around the house and, much to my dismay, he'd heard nothing to suggest that Beverly Thompson might still be alive and captive inside.

For the last nine days, the only remotely encouraging note in the otherwise frustrating investigation was that we had not yet been forced to confront the fact that McClain had killed Thompson too. Saving her life would hardly make up for the all the other lives that McClain had destroyed, but it would offer at least some small vindication of our efforts. And I clung to the hope that if the woman was not in the house we were watching, McClain might still lead us to her.

CHAPTER FIFTY-NINE

The radio in the kitchen snapped off in the middle of Springsteen's "Glory Days," and thirty seconds later, McClain walked into the bedroom carrying a couple of wine glasses and a Mondavi Reserve Cabernet. Beverly figured that the wine must have set him back at least a hundred bucks, and she wondered what in the hell the bastard thought he was trying to accomplish. He'd opened the bottle in the kitchen. Now he poured an ounce into her glass and waited for her to taste it. She took a sip and nodded her approval.

"Very nice."

McClain poured her a third of a glass, poured some for himself, and then went back to the kitchen. He returned, using hot pads to carry two plates, and set one of the plates down in front of Beverly. "Watch out," he cautioned. "The plate's extremely hot."

Dinner consisted of the steaks, baked potatoes, and the vegetable du jour, which tonight was glazed carrots rather than another variation of green beans. Beverly swallowed the first bite of her steak and looked up at McClain. "I'm sorry to keep repeating myself, but this is an excellent steak—as good as any I've ever had in Mastro's or Ruth's Chris. I think you really could have a vocation as a chef."

McClain shrugged, seemingly embarrassed. "Yeah, well, I found a place that sells prime beef. It'd be pretty hard to screw it up."

Beverly nodded at the wine. "You went to a lot of trouble tonight."

Looking at his plate rather than at Beverly, he said, "Well, I figured I owed it to you. Besides, I was afraid you'd probably kill me if I showed up with another damn pizza."

Beverly looked down at her own plate and the room fell silent. Then McClain shook his head. "Jesus, I'm sorry. Bad joke. Sometimes my mouth gets way ahead of my feeble excuse for a brain."

Beverly looked up and made eye contact for a moment, then gave him a slight nod and returned to her steak. They ate in silence for the next few minutes, and McClain poured himself some more wine. Holding the bottle, he looked at Beverly's glass. "You don't like it?"

"Oh, no," she assured him. "It's excellent. I'm just savoring it."

She took a sip and let him pour another ounce or so into her glass. Then she ate another bite of her steak. "So what do you suppose you'll do with yourself when you're finished here, Carl?"

McClain set down his fork, took another sip of wine, and shook his head. "I'm not completely sure. The one thing I do know is that I'll be getting the hell out of Phoenix. Leaving aside the obvious reasons why I'd want to put some distance between myself and the local authorities, I have absolutely no desire to live here anymore."

He took another drink of wine and waited for a moment, lost in thought. Then he looked up to meet her eyes. "You can't begin to imagine what it was like, Beverly, getting off the bus from Lewis and seeing Phoenix for the first time in seventeen years. I felt like Rip Van Fuckin' Winkle, or like I'd just stepped out of H. G. Wells's time machine."

She allowed him a small smile, and he shook his head again. "No, I mean it. Really. When I was a kid, this valley was a pretty decent place to live. But now . . . Jesus, what with the number of people who've poured in, the endless sprawl, and the air pollution, not to mention the goddamn traffic . . . Seriously, how in the hell do you stand it?"

"I don't know"—she shrugged—"but I can certainly understand how disorienting it must have been for you. The Valley *has* grown and changed a lot in that time, and I realize that it must have been one thing to read about it in isolation and another thing altogether to suddenly experience it . . ."

She pushed a couple of carrots around on the plate with her fork. "I guess that living through all those changes, I experienced them gradually. And like everybody else who's lived here through that time, I adjusted as I went along. I agree with you that I absolutely hate looking at the mountains and seeing the pollution hanging there, especially on those winter days when it's really bad. And sometimes the traffic really does suck. But at least the freeway system is a lot better than it was seventeen years ago. And most of the time, except at rush hour, it doesn't seem to take me all that long to get most of the places I need to go.

"Besides, I still really love the weather here, especially at this time of year—and the recreational opportunities. Even with all the additional people who've moved in, you can still take advantage of the mountains and the parks and not feel crowded . . . I've been to a lot of other cities in the last ten years or so, and while I like visiting them, I don't think I'd want to live permanently in very many of them as opposed to here."

McClain finished the last of his steak and poured himself some more wine. "Well you're ahead of me on that score, of course. And I do want to get out and see what the rest of the country looks like after all this time. But I need to find someplace smaller and a helluva lot less congested. Phoenix just doesn't work for me anymore."

They sat in silence for the next few minutes as McClain continued to drink his wine, occasionally looking at Beverly and then looking quickly away. She toyed with her glass, occasionally taking a small sip, hoping that he wouldn't notice that she was allowing him to drink the bulk of the wine. With about a quarter of the bottle remaining, McClain let out a long sigh.

He got up from the table, closed the bedroom door, and snapped off the overhead light, leaving only the small lamp on the nightstand to illuminate the room. Then he walked back to the table and touched his hand to Beverly's shoulder. She sat, staring at her wineglass, refusing to meet his eyes. He waited a few seconds, then said in a soft voice, "Take your off clothes, Beverly."

She sat for another moment, her eyes squeezed tightly shut. Then she finished the last of her wine, set down the glass, and rose from the table.

CHAPTER SIXTY

By ten o'clock, we were increasingly resigned to the fact that McClain would probably not be leaving the house again before morning. Maggie and I remained in the small surveillance van closest to the house. Chickris was still in a truck at the back, and Al Harris continued to direct the Special Assignments team from his command truck two blocks away. Otherwise, the second shift of the Special Assignments team had rotated into place, all except for Curt Hesler, who insisted that he was still good to go, at least for the time being.

A patrolman had slipped into our van with a take-out pizza and some soft drinks, and for only the second or third time since we'd been teamed together, Maggie made no complaint about eating fast food. We sat on stools in the back of the van along with two members of the Special Assignments team, taking turns watching the front of the house, while all of us continued to listen to the radio chatter through our headphones.

Unfortunately, there wasn't all that much to listen to. Vehicles continued to pass on the street in front of the house, and the occasional pedestrian walked or staggered by. Light continued to show from McClain's living room and kitchen, while the back of the house remained dark. As the evening progressed, Hesler made several more trips around the house but reported hearing nothing, save for the occasional sound of muted voices coming from the one bedroom. But he was still unable to determine whether the sound was coming from people conversing in the room or from a radio or television set.

At ten twenty, I drained the last of a Coke and watched as Maggie stifled a yawn. I touched her knee and said, "You want to take a break—go home and sleep for a while? This asshole's not going anywhere tonight."

She shot me a skeptical look. "Yeah, Richardson. I'll go home and take a nap about the same time you do."

She stretched briefly and rotated her head around her neck. "I just hope to hell we don't sit here all night and discover tomorrow that this asshole's just a freelancer who was hoping to score a story that he could sell to one of the papers."

"Oh, Jesus, Maggs, don't even suggest it. But if that's the case, why is he renting this house using the name Alan Fischer and then trying to set up the interview with Mike Miller as Jason Barnes? More to the point, why can't we find any record of Jason Barnes at all, and no record of Alan Fischer that goes back more than three months ago?"

"Yeah, I know," she sighed. "It's gotta be McClain. But if it's not, I'm gonna ream the fucker a new asshole."

McClain pulled on his T-shirt, underwear, and jeans, then felt his way toward the door, leaving Beverly naked and crying softly on the bed behind him. He opened the door, and light from the hallway flooded into the room. McClain went back to the table, picked up his glass and the bottle of Cabernet, and then left, pulling the door closed behind him.

For the first time since he'd abducted Beverly, he'd been unable to go through with the rape. On his order, she had obediently gotten up from the table, stripped off her T-shirt, sweatpants, and panties, and lain down on the bed. He'd slowly taken off his own clothes, looking at her body and watching her reaction as his erection firmed up.

A tear fell out of her eye and slipped down her cheek as he climbed on top of her. He wiped the tear away with his thumb and lowered his mouth to her breast. She began sobbing even harder, and in a soft voice, she pleaded again, "Why are you doing this to me?"

McClain reached out and slapped the lamp off the nightstand and onto the floor, breaking the bulb and plunging the room into darkness. He grabbed her wrists and, using one hand, held them together above her head. With his other hand, he roughly forced her legs apart, willing himself to ignore the sound of her crying as he attempted once again to summon up the rage that had first brought him to her door nine nights earlier.

But it was useless. Struggling to force himself into her, he felt his erection slipping away. He released her wrists and lay still on top of her for another minute or so, listening to her cry. Then he pushed himself up to his elbows and touched her cheek in the dark.

"I'm sorry," he said quietly.

And then he was gone.

Beverly listened as McClain made his way across the room and pulled the door closed behind him. Then she opened her eyes in the darkness and wiped them with the back of her hands. She swung her legs off the bed and was just about to set her feet on the floor when she remembered the broken lamp. She crawled across to the other side of the bed, got up, and slowly felt her way around the room to the door.

She flipped the light on, made her way to the bathroom, and took a hurried shower in the lukewarm water. Even though McClain had not successfully penetrated her, she was nonetheless desperate to scrub the memory of his touch from her skin.

She toweled herself off, went back into the bedroom, and used the T-shirt she'd been wearing earlier to push the fragments of the broken lightbulb into a small pile out of the way up against the wall. Then she pulled on a fresh pair of panties, a clean T-shirt, and her sweatpants.

Back in the bathroom, she closed the door and picked up the plunger from beside the toilet. She took a deep breath, said a silent prayer, and then flushed the noisy toilet. As the water gurgled out of the tank and into the bowl, she snapped off the handle of the plunger.

It made less noise than she thought it would, and in her right hand, she now held the top eighteen inches or so of the handle, which tapered down to a broken jagged point. She turned off the water, dropped the rest of the plunger into the wastebasket, and covered it with the *Newsweek* that McClain had bought her on Valentine's Day.

Holding the weapon at her side, she cracked open the bathroom door and looked into the bedroom. Thankfully, the room was empty and the door to the hall was still closed. She turned off the bathroom light, moved quickly to the bed, and lifted up the mattress. She stuck the broken handle under the mattress right at the place where her arm would naturally fall when she was lying with her head on her pillow.

That done, Beverly walked over to the door and snapped off the light. Then she felt her way back across the room, lay down on top of the covers, and waited for Carl McClain to come back to bed.

Chapter Sixty-one

At ten twenty-eight, we watched the light disappear from McClain's kitchen window, and a couple of minutes later, the living room went dark as well. I picked up my radio and keyed the mic. "Greg, he's turned off the lights in the front of the house. What's happening back there?"

"Nothing. It's still completely dark. I haven't seen even a tiny glimmer of light from the back of the place since I got here."

"What's he got for window coverings back there?"

"There's one small window that I assume is in the bathroom. It's completely black. The other windows have shades in them and what must be white curtains behind the shades. The shades were closed when I got here, and I could see a narrow strip of white cloth around the edges of one of them. But nobody's touched the shades during the time I've been watching."

"And there's no light at all showing through any of the windows back there?"

"Nope."

Curt Hesler had worked his way around to the back of the house again, and I asked him if he could hear anything.

"No, sorry, Sean," he whispered. "I'm not picking up a thing back here now."

"Well shit," I sighed into the radio. "It looks like he's giving it up for the night. But everybody stay alert. If he hasn't gone to bed, don't let him slip out of there in the dark without us seeing him."

* * *

McClain snapped off the light in the kitchen and made his way to the living room with his glass and what remained of the bottle of Cabernet. He dropped into the easy chair, poured himself half a glass of the wine, and set the bottle on the table next to the chair. Then he propped his feet up on the ottoman and turned off the floor lamp. Alone in the darkened room, he took a healthy drink of the wine and tried to figure out what in the hell he was going to do about Beverly Thompson.

He understood now that he should have finished with her after the first two or three days, back when he still knew for certain that she was the stupid, incompetent bitch who'd let them send him to prison for life—back before he'd begun to wonder if she might have been some other woman all along.

But of course, that was then and this was now. And he realized that despite the doubts that might be gnawing at him, he had no real choice in the matter. His only option was to finish what he'd started here. His own survival depended on it.

He drained the last of the wine and sat there for another thirty minutes, his mind running in circles. Finally, he pushed himself up out of the chair, and for a few seconds, the floor seemed to be shifting under his feet. He was somewhat surprised to realize that he was slightly drunk, but he wasn't so drunk that he didn't know what needed to be done.

Attempting to move quietly, he walked down the hall in his stocking feet and stopped in front of the bedroom door. He unbuckled his belt, pulled it free of his jeans, and looped the end of the belt back through the buckle. Then he slowly opened the door, slipped into the room, and made his way toward the bed.

After sitting in the dark for thirty minutes, his eyes had adjusted to the little ambient light that filtered into the house from the outside, and he could just make out Beverly's vague shape lying on top of the covers. He stood beside her for several long minutes, holding the belt and willing himself to get it over and done with.

Beverly's head was turned away from him and she was breathing softly and regularly. McClain reasoned that it would be a fairly simple matter to quickly slip the loop in the belt over her head and pull it tightly around her neck. With any luck, she'd be dead before she was even awake enough to realize what was happening to her. But his hands remained at his sides, stubbornly refusing to execute the command that his brain kept repeating insistently.

Finally, after wrestling with the issue for another couple of minutes, it occurred to him that the better plan might be to wait until morning when he was completely sober and thinking a bit more clearly. He could get up early and get his things packed into the Taurus. Then he could finally finish with Beverly and be out on the road immediately after.

Relieved at having conjured up a more sensible approach to the problem, McClain reached out and lightly touched Beverly's leg. Then he sighed and walked slowly around to his own side of the bed. He slipped out of his jeans and lay down beside her, setting the belt on the floor next to the bed. Tomorrow morning would be soon enough.

CHAPTER SIXTY-TWO

Lying on the bed in the dark, Beverly had no way of telling how much time had elapsed since McClain had left the bedroom, but it felt like it was taking a lifetime for him to finish whatever it was he was doing before coming to bed.

She thought about the way he had touched her before leaving the room, and about the way his voice had broken when he said he was sorry. For the first time he'd actually sounded like he meant it, and Beverly wondered whether he might finally be having a belated attack of conscience.

What if he was, at long last, actually experiencing some sense of guilt and shame? What if he'd decided that he couldn't face her again tonight? What if, God forbid, he'd finished the bottle of wine, but instead of coming to bed as she had hoped, with his senses dulled by the alcohol, he'd simply passed out and was sleeping it off somewhere else in the house?

As the thought crossed her mind, she reached down and touched the tip of the plunger handle. And just as she did, McClain quietly opened the bedroom door.

The hall outside the bedroom was not nearly as pitch-black as the interior of the bedroom itself, and she could see him standing as a dark silhouette in the doorway. Then, without closing the door, he began moving slowly across the room in her direction.

Beverly closed her eyes, turned her head away, and tried to force herself to breathe slowly and regularly as if she were asleep. She could feel him standing beside her in the dark. Was he going to try to force himself on her again?

The time dragged on interminably. Then, through the sweatpants, she felt the touch of his fingers on her calf. She heard him move around to the other side of the bed and take off his jeans. He lay down on the bed beside her—carefully, as if he was trying not to disturb her. Still feigning sleep, she rolled onto her right side, facing away from him, and brought her hands up together near her face.

She lay like that for the next hour, breathing slowly and regularly while remaining alert to McClain. He continued to lie on his back, as he had since coming to bed, sighing occasionally and apparently unable to sleep. She sensed that he was wrestling with some dilemma, and she could feel the blankets and the mattress shift slightly as he clasped his hands together, first behind his neck and then across his stomach. Finally, after perhaps an hour had elapsed, he settled into one position and began to breathe more regularly. Fifteen minutes later, he was still lying on his back and snoring softly.

In the middle of most nights, when he was totally dead to the world, McClain's snoring would have drowned out the whine of a twenty-year-old chain saw, and Beverly struggled, willing herself to remain patient and motionless until he had fallen into his deepest sleep. But after another ten minutes, her heart was pounding and the adrenaline was raging through her system. What if he were to wake up to go to the bathroom or some such thing? What if he got up for some reason and then didn't come back to bed?

Beverly drew a deep breath and held it. With her senses on highest alert to any movement by McClain or to any change in the rhythm of his snoring, she slowly reached down with her left hand and found the tip of the plunger handle. As carefully as she possibly could, she eased it out from under the mattress and transferred it to her right hand.

She rolled slowly onto her back and lay quietly for a couple of minutes, holding the weapon beside her while McClain continued to snore next to her. Then she dropped her left elbow to her side and dug it into the mattress to brace herself. As she did, McClain shuddered and shifted his position on the bed ever so slightly. Beverly froze, terrified to move or even to breathe. Then, perhaps thirty seconds later, McClain's snoring settled back into a steady tempo.

Beverly slowly rolled up onto her left side, holding the plunger handle in her right hand behind her. In the dim light, she could now see that McClain was still lying on his back with his hands at his sides and his abdomen exposed. She squeezed her eyes closed for a moment and into the darkness she whispered, "I love you, David."

Then she opened her eyes again. In one swift fluid motion, she rolled up to her knees and raised the plunger handle above her head, gripping it tightly with both hands. And then, summoning all of the strength she could possibly muster, Beverly drove the makeshift weapon straight down into Carl McClain's stomach.

CHAPTER SIXTY-THREE

"Heads up, everybody! Heads up! Something's going on in the bedroom back here."

It was just before one in the morning. I was scanning the front of McClain's rented house with my night-vision binoculars while one of Al Harris's men monitored the neighborhood around the house. His partner was catching twenty winks in the driver's seat, and Maggie was taking a catnap in the back corner of the van when Curt Hesler whispered excitedly into our headphones.

I keyed my radio and asked him what was happening.

"I can't tell for sure yet. I attached the mic to the bedroom wall where I was hearing the conversations earlier and settled in under my headphones. I haven't heard a single sound in the last two hours and then someone—I'm sure it was a man—just screamed like he was in terrible pain. But that was it, just the one sound. I'm not hearing anything now. I suppose it's possible that the guy's just having one hellacious nightmare, but he sure got my attention."

"Okay, Curt. Hold your position and keep listening. Let us know the instant you hear anything else."

The interruption brought Maggie to full alert and as she scanned the front of the house, I said into the radio, "Did you copy that, Al?"

"Yeah, what do you want us to do?"

"Hold your position for the moment, but get your entry team geared up and ready to go at my signal. If Hesler hears anything else, we may want to go in immediately."

"Copy that. They're suiting up now."

I set the radio down beside me and retrieved my binoculars. But I could still see no light in any room of the house and no activity in or around the house.

The plunger handle knifed into McClain's stomach, and a split second later, he sat halfway up on the bed and let out a bloodcurdling scream. As he did, Beverly scrambled off the bed and raced out of the room. In the hallway, she ran to the right, in the direction of the kitchen, and found a light switch at the kitchen door.

Her heart was pumping so hard it felt like it was about to burst. She snapped on the light and risked a glance back over her shoulder at the bedroom door. She could hear McClain moaning in agony, but he was nowhere in sight.

Next to the kitchen at the far end of the hall was the door that she had seen two nights earlier. Beverly raced over to the door, twisted the knob, and attempted to pull the door open. But it refused to budge, and her heart sank when she saw that like the bedroom door, this one—wherever it led—was secured by a dead-bolt lock that could be opened only with a key.

From behind her, she could hear the sound of McClain still moaning in agony. Trying not to surrender to the panic that threatened to immobilize her, Beverly ran back into the kitchen and pulled the shades up off the window.

In the dim light cast by the streetlamp on the corner, she could see a handful of vehicles parked along the street in front of the house, but no one was moving outside. She found the window latch, released it, and strained to push the balky window up. As the window squeaked in protest, she managed to force it up about six inches, only to realize suddenly that the window was protected by iron bars that would prevent anyone from getting in through the window—or out.

In desperation, she reached out and grabbed one of the bars, but it was anchored securely. She would never be able to wrench the bars aside and escape through the window.

She could no longer hear McClain moaning, and the thought of having to go back into the bedroom and somehow force him to give up his keys terrified her, but she knew that she had no choice.

Turning away from the window, Beverly saw that McClain had cleaned up the kitchen after dinner. The dishes were put away and the counters were wiped down and empty. She ran over to the cupboards and started feverishly pulling open the drawers. In the third drawer, she found McClain's kitchen knives, washed, sharpened, and carefully put away. He'd bought himself a beautiful new Wüsthof chef's knife with a ten-inch blade. Her hand shaking, Beverly reached into the drawer, drew out the knife, and reluctantly turned back in the direction of the hallway.

At the kitchen door she could see no sign of McClain, and looking at the floor in the hallway, she could see no trail of blood to indicate that he might have left the bedroom. She stood in the kitchen doorway for another thirty seconds, straining to hear any sound. But the house had gone silent.

Gripping the handle of the knife in her right hand, she forced herself to move out into the hall and then inched her way back toward the bedroom. As she reached the bedroom door she pressed up against the wall and stopped to listen again for a moment. Still, she heard no sound coming from anywhere in the house.

Her heart pounding, she turned into the doorway, holding the knife out in front of her. In the light from the hallway, she could see that the bed was empty. She turned to look in the direction of the bathroom, and as she did, from the opposite side of the wall, McClain clamped his hand over her outstretched arm and jerked her back into the bedroom.

CHAPTER SIXTY-FOUR

I'd only just set my radio down again when a light suddenly showed around the edges of the kitchen blinds. I picked up my binoculars, and ten seconds later, the blinds flew up and I was looking into the face of a panic-stricken Beverly Thompson. I grabbed my radio and hollered, "Al, get your team in there right now! Thompson's in the kitchen and she's trying to get out!"

Harris shouted back, "Copy that. We're rolling!"

I clipped the radio to my belt and leaped out of the van. As Maggie jumped to the ground behind me, I could hear the sirens of Harris's SWAT team screaming to life a couple of blocks up the street. I grabbed Maggie's shoulder and said, "Take the team in through the front door. I'll take the back."

As three SWAT-team vehicles raced around the corner with their Mars lights blazing, I vaulted the chain-link fence and ran over to the door at the side of the garage. I drew my pistol, braced myself, and kicked through the door, shattering the jamb as the lock broke free. I jumped back and flattened myself against the outside wall of the dark garage, but heard no one moving inside.

Crouching low, I crossed to the other side of the door, peeked in, and found myself looking at "Jason Barnes's" gray Ford Taurus. Still staying low, I slid my hand up the wall next to the door, found a light switch, and flipped it on. I took another cautious look into the garage but could not see or hear any activity inside.

I moved quickly to the corner of the garage, looked around, and saw Maggie and the SWAT team assembling at the front door of the house with a battering ram. Ducking back around the corner, I slipped into the garage and headed toward the door that led from the garage into the house.

As McClain jerked Beverly into the bedroom, the chef's knife flew out of her hand and clattered across the floor in the direction of the bed. Beverly screamed and McClain wrapped her body up against his. Beverly was facing away from him and he clamped his left arm around her neck to hold her there. "You fucking bitch," he cried in a strained voice. "I'm really going to hurt you now, Beverly."

Beverly could feel the life being squeezed out of her. Struggling to breathe, she tried kicking back at him while pulling at his arm with both hands in an effort to loosen the pressure at her throat. McClain began dragging her in the direction of the bed, and suddenly the night air exploded with the wail of sirens.

McClain stopped in the middle of the room. In a voice wild with shock and anger, he said, "What the fuck did you do, Beverly?"

He held her still in the middle of the bedroom for another couple of seconds. Then he released the pressure on her neck a bit and began dragging her back toward the hallway. "Walk with me, Beverly," he commanded. "And do exactly as I say or I'll snap your goddamn neck."

He dragged her back out into the hallway, then down the hall and into the second bathroom. From the kitchen end of the hallway they heard the crash of someone battering down the door into the garage. Through the living-room walls, they could hear the shouts of people racing toward the front door.

Beverly could feel the blood seeping out of McClain's wound and soaking into the back of her T-shirt. She had no idea how badly he was hurt, but he was obviously not incapacitated. She prayed that he was in shock, running on adrenaline, and that he would not be able to sustain for much longer the strength he was now demonstrating. She struggled against him, and again he tightened his choke hold around her neck.

The noise outside the house intensified, and something exploded against the front door. But McClain's barricade withstood the blow and kept the intruders at bay, at least for the moment.

McClain leaned back against the bathroom wall, then slid down the wall a couple of feet, pulling Beverly with him. She heard the sound of a zipper and realized that McClain was opening his backpack, which was sitting on the floor against the wall. He reached into the backpack and came out with the gun he had used to murder David. And as he did, someone kicked in the door at the kitchen end of the hall.

CHAPTER SIXTY-FIVE

The door from the garage flew open into the house, and as I regained my footing, I found myself looking down a dimly lighted hallway toward the opposite end of the house. To my right was the kitchen where I'd seen Beverly Thompson struggling with the window less than two minutes earlier, but the room was now empty.

Holding my gun out in front of me, I began moving slowly down the hallway. The entry team slammed the battering ram into the front door a second time, and the whole house seemed to shake. An instant later, Carl McClain popped out of a room ahead of me, shielding himself behind Thompson and holding a pistol to her head.

Thompson was dressed in a T-shirt and a pair of sweatpants. McClain, wearing only a T-shirt and a pair of black briefs, looked nothing at all like the photos and sketches we'd been circulating. He was much thinner and fitter than I ever would have imagined. He'd also gotten rid of the geeky glasses and had shaved his head. After hunting him for the last four days I could have passed him on the street and never would have recognized him. Waving his pistol at me, he shouted, "Tell those fuckers to get off my front porch right now!"

Still holding my own pistol in my right hand, I pulled my radio from my belt with my left, keyed the mic, and said, "Hang on, Maggie. He's got Mrs.

Thompson, and he wants the SWAT team off the porch. Pull back for now."

Maggie acknowledged the message, and I clipped the radio back onto my belt. McClain cocked his head and listened for a moment. As the team outside fell silent, he gestured at me with his pistol. "Drop the fuckin' gun."

"Don't listen to him!" Thompson begged. "Please. Just shoot the son of a bitch right now!"

McClain was holding the woman, her back pressed up against him, with his left arm clamped around her throat. Using his right hand, he slammed the gun into the side of her head. In a deliberate voice he said, "Shut up, bitch." Then to me: "I said drop the fuckin' gun, asshole."

With my pistol trained on McClain's forehead, I slowly shook my head. "I don't think so, Carl. I can't see any percentage in giving up my gun. This place is surrounded. You can't possibly escape. Your only chance to get out of here alive is to drop that gun and surrender to me right now. Shoot either one of us and thirty seconds later you'll be a corpse."

McClain coughed and a trickle of blood dribbled out of the corner of his mouth. "I'm a corpse already, shithead. There's no goddamn way I'm going back to the pen and so I've got absolutely nothin' to lose here."

"Listen, McClain, it doesn't have to go down like that," I countered. "You're hurt. At least let me get someone in here to look at you."

He shook his head as if amazed. "Fuckin' bitch stabbed me. Can you believe it? Got me feeling sorry for her and then attacked me in my sleep."

Thompson began struggling against him. "Please," she pleaded again. "I don't care what happens to me. Please, just shoot him."

McClain tightened his grip around her throat and I held up my left hand. "Let her go, Carl. I'm not going to shoot you. Let me get somebody in here to look at your wound, and we can go from there."

Again he shook his head. Then he lifted the pistol away from Thompson's head and pointed it at me. "I have a better idea," he said. "You back out the door behind you and send the medic in. I'll hang on to Beverly here for insurance. While the medic patches me up, you bring a car up into the driveway and tell everybody else out there to pull back. I'll come out with Beverly. She and I will get into the backseat, and the three of us will go for a ride."

My turn to shake my head. "No way, Carl. You know that's never gonna happen. Give it up. Yeah, you'll wind up back in the pen, but that's still a helluva lot better than buying yourself a ticket to the boneyard."

He coughed again, now spitting a few drops of blood onto Thompson's shoulder. "That's what you think, pal. We do this my way or I take the both of you to hell with me."

Again McClain coughed, harder this time. As he did, Thompson pivoted slightly away from him, clasped her hands together, and slammed her right elbow back into his bleeding stomach. He screamed in agony and doubled over slightly. Using both her hands, Thompson reached up and managed to break his grip on her throat. She threw herself to the floor in front of him and as McClain moved his gun off of me to follow her, I shot him in the head.

McClain dropped to the floor next to Thompson, and I quickly closed the distance between us. I kicked his weapon away and shouted into my radio, "He's down and disarmed. We're clear in here!"

As I holstered my gun, Thompson rose to her feet. She stood for a moment, sobbing over McClain's body, then raised her bare foot and smashed it down into what was left of his face. In a voice brimming with a stew of pain and rage, she cried, "That's for David, you pathetic piece of shit."

Then, leaning against the wall, she slipped down to the floor, pulled her knees up to her chest, and began weeping uncontrollably.

CHAPTER SIXTY-SIX

The crime lab quickly confirmed that Carl McClain's pistol had been the weapon used to kill Alma Fletcher, David Thompson, Karen Collins, Harold Roe, and Larry Cullen. The techs were not able to tie McClain conclusively to the murder of Walter Beckman, but we had absolutely no doubt about the fact that McClain was responsible for the judge's death. Beverly Thompson told us that McClain had boasted of committing the murder, and the case was declared closed.

No one stepped forward to assume the responsibility for McClain's burial. The afternoon after his death, Amanda Randolph appeared at my office, looking tired and anxious. "I hope you don't think me a horrible person," she said in a soft voice, "but the truth is, I'm glad that he's dead. Especially given what he's done in the last few weeks, the thought of him being out there alive . . . the thought that he might have attempted to see Tiffani . . ."

"What have you and Mr. Randolph decided to tell Tiffani?" I asked.

"Nothing," she replied, shaking her head. "When we joined her in California, we simply told her that we'd decided to take a break and come over to watch her play in the tournament.

"She knows, of course, that Richard is not her biological father, but she has no idea that Carl McClain was. Several years ago, when I thought she was finally old enough to discuss the matter, I told her that I'd been in a relationship with a man and that I'd gotten pregnant. I told her that the man had not loved me, or the child he had fathered, enough to stick by us. I told her that he had abandoned me and left the state—that I had never heard from him again and that I had no idea where he might be.

"Tiffani loves Richard, and she knows that Richard loves her. She understands that by any meaningful definition of the term, he is and always has been her father. After our discussion of the issue, she's never expressed any curiosity about her natural father, and I'm hoping desperately that no one will ever discover that I was Carl's wife and that Tiffani was his daughter."

In McClain's backpack, we found a safe-deposit-box key that we ultimately traced to the bank where he had rented a box under the alias Alan Fischer. In the box, we found just under $100,000 in cash, two additional sets of fake ID, a tarnished Saint Christopher's medal on a broken chain, eleven major-league-baseball cards bound in a rubber band and dating back to the middle nineteen seventies, a faded picture of a woman we assumed to be McClain's mother, and a note indicating that in the event of his death, McClain wanted to be cremated with no services of any kind. Underneath the note was a small studio photo of McClain's daughter and his former wife that I managed to palm and slip into my pocket while everybody else was distracted by the sight of all that money.

In accordance with McClain's wishes, his remains were cremated and the charges were deducted from the money found in his safe-deposit box. A week later, one of Larry Cullen's ex-wives filed a lawsuit claiming the balance of the money in lieu of the alimony she would have received had McClain not murdered her ex-husband.

Beverly Thompson spent several days in the hospital recovering from the abuse she had suffered during her captivity, but a week after her escape she was able to attend a memorial service for her husband and to see him properly buried. After an extended break, during which she moved into a condominium and sold the house where her husband had been killed, she returned to work at the end of April.

And early in May, while Elizabeth was back in Minneapolis volunteering at a celebrity golf tournament, Julie contracted pneumonia. Her immune system, which had been steadily weakened during the long months of her illness, was unable to repel the virus that now assaulted her lungs. For two days and nights, I sat at her bedside as her condition steadily deteriorated. And at ten twenty-seven on a beautiful spring morning, I held her in my arms as she died, a week before her thirty-fourth birthday.

21045734R00182

Made in the USA
Charleston, SC
06 August 2013